FANG VOLUME 11

FANG VOLUME 11

Edited by

SPARF

BAD DOG BOOKS

FANG Volume 11
First publication 2023

Edited by Sparf

Cover by Rukis

Published by Bad Dog Books
www.BadDogBooks.com

An imprint of FurPlanet Productions
www.FurPlanet.com
Dallas, TX

All stories copyright their respective authors.
Print ISBN: 978-1-61450-588-4
Electronic ISBN: 978-1-61450-589-1

FOREWORD

I have always loved tales of sorcery and knights and shadowy thieves stealing magical items. Tabletop fantasy RPGs have certainly experienced a renaissance in the last few years, becoming something of a mainstream pop-culture star. It is fitting then that this volume of FANG arrives on shelves only a few months after the release of a very big-name film adaptation of one of those RPGs.

Within these pages you'll find mystery and magical adventure, coupled with a healthy dose of love and lust. I truly hope that these excursions to other worlds by this amazing array of authors delight you.

-Sparf

BAD DOG BOOKS

CONTENTS

UNRAVELED

FAORA MERIDIAN

Booted feet stomped across the grates above. Dust shook loose as thin rays of sunlight were briefly snuffed out by the passage of people. There was a practiced rhythm to each footfall that betrayed military training. The cadence of soldiers on a brisk march. A hunt.

In a musty tunnel below, a ferret carefully lifted a paw to shield his eyes from the falling dust. He watched as he hopped nervously from foot to foot, his other arm protectively wrapped about his midsection. The brown of his fur and robes both were stained with red as he grit his teeth. "They must have locked down all of Kadara," he whispered.

"At least the market district," came the equally quiet reply from behind him. The ferret turned to see a slightly taller fox in what had once been gleaming silver armor seated on a half-shattered wooden crate. His armor dented and scored with black, and the sword that lay across his lap was slick with blood. "The rest of Kadara won't take much longer." His eyes lifted from his sword to meet the ferret's. "You've got to do it now, and you know it."

The ferret's eyes narrowed, and his nervous hopping came to a sudden halt. "I've never unraveled so much time before," he hissed back. Was that anger in his tone? He'd not meant to be angry. Forceful, yes. Afraid, even.

It didn't seem as if the fox minded, though. He stood. Swayed a little on his feet. "If you don't, they'll kill you," he reasoned as he made his way over to the ferret. His sword was clutched tightly in one paw, and the ferret eyed it warily. "They'll use me to find you, they'll kill you, and then they'll kill me for betraying them."

"They'd have to catch me first," protested the ferret, though he didn't sound convinced even to his own ears. He chewed on his lower lip nervously, his ears twitching as he began to hop about again. "I don't know about this, Azraff. It's dangerous. I could unravel more time than I intend. I might not unravel enough."

"More dangerous than letting either of us be caught?" The fox sheathed his sword with a sickeningly wet *schluck* sound and reached out to gently take the ferret's shoulders into his grip. "I won't be responsible for your death. I'd sooner die myself." His fingers kneaded the ferret's shoulders. The shorter male's hopping once more fell to a halt. "Naim. There's no more time. We both know that."

Another cloud of dust rained down over the pair as more soldiers marched past above them. Naim held the fox's stare.

His brow furrowed as his ears continued to twitch. His mouth opened, but his jaw remained clenched as his eyes welled up. Words didn't come. They couldn't.

Azraff sighed. He closed his eyes and leaned forward. The fox touched his forehead to Naim's as his arms slid slowly over the ferret's shoulders to pull him into a soft, loose embrace. "It'll give us a chance," he whispered.

"It'll take you away," Naim countered. His body began to tremble, then jerk with barely restrained sobs. "I'm going to lose you. You're—"

"I'm going nowhere," Azraff interrupted as he pulled back. The fox brought one of his paws back around to tilt

Naim's chin up. The ferret's cheeks were streaked with tears that matted his fur, but he stubbornly held Azraff's gaze as the fox's paw trailed down to press gently against the ferret's chest. "I'll be here, no matter what happens."

Naim bared his teeth, as much to clench his jaw and keep himself from bawling in front of the fox as anything else. His eyes continued to swim as he shook his head. "I never wanted that. I never wanted *you*."

"I know." Azraff leaned back in again to rub his muzzle along Naim's. "You have to do it now. We don't have the time to waste."

As he spoke, he reached down to the ferret's sides. He took Naim's paws in a tender grip. Ran his thumbs over them as he lifted them closer. He even gave them a little squeeze. Reassurance. Acceptance.

Naim didn't fight him. He let the fox lift his arms, and his fingertips brushed through that brilliant crimson fur at the sides of his head. His paws lingered there as Azraff's fell away again, left to cradle the fox's head. He held it in his paws and shook his head again. "There will be pain," he warned.

"You'll be with me," Azraff replied, and the fox gave him a warm smile as he patted his own chest with one paw "Right here, all through it. Always. It won't hurt a bit."

A tear ran down the line in the ferret's cheekfur as his fingers tightened their grip for a moment. "Goodbye, Azraff."

"I love you, Naim," the fox replied.

Naim shut out the words. He shut out that smile. He shut out his fear and his pain and he shut out the world around him. He reached in. Stretched out as he'd been trained, while his golden eyes took on a soft glow. Felt the essence of the fox before him in a way so few ever could. Took hold of the essence of his character. All his best qualities. The best of him.

And then, piece by piece, Azraff began to unravel.

———

—he almost buckled under the clang of steel on steel. Azraff grit his teeth as he forced the sword of his fellow hunter back and kicked out with one foot. The boot caught the rabbit in his stomach. He doubled over, despite his armor. A backhand from Azraff's gauntleted paw turned him aside, and the fox slammed the hilt of his sword down into the back of the rabbit's neck. The other hunter went limp and hit the floor.

His eyes went wide as he glanced over at Naim. He was locked in battle with the rogue magus; lightning surged all around the ferret's body but did not touch him. Naim was a calm center in a storm of arcane energy, and all of Azraff's concern for him had to be put aside. The ferret had the rogue's attention locked firmly on him. If Azraff could get in close enough, he could end the fight.

Only one more of the ensorcelled magus hunters stood between them. The large bear was almost twice Azraff's size, but she lacked any of the fox's speed. He growled at her as she swung her massive warhammer in his direction. "Don't make me hurt you, Ketifa," he warned her.

But the bear's eyes were relatively dull and glassy. The warning fell on magically deafened ears, and she snarled back at him as she brought her hammer down in a terrifying overhead strike. Azraff ducked and rolled to the side, and the blow hit the ground with such force that it cracked open a hole in the floorboards. She tugged the weapon back, but it was no use. It was stuck.

That was his chance. Azraff darted up and leaped into the air. He came to a rest on the haft of her warhammer for a moment before he jumped up again, just in time to avoid an angry swipe of her arm. The crook of his elbow caught around Ketifa's neck as he moved past her. The sheer momentum of his leap was enough to knock her off-balance. The bear tumbled backward with him, and Ketifa almost landed on top of him as they crashed to the floor.

Azraff winced as he hit the ground, but he didn't loosen

his grip on the bear's throat. He held there, gripping his arm with his other paw and squeezing tighter. She flailed and gurgled in an attempt to knock him clear and free up her airways again. The fox remained grimly attached however as she flailed at first more desperately, and then weaker, and then finally not at all. Azraff held her there for a few moments more—she was a big girl, after all—before he let her go. He scrambled back to his feet and looked around.

Most of the other hunters he'd dazed were about to get back to their feet, too. There wasn't time. Not if they were going to end the fight. Azraff grit his teeth as he turned back to Naim, and the enraged rogue magus before him. The equine dwarfed Naim by a sizable margin and his eyes were alight with bright blue fury as that torrent of electric magic surged at Naim. The ferret's eyes were squeezed shut tighter. He doubtless couldn't hold out for much longer.

The fox moved. He squeezed his sword tight—the thing hadn't stopped humming at him since they'd entered the building—and charged full-tilt at the horse. He raised the sword as the horse turned slightly toward him and shifted a hand. The first bolt glanced off the sword, and its hum briefly froze as the arcane energy was redirected. The second slammed into Azraff's chest and left a searing black scorch mark across the fox's battered, dusty armor. The third missed as panic seemed to set in.

The fourth never came, as Naim reached out a paw and wrenched it to the side. The horse's hand turned back toward its owner, and it was only by reflex that the horse was able to keep from electrocuting himself in the face. It proved to be too much of a distraction. Azraff roared and threw himself upon the horse. His sword preceded him, and it dove deep into the rogue magus just before the fox's body slammed against him.

It was much easier to bring the horse down compared to Ketifa, though Azraff was thrown off halfway through their tumble. He hit the ground with a grunt and rolled to the side.

A glance up showed Naim rushing to his aid and, behind him, the horse beginning to rise.

Azraff's sword protruded from his chest, but it didn't seem to have stopped the rogue too much. He grinned through bloody teeth at Azraff just as Naim skidded down beside him, and fresh lightning flashed between his fingers. The hunter's eyes went wide as the horse turned not to him, but Naim. He stretched out his hand.

Azraff moved instantly to dive across the space between the two. The bolt of lightning that the rogue loosed hit Azraff in the armored chest, and this time the enchanted metal was only able to absorb a fraction of the energy. The fox cried out. His body twitched as he hit the ground. His armor was blackened where the bolt struck him, and he rolled onto his back with a groan. Out of the corner of his eye, he could see the horse turned back toward Naim again. Azraff tried to warn the ferret.

He needn't have bothered. Naim was faster. The ferret reached out with an empty hand and, anger in those glowing, golden orbs, wrenched his arm toward the ceiling. The horse's eyes went wide for a brief moment before the sword buried inside him followed Naim's motion. It ripped through the rogue magus' chest, throat and head in one clean motion. The blade buried itself in the ceiling as the horse fell apart, his body bisected from the ribs upward. His blood spilled across the floor as the hunters all around them similarly collapsed.

When Naim turned back to Azraff, the fox looked at him with shock. "I didn't know you had that in you."

"He would have killed you," Naim replied, though there was a note of pain in his voice. He glanced around at the stunned hunters. "They won't be out long. I need to unravel them before we make our escape."

Azraff nodded, and he turned to where he'd downed Ketifa. The bear's hammer had cracked the floorboards, and there below the ground was a small tunnel. A new access point to the network under Kadara. "Make it fast," he said as he pushed to his feet again. "We won't have long until the next hunters arrive. We still need to find a safe place for—"

"Stop talking, please," Naim growled. A glance showed the ferret crouched over Ketifa with his paws pressed to both sides of her head. "This is difficult enough at the best of times. Don't remind me of what comes next."

The hunter grit his teeth again as he gave a nod. Naim was right. Best they not think about what was still to come. Azraff offered a silent prayer to the gods as he closed his eyes for a second. "Give me strength to face what must be done," he whispered, "and give me wisdom to find my way back."

He looked over at Naim. The ferret had moved off to the rabbit then, his eyes aglow once more. Azraff would miss those eyes. He sighed as he pulled his sword free, and the wood around it splintered and—

———

—cracked in the distance. The slumrats cried out in terror as they fled in all directions, and Azraff felt himself buffeted by bodies as they streamed past him. He glanced back over his shoulder as another window blew out of the small building on the edge of the slums, accompanied by another jolt of lightning and burst of thunder. "Damn it all," he muttered. His sword hummed constantly at his side. It was a wonder the thing hadn't shaken loose of its sheath.

The fox was forced to push a familiar doe aside as she bounded toward him at speed. She hit the ground as her momentum was shifted. Azraff stifled a curse and paused long enough to help the doe up. She babbled her thanks as she sprinted off again. Would that he was so lucky.

A sigh of relief broke from his muzzle as he caught sight of a golden flash in the crowd. It was lost for a moment in the sea of bodies, but then he saw Naim. The ferret was barking orders at the other residents of the slums, instructing them in different directions to help each other. Azraff felt a swell of pride at the sight of his lover. Ever the altruist. That swell was swiftly swallowed up by the cold realization of what he was about to ask. "Naim!"

The call roused the ferret's attention immediately. He looked up for a second to lock his gaze on Azraff. The fox could see the way Naim's eyes went wide with sudden fear. It was like he knew what he was about to be asked. He watched as the ferret gulped and nodded, and he quickly shuffled the nearby slumrats on their way as Azraff jogged over to him.

No sooner had he arrived than Naim shook his head. "You can't."

"Look at what he's doing!" Azraff countered. He waved a paw at the building as his sword began to hum again. A moment later, another window was blown out by a crack of lightning. "They've already sent in six hunters. He's not just shredding us with magic. He's *using* us."

Naim gulped as he looked back at the building. Small flames had started on its inside, what with all the magical energies being expended within. "He's a mindthief."

Azraff nodded. "We've only got two bodies back. He's turning the hunters on anyone who comes after him." The fox reached out to grab one of Naim's paws in both of his. "I need you. Before he kills anyone else."

"He's a *mindthief*," Naim repeated as he tugged his paw free. "You go in there and you take him down, and you know what they'll do when you get back to the guildhouse!"

"And that's why it has to be you." Azraff let his arms fall back to his side. His tail tucked up between his legs. "It *has* to be you, love. They'll sift me to make sure I'm not under his control, and they'll learn about you, and…" He took a deep breath as Naim stared back at him. The ferret tried to put on a brave face, but Azraff could see through it. He could always see through it. "You have to help me, Naim. And then you'll have to unravel me."

The slap came faster than Azraff could blink and it hit harder than he'd expected it to. His head snapped to the side under Naim's blow, and when he turned back to the ferret it was with a look of anger on those beautiful features. "You bastard. How can you ask that of me? After everything we've been through? Everything we've—*you've* done?"

"Because if they sift me, they'll find you." Azraff braced for another slap as he saw the ferret's shoulders tense. It didn't come. "I won't let that happen. If you don't unravel me afterward, then I'll have to die."

Naim's eyes narrowed as he began to bounce from foot to foot. "You wouldn't dare."

"To protect you? You know I would." Azraff held out one paw to the ferret. He placed the other on the hilt of his sword. "My job's to protect the city from rogue magi, but all I want is to protect you. *Just you.*" His eyes were wide as he lifted his offered paw ever so slightly. "Please, Naim. Help me do that."

The ferret's teeth ground together as he eyed the offered paw. In the distance, another thunderous crack shook the slums. The hunter's sword hummed fiercely in response. "You're asking me to take you away from me," he said. "You're asking me to lose you."

Azraff nodded. "And I'm asking you to help me save hundreds, maybe thousands of lives in the process." The fox's ears twitched back. "It's a fine bargain, and you know it."

"Lopsided deal," Naim muttered. His eyes lifted, and for the first time ever Azraff could see true terror in there. It was reassuring, in some twisted way. Naim was so afraid to lose him. The ferret did care, after all.

A scream of pain from the direction of the compromised building sent a jolt through Naim, and the ferret seemed to shrink into himself in turn. Azraff's shoulders drooped as he felt Naim's paw slide into his. "One last transaction, then?" the ferret asked. His eyes were uncharacteristically dull.

Azraff smiled sadly and squeezed that paw. "One last transaction," he agreed, and he pulled Naim into a tight embrace as the ferret—

———

—all but collapsed under him. Azraff grunted as he was pulled by the knot down atop Naim. The magus took the extra weight surprisingly well, though he still gently elbowed the fox to the side so that he could roll carefully over with him. He chuckled as he ran a pair of fingers gently down the ferret's side. "I swear, you just like tugging on me."

"You're the one who can't help it," Naim countered. He bore back a little, wriggling into Azraff's embrace as they lay on the rug. The dim afternoon light had begun to give way to twilight, but the fox could still see the outline of the ferret's face as he leaned back to nuzzle up against his cheek. "Whatever happened to, 'They might summon me at any moment,' and all that?"

"Oh, I don't know." Azraff smirked as he slid his paw down to the ferret's hip and drew his hips back. His knot, still trapped by those hot, now considerably slicker insides, barely budged as Naim gasped. "I think you'd hardly mind me struggling to free myself."

The ferret gave a quiet chuckle as Azraff relaxed again, and he squirmed once more around the fox's sensitive, spent shaft. "You say that as though you could ever free yourself from me," he replied. "You, noble hunter, have been trapped. Ensnared by me."

"Oh I have, have I?" Azraff asked, and he smiled as he leaned in to lick across the ferret's nose. "Ensorcelled me, have you? Stolen my mind?"

"Mmm. Just your heart, if I had to wager a guess." Naim's

smile faltered for a moment and he turned back away from Azraff. He didn't try to slide out of the fox's embrace, but he did lay his head down with a sigh beneath Azraff's chin.

The afterglow of their activities began to fade considerably faster at that point. Azraff's ears flattened. "Is something wrong?" he asked.

Naim was silent. The ferret squirmed—itself not too helpful, given what was lodged inside him at the time—but offered no words in response.

Azraff began to frown as one ear perked. "You're worried," he said as he gently ran the back of his paw down over Naim's cheek.

"I'm always worried, Az," the ferret sighed. He nuzzled gently into the fox's touch. "How long can we keep doing this? Being… *this?* It's only a matter of time until—"

"Hey." Azraff gave Naim a gentle squeeze as he snuggled in tighter against the ferret's back. "None of that. What we are… what this is? What we're doing? It's all up to you, love." Naim twitched against him at that last word, and Azraff sighed. "It still makes you uncomfortable."

"We've been at this for a year now," Naim reasoned as he closed his eyes. "A year of… of whatever this is. Every time, it could be the last. Every time, it could be another hunter who chances upon my work. Am I meant to seduce my way to freedom with whomsoever comes next as well?"

Azraff blinked. "That's not—" he began.

"Not for you." The interruption wasn't angry. Naim's words were calm, perhaps tired. "I can forget. Sometimes, I can just… forget what we are. Imagine what we could have been, were our lives different." He sighed as he curled in slightly. "But then I remember. Would that I could forget entirely, as you seem to."

"You don't…" Azraff cleared his throat. A sliver of fear stabbed his heart. "You don't think that… I don't care, do you?"

Again, Naim twitched. "No," he said after a quiet moment. "No, I think you do care. Truly. I know you do. I can feel the truth of it. Hear it in your mind."

The fox blinked. "So what's the problem?"

"One you are yet too blind to see." Naim fell still again, though he did lean back into the hunter's embrace. "I see an end coming, Az. Our end. A day, a week, a month… it's coming, and all because of who we are." He paused for a moment. "I would rather be ready. See it coming. Prepare for it."

Eyes closed as Azraff wrapped himself around the ferret. He didn't say anything. What was there to be said, anyway? What could he say? There was nothing that would help. Nothing that would assuage Naim's concerns. He was powerless.

It was all he could do to—

———

—cover his mouth to stifle his laugh. "That's madness," Azraff said, once he was able to speak again. "Absolute bedlam. And he got away with it?"

"Only until Master Saniyah sifted him and found the truth," Naim replied, and he grinned. "She made him smoke the whole lot in a single go. I've never seen such colors come out of a hookah. Isam wasn't the same for *days* afterward!"

Azraff didn't even bother to cover his muzzle that time. He tossed his head back and laughed up to the stars. "Never! Never let it be said that magi don't know how to have a fun time!"

His words were quieter than his laughter had been, but the sounds of the Kadara markets after dusk easily drowned them out. Nevertheless, a glance down at Naim revealed sudden nervousness. "You're worrying too much. This was meant to be a nice night for us."

"I don't often get to leave the slums," he replied, his own voice suddenly quieter as well. He leaned in against Azraff and hooked his arm in the fox's as he lifted his other arm. He flapped about the loose-fitting sleeve of his robe, clean and new and a bright red that matched Azraff's fur. "Or have nice nights. And this… you didn't need to buy me a new robe. I won't be able to wear it in the slums without being robbed. It's too nice."

The fox leaned in and nuzzled gently against the top of the ferret's head. "I wanted to do something nice for you," he replied with an easy shrug. "You do so much, and it's thankless work. I wanted you to feel… appreciated."

"Oh, I'm sure I'll be shown how great your appreciation is later this evening," Naim said. He cocked an eyebrow as he wiggled his ears.

"Only should you wish it yourself," he told the ferret with a shake of his head and an easy smile. "Our days of bargains and transactions are done. I want to prove that to you." Naim's smile faltered for a second, but it was an eternity to Azraff. "What? What is it?"

"You don't need to do this, Az." Naim shook his head. "Making up for it. Trying to convince me that you actually want me for who I am. This isn't about me."

Confusion touched Azraff. He felt his ears droop as he looked down at the ferret. Not for the first time, he wished he could sense Naim's emotions and thoughts the way the magus could sense his. "You seem sure. What is it about then, if not that?"

Naim continued to avoid Azraff's gaze. "You feel guilty. Uneasy, as you should, about how we have come to know each other so intimately. You mean to assuage my disgust at those memories, and your own guilt at what you impressed upon us."

The ferret slipped off Azraff's arm, though he didn't drift

far. Azraff could only stare after him. "Could it not be that I have come to genuinely care about you?" he asked.

"I most sincerely hope not," Naim replied. He turned a little further away. "Such a thing would be most dangerous indeed, for both of us."

"Then gods take the danger." Azraff reached out again to take a gentle but firm hold of the ferret's arm. He turned Naim back toward him, and the magus didn't fight but also didn't lift his head to meet Azraff's gaze. "Yes. I feel guilty. I took advantage of you, and I was wrong to have done so. I abused your position of weakness from my position of strength, and I was wrong to have done so. And as I have said before, and as I will *always* say to you, I am so, so sorry.

"But we're here. Now." He waved his other arm about the markets. "And I gave you your chances to leave. You've had every single chance in the world to cast me aside, Naim. You didn't even have to come with me tonight. You haven't left, and I haven't wanted you to leave." He gently reached down to tilt the ferret's chin up, and those golden eyes shone up at him as he tried a little smile. "We've been through too much together these last few months, and if you truly feel this way, you would have left. Why haven't you?"

Naim glanced aside for a moment, but when his eyes met Azraff's again they seemed softer. Warmer. "Could it not be that I have come to genuinely care about you?" he asked.

The words sent the warmth in Naim's eyes all the way through Azraff's heart, and his smile widened as he squeezed gently at the smaller ferret. "Such a thing would be most dangerous indeed, for both of us," he replied, and leaned down.

His lips met a finger. Azraff leaned back, confused as Naim shook his head. "Yes," he replied, and he seemed to sag in Azraff's arms. "Yes, it would be."

Azraff gave him another little squeeze. "Gods take the danger?" he suggested. He wanted to hear the words. He wanted to hear Naim say them. He wanted it more than he thought he would. More than he'd wanted anything in the world.

But he—

————

—wasn't where Azraff normally met him. The fox frowned as he glanced around. There were few quiet, deserted places in the slums where they were able to meet, and for him to go directly to the ferret's hut every time wouldn't have done anything but arouse suspicion. Their little nook in an alley by the city's outer walls was as good a place as any, but for the first time Naim wasn't present. A moment's fear gripped Azraff, but it passed. The ferret was probably just busy.

No sooner had he left the nook and started back toward the main road through the slums however than that fear returned. The massive figure of Ketifa, a fellow hunter, stood in the middle of the road. One meaty paw was on the warhammer strapped to her back. The other…

The other rested on Naim's shoulder.

Azraff couldn't hear what they were saying from where he was, but a mage hunter only stopped someone for one reason. The fox's blood ran cold. Naim was in trouble. He started to make his way over toward them.

Naim must have noticed his approach, since the ferret's eyes flicked in his direction. It was enough to alert Ketifa, and she turned even as she squeezed Naim's shoulder tighter. The ferret cried out in pain at the bear's grip as she smiled down at the fox. "Azraff."

"Ketifa." He nodded to her as he folded his arms. "And… what is this?"

"This?" She turned back to Naim for a moment before she pushed down hard with the meaty hand that held the ferret. Naim hit the ground, crumpled by the shove as he cowered beneath her. "This slumrat set off my weapon. He is a magus." Her eyes narrowed as she glared down at him. "Unregistered. Rogue."

"I see." Azraff followed her gaze down to Naim. The fox was forced to adopt a similar sneer of derision as his mind raced. He didn't have much on him. Nothing that could solve the problem bloodlessly. "And he has demonstrated his powers?"

Those words drew a scowl from Ketifa. She turned her glare on Azraff a moment later. "He has not. In fact, he has denied that he is a magus. Says that it's a false reading."

"It is, but!" shouted one of the other ragged denizens of the slums from behind the bear. "Naim ain't got no magic! He just begs, like the lot of us!"

"Yeah!" called out another. "No magi here, big girl! Run on back to your guild house, huh?"

A growl rose in Ketifa's throat. "I hope you're all telling the truth," she warned them as she glanced around. "If I find he's a magus and you're lying to me, your punishment will be the same as his."

That silenced the crowd, just as Azraff had a moment's inspiration. Maybe… if Naim was as quick-witted as he seemed, this could work. "Have you searched him?" he asked.

Naim only looked confused as Ketifa scowled at the fox again. "Why?" she asked, suddenly suspicious.

His reply was an exaggerated sigh as he crouched down close to Naim. He began to roughly pat the ferret up and down and took a moment to lean in over his shoulder. "Left pouch," he whispered into Naim's ear. Any louder, and Ketifa would have heard him. "Quickly!"

He continued to search the ferret, until at last he felt Naim draw back again. "Ah. Here!" he announced, as he blocked Ketifa's view with his body and grabbed what was in the ferret's paw. He stood and yanked Naim upright with him and revealed the contents of his paw: a small, pewter ring. "This. This is what you detected."

She looked skeptical. "A ring. I detected a *ring*."

"An enchanted artifact," Azraff said. He held it up for her to inspect. "Market's been flooded with these lately. Low-level thing. Harmless really, but completely unregulated. I've been keeping an eye out for them." He frowned up at the bear. "You really should listen to the commander more often, Ketifa. You're getting sloppy."

She sneered down at the fox. "It doesn't look magical to me, Azraff," she countered.

He rolled his eyes. "Because it's not been activated," he replied, and slowly, obviously, lifted his other paw as he glanced at Naim. "But if I rub it like so…" Slowly he lowered his paw, extended a finger, and stroked it across the side of the ring.

Naim's head was bowed to cover the glow of his eyes, but Ketifa's attention was focused on the ring. It began to vibrate in Azraff's paw, and then both his sword and Ketifa's hammer began to hum. "You see?" he said as he closed his paw over the ring again. He fought back the sigh of relief that threatened to slip out. Naim had done his part.

Ketifa, for her part, looked disappointed. "I was so sure."

"Go," Azraff told her with a dismissive wave of his paw. He tucked the ring back into his belt pouch and then reached out to grab Naim. "I'll get the information about which merchant sold it to him and shut them down." His eyes narrowed. "And remember. The slums are *my* hunting grounds."

She glared back at him but nodded gruffly and turned away. The bear marched right back up along the main road, and a crowd's worth of eyes watched her leave. Azraff didn't dare move a muscle until she was well out of sight. Even then he didn't say anything until he pulled Naim off the road. "Gods all… are you alright?"

"Fine, fine," Naim muttered back again, though the ferret clearly looked shaken. He shook himself clear of Azraff's grip and brushed down his robe. "You didn't have to do that."

"Looked to us like he did," said someone on the street; the first voice from before.

"We don't know what we'd do without you, Naim!" said another.

"Thank you, good hunter!" said a third.

That last one flattened Azraff's ears with embarrassment. "I'm just glad you're safe," he said.

Naim frowned as he looked up at him. "Why?" he asked. "Because it's time again? Time to bargain? Another transaction?"

"No." The word surprised the ferret. "That's what I came down to tell you. No more bargains. No more transactions. I'm done with that." He shook his head as he crouched down for a second, and then came to rest on his knees before Naim. "I'm so sorry. You are a good person, doing good things, and I… have mistreated you so, so badly. I cannot ever beg your forgiveness, and I do not deserve it. I came to say goodbye, Naim.

Shock was written across the ferret's face as Azraff bowed his head. He seemed stunned to silence. "I…" he began, then paused and shook his head. "Thank you. Not only for this, but… you saved my life." He shook his head and gently reached out to lift Azraff's face again. "I suppose perhaps now we are even in the latter regard, yes?"

Azraff smiled. "I suppose we are," he agreed, even as he began to frown. "Does that mean you would… not be averse to seeing me again? Not just to check on you and make sure you're okay, but…"

Naim held up a paw to stop him. Azraff felt his heart sink for a moment. "You saved my life," he said. "That does not undo our history. I need… time."

The fox tucked his tail and nodded. That was fair. "And

you shall have it," he told the magus with a nod. "But if I need your help again with threats to this city… could I count on you to help me?"

That nod came much faster, and it brought a sigh of relief to Azraff's muzzle. "I suppose you can," Naim said, and the ferret even gave a small smile of his own. He—

———

—couldn't have gone too far. "Anything?" Azraff hissed. The sword in his hand was silent.

No more than a step or two behind, Naim sighed. "I told you that I would let you know when I have something," he growled back. A glance at the ferret showed his glare filled with frustration.

Azraff sighed and turned his gaze forward again. The tunnels and caverns under Kadara, left over from when an old guild of thieves operated in the city with impunity, were seldom traveled. The air was stale. Dust clung to every surface. It rained down over them as people, ignorant of the hunt below, continued their lives above. "Naim," he insisted.

The sword in Azraff's paw began to hum as the ferret closed his eyes. Azraff glanced around again. The tunnel split into three passages. His quarry could only be down one. The dust beneath their feet looked equally undisturbed at all three passages. There was no way to know which his target had fled down. Not without Naim's help.

A sudden weight slammed into Azraff's back as the hum of his sword intensified dramatically. The hunter grunted as he tumbled to the ground and rolled across the floor, a cloud of dust kicked up all around him. He lifted his head to see a stone spike raised from the ground where he had been, and Naim with his paw outstretched. The ferret stared back at him, his eyes wide as Azraff blinked. Surely he'd not tried to kill him!

The rise of a second spike stole those thoughts away. Naim danced lithely to the side as the ground trembled beneath him and erupted up. The spear missed him, and he rolled to the left then as another spike rose out of the ground to strike. Naim's eyes lifted. Azraff followed his gaze.

There. The wolf was pressed up in a corner of the cavern, his feet braced against outcroppings of stone. His eyes burned with an intense orange light as he thrust an arm upward, and another spike of stone exploded out from beneath the ground. This one too missed Naim, but it was closer than the others. The ferret didn't have long.

Azraff thought quickly. He unbuckled his sword's sheath from his belt and cocked back his arm. The wolf tried to impale Naim again as Azraff lined up his shot. Took a second to check his aim. Exhaled. Hurled it with all his might.

The wolf seemed surprised as he turned toward the incoming sheath. He cried out more in shock than pain as the arc of its trajectory saw the end of it jab into his gut. It didn't pierce flesh, but it disoriented him enough that he lost his footing. His cry turned into a yip as he hit the ground back first, and a groan followed as he writhed on the floor. Azraff dusted himself off as he started over to the hurt magus. "You," he said as he waggled his sword at the wolf, "have been nothing but trouble."

The groans cut off as the wolf rolled his head toward Azraff. The glow was gone from his eyes, though it impotently sputtered and sparked as the wolf grit his teeth. A line of blood began to run from the corner of his mouth as he stared angrily up at the mage hunter. "And you consort with a rogue," he growled back. "Your guildmates would not approve, hunter."

"No." Azraff paused above the wolf. "They would not." And with that, he reached down to draw the blade of his sword swiftly across the wolf's throat.

He didn't bother to linger on the lupine magus as he

gurgled his last on the ground. Instead, he stepped over him and made for Naim. The ferret stared at his fellow magus. "Are you hurt?" he asked.

The words seemed to snap Naim's attention back again. "I'm sorry?" he asked. Behind Azraff, the wolf's back arched one last time as he fought for breath. Finally, he slumped down and lay still.

Azraff reached up slowly to lay his paw on the ferret's shoulder. "Are you injured?" he asked again as he looked Naim over. The robes didn't seem torn in any new places, but that wasn't saying much. "Did he—"

"I'm fine," Naim replied and brushed the paw away. "He wasn't anything special. Probably no more than an initiate. His magic was sloppy."

"Not so sloppy that he didn't kill eight people," Azraff countered. He looked down at the ground. He'd never seen a magus use it as a weapon against him before. If not for Naim… "You saved my life."

"That is what I do, hunter," Naim said. He shrugged, but his eyes drifted down to the wolf's body. "This, however, is what *you* do."

Azraff followed his gaze and perked an ear. "You're defending a murderer?" he asked. "The same murderer you just helped me to eliminate?"

Naim began to hop from foot to foot in the way that Azraff had come to associate with nervousness or frustration. "Of course not. That is why I helped you. There was a risk to the people of this city, and while I may not be a member of the Order of Magi anymore?" He drew himself up tall and proud. "I do not shirk my duty to my home. Not ever."

The fox perked an eyebrow. Naim's sense of righteousness was enviable. "And that was the only reason you decided to aid me?" he asked.

"That it served as alternative payment for your benevolence is not unwelcome," Naim said, and he rolled his eyes as he bit the words out.

"And yet you saved me." Azraff frowned as he waved a paw at the wolf's body. "You could have let him kill me. Perhaps escaped the city with him."

The ferret's eyes flashed for a moment, and Azraff briefly felt his sword briefly begin to hum again. "If you think I would have done anything other than what I did, then you clearly know me not at all." He tilted his head up. "I have done as you asked, hunter. Am I free to go?"

Azraff sighed. Why did Naim have to always be so difficult? "Yes," he said. "Of course you are."

Naim tilted his head to the side. "And the arrangement?"

"Is already paid for by your service to me in this matter." Azraff shook his head. "You won't have to see me again for a month. Just as we agreed."

"Good. Some peace will do my mind a true kindness." The ferret nodded as he turned and started back the way they'd come.

Azraff winced as his tail tucked up between his legs. "Naim?" he called after the ferret.

Naim paused where he stood and sighed. He hung his head low for a moment before he turned to face Azraff again. Irritation was spread clear across his face. "What? What is it now?"

In spite of the glare leveled at him, Azraff favored the ferret with a little smile. "Thank you," he said. "Not just for helping me, but... you saved my life. You didn't have to, but you did. Thank you."

The ferret's muzzle opened as if to snap some witty and frustrated words back at Azraff, and the fox was all prepared to bear them. But then Naim's muzzle shut again and he glanced aside for a second. Paused. Seemed to consider what he'd said.

Azraff had been about to turn back to the wolf's body

when Naim finally replied, "You are welcome, hunter. As I said, protection and healing are what I do. I am… glad to have saved at least one life today."

At that, the fox's smile became a little wider. Perhaps there was hope for Naim yet. He nodded to the ferret, and the nod was returned as Naim—

———

—drew a moan from the fox's muzzle as he arched his back. Naim's own muzzle made its usual sounds as it slid smoothly up and down along the fox's shaft, and they sounded especially loud in the darkness of the ferret's hovel. Every brush of the ferret's lips along that sensitive flesh sent sparks of pleasure through Azraff's mind.

The first time had been intense, but short. The second, longer but no less overwhelming. By the third time he'd sunk into that seemingly bottomless muzzle, Azraff knew he'd made the right call. The bargain was sound. No one was hurt. Everyone won. Especially, as a shudder rolled its way up the fox's spine, Azraff.

His fingers curled around the shorter magus' little ears, though he didn't squeeze or tug at them. He rubbed slowly, caressed them in time with the bobs of Naim's head below him. The ferret's tongue teased up and down along the underside of his shaft with every motion, as though Naim's ears controlled it. It felt as though he was manipulating the ferret's body directly, and it drew a fresh moan out of Azraff.

A throb in the midst of that moan saw an echo sound through the hut. Azraff's eyes widened as he glanced down at the ferret below him. The sound had been muffled, but there'd been no way to mistake the way it had vibrated along his shaft. Naim had moaned. The ferret was *enjoying* himself too. That knowledge sent another throb through Azraff's length, and rewarded Naim with another surge of slick, warm pre. The sound didn't repeat itself, but it did reinvigorate the ferret's bobbing.

His lips pressed tighter around the fox's length, and they bumped firmly into Azraff's knot as it swelled rapidly at his base. Naim moved faster as Azraff moaned again above him, and it was without any control at all that the fox's hips began to twitch and hump forward. That little moan from Naim had done more for him than he'd expected. It was a whole other thrill; reinforcement that the ferret was getting something out of the physicality of the bargain as well.

It took everything Azraff had to control his hips. Even as he slowed down he felt Naim pick up the slack. The ferret all but lurched forward to take Azraff right down to the base, and the fox's back arched as he could do little more than grind his knot against the magus' lips. "Gods all!" he managed to gasp. Fingers tightened inadvertently on Naim's ears.

The ferret didn't seem to notice all that much. It certainly didn't affect his performance. His tongue teased down around the top of Azraff's knot each time he bottomed out. The fox felt the tightness of Naim's throat swallow him up quite literally, as though the magus wanted to take him further still. Azraff's knot was too large though, and the fox could do little more than grind against that hungry muzzle while Naim tried to rectify the situation.

It was never going to work though, and it seemed Naim knew it. He pulled back, set to resume his rapid bobbing under Azraff's paws as the fox felt his shaft pulse once more. He throbbed harder and grit his teeth, his ears pinned back as he squeezed his eyes shut. "Naim, I—" he warned. Whether it was to entice the ferret to slow or continue he didn't know.

But it didn't matter, either. Naim wasn't about to stop, and the ferret redoubled his efforts again. One paw squeezed at the fox's hip while the other slid up from his thigh to hook fingers in behind Azraff's knot. The hunter saw stars. The whole world exploded out of view around him as Naim squeezed and once more took him into his throat. Control vanished. Restraint was gone. He pulsed in warning once. Again.

His moan echoed off the walls as he peaked. His fingers tightened around those cute little ears again as he pulled Naim in for a brief moment. The first surge of his seed passed the ferret's muzzle entirely as he remained thoroughly impaled on Azraff's shaft. The fox shuddered with the second shot, fired so hard that he feared he might hurt the ferret beneath him.

If Naim was even remotely discomforted, he didn't show it. The ferret stuck to him doggedly, his lips sealed around the top of Azraff's knot as his fingers teased and squeezed and milked it from behind. He didn't move, save to gulp and swallow around the tip of the fox's length as it continued to pulse and spurt right down into his belly. Not a drop escaped. Not a moment passed where he wasn't swallowing.

At least until the flow started to subside. Naim slid back and relaxed his grip on Azraff's knot as the fox sagged forward, only the tip left inside his muzzle as the last of his orgasm drooled out of him and across the ferret's waiting tongue. That tongue teased the underside of Azraff's tip in just the way Naim had learned he liked, and it rewarded the ferret with one last spurt before the flow tapered off once again. "Gods," Azraff panted.

There was no answer from Naim. He was still hard at work, tending to the leaking shaft between his lips and swallowing down everything that dripped out. He remained there, silent for a good minute or so before he finally popped off of it and looked up at Azraff. "And are you satisfied, hunter?" he asked.

Azraff opened his eyes and looked down at the ferret. Those gorgeous golden eyes stared back up at him, but they were absent the bitterness that usually followed in the wake of their little 'transactions.' There was a hint of red under the fur of his cheeks, and he could see it had spread as the fox released the ferret's ears. "As ever," he said after he took a moment to gather his breath. "You are... *very* good at that. I had no idea you enjoyed it so much yourself."

There was a moment's indignation that flashed across Naim's face, but the moment passed as his gaze drifted aside. "I would not have offered such a thing were I not already inclined to it," he reasoned. "I find the act itself enjoyable, yes. I take what pleasure I can to dull the shame of it. I would find this arrangement considerably more pleasurable were it not under duress."

The waves of pleasure in the aftermath of Naim's talented muzzle crashed on the shores of guilt. Azraff's ears flattened as he too looked away from the ferret below him. "I... expect so," he replied. Lamely, he thought to himself as Naim stood up again.

As he stood though, Azraff could see something else. A damp spot in Naim's old robes, where he'd been crouched. His eyes widened. The ferret really had been enjoying it. "Wait a moment," he said, and reached out to Naim's arm.

His paw was batted away by the ferret though, and Azraff blinked in surprise as Naim turned a glare on him. "You have what you came for," the magus growled. "My part in our bargain is done. Now is the time for you to uphold yours. Leave me to my work. I have many people to help in the slums."

The fox frowned as he perked an ear. "You misunderstand me," he said as he folded his arms. "I meant to... I mean..." He coughed as he cleared his throat and nodded down to the ferret's dampened robes.

Naim glanced down along his body, only to look up again with a frown. "Oh? You would sully yourself by pleasuring some filthy slumrat? Debase yourself for his release?" Those golden eyes narrowed. "Oh no, noble hunter. I'd not dream of forcing you to my level. Heavens forbid." He swept an arm toward the flaps that protected the entrance to the little hut. "By your leave. *Hunter.*"

The dismissal was clear, and it only amplified the guilt that Azraff felt. Naim must have been able to sense it clearly too, but it did little to change the ferret's demeanor. He thought to argue for a moment; perhaps to insist on it as a part of their deal.

A look at Naim's face stole that thought from his mind. Such a thing would only compound the ferret's hatred for him. Instead, Azraff nodded. There was nothing for it but to leave, and so he—

———

—saw him across the shanties. Azraff was certain of it. He'd seen the ferret and his ragged old robe a couple of times in the eastern corner of the slums, when rogues had gone to ground there. Never for long, and never more than out the corner of his eyes. Now, the way his sword hummed at his side, the hunter knew why.

This time was different. The ferret hadn't seen him yet. His focus was wholly on a young doe sprawled out on a table before him. She writhed as if in pain, and Azraff made his way over as the ferret ran his fingertips across the female's leg. Up and down, up and down, until he saw the fox.

Azraff didn't stop his approach, and the ferret's motions only froze for a couple of seconds before he resumed them. His eyes were aglow; their golden color amplified and lit from within by the same magic that set Azraff's sword humming. He didn't run as the fox drew closer, and Azraff felt a moment's confusion.

That confusion only doubled when he reached their side and the ferret lifted his other paw. "You'll have to wait a moment," he told the hunter. "I'm busy."

Confusion gave way to surprise, and then even admiration. This magus had balls. "I've got time," he replied.

The ferret snorted and returned his full attention to the doe. Azraff watched on, and with his new vantage point could see what the magus worked at. The doe's leg bore a deep gash, but more than that a sickly, foul-smelling pus seeped from what had to have been a relatively nasty wound. As the ferret's fingers stroked along the cut, that viscous goo seemed to bubble and steam away. "What are you doing?" he asked.

"What does it look like I'm doing?" Those golden eyes rolled, though the ferret remained focused. "If I cannot stem the infection, she will die."

"And do you have your papers on you, magus?" Azraff asked. He felt the corner of his muzzle turn up slightly as an ear perked.

"Like I said," the ferret bit out as he closed his eyes, "you'll have to wait a moment."

The smirk only grew on Azraff's face, and the fox nodded once as he felt his tail twitch. No registered magus would be caught dead in the slums. No registered magus would make a member of the hunter's guild wait for him. The ferret was his quarry, and there would be no escape this time.

The minutes wore on though, and the ferret's breath became more and more labored. The wound continued to close and clear as Azraff watched on, but it was clear the ferret's strength had begun to flag. The doe's writhing had slowed, and her pitiful groans had grown quiet. Azraff wondered if that meant she was recovering, or if she was fading.

But then she gasped, her eyes wide, and sucked in a deep breath of air. The ferret slumped over her, and Azraff reached out to catch him by the shoulder before he fell across the doe's legs. "Easy, there," he said, as he gently pushed the ferret back into position. "Breathe, magus."

The doe yipped from the table as she finally saw Azraff.

The fox's eyes flicked to her as he flattened his ears and reached his free paw for his sword. Almost faster than he could blink, the doe scrabbled back and off the makeshift table and to her feet. It was a testament to the work of the magus that she bolted faster than Azraff had ever seen anyone move.

"Breath comes easy," the ferret muttered as he looked up, and Azraff was once again struck by those golden eyes. Even without the glow, they were stunning. "What comes next, perhaps not so much."

At that, Azraff would have normally smiled. Instead, his expression was neutral as he felt a pang of guilt. "You have no papers."

"And you're a magus hunter." The ferret's tone was matter-of-fact. "I know how this plays out, fox. You take my head. I'm too dangerous, aren't I?" At that the ferret gave a joyless smile of his own. "I mean, these slums rather won't heal themselves, will they? Best off me before I can do something horrible like set some more bones or conjure some clean water."

Once more there was that pang of guilt. This was the first time Azraff had encountered a magus like the ferret. The others all fought. Ran. Killed. Were killed. "You're a healer."

"I *was* many things," the ferret replied. He brushed the paw off his shoulder as he stood a little taller. Azraff's fingers tightened on his sword, but the fox left it sheathed for the moment. "You are one. You're here to do your job." The ferret spread his arms slightly. "Get it over with. I don't have all day."

Azraff blinked. "You want me to kill you?" he asked.

The ferret's eyes narrowed, a hint of irritation entering his gaze. "The guild doesn't allow for leeway. You're here on the hunt for undocumented magi. You found me. Don't waste my time."

He was right, of course. The guild charter and the law of

the land was clear. The ferret wasn't documented. He was a rogue. And yet, there was a softness behind the frustration in his gaze. The male was gentle. He offered the lowly wretches of the slums comfort and aid even though it put him in danger. He was no threat. If he'd not seen it for himself, he'd not have believed it.

He remained still and silent. The ferret sighed. "Do you need me to give you a reason?" As Azraff looked up into those eyes again, he saw something else behind them. Tiredness, and something more. A profound sadness. "There's no other way out of this, is there?"

"Perhaps not." Azraff stepped back and squeezed gently at the hilt of his sword again. Its hum had long since faded as the ferret's magic ceased, but it had seen the truth as surely as Azraff had. The ferret sank down to his knees and bowed his head. Azraff rounded the table and stood before him. A flicker of thought struck him; under different circumstances, this scenario and their respective positions could have been fun. Alas, it couldn't be.

"Wait." The word came from beneath him, and Azraff frowned as the ferret lifted his eyes. "You... fancy me."

Suspicion wormed its way through the fox. "You're a mindthief."

"Magus," the ferret corrected him, and he glanced side to side as he shuffled a little closer to Azraff's legs. "No matter what they do to cast me out: magus. And sensing your surface thoughts is easy. Especially such... lascivious ones." The ferret looked up at him. "Perhaps there *is* another way out of this after all."

"You're not seriously suggesting this." Azraff shook his head, though he knew the perk of his ears would have given his interest away.

The ferret shrugged. "If you're busy, you've no reason to take my head off," he reasoned. "If I still have my head, I can still help the people down here. Do some good." The ferret set his jaw as he looked up at Azraff. "Or you can just end it now. The choice is yours. The offer's on the table only so long as my head's on my shoulders."

The hunter glanced about. This little corner of the slums was relatively empty for the moment, but this was hardly the place to engage in such things. If he was interested. Which, of course, he wasn't. But if he was—if he *would*—then surely it wouldn't be the worst thing that could happen.

Could it?

The fox licked at his lips as he looked down again at the still—kneeling ferret. His expression had changed from irritated and saddened to resigned. He knew Azraff's answer even before Azraff had needed to say a word. "Alright," he said, and unbuckled—

———

Azraff's eyes opened.

The glare of the afternoon sun forced him to close them again all of a sudden, and the fox gasped as he sat sharply up. His head throbbed, and he groaned as he pressed a paw to the side of it. "Gods take me," he muttered as he slowly began to shake his head.

"Easy there, friend," came a voice from his side.

He whirled and forced his eyes open again, despite the brilliant light. The figure resolved itself into the form of a smallish ferret in the tattered rags that passed for clothes among the slum-dwellers of Kadara. He shrank back from Azraff's glare and immediately dropped to a knee before him. "Do not be afraid, noble hunter," the ferret said, his eyes firmly locked on the ground. "I mean you no harm."

"Doubtful," grunted the fox as he cast his gaze around. They were on the edge of the slums in the eastern quarter. Somehow this meek little slumrat had kept him secure from the rest of the scavengers of the quarter while he was unconscious. "Do you know the punishment for stealing from a mage hunter, wretch? I assure you, it is *most* severe."

"A thousand pardons for startling you, noble hunter," the ferret told him again. Azraff blinked in surprise at the sound of his voice. It wavered. Had this ferret been crying? "I don't know what brought you here, but… you seemed to be in pain. I thought to sit by you… to wait for you to awaken. I would never dream of stealing from one of your station."

Again the fox snorted. He shook his head as he looked back down at the ferret. He trembled before Azraff, as well he should. "How did I come to be here?" the fox demanded as he forced himself to his feet. He drew his sword, and the thing gave surprising resistance to the tug. It became clear why, as the blade was covered in congealed blood and gore. Azraff's eyes widened. "What in the gods names has happened to me? Answer!"

"I cannot say, I swear!" babbled the ferret as he lifted his head. Azraff could see there that he *had* been crying. His cheeks bore the wet troughs of tears, and his eyes were reddened with some grief or other. A paw idly twisted a small, pewter ring on a finger.

"Humph. Useless wretch. Stand aside!" The fox stretched his legs and arched his back as he moved to where the ferret stood. The feeble creature scurried to the side, his back still stooped as he remained low. Fit to his station. "I was in a fight."

It was no question, and the ferret nodded along. "There was a great battle, yes," he told the fox. "A sorcerer was warping minds. We heard about it even down here. I went to see… found you." His eyes lifted again for a moment, and they sparkled before the ferret dropped his gaze once more. "I wasn't going to leave you."

Azraff grunted and swung his empty paw at the ferret. The backhanded blow was weak, but it still collapsed the wretch where he crouched. "And by taking me from where I was, you likely prevented my fellow hunters from locating me! Fool!" He raised his paw for another blow as the ferret cowered beneath him.

Paused.

His paw twitched. Shook. He felt a moment's… what was that? Regret? Sympathy? Pain? Azraff forced it down as he watched the ferret curl inward before the hunter. "Who are you?" he demanded. His paw dropped back to his side. "Name yourself. Now."

"No one of consequence," the ferret replied, and Azraff found himself struck in turn. Something about this voice was familiar. Perhaps they'd crossed paths before. "No name of consequence. Just one of many in the slums. Just another one unworthy to even behold the might of the hunters. Please, I beg you. Forgive my offensive form and words."

Whoever that ferret was, he'd been educated. His dialect was cleaner than most of the slumrats Azraff had the misfortune to cross paths with. He'd probably once been someone of import who'd crossed the wrong lord or some such. "Pick yourself up off the ground. Let me get a look at you."

The ferret hesitated, but he complied in a moment. He brushed the dirt from his robes as he hugged himself about his middle, though his eyes were hidden by a downcast stare. "We have not met before, have we?" he asked the ferret. The fox began to frown as he looked the poor male up and down. He seemed so familiar. Something about him…

But the ferret shook his head as he glanced aside. "I doubt I am worthy of remembrance, noble hunter," he replied. His voice hitched near the end as his eyes began to well up once more.

"So few in the slums are," Azraff agreed even as he reached out. He delicately tilted the ferret's chin up with a fingertip to take a better look, and it was with obvious reluctance that the ferret's golden eyes met his. He was attractive, yes, and there was still that lingering familiarity. He just couldn't place it. "You... I feel like I should know you."

"I ought feel threatened if you did, noble hunter," the ferret told him with a shake of his head. One of the ferret's dusty paws came up to wipe away his tears, and only succeeded in smearing dust into his fur. It mixed with the dampness already there to muddy his face up, but it did little to diminish his beauty. "Someone remembered by a mage hunter would likely be their quarry."

The fox hummed his agreement as one of his ears perked up. He leaned in a little closer as he drank in every last detail of the ferret's face. He was so close he could taste it, and yet... "You should be so lucky," he muttered as he began to draw back. "No. No, even if a magus unravels memories, some trace remains. If you were my target, I would *know* it."

Those bright, golden eyes softened for a moment—the sight of them filled him with more warmth than the sun had rays, but why?—before the ferret bowed his head. "Then I am grateful that I am... nothing to you, noble hunter. I'm sorry. I only wished to provide you aid. I won't keep you a moment longer."

Azraff frowned as he reached out. His ears flattened as he watched the ferret flinch back from his paws. That feeling of guilt and shame rose inside him again. Where had that come from? He held still for a moment and remained silent, and he waited for the nervous bouncing of one of the ferret's legs to still before he reached out again. His paws found the ferret's shoulders; the smaller male trembled under his grip and looked anywhere but at the fox as he was studied.

Azraff still couldn't place him, but that didn't matter. He began to gently dust the ferret's robes down. At first the ferret's trembles turned into veritable quakes of fear, but they began to ease back as the ferret relaxed under his touch. "I... beg your forgiveness, sir," he said at last. The words were unlike him, but they came naturally nonetheless. "I should not have struck you. I was dazed and confused, but… that's no excuse. One such as I must be held to a higher standard."

"You have nothing to beg forgiveness for," the ferret replied after a moment. He looked as surprised as Azraff felt. "I was in the wrong. I am sorry."

"No, you have tried to help me. Your service to the hunter's guild will not be forgotten." Azraff stepped back to admire his handiwork, and his ears remained pinned back as he scowled. He'd not been able to tidy up the ferret's rags all too much, but it had been something at least. "May I do something for you, in turn? A reward for your good intentions."

The ferret's eyes widened, but he bowed his head and shook it quickly. "I appreciate the offer, noble hunter, but it is not necessary. Would not your colleagues wonder?"

Azraff cracked a little smile. Why was he smiling? The thought sent a tendril of warmth through him. "Perhaps they would, at that," he replied at last, and took another step back. "Very well. Good day, sir." He nodded to the ferret and turned to leave.

"Naim."

The fox paused in mid-step. He planted his foot in the ground and perked his ears as he turned to look back over his shoulder. "I'm sorry?"

The ferret stood there. His eyes were still on the ground and he clutched tightly at one of his arms, but he stood tall again. "You wanted to know who I was," he told Azraff, and his head lifted ever so slightly to allow the setting sun to catch his eyes. They sparkled in the light as Azraff felt his breath hitch in his throat. "It's… I'm Naim."

"Naim." Azraff turned the word over in his mouth as he watched the ferret in the light of the dying day. "It's beautiful. And should you wish it, mine is Azraff." He smiled and nodded to the ferret as he turned to leave the strange, familiar ferret once more.

The warmth vanished and a shiver wound down his spine as he heard the ferret give a sad little sigh behind him. "Goodbye, Azraff," he said. The words were quiet enough that the fox wasn't even sure it wasn't the wind. He gulped as he found his feet frozen again. His tail tucked up between his legs as he hesitated, and he had to forcibly shake himself out of his stupor. His fellow hunters would be looking for him. Something had happened, surely. He would attend to his duties first, and the strange ferret could wait. Couldn't he?

And yet with every step away he took, it felt like the setting sun began to leech Azraff of all his body heat. The memory of those golden eyes still shone in the back of his mind, and Azraff paused one last time as a cool breeze ran through the slums. He frowned. Turned. Tail drooped. Naim was gone.

For the moment. Only the moment. There was something about the ferret that Azraff couldn't place. He would go back to his guild and they would sift his memories. Find out what had happened, if anything was left of them. He'd rest and recover. Then, however?

Then he would find this Naim again. He would find answers. He would find that warmth. He would find understanding. He didn't know why, but that didn't matter. Only one thing did.

He *would* find Naim.

He had to.

MORE VALUABLE THAN GOLD

LINNEA CAPPS

"There are things magic can't do."

It had only been three days and Gil was already miserable from his time in the tent city. Mud caked the fur on his foot paws, staining the natural cider color he took pride in. Even with the pillow a kind fox had offered him, sleeping on the hard ground left him unrested and irritable. His one meal of the day at the soup kitchen several blocks away was the only thing he had to look forward to and that wouldn't be happening until the evening.

That line in Bayard's voice repeating in his head was the only thing that kept him motivated enough to not give up casing their newest target on the first day. If the fellow residents of the tent city knew just how much gold was being stored in what appeared to be an abandoned warehouse nearby they likely would have stormed the place en masse, consequences damned. Gil needed a stealthier approach. If he or the gold were tracked down once stolen, Bayard might never be able to finish paying his debts.

Gil whistled in the way only a dhole could, pulling out the walkie talkie he had stashed in the pillow, pressing the button on its side and whispering into it.

"I hate this place."

He waited patiently for a response. These tin-circuited models were finicky, but Gil had always felt that splurging for proper gold versions would be wasteful.

"You just hate that you're not at home in bed with me."

The dhole's tail wagged gently, the fur making scratching synthetic sounds against the floor of his tent. He wanted so badly to take the small chunk of pure gold from his pocket, carve out a small sliver, and say 'beszélj' to cast the spell. He wanted to hear Bayard with crystal clear clarity instead of through tinny static. Gil knew he would have to settle for this, however. Magic was far easier to track than old tech like radio signals.

"Yes, but I hate that you might have had to live like this. Hell, that anyone has to live like this at all."

There was a short pause before the bush dog's voice responded.

"We could always dispel the tracker on a few extra bars and donate it to the soup kitchen if that would make you feel better."

Gil considered it a moment then nodded, before remembering he had to speak into the walkie talkie.

"It would. In fact I order you to add two more bars to our tally."

The bush dog's squeakily giggled response made the dhole feel warm inside.

"Hey, you don't get to give orders until after the job is done. You know the rules. You made them! Now stop talking to me and keep an eye on the place. We gotta know if they ever post guards."

"Fine, but don't whine when I go all out. You have to learn a lesson for using that cheeky tone with me."

The nervous peep in response let Gil know he got the reaction he wanted. The fun of teasing Bayard was too tantalizing to resist.

"Good boy, over and out."

———

Gil was returning to the tent city from the soup kitchen, stomach not truly filled but at least not complaining of hunger. He was chatting with Jasper, the fox that had given him the pillow and several other small things that made tent life a bit more tolerable. The dhole felt guilty about giving him the cold shoulder even though he needed to be incognito during his stay. So he had chosen the most common name he could think of and allowed the fox to get to know "Liam" over the past few days.

"You know Liam, I put out a bucket for rainwater. I could help wash up those muddy paws of yours. Want to come hang out in my tent?"

Gil looked at the fox, taking a moment to weigh his options. He felt certain the fox was harboring a small crush for him and was equally certain this was a way for Jasper to have the two of them alone in his tent. Gil didn't want to lead him on, after tomorrow his tent would be empty and "Liam" would no longer exist.

Still the dirt coating his paws had been most maddening to the dhole that was used to studiously grooming his fur. It would certainly mean spending less gold on the "mosás" spell. Gil's paw prints weren't in any databases he knew of, but he wasn't about to risk finding out by leaving muddy ones behind.

"Honestly, that sounds like a treat Jasper. You're sure it's not too much trouble?"

The fox's tail whipped through the air behind him. "No problem at all!"

Jasper took the dhole's paw in his own and started pulling him towards his tent, Gil suppressing a teasing whistle at the fox's enthusiasm. In the end the dhole figured Jasper would respect being told no if he tried to make serious advances. The dhole needed the cover of darkness anyways. This could pass the time until the watchful eye of the sun sank past the horizon.

Jasper stopped in front of a tent more impressive than most, not that much stood out in the camp. Four worn wooden posts held up the blue wrinkled tarps that formed a square canopy over the tent, a cuboid model with more floor space than the pyramid style Gil had been sleeping in. A worn floral blanket hung as a door over the entrance, Jasper reaching with a paw to pull it aside.

"Welcome to my humble abode! Emphasis on the humble. Sit down, I'll snag the bucket behind the tent."

Gil dipped his head to lean inside, ears rising in surprise. A stuffed futon mattress lay in one corner adorned with pillows and a blanket. He sat down to make himself comfortable, sneezing as strong fox musk overwhelmed his senses.

Jasper made his way into the tent, water sloshing in the bucket as he sat it down, tail wagging.

"I literally can't remember the last time I had a guest over. Was it before the tent life chose me? Anyways, paw please!"

Gil hadn't had his paws washed like this since he was a puppy, but still he complied. Jasper got his forepaws soaked in water before starting to work. Gil could feel the gentle pressure of Jasper's claws working their way through stubborn bits of mud along the dhole's ankle. The cool water and attentive claws trying to comb fur into neat rows sent delightful tingles up his leg, helping him relax.

"So, I didn't know someone could even have a tent this nice out here, especially with a bed. How many ounces did it cost you?"

The fox barked in laughter, motioning for Gil to present his other ankle for grooming.

"I used to like camping sometimes for fun. I guess I was investing in my future without really thinking about it."

The dhole yipped in response. "I guess that's one way to look at it, though hopefully something better will come your way."

Having gotten the ankle clean, Jasper moved onto the paws. Tension drained from Gil's body from the kneading, each rub and touch removing pieces of mud and stress. Waves of warm static pulsed through the back of his leg, only ending once they reached his pelvis. Gil couldn't hold back a low whistle of pleasure, his tail dusting behind him.

"Hey Liam, can I be honest a second?"

It took Gil a moment to remember through the haze of relaxation fogging his brain that he had chosen that as his fake name.

"Ohhhhhh I uh, oh. Yeah? Of course you can."

Gil noticed the fox's ears were turning back, tail curling between his legs as he knelt and continued massaging.

"It was probably pretty obvious how hard I've been trying to come onto you. But I don't think I can, you know. Not to lead you on or something! Just…"

Gil roused himself fully from his stupor. He had expected Jasper to make his move now and had been preparing to turn him down. The dhole was left off-kilter, unsure of how to respond.

"I uh, well, I honestly thought I was just getting my paws clean here. Sure, it felt incredible, but you don't owe me sex or something like that just because you made me feel good. I couldn't forgive myself if you felt pressured into something like that."

The fox barked a sorrowful laugh. "I'm glad to know I'm doing a good job. I'm a massage therapist you know. Or at least that's what I try to be. That's not really it though."

Gil's head tilted, patiently waiting for an explanation. He didn't want to put any more pressure on the fox that seemed to be wilting before his eyes.

"My boyfriend, he's stuck in a mining camp. We fell

behind paying rent on my old massage parlor. I've been trying so hard to help pay off his debts, but we still owe at least a bar, not to mention how many ounces in fees…"

Gil winced, knowing no one could mine enough gold to pay back the cost of food they ate at the mines alone. Even with three meals a day and a roof over their head, no one wanted to sacrifice their freedom for the endless cycle of forced labor.

The dhole clucked, trying to suppress a full growl in his throat as to not scare Jasper. There were very few words still documented in the magical tongue and few would risk the gold to cast spells that might do nothing. Or worse, cause some sort of catastrophe. Since pure gold was required to cast a spell and would dissolve into nothingness after, it had become standard currency.

A select few held the word for "grow" which allowed plants to grow in soil spoiled by the countless wars that had taken place too long ago for anyone to remember. All that one of the agricultural moguls would need to do is simply share the word with the world and then no one would go hungry ever again.

Instead, those who couldn't make enough gold to eat and still rent from a slumlord were forced to live in places like this. Gil had seen the residents of tent cities were often disproportionately ill compared to most, medical bills that could not be overcome forcing them into tents.

"W-Well you see, he knew we'd be apart for a long time so… Well people have needs. You're a dhole just like him, and I thought… But I can't. I just can't."

Jasper broke into yapping sobs, Gil moving to wrap his arms around the fox in a comforting hug. The sorrow flooding through the fox's eyes caused an inferno of rage to blaze within Gil's belly. He was reminded once more that if it were not for lucky circumstances, he and Bayard would be in the same position.

Gil pulled out the small chunk of gold in his pocket, claws carving off some for his new fox friend.

"Spend this how you want. Call your boyfriend, pay for something you need, whatever will make you happy."

"Liam I can't, you n—"

Gil interrupted the fox as he made his way out of the tent. "You won't be convincing me otherwise. Payment for the best paw massage of my life."

Jasper's silent nod went unseen with night blanketing the camp. Gil exited the tent, marching with determination towards his own. The memory from his week living in the city made for a good guide despite the darkness.

Once he reached the tent, he snatched up the pillow, taking the walkie talkie from inside.

"I lied. We're adding four extra bars. Sorry for the last-minute notice, we'll rendezvous at the target. No need to respond, over and out."

The dhole turned off the walkie talkie, stowing it away in his pocket. He knew Bayard would be there to meet him soon enough. He kept the worn pillow clenched in his paws as he left the tent, knowing it would soon come in handy.

Gil took one last look at the building, illuminated by a lone streetlight. It was made of rugged clay bricks, looking unremarkable in every way. If anything, it looked dilapidated, windows broken in places, likely infested with vermin. The perfect facade for a gold storage facility no one would expect.

It only took a single well aimed pebble hurled at the streetlight to plunge the entire street into darkness. Gil's ears raised, hearing the rustling of bodies in tents trying to find comfort on the hard ground. The sudden shattering of glass had not been deemed worth investigating to the weary minds of those in the tent city. Perfect.

He padded silently across the street, making his way into an alleyway, the 'pissway' as the residents called it. He ignored the scent of ammonia in the air, knowing someone might need some middle of the night relief at any moment. The dhole needed to work quickly.

Gil focused on the building before him, knowing he needed the area for the spell clear in his mind before casting. He pulled the chunk of gold from his pocket.

"Észlelet."

His ears lifted as his eyes scanned the building. Even in the dark the wavering threads of green and yellow could be seen only by him, spells set to catch anyone attempting to sneak inside. It had been the reason no one in the tent city dared risk breaking in. Even with a roof over your head, an easy to track trespassing spell could get you caught and sent straight into the mines.

Bayard was in charge of dealing with tech, likely hacking into the camera system he had discovered after Gil had called him on the walkie talkie. It would be Gil's job to find a way in.

During his week of observation, it had seemed that the main point of security was being nondescript. Whoever had been in charge of security spells would have likely been on a tight gold budget and rushed through the job, the owners not wanting to draw attention to the building.

Gil spotted it: a single window five stories up that had been missed. He ended the spell, memorizing the position of the window in his mind while massaging the gold with paw pads, gauging just how much was left.

The dhole would need to cast a levitation spell, which ran through gold rapidly. It was likely the window would have a physical iron lock. Busting through the window itself with force would be too noisy, too many cuts through his fur, too messy. Bayard would already be on his way. With four extra bars to dispel they needed every second they could get. If only he hadn't given that extra gold to Jasper, this would all be easier.

Gil set the pillow on the ground, focusing on it as he stepped onto its lumpy form.

"Lebegés"

The pillow soared with him on it upwards, a fuzzy sensation rippling through the dhole's head as the gold dissolved in his paw. Upon reaching the window he needed it was too dark to properly see the lock. With seconds left before he would plummet to the ground Gil turned his focus to the entire window, letting his levitation spell break.

"Feloldás!" he gasped, sinking his claws into the brick of the window as the pillow began its descent to the ground. His digits burned, arms trembling from the exertion of holding his weight as he dangled from the windowsill. Once the small metallic click signaled that the lock had finally come undone he used the last of his arm strength to push the window open and pull himself inside.

Panting heavily, he planned his next course of action. His paw was empty, not a single sliver left for casting a spell. There was potentially broken glass scattered across the floor of the pitch-black building. He knew the actual storage facility was two floors higher, he had seen a higher concentration of what must be tracking spells attached to the bars of gold there.

With no gold to undo the lock that would most certainly be on the door to the room, let alone burn through whatever walls might be surrounding it, there was no point possibly injuring himself wandering through the dark. He would have to wait for Bayard to arrive.

A familiar lumpy pillow collided with the back of Gil's head, a shorter stocky canid levitating in after it through the window.

"I saw the pillow falling and it scared me half to death thinking it was you Gil!"

The dhole popped up from the ground, hugging his much shorter bush dog boyfriend tight, ignoring his grumpy mumbling.

"I missed you too, didn't think you would get here so soon. I wanted to get a head-start, the gold is a couple floors up."

Bayard pressed a button on a headlamp, shining a small stream of light through the room. Gil let him go so he could lead the way towards the stairs, following close behind. There would be time for catching up later.

It was obvious once they reached the room with the gold, a steel structure had been built inside, a room inside of a room, with an electronic lock system attached to its door.

"It's a Barksa, B-50x." Bayard muttered as he approached the door.

"Can you get us in?" Gil inquired. He was quite certain even with the reserves of gold the bush dog would have brought with him there was no way they could cast a spell strong enough to break through the steel enclosure.

"I got us in a Barksa on our last job, this is just the newest model. It should be just fine."

"Well, you'd better or there's going to be some serious punishment for making me live out of a tent for a week for nothing."

Gil didn't need the light to know Bayard's ears were pinned back, he could hear the usual flustered squeak that accompanied the bush dog's expression. It didn't matter just how risky the job was, Gil couldn't help but tease.

The dhole did know better than to distract Bayard while he got to the serious work however, so he behaved himself as the bush dog pulled out his gear and set to his task.

"Okay rerouting the touchpad... Cut this wire here...."

Gil's tail wagged, he had always found Bayard's constant description of what he was doing adorable, even if he couldn't remotely understand what was going on. He had never been tech savvy.

Suddenly there were several beeping sounds in rapid succession, followed by a small puff of smoke. The two thieves tensed, ready to dash in case an alarm sounded.

The two both sighed once there was a clanging of metal gears, the door opening out to let them inside. The headlamp shone against the hundreds of sparkling bars of solid gold kept within.

"Not even a single guard for all this? They should have put this in a proper vault" Gil muttered.

"You know as well as I do it'd cost half the gold in here to do that. It's not like there's many professionals like us stealing out there anyways."

Gil agreed, nodding even though the bush dog's light was focused on the gold so he couldn't see.

"Alright, in the time it takes for the casters to notice, call up security, and get people our way we'll have about five minutes tops. Less than a minute per bar to get all six. You're going to have to help dispel this time Bayard."

The bush dog reached into a pocket as they walked into the room, pulling out a miniature bar of gold and placing it in Gil's paw.

"Got it, don't get stuck on any fun puzzles this time okay? This is hard enough as it is."

The dhole barked in amusement. "Come on, that 3D maze was amazing! I'd never seen anything like it!"

Gil was certain his boyfriend must have been rolling his eyes as they each chose a bar to start with.

"Alright on the count of three. One… Two… Three."

The two murmured "Eltávolítás" and begun their work. Each bar had its own tracking spell with a security measure placed on it, each unique to the person that cast it. Unfortunately for those wishing to protect the gold, the security spell, "biztonság" contained an unusual quirk.

Each instance of security could not be locked down with something secure like a password. Instead a challenge would have to be completed for the spell to entirely vanish. It could be anything from a maze to a puzzle that must be solved. Whenever dispelling was attempted, the caster would be informed by a buzzing sensation at the base of their skulls. If they hadn't been informed dispelling would be taking place, police would be called.

Most specialists in tracking charms worked for several different clients. It normally took time mentally checking through all of their spells to locate the exact location where a tracking spell had been removed. Just enough time for them to complete their heist. Gil had raced through a sliding number puzzle he had seen countless times before in under thirty seconds, starting on his second bar before Bayard could complete his first.

He hefted the gold bar into the backpack Bayard had brought with him. At 27 pounds of gold a piece he was always amazed that the bush dog had the muscle to carry their entire quarry home after each heist.

"I'm sorry Gil, I can't get this one. These shapes are too weird, I can't separate them."

Gil grunted, having raced through a spiral maze that had been presented to him on his first try. "It's okay babe, set it down and move on. If you can't get it in under thirty leave it."

Bayard did as instructed, picking up another bar and got to work. The dhole's ears were perked, trying to ignore the ramblings made by his boyfriend attempting to solve a cube puzzle. He had finished his third bar when he picked up the faintest sound of sirens. The police were already on their way.

"Shit, cops are coming. how many have you got?"

"Just the one, damn it I'm sorry G-"

"No time! Take what you've got and head out. I'll get the last two."

Bayard stomped a foot and looked ready to protest but Gil interrupted any argument by firmly saying, "Eltávolítás" and beginning on his next bar. He was determined to bring home a full six bars as he had planned.

The bush dog whined but Gil knew he would do as he was told. He never ignored a direct order from the dhole. As he hefted the now heavy backpack onto his shoulders, Gil managed yet another sliding number puzzle. The wailing of sirens was growing louder.

The bush dog was already padding away on his stubby legs. Gil knew he was a slower runner and would need the head start.

"Eltávolítás, oh fuck too hard come on! Eltávolítás!"

The sound of sirens would have woken up the entire tent city at this point, police ready to rush the door. He would still have time to fly away if he could only manipulate all of the colored cubes to match on each side with his mind fast enough.

He solved the puzzle the moment he heard the door slam open on the bottom floor. Thanking his lucky stars that the police force was too underfunded to use spells to float as he did, he removed the pillow he had carried from its case, placing the bars inside. Hoisting it over his back he dashed down the stairs, knowing he would need to reach the fifth floor before the cops.

He saw the light of large flashlights flooding the staircase as he dashed towards the window he had entered at, heard yells of "perp spotted!" and "We've got him!" as he dove headfirst through the open window, clutching the pillowcase to his chest.

"Lebegés!" he cried, letting the magic rocket him forward. He felt the rapid beating of his heart in his throat, his entire body trembling with adrenaline and fear. He urged the spell on faster with his mind, heading towards the more populated area of the city. There would be plenty more buildings and alleyways to float behind, making the police lose sight of where he would eventually land. He could always find his way home from wherever he touched down.

———

Gil had long since evaded the cops, now taking the elevator to the third-floor apartment he shared with Bayard. The dhole was whistling happily. They had never managed more than four bars before in a single heist, he was incredibly proud.

A small ding let Gil know the elevator had reached the correct floor as the door opened. He walked down to the end of the hall, knowing the door would already be unlocked for him as his partner in life and crime would have already made it back.

He had barely gotten inside before the enraged squeaking began.

"You will NEVER do that again you hear me Gil? I was so fucking scared!"

Gil clucked, taking the pillowcase and setting it down next to the backpack filled with gold on the floor. He didn't want to deal with the over 50 pounds of weight any longer and wasn't willing to admit he was lucky it hadn't ripped through the case while he flew. He didn't want to give the bush dog more ammunition for his worrying.

"Alright, I know I give the orders but this time I did go a little too far."

Gil could see the tension leaving his boyfriend's body, noticing his stubby tail swaying side to side. "Good! Now why the hell were we stealing six—"

Gil strode confidently towards the bush dog, effortlessly shoving him towards the bedroom to interrupt him.

"H-Hey come on Gil, just—"

"I have waited an entire week away from you. Questions can come later; I want to cum now."

Bayard started the flustered squeaking and squirming Gil loved so much. Gil had always taken the lead in the bedroom and he didn't want to waste the adrenaline induced rush he was feeling now. He knew if Bayard actually wanted his questions answered first he could always say 'red' and Gil would respect that. Since he wasn't saying it, however, the dhole growled playfully.

"Good boy."

Gil used his superior height to press against the bush dog, moving him towards the bed before pushing him forcefully onto it so he fell onto his back, stubby bush dog legs dangling off the end. The dhole moved to pin his boyfriend's wrists above his head with one paw, the other grasping his lover's chin, tilting it up.

Their muzzles met, lips brushing together as the dhole straddled the bush dog's waist. Their tongues rolled over each other, a passionate dance of reconnecting after being so long apart. The dhole could feel tugging from the paws he had kept pinned down. He released them, savoring the sensation of the now free paws brushing and stroking through the fur beneath his shirt.

By the time they pulled apart, lips barely touching, both were panting with a desperate need.

"Clothes off. Now."

Gil removed himself from the bush dog, painfully aware of the length tenting his pants. He could always give himself attention in a bit, he needed to get Bayard hard first.

He gazed over the bush dog's form, admiring it as Bayard removed his shirt. The luscious umber fur of his muscular chest hid the two scars he knew adorned the underside of his pecs. Short but strong arms scrambled to remove pants, revealing his lover's sheath, his cock still waiting to be coaxed out within. It looked slightly different than most, but it did not stop the yearning ache to have it buried inside him.

This was Bayard's body. The body Bayard had needed modified to truly feel like himself. The body they had needed to steal gold to pay for. The body that ignited the burning lust that crept warm under Gil's fur. There were some things magic couldn't do but Gil could show his partner just how gorgeous he found him.

Gil rubbed his paws through the soft fur of Bayard's chest, loving how the touch made his boyfriend shiver and whine needily. Voice laced with arousal, he growled, "I'm coating this chest in cum. You're gonna look good in a pearl necklace."

The bush dog loosed a squeaky whine, his body trembling. Gil let him steep in carnal want, tantalizingly slipping off his own shirt, slowly revealing his muscles that carved small hills in his cider fur. The dhole stood still, allowing Bayard to take the image of him in, letting the needy tension build until it snapped from the bush dog's maw.

"P-Please, no more teasing." Bayard spluttered. "I need you, to be inside you. Please…"

Gil barked a dark chuckle, shaking his head. "Such a needy little thing, aren't you? I suppose you've been a very good boy tonight…"

Gil sank to his knees, wetting his lips while Bayard eagerly moved to sit at the edge of the bed. The dhole gave Bayard's sheath a tender nuzzle, the fur of it tickling his nose as he breathed in the familiar musky scent. Gil traced a paw pad along the bush dog's thigh, he knew how to turn his man on.

Gil gently cupped Bayards balls with a paw, the other finding its way to feel his lover's pulse from his groin. The dhole took pleasure in the masculine salty taste that met his tongue as it slipped inside the sheath before him. He caressed the pump hidden under the sensitive scrotal skin, slowly bringing his lover's length to life to the rhythm of the bush dog's beating heart.

That heartbeat was rapidly increasing, heavy breathing punctuated by eager moans to urge the dhole on. Bayard reached his paws down to rub along Gil's ears, a spark of pleasure crackling through his body at the touch.

Gil dipped his tongue into the opening of his partner's cock while it swelled larger from his eager attention. He engulfed the length in the wet heat of his maw, urging it to grow even larger with the digits of his paw, until it touched the back of his throat. The dhole made a show of swallowing around it, pulling up for breath with a small cough.

"God babe, you're so big…"

Gil knew the moment of validation would swell within the bush dog, confirming it upon seeing the nervous grin spread across his partner's maw. The dhole gently nudged at him with his paws, urging him to get onto the bed proper.

"Think I can even fit this monster inside?"

Gil rubbed his paw over the cock slicked with his saliva. He had helped Bayard grow to his full length but had stopped before allowing his knot to swell. The bush dog would have to do that work himself.

He allowed his pants to fall away to the floor, his own length finally free from their prison. Every twitch marking his need to be filled to the brim, knotted by the male who was now laying back on the bed.

The dhole began climbing on top of him, resting his rump against the now large cock below him.

"Your paws, my cock, now."

The bush dog eagerly complied, needing both webbed paws to wrap around Gil's length. The gentle pressure of Bayard's soft paws milking away at his length caused him to shudder. It would be hard to last long, a week's worth of need pooling as pre at the tip of his cock.

Gil pressed a digit against Bayard's lips, forcing past them to prod into the bush dog's maw. He slid it in and out, as deep as the cock had been inside his own throat, only finally relenting once he had found it slick enough.

Bayard trembled, gasping for breath while the dhole casually lifted his tail, using his lover's spit to lubricate his hole. He reached behind him to grab the bush dog's cock, using it to tease at his entrance.

"Does my good boy want his cock inside me?"

Bayard nodded rapidly, unable to hold back a tide of

squeaky whines. Gil chuckled at the adorable reaction, wanting to bring his desire to a fever pitch. He knew the more he egged his partner on, the harder he would get fucked. Gil wanted the ride of a lifetime.

"Beg for it."

Bayard's ears were pinned back hard, his entire body shaking as he held back from thrusting upward. Gil knew he wouldn't until given permission.

"P-Please Gil come on I need it so bad. It's been a week, ple—"

"I didn't tell you to stop stroking my cock!"

Bayard had been too distracted by the well of desire bubbling inside him to keep his paws focused at the task. Gil twitched powerfully in the bush dog's paws, indicating just how good it felt.

"S-Sorry Gil, it won't happen aga— oohhhh fuuu-uccckkkk!"

Gil had leaned himself back, applying just enough pressure to pop the tip of Bayard's length inside him. He barked and chuckled, seeing just how much effort it was taking the bush dog to keep stroking and not buck his hips to sink all the way inside.

"What was that? That didn't sound like proper begging to me."

Bayard whimpered, his entire body now vibrating in desperation. "Please! Please Gil let me fuck you. I'll be a good boy and make you cum I swear! Just please! Pleeaasseee!"

Gil cracked a cocky grin. "Okay you have my permission t — oof!"

It was his turn to be cut off, the bush dog's paws darting to grab onto his hips, claws sinking in. The sudden impalement by Bayard's cock knocked the wind out of him, a shockwave of delight rocketing powerfully through his body.

"G-Good boy!" Gil hated that he had stuttered but it couldn't be helped, Bayard's animalistic hunger to fuck him was stronger than he had ever known it. His hips kept being pulled down harder with each thrust, dangling orbs slapping up against his rear. Each impact caused the bush dog's knot to swell up a bit more.

Still it wasn't large enough. Gil wanted to be tied, connected to his love in an intimate way only a canid could, trapped together in utter orgasmic bliss.

"That's my good boy, you want me to mark you with my cum?"

Bayard responded with nothing more than an increased fervor to his thrusting accompanied by grunts and groans. The couple were panting desperately. The scent of sex, strong enough to intoxicate them both, floated through the air.

With each slamming of hips to rear the knot got a little larger, stretching out Gil's hole as it entered and leaving with a sloppy pop as it slid back out. Gil's cock was bobbing with no paws around it, pre flying from its tip to leave iridescent drops across the bush dog's belly. Each failed attempt of the knot to tie sent a wave of static splintering out, an electrical storm forming in his groin that needed to release.

Bayard jerked Gil down a final time, his knot swollen enough it took effort for it to break past the tight warm wall before it. This time it stuck. As the bush dog became a panting mess of delight beneath him, Gil felt the world around him dissolving into pleasure. The pressure that had built over a week shooting outward, warm ropes painting the umber fur of Bayard's chest with iridescent white.

Time seemed to slow, both canids lost in the haze of post orgasmic bliss. Gil carefully laid down on Bayard's chest, a lifted ear listening to the joyous thumping of his heart. The dhole didn't care that his cum would get into his fur, the two could always shower later. Now was the time to enjoy the stubby arms wrapping around his back to hold him close and savor this moment with the man he so deeply loved.

———

It had taken weeks to convince Bayard it was finally safe to return to the tent city. Gil had been chided about how corny it was to return to the scene of a crime, but the dhole knew he had a task too important to ignore. There were some things magic couldn't do, but this was something he could do himself.

He had kept his promise to come while it was dark for the most part, the sun was close to rising. The dhole hadn't wanted to be recognized, but he had to be sure the package he was delivering would be found by the proper recipient. He quietly lifted a floral blanket door aside, setting the two bars of gold wrapped in a worn pillowcase inside before setting a note on top.

Jasper,

I'm sorry I couldn't give you my real name, it's too risky in my line of work. This should be enough to get your boyfriend out of the mining camp and get you back on your feet. Keep him close. I know it's cheesy, but his love is more valuable than gold. Live your best life, you deserve happiness.

- "Liam"

CARNIVAL OF JUBILATION

SKUNKBOMB

It was strange not seeing James's desk covered with notes from leads, the stack of empty coffee cups, or the tennis ball he chewed on when struggling with a story. His walls were bare. They used to be covered in framed stories from his career: profiles from generals to foot soldiers from the war almost a decade ago to the sorcerers that had become indispensable to either side.

We joked that James, a bloodhound, could literally smell a story. Not just from events, but people. He was an amazing profiler who came in with just the right question to put the interviewee at ease or throw them off their game. James was one of the good ones.

But the war ended, and our sleepy town settled back into something resembling normalcy. James's nose led him away from the *Shiner's Post* to an editor-in-chief position in a neighboring city.

My rabbit bobtail twitched. The Assistant Editor position was open, and it was going to be mine.

I slipped my hand into my coat pocket, touched my inhaler, but then thought better of it. It was best to save it for when I really needed it, and I didn't want to look nervous. I filled my shitty lungs with as much air as I could and marched into the head editor's office.

"Sir, a word?" I asked as I stepped in.

The badger glared at me, though that was nothing new. Eli always had a look of a disapproving father. "Seeing as you've already waltzed right in without knocking—"

"I'd like to throw my hat in the ring for the Assistant Editor position."

"And you'll be considered."

I straightened myself up, though I tried to keep my long ears from looking too tense. "Now that James is gone, I'm the most senior writer on staff, so—"

"This isn't your job interview," Eli said, his eyes back on some notes. "Give me a few days. I've got my work and James's to take care of."

"I'm happy to take some of James's tasks off of your plate."

Eli opened his mouth, but then seemed to think better of it. He dug through one of the drawers of his desk and tossed a folder at me. "James was due to cover this story today. I've got phone meetings starting at noon and my ass will be glued to this chair until further notice."

I opened the folder and glanced at the notes. "A carnival? Not much of a story on its own. What's the hook?"

The badger leaned forward. Something resembling a smile played at his lips. At times, I forget he was once a staff writer himself, chasing stories around the town. "Carnival's run by a skunk named Isaac Wistman. Get this though. Before that, he was a military sorcerer. That's one hell of a career hop. Apparently, he's got a bunch of sorcerers in his carnival slinging around magic. Real magic. None of that smoke and mirrors crap."

My foot tapped as I tried to picture this skunk. Most sorcerers with notable talent went into the military. Becoming a carnival performer seemed like a demotion. "I'm sure if I bring back a good story, that'll help my chances with getting the Assistant Editor position, right?"

"It won't hurt," the badger said. He got up from his desk. "I've got a phone call in ten. Scram. Get the story." Once I had scooted out the door, the badger shut it and drew the blinds.

So there was a chance. If I became the Assistant Editor, I'd get juicier assignments, and better ones still once I became Head Editor. I'd get the kinds of stories that won awards and were read nationwide by millions of people. I'd no longer be some nobody in a small town writing about church bake sales. I kept my hand on the inhaler in my pocket. The excitement was squeezing my lungs, but I could still breathe for now.

———

I grabbed the morning's *Shiner's Post* and skimmed it while on the shuttle bus to the outskirts of town. Usually, I'd skip to my article and question whether or not it could have been better. Instead, the headline caught my attention.

Tensions Rise Across the Border: Are We Heading for Another War?

Most of the front-page articles for the past few months had talked about a potential war with the north. And it seemed like we'd just gotten out of a war not long ago. At this point, it wasn't a question of if, but when, the first shots would be fired. Would it be another year? A month? Sooner? It was like watching a pot boil. A whole lot of nothing until tensions eventually bubbled to the surface.

The shuttle came to a halt outside a cluster of large pink and green-striped tents near the forest. I rolled up my newspaper into my bag. Anxiety over war could wait for now. I had an interview to do. Perhaps Isaac Wistman would be called into service again.

I stepped off the shuttle into a group of over four-dozen people waiting in line to buy tickets. Luckily, as a member of the press, I was allowed to bypass the line. Through the intermingling scents of all the different species, the aroma of warm, sweet treats rose above it. There were sugared pastries shaped like flowers, ice cream cones surrounded by a mane of cotton candy, and curious bottles of glowing blue liquid. A deer cub took a swig of it at the goading of his friends.

"Hold it, hold it," said the tiger cub with him. "Now blow it out!"

The blue mist the deer blew out formed into the shape of a dragon, which breathed a misty blue flame.

"That's what I was thinking of!" The deer said.

Memory Mist! I'd only read about the liquid that could bring thoughts to harmless life, but it was difficult to find. And here it was, just as available as a soda. I fought the temptation to get in line for a bottle. Work first, and then I could play later.

According to the person I spoke to earlier on the phone, Isaac Wistman would most likely be in his tent near the back-right side of the carnival. One tent glowed while another billowed purple fog. The fog didn't smell of water vapor or chemicals. It was unearthly. Mystical. This really was a carnival of magic, real magic. Maybe I could leverage Isaac into allowing me to see his fellow sorcerers' spells up close. There was a certain skip in my step as I continued my search for the skunk's tent.

Isaac's quarters had a black flap with a white stripe for a "door." Knocking seemed silly. Tents didn't have doors to knock on. Instead, I cleared my throat and lifted a corner of the flap.

"Hello?" I said. "Isaac Wistman? I'm Simon Driscoll with the *Shiner's Post*."

"He might be out now."

My foot tapped. "Yes it seems—"

A skunk in a green vest and a pink bowtie stood beside me. He clutched a cane with a head shaped like a sparkly purple cloud. I could see his military background peek through in the crispness of his attire, though the color and the cheeky smile gave him a more playful air.

"Isaac Wistman, I presume," I said. "Thank you for agreeing to the interview."

The skunk bowed. "The pleasure is mine. The more folks who know about my carnival, the better. Please, come inside."

Outside, the skunk's tent looked like one of the smaller ones, but when I walked inside, it was clear some magic was in place. Isaac's tent was at least twice the size of my one bedroom apartment. If I hadn't just walked inside from the carnival grounds, I would have thought it was a cushy residence from the wealthy section of town.

"Why don't you have a seat?" Isaac said, pointing to the sea of large, soft-looking armchairs surrounding an unlit fire pit. He placed his cane against one of the armchairs. "Can I interest you in an affogato? We make the ice cream in house."

"It's barely past nine A.M."

"Yes, hence the espresso."

"No thank you."

As he brewed the espresso, I took in the rest of the room. The chandelier that didn't appear to be hanging from anything kept the room well lit. A bookshelf was built into the wall, containing thick tomes with magical language on the side. I flexed my toes against the soft carpet and took a discrete sniff. Maybe it was the candles, but the room smelled like afternoon tea in the garden, floral and sweet. At the end of each sniff was a sharp skunk note.

Isaac reached to the back of the freezer. The white stripes of his tail ran along the edges until at the tip, where both stripes dipped. It was sort of like a heart.

"Ah, always forget the new cartons are in the bottom freezer." The skunk bent over in his tight green trousers. His tail arched up. He looked over his shoulder. "Could I get you anything to drink?"

I turned away. "No, I'm fine, thank you." I tugged on one of my whiskers. What was I doing looking at him in such an unprofessional way? I couldn't jeopardize my job over the skunk's nice rear. I took a deep breath. From here on out, I would be nothing but the picture of professionalism.

Isaac sat down in one of the chairs next to me rather than across. I turned in my seat to face him while he ate his ice cream and espresso.

I cleared my throat. "Well, shall we? Can you tell me about who you were before starting the Carnival of Jubilation?"

The skunk swallowed a mouthful of ice cream. "I was born on the Summer Solstice to a family of five children barely hanging on to the status of 'middle class'. My family didn't possess any notable amounts of magic, though one of my sisters could turn her tail into a feather duster. She still complained about doing chores though."

"Magical studies aren't cheap," I said as I took notes. "Were your parents able to pay for it?"

"They scraped by somehow," Isaac said and shrugged. "Once I'm able to see my family again, I'm going to give them some of the money the carnival's made so far. It's the least I can do."

"Carnival keeping you busy?" I said. "I know how it is. Work just never seems to let up."

"Not just the carnival," the skunk said. He pushed around the ice cream and espresso without actually scooping of it up. "Ever since I graduated from college, getting to see my family…well, it's gotten harder."

"And when and where did you graduate?"

"St. Artemis about—,"the skunk coughed. "—years ago."

My smile widened. "Could you repeat that for the record, please?"

"Nine years ago." Isaac sighed. "Nine long years."

"And what exactly was your magical area of focus?" I looked down at my notes. At least, I thought I did. Nothing was written down. Instead, I found myself holding a rose instead of a pencil.

"For me?" the skunk said, his eyes big and bashful. "Why thank you." He took the rose, and the skunk bloomed as if turned into a living rosebush. The floral aroma flooded the room.

A breath from next to me tickled my ear, and I shuddered. The skunk rosebush blew away.

"I specialized in illusions," Isaac said, suddenly right next to me on the arm of my chair.

I flinched, and my page of notes and pen fell to the carpet. I'd seen magic before, but only minor things: levitation to grab a pen across the room or lighting a match with a finger. Magic has never appeared in front of me in such a large, enveloping way.

Isaac picked them up and handed them to me. Our fingers briefly touched in the exchange, and they seemed solid enough. Then again, he seemed real just a few minutes ago. "Is that all this carnival is? An illusion? Is it all magic?"

"I'd argue there's magic everywhere," Isaac said. "But if I'm using your definition, we mostly use our magic to enhance what's already there. I assure you we aren't just watching the townsfolk run around an empty forest staring at trees and eating leaves."

My heart still pounded. Isaac was thrilling, certainly. And even though professional courtesy dictated he shouldn't sit so close to me, I wanted him near. Unfortunately, this was all for work. I needed to get back on track. "I'm sure your magic was helpful on the battlefield. Could you tell me about your time in the service?"

Isaac's tail stiffened. "I entered the military right after graduating from St. Artemis's. The war began after that, and I served two tours. Then after the war ended, I was honorably discharged." He tapped his knee with his cane. "Doubt I'll be called back into action after my injury."

"And what exactly happened to your knee?" I asked. "Was it gunfire? Shrapnel?"

"I'm sorry," the skunk said. "What does this have to do with the carnival? Isn't that what this article is about?"

"Just getting some background information," I said, my tone neutral. "Going from military sorcerer to carnival ringmaster is quite the career jump."

Isaac leaned back against the arm of my chair, his smile less strained now. "Yes, took quite a bit of soul searching after all the unpleasantness. But then I realized I'd rather bring joy to people, not pain. That's all I ever wanted to do with my magic. I gathered up some likeminded sorcerers, and we came together to create this wonderful Carnival of Jubilation."

"Now, the other sorcerers at the carnival," I said. "Were they also in the military while you served?"

The skunk sat up. "It's too nice a day to spend in here. Let's take a walk, shall we? We can see the whole carnival, since that is what the article's about."

Isaac was clearly hiding something, but now didn't seem the time to push him. If an interview subject got too hot and testy, they'd shut down completely and I'd never get the story. I did want to take a look around the carnival and interview some of the other workers and performers. Maybe the walk would calm the skunk down and loosen his tongue.

Isaac picked up his cane and extended his arm to me. "Would you mind? Walking the whole carnival on this knee's a bit rough without some help."

I hesitated. There were professional boundaries one doesn't cross as a journalist, and walking arm in arm with the skunk was something done between lovers. Still, it would be rude to refuse. I could support him without it being unprofessional. "Very well."

He took my arm and drew me closer. All at once, I got

another whiff of his scent of sugar and flowers overtop the skunk odor. Even outside, the scent was cloying.

Most of the food stalls were in the front of the carnival. Starting near the back, we witnessed a few performers practicing. A polar bear, The Canvas of Tales, painted her white fur, and each stick figure and symbol came to life in the form of a play along her minimally clothed body. In another tent, a pig acrobat by the name of The Windy Aerialist, flipped to the ceiling of the tent with the aid of "digestible propulsion."

The interviews with the other sorcerers were brief and frustrating. When I asked where she grew up, The Canvas of Tales said she had to get ready for her next show and began undressing in front of me. For the sake of modesty, I hurried out of the tent. When I asked The Windy Aerialist where he attended college, it suddenly became important for him to 'burn off excess propulsion'. I quickly cut the interview short to flee for fresh air. All the interviews followed that same pattern. Most maddening, the sorcerers I spoke to only went by their stage name.

"To know their name would break the otherworldly air I so carefully crafted for this carnival," Isaac said. "Surely you don't mind that, do you?"

"Then why no stage name for yourself?"

The skunk adjusted his bowtie. "I'm too vain for one. Let the world know my name."

The next tent was one of the bigger ones. Before I could take more than two steps inside, Isaac held me back. "Best we give him some space."

A wolf stood in the center of a dark room. With a wave of their hands, a pair of shooting stars flew, flipped, and spun past planets. The pair of stars touched like lovers kissing, and little sparks flew through them. I was ready to believe the planets were just as magical as the stars until they collided with Pluto. It may have been the smallest planet, but it shook the ground as it landed with a metallic clang. I held my long ears.

The wolf rushed over and hugged the skunk. "I'm so sorry! I got careless, and I didn't know you were here. Are you okay?" The wolf held the skunk's head gently in his large hands. His thumbs rubbed the skunk's small, rounded ears.

What was left of Pluto rested several feet away from us. Had Isaac been struck by shrapnel? I didn't see any blood on him, though the wolf had the skunk's face pressed against his chest.

After a few seconds, the skunk pushed away from the wolf and chuckled. "I'm fine, Star of Night, perfectly fine!" He smoothed out the fur on his striped tail, which was still on end.

"Are you sure? Do you need—?"

It was Isaac's turn to rub the wolf's head. "I'm *fine*. Simon, are you okay?"

I nodded, and then turned to the wolf. "Sorry for interrupting your practice. We'll leave you be."

Star of Night's ears were still folded back when Isaac and I left. Isaac held me closer as we walked, his tail still halfway cocked.

"He seemed rather upset," I said, trying to sound as conversational as possible. If I made it sound too much like an interview question, the interviewee tended to put their walls up.

Isaac chuckled. "Simon, I don't think I need to explain why it's not a good idea to startle a skunk. I don't know a skunk that would spray just from being spooked, but it's a myth we live with daily. I'm sure Star of Night was worried that awful smell would ruin his tent, or the whole carnival. Oh, and that wolf nose of his would be smelling it for days. Terribly unpleasant." The skunk's hand was clenched tightly around the head of his cane.

"Right, of course."

The skunk steered me toward the center of the carnival.

"I think a tour would be incomplete with a ride on our Ferris wheel. How are you with heights?"

I tried to keep my face neutral, and I fought a twitch in my ears. "Decent."

Isaac pulled me closer so that our hips brushed. "I assure you all of our rides are stable, but if it helps, you can hold onto me."

"Thank you," I said. What I didn't say was that the skunk had a certain way of drawing attention to himself. Yes, there were his scent and stripes and his foppish attire, but it was all in the walk. I wouldn't call it lewd. At least, it didn't seem outwardly so. Perhaps it was the way he, like many skunks, are pear-shaped. There was a sway in the hips that was rhythmic and inviting. I fought the urge to slip my hand down to his lower back, just above the tail, and feel the sway of his hips. I cleared my throat. "I'd like that."

I glanced at him looking at me looking at his rear. Even though I looked away, he said nothing. His pleasant smile remained, though perhaps the corners turned up slightly more. Isaac's hips swayed just a little bit extra.

It took a few minutes to get onto the Ferris wheel. The ride operator immediately ushered us over upon seeing Isaac, but the skunk declined.

"They've been waiting longer," Isaac said, indicating the line. "Let them go first."

Once at the front, we climbed into the acorn-shaped cars. Instead of sitting across from me, the skunk slid to my right. The bench seat easily sat three people, and yet here he was brushing up against me. The car rocked as he had climbed in. I grabbed the seat, and my other hand slipped into my pocket around my inhaler. Maybe heights weren't my favorite, but if I panicked, I'd need to take a puff.

Isaac set his cane on his lap, placed his hand around mine, and gently drew it off the seat. "I promise you won't fall."

The ride operator closed the door. It was just Isaac and me now.

The ride took off as gently as a leaf on the breeze. Instead of going around in a circle like most Ferris wheels, this one corkscrewed around the "trunk" of the thick tree.

"I like to ride this every day," the skunk said as he looked over the edge. "I get to see so many people. Even if I'm too high up to see it, I can feel their smiles."

I sat still, but tried to throw on a smile. "A king surveying his kingdom."

The skunk waved me off. "I don't have such lofty aspirations. Besides, I don't need to sit high up to see what's going on in the carnival. Or what's happening here."

Isaac's cane brushed the inside of my thigh. It searched all the way up until it pressed up against my crotch.

I stiffened, and was beginning to stiffen in another way. Outside the car, the tree and the other cars disappeared as we rose into the clouds. The ride wasn't nearly so tall when I first saw it. Was this another illusion?

"You've got such lovely dark, roving eyes," the skunk purred. "It's all right, you're not in trouble. Quite the opposite. If you're so fond of my rear, I could show you more of it. You could do more than look."

Isaac moved his cane away from my groin. He made a little show of lifting his tail up and settling down in my lap. His bushy, fragrant tail tried to slip around my back, but I had pressed myself hard against the back of my seat.

"Oh! Well," the skunk said, settling further against my crotch. "Always good to know the audience enjoys the show." There was an uneasy chuckle in his tone. "Is this enjoyable? This goes much better when you say something."

Isaac was undeniably attractive. The skunk was giving clear indications he wanted me as well, possibly right here in the Ferris wheel car. My mind was quickly fogging up with the single-minded lustfulness that comes from arousal. I could easily allow Isaac to drop his trousers, work myself out of mine, and fuck this skunk I was assigned to interview for a chance at becoming an Assistant Editor.

"This is greatly appreciated," I said, "but I'm here on business. I can't compromise my work like this. Even though it's terribly tempting." I bit my tongue. That last bit was taking it too far.

Isaac kept his smile, though his tail drooped. "Ah, yes, of course." He extricated himself from my lap and sat down next to me, this time at a proper distance. "I've been told I come on a bit strong."

The clouds rose away from us. The tree trunk and the other acorn cars rose and descended around us. The car shook again, and I grabbed my seat.

The skunk grasped my hand. "Would this be all right until the end of the ride?"

I nodded. "Thank you."

"Once you're done with this story of yours, would it be considered unprofessional to stop by my tent?" Isaac's thumb circled my hand in his grasp. "The carnival will be in town for three more days."

"I suppose it would be okay. More than okay, really."

The skunk glanced at my crotch. "I figured as much. You may want to think about baseball. Actually, I could use a bit of my illusionary magic to make it look like you haven't got an erection."

If my ears were any hotter, they'd melt the car we were in. "Hadn't we just agreed on professionalism?"

"Just wait until you see how much 'professionalism' you're showing when we get off the ride," the skunk said, smiling. "Then you'll be begging for my help."

By the time we got off the Ferris wheel, I was thankfully back to normal. Isaac walked me to the front gate of the carnival. We each looked at each other, unsure who would unhook their arm first. I found myself reluctant to do so.

"You should come by tonight," Isaac said as he released me. "It's the big show where all the carnival sorcerers come together for one spectacular act."

"I'd like that."

The skunk waved me off. "I'll save you a seat."

Even though my ears felt droopy, I wasn't too sad to part with the skunk. I just needed to write this story and then I could be back at the carnival, hopefully in his arms again.

———

I usually wrote my stories at my desk at the *Shiner's Post* office. If all went well, I could write up my assignment by the time lunch ended and have the article out in the next issue. When I walked into the office, Eli's door was shut. Eli was talking to someone, but it wasn't on the phone.

"Your work speaks for itself. I think you'd make a fine Assistant Editor."

"I'm glad you think so. I can start anytime, just give me the word, Eli."

"Well, there's still some names to go through, but I won't lie, Jacob, you've got a good shot at this. We'll talk more later."

The door opened up. Jacob, a coyote, had a bit of wag to his tail.

Before the badger could close his door, I slipped inside.

"You're interviewing Jacob?" I said. The coyote had half the experience I had and a quarter of the writing ability. Even after five years at the paper, he had to rewrite every other article because of his habit for listing events instead of showing the story.

Eli sighed and shut the door. "He's in the running. I haven't made a final decision yet."

"You sounded like you'd made up your mind. And what happened to being so busy you couldn't interview anyone this week?"

The badger walked behind his desk as if to hide behind his authority. "You were eavesdropping?"

"Not intentionally," I said. "I just came back from my assignment and was walking by your office."

"My door is shut for a reason, Simon," Eli said. He tapped his desk with his claws. "That's an invasion of privacy, unintentional or not."

"Don't change the subject!"

"We could have been discussing anonymous sources," Eli continued. "Do you understand? You're usually the professional around here, but here you are sticking your long damn ears where they shouldn't be."

My nose twitched, and my chest tightened. "It won't happen again, sir, but—"

"Just get out of my office," Eli said. "And you better have that carnival article ready to go for tomorrow."

I opened my mouth, but I couldn't force anything out. Whatever air I drew in wasn't nearly enough.

"Take that fucking inhaler already before you choke," Eli said.

I dug my inhaler out of my pocket. Eli waited.

Then I bolted out of his office. I wasn't about to let him have the satisfaction of seeing me so weak.

I stumbled down the hallway that I remembered being much shorter than it felt now. The moment I stepped outside the office, I leaned against the door and took a precious puff from my inhaler. Slowly, my lungs filled, and I took greedy breaths.

Perhaps I shouldn't have been shocked I was getting passed over for the Assistant Editor position, and yet, here I was. I just didn't expect Eli to pretend I had a shot in the first place.

Once I fully caught my breath, I walked over to the nearest bus stop. I'd get the story done before the end of the day, but if Eli was going to accuse me of being unprofessional,

I was going to be unprofessional on my own terms. It was time for me to experience the carnival to my fullest.

———

Isaac wasn't at his tent. I found Star of Night, the wolf with that dazzling light magic, and he pointed me toward the food stalls. My stomach growled. After everything earlier at the carnival and at my office, I'd forgotten it was late into lunchtime.

I walked past booths offering spiced kebabs and octopus-shaped buns filled with black bean 'ink'. Isaac walked away from the crepe booth. He had a smudge of hazelnut spread on his muzzle.

"Back again?" Isaac said. He held out his crepe. "Care for something sweet?"

I pressed my muzzle to his. He tasted slightly nutty and fruity, but even without the crepe, the skunk would have been sweet. It was cloying, intoxicating. Isaac Wistman was the dessert of skunks: probably bad for me, but just what I needed to turn a bad day good.

I pulled away first. Now that I'd gotten a little taste, I was acutely aware some folks in line were watching like a performance underneath one of the many tents.

"Let's go back to my quarters, shall we?" The skunk placed one hand around my lower back and walked me toward his tent.

By the time we arrived, he had scarfed down his crepe and was licking his fingers clean. We walked right past his expansive living room and through the drape in the back. Inside was a large circular bed surrounded by candles. Isaac snapped his fingers, and the candles lit up. A rain of rose petals fell onto the sheets. It may have been the candles, but the room was just a bit too warm for clothing.

The skunk tossed his cane aside. He trailed kisses along my

jaw, nipped at my neck, and unbuttoned the top buttons of my shirt.

"Is any of this real?" I said. I fumbled for his bowtie, but I couldn't get it undone.

Isaac held my trembling hands. "It certainly feels real, doesn't it?" He undid the last couple buttons and drew me out of my shirt and coat. They dropped to the floor.

I was tempted to grab my inhaler, but decided against it. It had been a while since I'd last had sex, but I could get through it without triggering an asthma attack. "I just don't want to come to and find out I've been humping one of the pillows."

The skunk whipped off my belt in one smooth yank. "Trust me, I'd rather not waste your seed on the bedding, and the cleaning would be a headache." Isaac undid the tail latch and slipped out of his striped trousers and underpants in one go.

He did seem rather eager. His cock, just a couple shades pink away from the pink of his outfit, bobbed at half-mast. The candles and rose petals did nothing to cover the musk wafting off the skunk. If I was walking down the street, this might have been unpleasant, but here in the bedroom with a growing erection, it was alluring. I slipped off my underpants, freeing my cock.

The skunk tossed his coat and vest onto the floor and loosened his bowtie. He didn't bother with his shirt. "Now, please keep in mind what I'm about to do is an invitation, not a warning." The skunk got on all fours on the bed and lifted his tail. His pucker was on full display.

"Wait, you don't have to," I said. "Not with your knee."

"My—?" The skunk froze. Then he laughed and rolled over onto his back. "Yes, excellent point. Thank you. Lube's in the nightstand. First drawer. Or I could use my muzzle."

I grabbed the jar of lubricant and began slicking myself up. "No, I want to take you from behind. It's what drew me to you, after all."

"Not my sparkling personality?" The skunk chuckled. He laid his head back against the bed. "I trust you've blunted your claws?"

I knelt by the end of the bed so my face was level with his rear. Isaac's fur was white along the inner thigh all the way up to the inner parts of his behind. If he wasn't spread, I'd of thought his rump was entirely black. "Of course. Okay, I'm starting."

"Appreciate the head's—"

The skunk stiffened as I slid my tongue along his pucker. The scent, and the taste for that matter, were sharp. I looked up. "Too much?"

"Word of caution: my glands are close there," Isaac panted.

"Should I stop?"

The skunk sat up, placed his hand on the back of my head, and pushed my face closer to his pucker. "Be careful, but gods, keep doing that."

I quickly acclimated to the odor and the taste of his asshole and developed a steady rhythm. My tongue traced along his ring and slid into him. Isaac squirmed delightfully. He whacked me with his bushy tail more than once in his ecstasy. During one quick twist of his hips, my tongue nudged something bulbous. Isaac pushed away from me. The candles turned off like a light switch and the roses disappeared.

"Okay, that's enough of that," he laughed.

I ran my tongue along the inside of my mouth. "Was that your—?"

"Yes."

"Ah." I touched my damp muzzle and sniffed. Pungent, though I didn't smell skunk spray.

A considerable amount of pre ran down the skunk's length. "I'd say I'm more than prepped at this point."

I held up the jar of lubricant. "Almost." I scooped a generous dollop to two of my fingers. Then I slid them slowly into the skunk. Isaac managed to keep the squirming down to a minimum.

I sat on his bed and patted my lap. Isaac straddled me, and our cocks brushed.

"Are you ready?" I said.

"More than ready at this point."

Isaac hoisted himself up and slowly sat himself down on my cock. I slid into the skunk with little resistance. Isaac wasn't loose back there, but the lubricant and eating him out had certainly eased things.

The skunk grabbed me by the shoulders. His tail lashed about as I pushed his hips down on me. I took one hand off his hips briefly so I could play with his bushy, striped tail. It helped distract me from my lungs, which were already constricting from the effort of having sex.

Isaac was certainly vocal, but they were animalistic chitters and squeaks. Even if I couldn't understand him, there was a drunk-like smile on his face. If there was something wrong, I'm sure he would have said something. I laid back on the bed and thrust into the skunk, quickening the pace.

As much as we were enjoying this, I wanted to finish sooner rather than later. My chest was already tight and my lungs were closing up. Once we both came, I could suck in enough air to not use my inhaler. Maybe I could make a discreet exit into the bathroom to take a puff.

"There. Right there. I'm—" The skunk pushed himself against me to the hilt, stiffen, and painted my chest and chin with his seed. He relaxed and panted. "There we are."

I opened my mouth, but wheezed instead. Whatever air I could suck in wasn't enough.

Isaac blinked away his post coital bliss. "Simon? What's wrong?"

I tried to roll off the bed, but my cock, even though it was softening, was still inside the skunk. Even more than a release, I wanted air.

Isaac slipped off of me. "Do you need a doctor? I can grab them, just give me a second to put some pants on."

I tumbled off the bed and grabbed my coat, but both of my coat pockets were empty. My lungs seized, and my throat closed even more.

"Is this it?" Isaac held up my inhaler next to his dresser. It must have fallen out when we were undressing.

I reached for it.

Instead, Isaac set me back against the bed and pressed the inhaler to my mouth. He puffed three blasts in quick succession. It would have been better if I had done it, but it was working. My lungs were slowly filling with air. My shame grew with each breath.

Once I was done with my inhaler, Isaac set it down and clutched my hands. I couldn't look him in the eye. The pity in his gaze was as thick as his scent. I didn't have to sit here and take it though.

I tried to stand, but the skunk held me down.

"Just let me go," I muttered. "I don't need your pity."

"It's not pity," Isaac said. "It's an apology. I harmed you because I was too focused on getting off and, well…"

I glanced down at my flaccid cock. As embarrassed as I was, at least I gave Isaac an orgasm. Sometimes I couldn't get my partners off. I could give them everything if it wasn't for my awful lungs.

The skunk failed to hold me back as I got up. I quickly gathered my things. "Look, this was lovely, but it's ruined now." I walked through the doorway to the living area.

And stepped back into the bedroom.

I looked through both ends of the door. They both led into the bedroom.

"As ringmaster of the Carnival of Jubilation," Isaac said, "I cannot on good conscience have you leave without a smile. Could you let me try to make it up to you?" He patted the bed.

I could have tried to leave, but the skunk would just make me walk through this illusion again and again until I collapsed. I tossed my clothes aside and sat.

Isaac knelt between my legs and pulled them apart. "I want you to close your eyes and count to five. If you don't feel good, say so, and we'll try something else. Can you please trust me?"

I sighed and nodded. "Okay." I shut my eyes. "One... two...three...four..."

Waves crashed against the shore, and a breeze was coming from somewhere. I opened my eyes. "Five."

I was on a seaside cliff. Unlike the town, as far as I could see, no one had touched this land. My lungs filled with more air than I had ever felt.

Beneath me, Isaac took my soft length in his muzzle. It didn't take long at all until my cock began to harden.

It was certainly the most serene blowjob I'd ever received. I luxuriated in all the air I could take in my lungs. Was this how healthy people felt or was this even more air than average? It was like being drunk, but pleasantly so. There was no need to rush.

Then again, even after losing my erection, my loins were quickly remembering the tension from thrusting into the skunk. My shaft was at full mast now. My ship was quickly heading towards the shore, so to speak.

The skunk quickened his pace. He took the full size of my length like a sword swallower.

My foot tapped against the ground, and I took a deep breath. I didn't feel anywhere close to choking. "Almost there now."

Isaac reached out and rubbed the spot between my balls and anus. I stomped at the ground, and he gave my balls a full squeeze.

"Sit back," I barely gasped out.

The skunk drew off my length.

I rubbed myself briefly before adding a couple extra stripes to the skunk's face. Waves crashed against the shore. When I was done, I fell back against the bed. The shore and the rest of the expansive outdoors were nowhere to be seen. I may have been a little drunk on the afterglow, but my lungs still felt full of air.

The skunk stood up and took a bow. He smiled at me with one eye shut. "Enjoy the show?"

I stood and kissed him. "Thank you. I'm glad I stayed, even if I didn't have much of a choice."

The skunk smacked his lips. He walked over to his night-stand and grabbed a tiny tin box.

"What are these?" I said, looking at the little white spheres inside. "Magical revitalizing pills?"

"They're breath mints." Isaac said. In a stage whisper, he added, "your breath smells like a skunk's asshole."

I grabbed two mints and popped them in my mouth. My face wasn't damp anymore, though I wouldn't say it was presentable. "Can you magic us clean?"

"The best I could do is give the illusion we're clean," Isaac said as he dug into his nightstand again. "That's a lot of work. I picked this up a while ago though. Works wonders." He held up a blue spray bottle. "Feels a bit tingly, but it'll clean you up in a few minutes. Keep your eyes closed, okay?"

I nodded and closed my eyes.

"Hope you don't mind being sprayed by a skunk."

I managed to keep my mouth closed through my laughter. The liquid was indeed chilly. I felt like an ice cube in a glass of soda pop due to the tingles.

"If you don't mind me asking," Isaac said as he spritzed my muzzle, "What happened to professionalism?"

Once he focused his squirting elsewhere, I replied, "I had a disagreement at work with my Head Editor. He lied to me."

The skunk squirted my crotch liberally. "People in power have a tendency to lie. They don't want everyone else to see all the cards they're hiding up their sleeves. There, that should do it." He held the bottle out to me. "My turn. Wait, let me get some of this excess seed off my face." He ducked into what I assumed was the bathroom. As I held the bottle in my hands, I wondered what the ringmaster with the power of the carnival in his hands could possibly be hiding.

———

I stayed the evening with Isaac, and he graciously allowed me to write up my story in his quarters, but only after he brought me over to the food stalls. It was past lunchtime now, and I devoured more than a few tiny blossoms of fried onions, an assortment of crème-filled chocolates, and soda pop that changed flavor with each sip.

That night, Isaac got me a seat to the big show at the packed center tent. Every seat was filled.

"And where do you come in?" I had asked. "The big finale?"

"Oh, no," the skunk had said. "I'm merely here to get the show going and keep the whole carnival running."

The center of the tent filled with a dreamy purple haze. When it cleared, the ceiling glittered like the night sky. A spotlight shone on Isaac. Maybe it was magic or makeup, but his tail sparkled like a little milky way.

"Esteemed guests," the skunk said, his voice echoing throughout the tent. "Many of you gathered here today have no doubt seen the news about unrest and heard whispers of another war on the horizon. You are tired, bitter, and scared. Our country's last war is still a wound scabbing in your minds and hearts. It has stolen too much from you. We at the Carnival of Jubilation are here to say no country can steal our joy. No war can rob us of our sense of hope and wonder. Magic is not for war, but for the betterment and splendor of the people!"

The crowd erupted in cheers. A ferret child seated near the stairway leading down climbed onto the railing. He wiggled with excitement as he cheered. The boy, in fact, wiggled too much. His foot slipped, and he flailed his arms to try to keep his balance. A woman, I assume his mother, reached for him, but he tumbled off the stands. The audience gasped.

Isaac tossed his cane. I half expected him to cast a spell to save the boy, but what could an illusion do? Instead, the skunk dashed forward and leapt. Isaac scooped the boy up and tumbled to the ground.

A hush fell over the crowd. A moment later the little ferret sat up, smiling. The crowd cheered once again.

Isaac made a show of brushing the dirt off the boy before taking his hand and walking him back up into the stands.

"I appreciate the enthusiasm," Isaac joked once he brought the ferret back to his seat, "but let's avoid any more balancing acts on the railing."

The boy's mother was all thank-yous and tears, and Isaac took her hands in his. He bent down on what I now realized were two perfectly healthy knees.

As the skunk hurried down to the center ring to finish his speech, I got up and marched down the stairway. Isaac was right. Powerful men did hold secrets.

I walked out of the tent and found the flap that lead to the backstage. Performers were hustling around locating lost props, putting the finishing touches on their makeup, and squeezing themselves into leotards. They were all too occupied to notice me as I waltzed on through.

Isaac was handing a flaming baton to an otter who was on their way toward the stage. I had to fight to keep my tone neutral as I stalked toward the skunk. "We need to talk."

"Simon, what are you doing back here?" Isaac said. "You're missing the show."

I glanced over at the skunk's cane, which was resting on a nearby chair. "So your knee made a miraculous recovery?"

Isaac's tail stiffened. His eyes flicked to me to the cane and back. If he was searching for some excuse, he wasn't going to find it.

"Don't tell me it's some illusion," I said, stepping toward him. "Magic can't do everything."

At this point, the carnival sorcerers were looking at us. I didn't care. Still, my lungs were beginning to tighten up.

"You weren't supposed to find out," Isaac said. He wouldn't quite meet my eye, and he had a faraway look. "No one other than everyone here was supposed to know, especially not the folks drawing up draft orders."

"I can't go around giving false information in my articles," I said. I took a sharp breath. "If my editor found out, I'd never get the promotion. Hell, I could be fired!"

The otter with the flaming baton grabbed my shirt collar. "Hey, ease off the boss!"

I shoved the otter away from me. The otter stumbled to the ground, and his flaming baton struck a box marked 'fireworks'. The box hissed.

"Hit the deck!" the otter hollered.

We all ducked and dove to the floor as fireworks screeched and flew around the backstage. They erupted in ear-shattering explosions of color, and I held my long ears against my head.

The eruptions of the fireworks gave way to the quick snap of gunfire. Was someone trying to shoot the fireworks out of the air? Behind a row of costumes, I chanced a peek.

The skunk was positively vibrating. He hugged his long tail around himself and rocked as soldiers dashed through the backstage. Every now and then, one would collapse with a bullet in their head. Another screamed as their leg was blown off from some unseen force.

The wolf, Star of Night, dashed to the skunk and placed his hands over Isaac's ears. "Isaac, you're at the carnival, okay? You're not on the front lines anymore. You're safe. Please come back, Isaac."

Slowly, the soldiers faded away, though the scent of the spent fireworks and the destruction still gave the backstage the look of a battlefield.

The skunk's eyes refocused, but they remained wide as he surveyed the scene. "Oh gods I-I just—I'm so sorry everyone. Let me tidy this…" he reached for a scorched costume.

The wolf hauled the skunk to his feet. "No more apologies out of you. You didn't mean for any of this to happen."

"We still have a show to finish," The polar bear, The Canvas of Tales, said. She spoke firmly, but didn't raise her voice. "Everyone get to your places. If you don't have anything to do, start cleaning."

"We should get him to his tent," I said.

"*I'll* take Isaac," the polar bear said, an ursine growl escaping from her. "Star of Night, get that damn rabbit out of here."

The wolf grabbed me by the scruff of my neck and marched me out of the tent. Even when we got outside, the wolf didn't release me until we were at the gates of the carnival.

"Isaac helped me see that I didn't have to use my magic to kill anymore," Star of Night growled. His hands glowed like twin North Stars. "I promised I'd never take a life again. If you come back here, I'll break that promise." He shoved me toward the bus shuttle and stalked back toward the center tent.

Maybe the skunk had lied to me, but I shouldn't have yelled at him. If I made a false statement in an article, I could always write a retraction in the next issue. There was no retracting the harm I caused tonight.

"Let Isaac know I'm sorry!" I said to the wolf.

The wolf kept on walking.

———

I wanted to go back to my apartment and avoid everyone, but I couldn't go home yet. My things were still sitting at my desk at work. I just needed to take a quick detour.

The moment I walked into the *Shiner's Post* office, Eli stomped his way over to me. "Where the hell have you been? Tomorrow's paper is heading to the printer in less than an hour, and we need your carnival story now!"

I froze. Gods, after the incident backstage at the carnival, I completely forgot about my deadline. "I have it, but I need to type it up."

Eli grabbed me by the arm and dragged me over to my desk. "You sit your ass in that chair and get it done. If that story isn't in my hands in the next twenty minutes, you can clear off your desk and find a new job." He stood over me with his arms crossed. "Get to work, Simon."

Even though I couldn't draw in a full breath, I set to typing up the story. It was a shame I didn't have notes from the big show tonight for the article, but I still had enough about Isaac and the carnival to write something both entertaining and informative.

Before I was even a paragraph into the story, I paused.

Isaac no longer wears a sorcerer's military robes, though his pink and green attire is crisp and orderly, his cane, which he needs after injuring his knee in the last war, is spotless.

"Don't you go taking a break, Simon!" Eli said.

"Sorry, just deciphering my chicken scratch," I said. I typed the line up, and every line in my already-written story, without any changes. No, it wasn't professional to publish lies as if they were the truth, but I'd done Isaac enough harm tonight. The lie still made for a compelling story.

———

"I'd like everyone to give our new Assistant Editor a round of applause," Eli said. This was the first time I've seen him smile in days.

The other staff writers and I clapped as Jason's tail wagged.

"I know James had a lot more experience than me, but I'll do my best to make the *Shiner's Post* the best damn paper it can be," the coyote said.

As the writers disbanded, I walked back to my desk and dropped my smile. I wasn't even given an interview out of courtesy. It seemed like no one else was, unless Eli had been interviewing multiple candidates while I was out for the carnival story. It made it into this morning's paper just fine. Now life could continue from where it left off. Before I ever met Isaac.

Potential story leads sat on my desk like empty Christmas presents. There was one involving a poor carrot crop (I think there was a reason *I* was offered that one), the most uneventful store robbery I'd ever heard of, and an upcoming quilting contest. I tossed the stories on my desk and placed on head on them.

Someone in green trousers sat down on the desk next to me. "Morning, Simon."

I sat up. "Isaac?" My voice came out louder than I wanted it. I dropped down to a whisper. "I don't think 'sorry' can cover just how awful I feel about last night."

The skunk held up the morning's paper. It was turned to my story about the carnival. "I read it. Do you know a good place for breakfast? Someplace with waffles? Pancakes are good too, but waffles have the little syrup pockets." He spoke easily enough, but he ran his hand through his stiff tail as he looked around the office. "Or is this a bad time?"

"I know a place." I stood up and offered him my arm.

Isaac smiled. His tail eased as he linked his arm around mine and we walked out of the office.

We sat down in a booth at a greasy spoon. It wasn't nearly as fantastical or colorful as the carnival, but the booth had a little jukebox where we could play music. After we ordered, Isaac inserted a quarter. A slow jazzy song played softly.

"I started having those waking nightmares before I finished my first tour," Isaac said. He dumped two packets of sugar into his coffee. "The higher ups said that wasn't an excuse to exempt me from tour number two. 'Everyone gets nightmares' you see. After my second tour, I paid someone to forge paperwork to make a minor knee injury into something greater. According to my medical records, I'll never be able to march again. That's a language the military understands."

"It's not just you, is it?" I said. Even though I wanted to pull out my notebook and write this all down, this story wasn't meant for anyone but me right now. "Do some of the other sorcerers have those nightmares?"

The skunk stirred his coffee. "Some have demons they face. Others are AWOL soldiers and lovers who never wanted to be fighters. Some are refuges from countries that deem magic as the Devil's work. My carnival's not just a sanctuary for guests. It's a safe haven for all the sorcerers who have deserted."

"There's no way all of them could us their magic for war. Why draft them?" Sure, I could see how Star of Night and Isaac would come in handy, but what use in the battlefield did an army have of a sorcerer who could paint living art on themselves or propel themselves into the air with flatulence?

"That's the trouble with magic," Isaac said. "Magic can make the impossible happen, but people mistake that to mean we sorcerers can do anything, including becoming killers. But we don't have a choice."

"Or else you go to prison for desertion."

"More than that," Isaac said. "You see, at least in our country, the military put a sorcerer's family in a safe house until the end of the war. All for safe keeping, of course. But sorcerers never have a say in this. And their family is kept in that secret safe house, with no way to contact them or knowledge of their location, until the war is over. Kill enough of the enemy and stay alive. Then we get our families back."

I slammed my mug down. Coffee spilled all over the table, and the diners glanced at us.

I was about to shout when I noticed the skunk wincing, and I remembered the night before. "I'm so sorry. I didn't—"

The skunk held up his hands. "It's fine."

I grabbed a handful of napkins. "Let me clean this."

"I can help."

"No, it's my mess, it's okay."

Our hands brushed as we sopped up the coffee. Our eyes met. I wanted to crawl into the biggest, most comfy chair in his living room with him. I wanted to kiss him and every inch of his stripes. I wanted my own magic so I could cast a spell over Isaac and protect him from all the harm in the world. But I wasn't a sorcerer. I was a journalist.

"I want to help you," I said. I let go of the coffee-stained napkins and held his hand. "And all the other sorcerers the government has hurt. The world needs to know your stories."

"Would that work?" Isaac said. "I don't want to put the other sorcerers in danger. They're family."

I squeezed his hand. "It can all be anonymous. And they don't have to tell me their stories if they don't want to. I understand some wounds are still too fresh."

"And I'm sure some of them still want to kill you," the skunk said, chuckling.

I smiled. "Promise to protect me?"

"Only if you protect me too," Isaac said. "All of us."

We leaned over the table and kissed. We hadn't even had our waffles yet, but he tasted so sweet.

"Um, sirs? I have your order."

Isaac and I pulled away, and my ears burned as the server

gave us our waffles and a cup of coffee to replace the one I broke.

My mind raced as I ate breakfast. Two days ago, I would have thought about all the awards I could win with the article, or even a book, I could win for such an exposé. Now, all I could think about was this remarkable, dapper, handsome skunk with syrup on his whiskers sitting across from me.

"Would your newspaper go for this story?" Isaac said after we waited for the bill.

I smiled. "I was thinking it might be time for a change of scenery." After all these years, if I wasn't going to get promoted at the *Shiner's Post*, I never would. I'd rather go where someone saw my true potential. "You don't mind having a freeloader tag along, do you?"

The skunk grabbed me by the collar and kissed me hard. We were both grinning like madmen. "Running away to join the circus?"

"Can we have dessert back at the carnival?"

"Excellent plan!" the skunk said. "No meal's complete without something sweet. What are you in the mood for? Funnel cake? Ice cream? Both?"

"I was thinking we could go back to your tent." I slipped my foot up between the skunk's legs.

The got a delightful squeak out of him. "Oh, I've got something for you to eat. But can we get some real dessert too?"

Once we had paid, the two of us left the diner arm in arm and headed toward the shuttle to the carnival. I pulled myself closer to the skunk. Eli could wait for my resignation until I had my dessert.

IT'S JUST A GAME

ALISON CYBE

"Watch out!" he screamed.

Mikah moved his fingers quickly through the air. The motion left a glimmering golden trail, forming quickly into a bright arc. The light leapt from the tiger's hands, crackling triumphantly through the air, and completed its journey by landing on the hard chest of the most handsome wolf that Mikah had ever seen.

The lupine's health bar leapt quickly, scrambling from near-depleted state to well within what the tiger considered to be a safe average. Just in time, he thought, as the Hierophant of the Deathsfall Caverns brought his great-axe down in a heavy overhead swing towards the blue-furred lupine.

A reverberating clash rang through the air, drawing Mikah's attention back to the conflict. The hierophant had pulled himself upwards, levitating in the air above the arena, readying his massive spectral axe. Around the creature's fell form snapped and hissed the souls of the beast's victims, beckoning the party to join them. With a glint in his eye, the Hierophant began to intone words in a long-forgotten tongue. Mikah responded by throwing another fireball at the fiend. On the whole, he was unperturbed by the display, having killed the boss at least twelve times in the last few weeks. The dramatics of the display were quite worn off for him.

"Realms of Valeron" was the hottest MMORPG on the market, in no small part to its promise of a vibrant, friendly base of players. The game had hit the shelves eight months prior, to massive critical acclaim. Sales had skyrocketed, easily dwarfing every rival game on the market. News reports spread across the world, describing the game's success as a cultural phenomenon. It didn't even require a high-end computer system to run, making it accessible to gamers who might otherwise have been priced out of the expensive process of upgrading in order to run such a visually stunning game.

It was the visuals, in part, that had attracted Mikah to the game in the first place. He had yearned for a game like this, one that was bright and colourful, one that seemed truly magical. When he played games with his friends, he quickly grew bored of trudging through battered, war-torn cities, etched in washes of brown and grey and plastered with scorched craters in various shades of ash. He wanted colour, he wanted variety.

Then the expansion pack was announced. It had come so quickly after the release of "Realms of Valeron," and boasted a plethora of new content. New lands to explore, new monsters to fight, more spells to master and special loot to find. More than that, though, it was free. A full-sized expansion pack, released absolutely free of charge to people who had already bought the original game, promising to almost double the size of the already massive online world. Best of all, though, was the secret dungeons, hidden away by the developers, waiting for the enterprising players to discover and explore all for themselves: dungeons that only the hardest and most talented of the players would stand a chance of emerging from conquering. The expansion boosted the sales of the game threefold, quickly skyrocketing the players from three million to a phenomenal ten million.

Mikah hadn't had to think twice about buying the game. He had picked it up from a local store downtown, deciding that he would go to the shop and discuss his purchase to make sure that his computer would run it. The cashier quickly put his mind to rest, explaining that the game could easily run on even a low-end system like Mikah's. The cashier, a tall man with an unkempt beard whose name tag proudly proclaimed his name as Rusty, had told him that if he played on the same server, he would happily send him a few in-game items to get him started. Sadly, Mikah had completely forgotten the name of the server that Rusty played on (fire-something, perhaps) in his eagerness to create a character. After playing around with the character creation screen for almost half an hour, he eventually settled on his first character—a tiger cleric, skilled in the arts of healing and slaying the undead through divine prayers.

Another swing of the axe. A vast, spiralling pattern etched itself onto the floor, indicating the direction that the attack would strike. With a deft spring, the wolf pushed his way out of the range of the attack, barely missing the impact before the ground beside him exploded in a fiery cascade of sparks.

Mikah hoped that the wolf was alright. Normally he didn't mind so much if the tank—the person responsible for receiving most of the damage in a party—took a few hits. But as the tiger found his eyes lingering on this particular tank he found that he didn't want to let any harm come to him. Smooth folded ears hung lightly on either side of his head, framing a long and flowing. The stranger slid his blade back into the scabbard that hung around his bare hips. Noticing this, Mikah felt his eyes trailing over the stranger's avatar. The wolf was topless, the muscles of his chest firm and powerful.

Quietly, Mikah whispered a small prayer of thanks to whichever algorithmic gods managed the game's in-built party finder.

The wolf finished his lap of the arena, tail swaying behind him, moving gradually out of the way of the Hierophant's

Malefic Tendrils spell. Then, once clear of the spell's area of effect, he turned back around to face the monster. He charged forward, bringing his sword up in a frantic, wild arc.

The Heirophant buckled, stumbling backwards, and collapsed. Blinking, Mikah tried to rub his eyes. The large figure of the dungeon's boss hit the ground with a resounding thud.

The tiger paused, catching his breath. "Is… is that it?" he choked. "Did we kill it?"

"Sure did" replied the blue wolf. Turning his head, the figure shot Mikah a friendly grin. "All thanks to you."

Chuckling, Mikah shook his head. "I didn't do anything. I mean, a few fireballs, but mostly healing. You did all the heavy work. You really saved my tail there."

Restraining a chuckle, the wolf smiled. "Oh good" he replied. "I always love to save the pretty ones. I'm Arthur."

Slowly, the tiger's eyes turned downwards, his gaze sliding down from the wolf's torso to the plump front of his leggings. "I…" he started. "Pretty?"

That was enough to make Mikah's lips form into a contented smile.

———

Six months later…

Mikah's paw rested against the man's chest. Sliding his feline claws through the soft blue fur of his partner's pectoral muscles, he leaned closer and gently kissed the man's dark azure nipples.

In response, Arthur gave a soft moan. His back arched, pushing his taught body closer to Mikah's affections. The pair lay naked in the grass, tall blades softly flitting around them in the breeze. Arthur eased his hips forward, between the cat's spread thighs.

Flexing his bare feet around the lupine's waist, Mikah

purred contentedly. He squeezed Arthur's hips, urging him closer, deeper. Through half-closed eyes, he stared in blissful contentment at the man's body, his thoughts dwelling on how enthralling his partner's deep blue fur looked in the moonlight. His cock twitched eagerly, anticipating his lover's caress.

That, thought Mikah, was what had first caught his attention. Arthur was the first blue lupine that he had ever seen in the game, and even though the man who was now his in-game lover played as a heavily armed tank class, he had no hesitation in showing as much of his well-toned fur as he could. When Mikah had first seen him, he wore little more than leather armbands and denim. His broad chest was restrained only by the bindings of a sturdy leather harness that matched his armbands. The man had enchanted him, even though Mikah had never thought of himself as being especially a fan of men with muscles, or of leather. But this one blue lupine had an air of both freedom and restraint to him; his virility straining against the material that confined him. He was Narcissus unbound and Dionysus in chains, all at the same time.

And, as Mikah had found out later that evening, his cock was huge too. Big enough to make the feline's knees feel weak. Of course, Arthur had shrugged that off, but Mikah was certain that he knew better.

The two writhed in their pleasured, moonlit embrace. The thought of their disparity brought a grin to Mikah's lips. He, a cat, bore short and speckled fur across his slender body, his naked chest and stomach smooth and pliant, whilst his lover's deep fur barely concealed a hefty frame of muscle that sang of strength. The two could not have been less alike, in species or in appearance.

Arthur slid downwards, sinking to his knees between Mikah's legs, his broad shoulders leaning back. He took the cat's taut, needy erection in his fingers and anointed it with kisses. The cat gasped loudly, his eyelids fluttering closed as he whispered gentle 'oh's into the air.

"I think" said the lupine, "after we are done here, could we go to the Deathsfall Caverns?"

Mikah didn't reply. Eagerly he arched upwards closer, his legs weaving their way around his lover's broad shoulders, toes flexing in pleasure. He gasped as he felt the head of his shaft slide between Arthur's lips, wet and warm. "Mmm" he moaned, "Please, I want to feel you inside of me…"

"It's just" continued Arthur, slipping the cat's cock from his mouth in order to lick at it tenderly, "I've still not got the helmet from there, and I really need it to raise my item level."

The cat pursed his lips. "Do we have to talk about this now?" he asked.

Slowly, Arthur shook his head and chuckled. "No" he said, "Sorry. I was just thinking ahead."

"While giving me head?" asked Mikah, a smirk spreading across his lips.

———

The dragon, whose name label readily identified him as Biggie, walked confidently down the path, a large musket rifle slung with one stony hand across his broad shoulders.

Mikah looked at the rifle, uncertainly. "How can you even use that?"

"IT IS HUNTER WEPON" explained Biggie.

The tiger gave a soft sigh. Even though he had tracked his way through well over thirty dungeons with the dragon, Biggie's unique linguistic habit of speaking every word at the top of his lungs, as though his claw were perpetually stuck on his caps-lock key, never ceased to be a source of amusement for him.

The cleric nodded, "Yes, I get that. But realistically, have you ever equipped a gun type weapon before?"

The towering dragon shook his head.

"Exactly" said the tiger. "I've only ever seen you with a bow. A gun is completely different to a bow, right? I mean, they operate entirely differently."

Biggie hefted the rifle from his shoulder and stared at it. "IT IS HUNTER WEPON" he reiterated, enthusiastically.

Mikah thought to himself that he really should know better than to get into a discussion about this with the dragon. Ever since he had joined the guild two months prior, the two had become regular party members. Unlike Arthur, Biggie's skill at ranged combat meant that Mikah rarely had to worry about the dragon taking excess damage during the heat of battle, something that the rookie healer was extremely grateful for.

The cleric shook his head, "Just because you can use a bow doesn't mean that you can use a gun. That's what I mean."

The dragon scratched his crag-like head. "IT IS HUNTER WEPON" he repeated, pleading his case.

"But, logically, there is no way that you should be able to just pick it up and use it, not if the only weaponry experience you have is with a bow" explained Mikah. "It doesn't make sense."

Biggie glanced around for a moment. He looked around the forest, examining the tree line. Then, with a smile, his eyes feel onto a small fox. He pointed towards it, and Mikah turned to glance. He noted that it was a level five critter and was labelled as a Densewood Forest Fox, presumably to differentiate it from every single other fox in the world.

The dragon brought the gun to his eye and, with a resounding explosion of gunpowder, blew the very tip of the creature's tail off. Mikah blinked a few times in disbelief at the shot. Slinging his rifle across his shoulder again, Biggie explained with finality, "IT IS HUNTER WEPON."

Mikah turned towards Arthur. "How does this even make sense?" he demanded.

The tank shrugged. "It shouldn't, but bows and guns both share the 'ranged attack' skill, along with crossbows and javelins."

"Wait," Mikah asked, holding his paw up, "Javelins? Shouldn't they use the 'throw' skill?"

The wolf shook her head, "No, the 'throw' skill is only ever used by the assassin class for throwing shuriken."

Mikah blinked. "But… But none of that makes any sense!"

Arthur glanced over towards Mikah. "Hun, you've been unusually down today. What's wrong?"

The comment forced Mikah to think for a moment. He had been rather down. He hadn't even realised it, but he definitely wasn't feeling his usual chipper, optimistic self. "I'm sorry," he said. He tried to think what might be causing it. Quickly, he managed to rule out any real-life factors. His friends were good, his social life fairly active. His work life was a monotonous, but ultimately non-challenging drawl, which left him with little real stress in his otherwise laid-back life. No, he thought, the only thing that was really stressing him out had to be something in the game. Then, smoothly as if it were wrapped in wet butter, the realisation of just what that something was came to him. "I guess I'm just worried," he admitted, "About us. I don't want all our effort to be for nothing."

Arthur stopped, mid-step. He glanced around to everyone else in the party, "You guys keep going ahead, I'll catch up." Then he turned to the cleric. "Mikah, really. I'm going to talk to you completely honestly here for a moment, okay?"

Mikah nodded.

The other three continued onwards, down the winding forest path.

The wolf smiled to Mikah, his tail flitting hesitantly back

and forth behind him, "I know that this idea is actually a massive longshot."

The cleric replied, "I'm worried that we're just setting ourselves up to fail at this" he admitted, reaching up to scratch behind one of his striped ears.

"Look" said Arthur, stepping closer. "We can't make any promises, and we can't get our hopes up. What happens in real-life might not follow what's happening in-game for us, and we need to be prepared for that. Are you sure that you're okay with that?"

Nervously, Mikah nodded. He hoped that he was, in fact, ready for it.

"It's getting late. Mind if we finish up for the night after this dungeon?"

"Oh" replied Mikah, his heart sinking a little. He had been hoping to spend more time alone with Arthur after the dungeon, perhaps even finish their intimate session from earlier. He swallowed a little, reminding himself that Arthur didn't have as much free time as he did. The guy was a university senior after all, he thought, and it's exam season. "Yeah" he said aloud into his mic, "that's cool, no worries. Still up for next weekend?"

The question hung heavy in the air. The entire process of asking Arthur to meet up with him had been a huge moment, the lead-up for which had all but left Mikah a nervous wreck. The last two months had been a blur of making plans, of trying to tether his hopes and not allow them to pull too eagerly on him. Mikah tried not to hope that everything would go as smoothly as it had in-game. But then, how could it not?

"Yeah" replied the lupine, drawing up his sword and smashing it fiercely into the hierophant's chest plate. "Definitely. But, eh, let's talk about it tomorrow?"

———

"What is it?" asked Mikah.

"THAT BOSS" said Biggie, "I THINK."

Arthur perked up. "I've just checked the website, it's definitely correct."

They stared across the great temple hallway. Vast ruined pillars were scattered from corners to lie crumbling in the dirt. Above, a huge domed ceiling rose above them, letting in a powerful shaft of sunlight that cascaded with a golden hue, appearing almost celestial in its majesty. A torn and shattered altar lay in a broken pile at the far end of the chamber, and before it stood the boss. It was tall, three times the size of either of the party and glistened with a sickly and viscous shimmer. Its green mass shifted uncertainty as it wavered, uncertainly, but held its strong geometric shape. From within, the gelatinous creature emitted a low growl. It was the shape of the thing that the companions looked at in confusion. They had not expected its cube-like form to taper at the top into a fine point.

Biggie looked at the others. "WHUT?" he asked, "NOBODY SEEN GELATINUS PIRAMID BEFORE?"

"In general" explained Mikah, "the standard dungeon monster is a Gelatinous Cube. I've never seen any triangular ones before."

The hunter shrugged, "DOES IT MATTER?"

Arthur hummed lightly, and then added "I'm pretty sure this was a Gelatinous Cube back in the beta."

"DEY CHANGE IT" said Biggie, decisively, "TO AVOID LAWSUIT."

Across the chamber, the Gelatinous Pyramid burbled at them.

"It doesn't look very threatening" said Mikah.

"Looks can be deceiving" commented Arthur. "Okay, assuming that this is the same boss as I'm familiar with, just with a slightly different model, then the fight itself is divided into two phases. The first is a basic tank and spank, except for the adds which spawn at twenty second intervals. Biggie, you and Mikah will AOE them down. When the boss hits sixty percent health, it starts the second phase, moving around the arena. You'll want to avoid the ooze trails that it leaves behind it; they will give you a slow movement debuff. Biggie, you'll want to make sure that your pet's procs are up as often as they can be, as the bear is immune to this effect. I'll frenzy when the boss hits thirty per cent and if Mikah keeps his crits on cooldown, we'll be fine. Any questions?"

"I NO UNDERSTAND NONE OF THAT" said Biggie.

Mikah replied, "Just shoot it and you'll be fine". He turned and smirked to Arthur. "Tank and spank, eh? Wouldn't mind a bit of that later on."

"Down, tiger" replied the tank with a smirk, and then turned his attention towards the slime triangle. "Right," he said, "let's show this walking pile of copyright infringement how we do things in Valeron."

The party charged.

The pyramid lunged forward, slamming into Arthur as the wolf rushed to meet it. The two crashed into each other with a heavy wet squelch. Arthur snarled and batted at the Gelatinous foe. His blade splashed against its surface. "I don't think that this is doing much good" he grumbled. The sword lapped against the creature's viscous surface with all of the impact of a small duck landing on the surface of a pond.

Then, without another word, the creature pulsed. A large number of thin, flailing tendrils sprouted from its wet form, flailing around madly. Arthur took a step back, only for one of the liquid-like tentacles to grasp around him, coiling its way around the wolf's waist. He thumped at it with his blade, struggling valiantly.

"I don't understand" said Mikah, as he channelled up another spell. His holy flames seemed to be having almost no effect on the creature, as it tried to bat at him with one searching tendril. "The website didn't mention it having any kind of attack like this in the beta!"

Biggie levelled his rifle and released another resonating explosive blast. "WHAT WE DO NOW?" he called rather loudly through the voice channel.

A single snaking tendril wrapped its way around Mikah's legs. Squeezing them together, it started to pull. The tiger gave a sharp yelp of panic, tumbling haphazardly down to the cold floor. "It's got me!" it cried.

"Just stay calm" replied Arthur, smashing his two-handed blade with all his might against the tentacle that tightened around him. "It's still just a boss."

"Easy for you to say!" replied the tiger. The tentacle of slime slathered its way around his legs, pulling him closer. Mikah looked down, a gasp of panic escaping his lips. His eyes drew wide as another slippery tentacle started to wrap its way around his leggings, tugging them down. "I..." he stuttered. "Oh my word!"

"IF THIS TURN INTO A JAPANESE PORN CARTOON, I'M LEAVING!" barked Biggie, unloading another volley of buckshot into the Gelatinous Pyramid.

Mikah dropped his staff, feeling the cold of the dungeon air around his hips. He clasped his hands around the invading tentacles, straining to pull them away. Instantly, more tendrils sprouted from the ones that assailed him, growing into long and probing fingers. In an instant, the tiger's leggings were around his knees, and the slimy appendages were slathering their way around his bare crotch, massaging his thighs and cupping hungrily at the tiger's soft, fluffy sack. "Arthur!" cried Mikah. "Can't you keep aggro on this thing?"

"I'm trying" wailed the tank, batting ineffectively at the assailing tentacles, whacking against the wet gelatinous substance with all his strength.

His legs bound, Mikah gave a terrified wail as the tentacles began to encircle his naked thighs and slide around his crotch.

He felt their warm, clammy fingers slather their way around his nakedness, leaving a wet trail across his sheath, slathering his balls until they were wet. He tried to reach for his staff, only for another snaking tendril to drape its way around his wrists and pin them securely above his head. The tiger tugged at them viciously. Then, in that instant, he felt their wet probing sensation between the cheeks of his buttocks. "Try harder!" he yelled. "This was not in the game's manual!"

"I kinda have my own problem here" grunted Arthur, as his sword was plucked from his paws by a particularly nimble tentacle. "I just need t-mmmph!" His voice was silenced as a snaking limb wrapped its way around the tank's muzzle, sealing it shut.

Gritting his teeth together, Mikah writhed as the slippery tentacle started to work its way into him. He clenched, feeling the probing organ flexing around inside him. The jelly tendril moved deeper, slathering its way into him, feeling its way around every inch of his entrance. The tiger started to moan loudly, feeling a crimson flush pass through his cheeks. "Look" he grumbled, "I really don't think that this is what the game's developers had in mind..."

With a single triumphant grunt, Arthur reached out and grabbed hold of his sword. Pulling it along the ground closer to him, he took a firm grasp on it and started to once more hack at the tentacles eagerly. "Looks like I'm coming to your rescue once again" he grinned. A deafening crash echoed as the head of Arthur's great sword tore through the jelly, crushing the tentacle to the ground. It slowly started to uncoil from his waist. The wolf smiled, a sense of relief washing over him.

Not wasting a second, Arthur sprinted over to his lover, blade flashing. With each swing, he sliced through a writhing, wet tentacle. Each one fell to the ground, flopping damply against the ground. The Gelatinous Pyramid, bereft of its appendages, gave a disgruntled burbling sound.

Picking himself up, Mikah gave a sigh of relief. "Thank goodness" he proclaimed. "You saved me from a fate worse than a cheesy porno fantasy story."

Scooping up the final tentacle, Arthur hacked it free. The severed end fell limp, drooping and sliding its way from between the tiger's buttocks. "Not too shabby, eh?" announced the wolf.

Then, with a wet glopping sound, the broken end of the tentacle opened, blossoming wide like a great flower. Arthur blinked. From within the tentacle issued forth a massive torrent of wet green slime, crashing into the wolf with all the cascading force of a fireman's hose. The wolf stumbled back, wiping frantically at his shirt, shoving thick globs of goop from his armour. "Gross" snapped Mikah with a laugh, "you've been slimed!"

The wolf sighed, "I noticed" he grumbled as it became very clear that he would not get through this battle with his dignity intact either.

———

"You know" said the wolf, "we don't actually need to wash the slime off."

The pair sat, naked and wet, in the misty haze of the hot springs. Mikah's arms slid around the wolf's broad, blue shoulders from behind, occasionally splashing pawfuls of hot water across his lover's shoulders.

Arthur was right; the debuff that the pair had received from the Gelatinous Pyramid, a curious status effect simply called 'slippery', had only an hour's timer. But even so, the tiger had insisted that the pair get a thorough wash, for little other reason than to share in one another's intimacy. "Shh" scolded the tiger, playfully, "there's still some slime in your ponytail."

"I'm sure that there isn't" replied Arthur. "You know that there isn't really any slime. It's just a game, it's not real."

Mikah gave a soft sigh. "I know, I know," he replied. He kicked his leg, splashing slightly against the water. The hot baths were resplendent, a new feature built into the rocky cliff-side that hung over the city of Makwanek, a beautiful but mountainous city in the game's northernmost continent. Inhabited primarily by NPCs of the avian species, the city was divided into several levels, each one cut into the very surface of the mountain itself. The hot springs themselves were on the third level from the top, one above the busy marketplace, and neighbouring a games plaza in which players could spend their time enjoying mini-games in an attempt to win a secondary currency that could in turn be spent on additional items. Mikah had no real interest in such things. Instead, he slipped his arms around the wolf's shoulders, hugging him close against his chest. "But you can't blame me for wanting to play along, can you?"

The wolf turned, glancing back at Mikah. He gave the feline a soft kiss on the cheek.

"Are you excited?" asked Mikah. "I mean, it's two days."

The wolf leaned back slightly, a soft splash echoing as his tail lapped against the steaming surface of the water. In the moonlight, the blue lupine seemed luminescent.

Two days, thought Mikah. In two days' time, they would meet. Not online, like they did every day. No, they would meet for real. The excitement buzzed in his chest, exploding into tiny little butterflies that filled his stomach.

He wondered what Arthur would be like in real life. Would be as tall? Would he be as toned, with the same dark eyes that Mikah could lose himself in for hours at a time? Would they make love as vigorously and passionately as their digital avatars did?

"Mikah" said the wolf slowly. "I don't think that you

should get your hopes too high. Remember, reality is very different from fantasy."

The tiger smiled, and shrugged his shoulders. Playfully, Mikah ordered his avatar to execute a 'splash' emote. Small particles of water cascaded across Arthur. Without wasting a beat, Arthur targeted the tiger with a 'tickle' emote, and the pair collapsed into the water.

Gently, the wolf slipped his strong arms around Mikah's waist. The water between them both swayed, rocking lightly with the movement of their naked bodies. The tiger brushed his fingers against the bare, soft fur of his lover's bicep. "I trust you" mouthed the tiger.

With a softness born of tender affection, the blue wolf leaned down and trailed his nips lightly across Mikah's neck. Mikah leaned his head back, letting his brawny companion slide closer against him. A soft moan escaped the wolf's lips as he slipped his muzzle against the tiger's. They kissed, and Mikah's mouth was assailed by the taste of the lupine's tempting lips. He tried to form words, but found that he had been all but robbed of speech, passion overtaking him. He pressed his body eagerly against the wolf, until the lupine's body heaved against the edge of the pool. "Want you" he murmured, his breath laboured with eagerness and antic-ipation.

Mikah felt a shiver of nervousness. Glancing back and forth, he hoped that nobody would see. But, he thought, why even care. He pushed his nervousness from his mind and locked his hands around the pert wolf's heavy arms. Sliding his fingers through the smooth fur, he matted it with long strokes. He kissed him again, harder this time, forcefully, and slid his fingers lower. Down they wove, around the wolf's waist and hips. He squeezed, pulling Arthur's hips against his own, pushing their bodies together.

"Want you too" muttered Arthur, burying his muzzle against the tiger's neck. He kissed, moving his lips down across the nape of the wolf's throat. Beneath his fur, his skin bristled in the heat of their passion.

Arthur drew his fingers across Mikah's chest, lightly trailing the tips of his claws in soft circles. Steadily, his fingers slid further down – down, until Mikah felt his companion's fingertip run along the underside of his shaft. He inhaled, hard. His erection jumped lewdly to the examining fingertip. As Arthur began to brush over the tip, the tiger whimpered in eager anticipation. Arthur removed his finger, examining it. It was wet with the tiger's excitement. The wolf smiled.

Mikah moaned as he leaned his head back, his eyes closed, every sense in his body alight as he felt the wolf's soft lips kissing down across his chest. Down he went, further and further. The wolf inhaled, his nose pushing against the tiger's thick tuft of pubic hair, smelling him. He pushed closer, nuzzling his chin against the tiger's heavy member. Slowly he started to lick at his tip, tongue working his smooth underside.

Moaning quietly, Mikah leaned his head back, exhaling loudly as Arthur sucked on him. He pumped his lips heavily and wetly against his partner's heavy, full cock. The girth seemed to swell, growing wetly against his tongue, excitedly pinning the licking and flailing organ to the bottom of his mouth, leaving Arthur to suck against the tiger's meaty rod as hard as he could. Mikah could barely believe it—barely able to contain the heady thrill of the sensations that filled him and assailed his senses.

The tiger's heart pounded in his chest, hammering a frantic rhythm as he clutched his paws excitedly at his friend's shoulders. He had no idea that Arthur had been quite so eager, so hungry. The wolf's meaty fist encircled the base of the tiger's cock and barely managed to close as Arthur worked the tiger's eager erection with enthusiastic tugs, all the while slathering his tongue against his slick organ. Savouring the overwhelming taste, Arthur tried to wrap his mouth around it again, bobbing his mouth down heavily.

His chest rose and fell with residual enjoyment. Mikah caught his breath, eagerness burning in his chest. With a soft wet pop, the wolf let his lover's shaft slide from his lips. Rising to his full height, the wolf looked over the tiger eagerly, his thick shaft jutting plumply from between his thighs, strong and full and powerful. The tiger moved quickly, cupped his wet organ, gripping its heft with his large paw. Arthur grinned, and turned around, pressing his taut stomach against the edge of the hot tub and spreading his water-slicked thighs.

Wrapping his powerful fingers around the wolf's spread thighs; Mikah slid them further apart, sliding between the lupine's hard thighs. Arthur whined, his fingernails clasping for purchase against the bark as the heat of the tiger's arousal pressed against his soft rump. Mikah moved his thumb and forefinger to squeeze temptingly against the wolf's gentle cheeks. He clutched one, parting it, exposing the wolf's tender entryway. Arthur gave a soft whimpering gasp, the coolness of the night air penetrating him.

The wolf gasped, his shoulders rising and back arching as the tiger slid the tip of his heavy cock between the adventurers' spread cheeks. As Mikah worked his way in, Arthur bit down on his lip, straining at the considerable size. His ears folded back, hanging down on either side of his head, his wet hair swaying as the big feline's girth forced the wolf's entire body to rock against his penetrating thrusts.

"D-Damn Mikah" he moaned. "Didn't know you could hold aggro quite… Uhh… so well…" Whining heavily, Arthur's gasping quickly turned into loud, sharp little yelps of raw pleasure, as the pair writhed hard and passionately under the dappled forest sunlight.

The tiger wasted no effort, his strength claiming his lover's tight, soft ass with every movement, every inch and motion. "I…" he grunted, "always wanted to…" With each thrust, his muscular fingers explored his lover's body, sliding their way across his waist and teasing light tufts of fur against his chest.

Arthur cried out in ecstasy, trickles of perspiration dotting around the soft down around his body. "Harder," he groaned, "harder." And with eagerness to accommodate his lover's pleading begging, the tiger strengthened his heavy thrusts, slamming into the wolf's form with rampant enthusiasm.

Arthur threw back his head, moaning loudly as the cat claimed him, satiating his months-long hunger on the wolf. Mikah's speed hurried frantically as he pounded his heavy cock to its hilt into the wolf's tight, hot body. Each thrust drew a desperate loud gasp from Arthur, his ears flapping as his head rolled to and fro in ecstatic rhythm.

The tiger drew close, straining to hold back his imminent climax, but it was all for naught. His sexual eagerness overtook him, as the feline drove his full considerable length inwards, squeezing every last ounce of pleasure from the tiger's sweltering form. His orgasm hit hard, thick spurts pounding into Arthur's trembling tightness with just as much force as the cat's passionate lovemaking.

The wolf slid down, clutching against the wall for balance, his chest rising and falling in over-exertion. His body slumped down, staggering, his mind feeling, his rump feeling worn and exhausted. Arthur turned his gaze, glancing up at the tiger in ecstatic passion. The two slid their arms around one another, resting there in the warm summer sunlight, entwined in each other's loving embrace.

Catching his breath, Mikah figured that yeah, he was sure that it would work out between the two of them. Even if things weren't as simple as they were in this little fantasy game in real-life, he was sure that it would pan out.

"I…" whispered Mikah, a soft flush colouring his features. "I think I love you."

Arthur looked at him, and did not say anything at all.

———

The young man sat in the cafe, staring out at the train as it pulled into the platform.

Carefully he picked up his cup of coffee, sipped it, and set it back down on the table with a dull clink. The train on the other side of the window from him opened its doors, disgorging its passengers into the platform in an eager flurry.

For a moment, the young man looked up, watching the people as they hurried from the platform. Several of them made their way to the bridge. More walked out, through the door to the station and into the busy streets of London to continue on their bustling commute.

The young man waited, watching each of the people as they did. He wasn't too sure what he was looking for. Perhaps somebody who looked taller than the others. Perhaps with broader shoulders, or perhaps the slightest hint of blue.

In a few moments, the platform was empty.

Glancing down at his cup, the young man picked it up and sipped it. Swallowing the remainder of the coffee, he placed the now-empty mug down beside the other that had preceded it. The two mugs sat next to each other, a pair. The young man wondered if he should go for a third.

With a slight shake to his fingers, the young man reached down and flipped open his mobile phone case. He tapped the screen, pulling up the menu. Two trains had come and gone since he had arrived—arrived on time, his nerves at boiling point, his anxiety screaming in his ears. He had been certain, when the haze of passengers had finally cleared and left the platform empty, that the man he was waiting for would be on the next one. Then, after that, he had ordered another mug of coffee and resolved to wait for the next.

The clock on his mobile phone read four-twelve. He had arrived at two-fifty. He checked for any text messages. There were none.

Slowly, he got up from his table and limply walked to the counter.

The waiter smiled—a short man, barely out of his teenage years. Not much younger than he was, he noticed. "Another cup?" asked the waiter.

Nodding, the young man fished into his pocket to find a handful of crumpled notes. He pulled free a few, and dropped them onto the counter. "I might be here a little while longer" he muttered.

The waiter nodded. Sliding a mug from a stack, he placed it under the nozzle of the cafe's coffee machine and began to pour. "Waiting for someone?" he asked, his voice light and conversational.

The young man glanced down, and shook his head. "No" he said. "Nobody. I mean," he thought, reaching out to pick up a few sachets of sugar, "I thought that I was. But I guess that was just a fantasy."

Slowly, the waiter nodded. "I'm sorry, man" he said. "Tell you what. This cup's on me."

"You sure?"

The waiter nodded. "I understand how you feel."

Shooting another quick glance out of the window and toward the train station, the young man nodded. "I guess" he replied. "Thank you. What's your name?"

"Arthur" said the waiter. "Now finish your coffee, Mikah. My shift finishes in ten minutes."

THE DARKNESS IN THE LIGHT

NIGHTEYES DAYSPRING

Charexin glanced at the wrinkled map and then back up at the town in the valley below. The map called this place Chaucer and had a little tower above the name, signifying a keep or a castle. The town Charexin was looking at had no castle, no keep, and no defenses at all. Instead it was a small sleepy farming village, and from where he was standing on the hills above it, he wasn't even sure it was big enough to have an inn. It likely wasn't going to have a very good one if it did.

"Another dead end," muttered the wolf, rolling the map up and sticking it back into its scroll case. If there had been a wizard's tower here, why wasn't there one anymore? Hopefully someone in this town would be able to tell him what happened.

After shoving the scroll case back into his bag, he picked up his pack and started down the road into the village. He passed fields of wheat and small farmhouses as the lane wound through the valley. Nothing about this area seemed remarkable to the wolf's eyes. The people waved, but no one approached him, and he didn't see any signs of ruins. Most of the farmhouses were small wood frame buildings with thatched roofs on stone block foundations, but a few were actually made of stone.

The village itself was on a small knoll in the middle of the valley. Charexin did find an inn, and his ears perked up when he saw it, tail wagging in excitement. The structure was built against a thirty-foot long section of stone wall, likely the only remaining part of the keep from the map. The building was three stories tall, and the first two were built flush against the wall while the third story was above the battlement. A door out of the third floor connected to the top of the wall. The sign hanging from above the door had the image of a barrel, a mug of beer, and a wand on it. Underneath the device were the words, "The Wizard's Cellar," written in a flowery script.

While promising, Charexin noted the other structures nearby all seemed to have recycled leftover stone from what was likely had once been a keep of some type. The smoke coming out of the inn's chimney and the smell of cooking food at least told the wolf he'd find a good meal, so he entered the building to secure lodgings and to catch some gossip. Someone here likely would tell him the history of this place for a drink.

Most of the first floor of the inn was occupied by the common room with a kitchen in the back. A long bar with barrels behind it sat on one side with some private booths against the walls. A staircase led upstairs, and simple tables and chair filled the rest of the space. The crowd seemed to be made of locals, and everyone inside glanced at him while he entered and walked over to the bar, but none of their gazes lingered. He at least passed for an uninteresting traveler, and Charexin wanted to keep it that way. It made the work he did easier, if people didn't take notice of him.

The bartender, a cheerful looking badger, waved at him as he approached. "Ah, a fresh face in town I see. The name's Pilth, and if you are looking for a good meal and a place to sleep tonight, you've come to the right place."

"You seem to be the only place in town that I've seen," remarked the wolf.

"Indeed, I am, but I have not let the lack of competitors dampen my standards, good sir."

The wolf nodded. The smell coming out of the kitchen was mouthwatering, and his tail was still wagging. "Do you have a room to rent for the night? I'd like a private one if I can get it."

The badger nodded. "We've got plenty of rooms here. Not many people passing through Chaucer these days."

"No?"

"Not at all. We see a few merchants, but the farming isn't as good as it used to be. I can't think when the last time I had all the rooms here rented. Probably when the mayor's son got married three years ago, but I can't recall for sure. Regardless, can I get you something to drink, stranger?"

The wolf nodded. "You got any beer?"

"Oh yeah, I make it myself from an old family recipe. I've got a couple different types. Perhaps a good farmer's ale for you?"

"That would work," said Charexin. "I was hoping having 'cellar' in the name meant you also brewed."

"Oh sure," said the badger, going over to a keg on the back walk, "but that's not why the place is named the Wizard's Cellar."

Charexin smiled. Perhaps this trip wouldn't be a waste after all. "Why is that?"

"The inn is built over the remains of what used to be a wizard's tower. The cellar is part of the original structure. That's what the old stretch of wall comes from." The badger came back with a tankard and misread the wolf's perked ears for concern and not excitement. "Don't worry though, all of that arcane magic that used to be here is gone."

The wolf *aahed* and tried not to look disappointed as he

took the mug. That wasn't going to be useful. "Better for the town I imagine."

"Oh yeah, much better."

Charexin lifted the tankard and took a sip. The beer was excellent and that gave him an idea. "All of that magic is gone, you say? This beer is far better than what I've had in the cities. You sure you aren't using some type of sorcery to make it?"

The badger grinned. "Just knowledge passed down generation to generation. It's my understanding that what the wizard who lived here did was more likely to taint the land than enrich, but some clerics came after him and spent a lot of time blessing the ruins. If it's got magic in it, blame the clerics."

Clerics? That was a new one. From the age of the building, it looked like the wolf was at least a hundred years too late to find anything interesting here, but the fact that whatever mess this wizard created needed clerics to clean it up intrigued him..

He took another sip of the beer. "Well, glad the beer comes out good."

"If you like that, you are going to love the stew I've got going."

The wolf wagged his tail. He'd only had a little jerky earlier for lunch. "Then I would like to order a bowl."

———

The stew was excellent, putting to shame many of the meals he'd had back in the capital. Charexin had eaten a lot of tavern food over the years and the Wizard's Cellar certainly had some of the best he'd seen. If Chaucer wasn't so far away from any place the wolf wanted to be, he'd certainly be passing through town to stop here.

The room the badger gave him was simply furnished, but it smelled clean and had been swept. Yet as he sat on the bed and looked over the map, he couldn't decide what his next move should be. The people who'd sent him were expecting results, but so far, he had nothing to show for his hunt.

He'd already visited all the major ruins near the coastal cities. He was at a loss of what to do next. The next wizard tower on the map was at least a hundred miles south, and he'd even seen it with his own eyes as a pup. It had been ruined for a long time and he doubted he'd find anything of interest there. He could head back home and hope someone at the Scriptorium had found some clues to where the Sunstone was, but he doubted anything was going to come of that.

The wolf dug into his pack and pulled out an old book, flipping it open. He couldn't take his library with him on a trip like this, but he'd brought the most important books. Opening the volume to the marked page in it he reread, likely for the hundredth time, the words that had set him on this hunt.

"Where the sun touches the green fields and bathes them in gold, where the sky is the deepest blue, there is a tower of the finest stone. Upon the altar to the sky, the Sunstone rests, waiting to be called upon."

The prophecy was so simple and clear, and yet so useless. The sun touched all the green fields, and how was the sky to be bluer than it already was? Charexin had first thought it would be located in a magical place, but as he'd traveled, he'd started to wonder if it would be a place with renowned farms. The map had the same inscription written on the back in the old script, but what connection it had to the prophecy he'd not been able to suss out. The wolf hoped when he found the map, on a lucky trip to a bookseller who dealt in rare volumes, it would be a key clue in deciphering the prophecy. So far it had just led him around the kingdom.

The valley Chaucer lay in had a reputation for good farming, and while he did not see the sky as any different, the description might be an allegory for a particularly rich land. For this part of the prophecy, Chaucer was a prime candidate, and now that he'd seen the town, he could understand how it might fit the description. There was the problem of the tower though. If the Sunstone had been in town at one point, whatever had destroyed the tower or caused it to be razed would have long since disturbed its resting place on the altar to the sky.

If the tower had been blown up, it was possible the Sunstone still was here, but an entire town had been built over the ruins. Likely whoever destroyed that tower would have known about the artifact and made a search to recover it, or taken it before destroying the tower. There was also the problem of the clerics purifying the area. If the stone was here and they'd taken it, the clerics had kept their possession of the stone a secret for a long time.

The wolf looked at the map. A few small houses had been drawn next to the tower. Chaucer either predated the razing or had been rebuilt upon the ruins. Or the artist had taken artistic license and drawn the place to be more important than it was. It seemed weird that this small sleepy town could be so integral to the prophecy. He'd barely seen it mentioned in the chronicles at the Scriptorium outside of the tax rolls, and he'd never seen anything about the wizard tower here being destroyed. That was something someone adding to the chronicles would have made a note of.

Unless what happened here was so important, so critical to the prophecy, that it had been omitted from the chronicles to keep things like the Sunstone buried in the past. A strategic misdirection by the sages of yore to throw off anyone who went looking for it.

If there was something for him to find here, he was going to need to ask around. The tavern owner might know a few things he could use, but Charexin would need to see if the town had any archive he could access. It was also possible the cellar of the inn might give him some clues as to what happened here.

The wolf rolled up the map and sighed. He didn't know

what he could find here in Chaucer, but if there was some-thing to help his quest, he was going to find it. He wasn't the only one looking for the Sunstone either, so he needed to hurry.

———

The tavern was quiet in the morning when he descended the stairs into the common room. A stoat was wiping down tables while the badger from last night was tending the fire.

"Already working?" asked Charexin, walking up to Pilth.

The badger stood up after adding another log to the fire. "The life of a tavern owner is never dull. Will you be wanting breakfast?"

"If you have it."

"I've got some cheese and bread. I don't get many overnight guests, so I don't have anything prepared." He scratched at the fur at the back of his neck. "I should have asked you last night if you wanted something."

"It's no trouble. I was hoping to stay for a few days, so perhaps tomorrow then?"

"Of course," nodded Pilth. "I'll make some porridge in the morning. Is there anything else you need today?"

"Just the food," said the wolf, walking over to the bar. He waited while the badger brought his meal and placed the bread and cheese down in front of him. A mug of beer also appeared, and the wolf didn't ask why. He reached for the mug and took a sip. This beer was light and smooth, a different type then he had last night.

"What business did bring you to Chaucer, if I might ask?" the badger inquired.

The wolf set the mug down. "I'm cataloging wizard's towers in the kingdom. I found an old map pointing to one being here that I never heard of before. I see why it's no longer noted down."

"Yes, it's been gone for a while."

"Do you have any idea what happened here? I've never read of there being a big battle out this way."

The badger frowned. "People around here don't talk about that."

Charexin took another sip of his beer and broke off a piece of bread. "It's not remarked in the chronicles I've seen."

The badger nodded.

"Why?"

"Bad stuff happened here, but the clerics came and fixed it all."

"What kind of bad stuff?"

The badger traced a claw along the wood grain in his bar. "The type of stuff that people don't tell their kids about and certainly don't tell strangers about."

He wanted to ask questions, but the badger seemed resistant. He also needed someone in town who would give him a place to stay. He picked up the mug to take another sip. "Dark magic is never something to toy with, but some people can't resist the temptation."

The badger eyed him. "No they can't. What about you? What type of magic tempts you?"

"I'm not tempted by…" the badger was looking at him intensely, "…dark magic."

The badger cleared his throat. "I think you should leave."

"You don't understand," said the wolf.

"I understand enough. Anyone who comes here looking for a wizard tower is not any friend of mine. Chaucer is past that. We aren't going back," growled the badger.

The wolf put down the mug of beer. "I mean you and Chaucer no harm."

"Then you should leave."

"No," said the wolf. "I've been searching too long not to find answers."

"There is nothing for you here. You may finish your meal,

but please leave. I will not rent you a room again for the night." The badger walked off.

Great, this was already going sideways. Charexin looked down at his meal and picked up the bread to eat in silence.

———

By the time he came downstairs with his stuff, two guards carrying swords were in the common room, a male rabbit and a female lynx. They immediately stepped toward the bottom of the stairs to confront the wolf.

"A welcoming party?" asked CharexinHe glanced around to locate the badger; Pilth was talking to a fox who had his back to the wolf. The stoat who'd been cleaning up earlier was also nearby, and he was warily eying the wolf.

The lynx cleared her throat. "By order of the Townmaster, we are here to escort you out of the valley."

"Charming," said the wolf. "Am I not to be trusted to leave on my own?" The fox and Pilth had turned their attention toward him, but Charexin kept his eyes on the guards.

The rabbit spoke up. "I do not know if you understand the seriousness of what you've done, so we're here to make sure you do."

Seriousness? "I only asked questions."

"Dark magic is not welcome here," said the lynx.

The wolf growled. "Dark magic? Questions are dark magic?"

"Don't make this difficult for yourself," said the lynx as she pulled her sword out.

The wolf glanced around, and smirked. This would not do. He put down his pack. "No, I think I'm exactly where I need to be. You will answer my questions." He called out to Pilth. "If the barkeep would be so kind, pour some of your wonderful beer for everyone; I believe we can settle this amicably."

The rabbit frowned and looked back at the others in the room. "It's five against one," he said.

The wolf flicked his hand and the door to the inn bolted shut across the room. "Indeed. You should have brought more people if you wanted to threaten me."

The guards looked pale and the stoat stepped back, butthe fox who'd turned his attention to the wolf only glanced toward the door. He cleared his throat and spoke up. "Pilth, you should have told me we're dealing with a wizard."

"I didn't know…"

"No matter." The fox looked at the wolf carefully with an intensity that surprised Charexin. He was about Charexin's age and was carrying a staff of wood, something the wolf hadn't noticed at first. The sudden realization of recognition hit the wolf then. They both stared at each other, surprised to see the other. It had been ten years since either had spoken, and their words had not been kind for each other then. "Poor two mugs, Pilth, and I will talk to him alone," said the fox finally.

"Sir…" said one of the guards.

The fox made a gesture, and Charexin felt the tickle of arcane energy against his whiskers. The front door unlocked. "I'll be fine, but don't let anyone inside. You should also leave, Pilth, after you get the beer."

The badger squared his shoulders. "The hell I'm leaving my own inn!"

"Suit yourself, but you know the cost." He waved to the guards. "Wait outside please and make sure we aren't disturbed."

They looked at each other, confused. "And if you need help?" one of them asked.

"I'll be fine, but you'll know if I do. Now please wait outside."

"Yes sir!" they said and exited the common room with the stoat following them. The badger watched them nervously.

"The beer, Pilth," said the fox, walking over to a table and sitting down. He gestured to Charexin at the chair in front of him..

"Of course," said the badger, getting the mugs. The wolf sat down and waited for the beer to be delivered, which quickly came. Then Pilth stepped back and waited.

The wolf glanced at the badger. "You want this conversation to be overheard?"

"I trust Pilth," said the fox, pulling a mug over and sniffing at it. "It's you I don't trust."

Charexin put a hand to his chest. "Ibras, I'm offended. We studied together. I know it's been a while, but you should at least let me talk before you throw an accusation like that at me."

The fox narrowed his eyes. "You are here for a reason. It's my duty to protect this town."

The wolf picked up his beer. "I see. How does a graduate of the college end up here in a farming community as Townmaster? Do they know you're adept in the art?"

"Please Charexin, don't try and undermine my authority here for your foolish games. This isn't the college. You spent more time in trouble than anyone else. It's a wonder you graduated at all."

The wolf huffed. "Mm, well if you want to play it like that, we can get down to business. I'm looking for something."

The fox nodded. "It's not here. There's nothing here."

"Ibras, please don't try and play me for a fool. You're here, and that tells me there is something here. It may not be what I'm looking for, but I doubt you would spend your time here if there wasn't something worth protecting or investigating. You were not known for your charity back in school."

"People change, Charexin. Some of us learn from our mistakes."

"Ha, very funny," said the wolf. "Still bitter I see. Well I can't say you shouldn't be. People do change, but if you've changed, then perhaps I have also." He fished into his pack and pulled out the map tube.

The fox narrowed his eyes but didn't say anything as the wolf unrolled the map and spread it across the table.

"Tell me what you see first."

"It's a map of the kingdom."

"Indeed, but look harder. You too, Pilth. Tell me when you figure it out."

The badger walked over and looked at the map. "I don't see a lot of maps, so I'm not sure what I'm looking at."

The fox was glancing over the map curiously. "Someone charted where all the wizard's towers were."

"And?"

The vertical slit eyes narrowed as he traced a finger across the paper. "How old is this?"

"This copy? I made it myself, but the original is over three hundred years old."

The fox's finger stopped at the capital of the kingdom. He looked at it and then to where Chaucer was on the map. "The college isn't marked on the map."

"No, it's not, but the college is older than the map."

"It's a possible unintentional omission."

"I thought that too. I'm not so sure."

"What is this language?" asked Pilth, pointing to the side of the map.

The wolf replied. "It's an archaic form of common. It used to be written with glyphs before we switched to the runic alphabet."

"If so, what makes you think it's only three hundred years old?" said the badger.

Charexin pointed to a village outside of the capital. A bridge was drawn crossing the river. "That bridge was built three hundred years ago when the king's highway was built. You'll notice the king's highway is also present."

Ibras looked at the lettering on top of the map and translated it to himself. "Towers of the Mages of Thesau?"

"Actually, I had to look that glyph up. It says 'Hideouts of the Mages of Thesau.' I bought this from the bookseller who supplies the Scriptorium. It looked vaguely interesting, something I could put up on the wall, but I didn't think much of it until I studied it carefully. I think it is the key to something greater. Let me show you what's on the back."

Ibras pulled back and the wolf flipped the map over. There were more glyphs on the back and Ibras read them himself.

"That's the prophecy of the Sunstone."

"Yes it is. It's here, isn't it?" said Charexin. "That's why you are here, to guard it."

The fox pinched the bridge of his muzzle. "First, there is no Sunstone here. I'm here because my family is from here. I returned home to take my father's place after he passed."

"It's got to be here. I've searched across the kingdom and there are very few places I have not seen."

"If I might intrude, what is the Sunstone?" asked the badger.

Ibras glanced toward the barkeep. "A lost artifact that is said to allow the user to channel the power of sunlight itself. It's been missing for hundreds of years. It is said to be quite powerful. Who knows what happened to it. It may never have even existed for all we know."

"Chaucer is a perfect match for the prophecy," insisted Charexin.

The fox laughed. "Chaucer has no mages tower for the stone to rest in. That's been gone for a long time, and what happened here was very different. Even if it had been here, it's long gone. Have you really been spending your time searching for the Sunstone?"

The wolf huffed. "Why? Going to lecture me again about my duties and neglecting my studies?"

"I just wanted what was best for you."

"Did you? It felt sometimes like you wanted me to do what was best for you."

The fox sighed. "You haven't changed at all, have you?"

"I have." Charexin smiled, showing fangs. "I'm not the person I used to be."

"I would hope not. He was insufferable."

"So were you."

They lapsed into silence and the badger spoke up. "You two have a long history."

"Very long," said the fox.

"He used to cry out passionately in the night as I ravished him," said the wolf, "but then he left me in the gutter to rot."

The fox blinked and stared at Charexin. "You are a craven asshole."

"No, just bitter, but I directed my energy toward other things." He cleared his throat. "So, where is the Sunstone?"

"It's not here."

The wolf leaned over the table. "Prove it."

"Prove it? How the hell am I going to prove something isn't here? On what authority do you think I even have to?"

The wolf smoothed down his hackles. He hadn't realized they'd gone up, but the fox had always gotten a rise out of him in one way or another. "If you give me a moment, I can show you." He reached down into his pack, and pulled out a spell-book, setting it down on the table. He flipped it open and pulled out a letter tucked in the front cover, handing it to Ibras. "Here."

Confused, the fox took the letter and looked at the broken seal before he unfolded it. "The High Council sent you?"

"Tasked me is more the way to think about it. There isn't an exact destination to go to."

"'The *who* asked him to come here?" inquired Pilth.

"The High Council of the Mage's College tasked me to find the Sunstone and either recover it or destroy it. There are rumors other people are looking for it, and they don't want that falling into the wrong paws."

"They asked you?" The fox flipped the letter over to examine it. "You? Please tell me this is a fake."

"You miss a lot when you aren't in the capital, but it made sense not to ask a high-level mage to do it. They would draw too much attention."

The pull of magic was sudden and forceful as Ibras probed his mind. If he'd been prepared for it, Charexin could have resisted the spell, but he was taken completely off guard by the divination. Instead he slumped into the chair, falling out of it, when the spell suddenly released.

"The fuck! Is that the only way you can trust me?" sputtered the wolf on the ground.

The fox said nothing and regarded the wolf thoughtfully.

"What… what did you do to him?" asked the badger.

The fox's ears flicked in thought. "I read his mind."

"YOU READ HIS MIND?"

The fox looked up. "I needed to know if we could trust him."

The badger's face twisted and he made a warding symbol as the fox got up and picked up his staff. He started to pace around the room while the wolf sputtered.

"You dick," said the wolf, finally getting to his feet. "You have no right to go into my mind like that."

"You always were bad at divination. It doesn't surprise me you don't think about protecting yourself from it."

The wolf balled up his fists, snarling.

"I wouldn't waste your energy on that," said Ibras.

"After all these years, you still can't trust me to do what is right," spat Charexin. "Well, do you believe me now that you've been inside my head?"

The fox stopped pacing and turned to face the wolf. "Yes, but if the stone was here, I should have been able to sense it."

"And where did you learn magic like that?" asked Charexin.

"You aren't the only one who has been searching for secrets." The fox sighed and turned to Pilth. "We should show our friend here the basement. I believe he'll understand the situation much better then."

The badger nodded and walked behind the bar. "Let me get the key."

———

Pilth carried a lantern as he led them down a set of wooden stairs into the cellar. The room was dressed in carefully cut stone and was stocked with various barrels of beer aging along with casks of wine and liquor.

"This is quite the operation," said the wolf as he looked over the barrels.

"Thanks," said Pilth. "I really enjoyed the work, and I have an innate knack for it I guess."

"I swear you use some type of magic to make this," remarked Ibras.

The badger just shrugged.

Charexin cleared his throat. "So why are we down here?"

Ibras strode across the room next to a rack of wine barrels. "Come this way, and you'll see." Carefully the fox squeezed behind the rack, disappearing with his staff.

"Do you want to go before me?" the wolf asked the badger.

"I do not wish to go down there again. This is something I cannot assist with."

The wolf frowned and walked over to the rack of wine barrels. Behind them was a narrow gap about a foot wide that led into darkness. Carefully he pressed himself through the space, shuffling against the stone until suddenly he felt the wall end.

"Spooky, isn't it?" said the fox, his eyes shining from the little light escaping around the barrels.

"I can't see crap in here."

"Oh sorry." Ibras tapped his staff against the ground and a small ball of light formed at the top of the staff, illuminating the chamber behind the barrels. Against the back wall an iron grate covered a small opening, a lock hanging off of it. "I'm surprised you don't carry a staff. They're very useful thing."

"I've learned to work without one, but," the wolf snapped the fingers of his right hand and in his left hand a wooden staff appeared. "I've created a little pocket dimension to keep mine in so I can keep a low profile when traveling."

"Impressive," said Ibras, "not everyone can master that."

"Thank you."

"How long do you want me to wait for you," called Pilth.

"We'll be a while, so you might as well wait upstairs. If you feed the guards, I'll pay you back for that."

"Fair enough," called the badger. His footsteps retreated across the stone floor of the cellar and then the creak of the steps was heard.

Charexin walked over to the iron grate and peered through it. "This was part of the tower?"

"It appears so," said the fox, walking over and unlocking the gate with a key. He swung it open and the wolf started to enter the passageway down, but the fox stopped him. "Before you go, I want to say I'm sorry."

"You're sorry?"

"For everything."

The wolf's ears flattened. "Everything?"

"The spell, but also what happened back at the college. That spell lets you detect the feelings of someone, but it's dangerous to use on someone you love. Having a strong connection to an individual makes it more powerful. You learn things from it you shouldn't know."

The wolf frowned. "What types of things?"

"Well, for starters, I know you're not lying about why you're here, and I know seeing me brings back a lot of old memories, not all of them good. You regret what happened between us."

The wolf was silent for a moment. "You got all of that from a spell?"

"The last part is based on the connection we have. Had I not known you, it would not have been so thorough."

"This is what I hate about magic like that. It messes with people in ways it shouldn't. In ways I won't."

"Oh, it's dark magic, I admit, but just a little goes a long way when you run a small town and need to know if people are lying to you. That's really all it's good for, but if you know someone well, if you know them really well, it tells you a lot more."

"Please tell me you aren't charming people around here to keep the peace."

The fox shook his head. "Absolutely not. Mostly it's all paperwork and settling silly disputes, but this, this is why I'm here. I'll show you why the townsfolk don't talk about the wizard's tower with outsiders. It's why I went to the college in the first place."

If Ibras was guarding what lay below, it likely was of great importance. It must be the type of thing that had to be protected. "I see. Lead on then," said the wolf, both suddenly curious and worried.

The stairs descended straight down in a passage carved into the stone below the basement. The fox walked in front, using his staff to light the way, and the wolf followed, pondering what Ibras had said. The air in the shaft was still and damp. The only marks on the walls were where the pick-axes used to dig the tunnel had scarred the stone.

After descending a few hundred feet, they came to the bottom of the stairs. Stepping through a doorway, they entered a large room, carved out of the stone. Two rows of pillars supported the roof of the chamber where at the far end sat an altar.

Charexin paused to scent the air. It was dusty and stale, but there was a tang about it too. There was magic here, and he could feel it tingling at the edge of his whiskers.

"This is what I have to protect," said the fox. He waved his hand and a set of charcoal braziers hanging from the pillars in the room lit up.

"What is this place?"

Ibras pointed to the altar. "Go, you'll see."

The wolf stepped into the room, his claws clicking against the stone floor as he walked. His tail bristled as he felt the power in the room. Slowly he strode towards the altar, looking around. There were no runes on the pillars, no symbols or iconography of any kind. Only an altar that stood at the far side of the room with a slab atop it. The stone was large enough for a person to lie down on and a channel had been cut at the bottom to collect any liquid that dripped off it.

"They sacrificed people here?" said the wolf turning.

"Indeed," said the fox pulling a small dagger from his cloak. "Many people died down here to feed the land of the valley. It's why it's so rich."

The wolf's eyes narrowed as he looked at the dagger. He clenched his staff as the fox walked across the room toward him.

"Oh, you needn't fear," said the fox.

"You won't find me so easy to prey on when I'm prepared."

The fox chuckled. "You say that, but I'm not sure. I think we'd both enjoy a fight like that, but it's not you this dagger is for. Step to the side and I'll show you."

The wolf stepped back and the fox walked up to the altar. Ibras reached up with the small dagger and made a tiny cut in the pad of his paw, letting a drop of blood drip onto the slab. Immediately the stone glowed with a red light.

"Long before the wizard came and built his tower here, druids used to worship in this chamber. They believed by following the cycle of life and death they could bring prosperity to this valley. I can find no records of what rituals they performed in this shrine, but the farms in this valley were rich and prosperous. A town was built here. At some point, a powerful wizard came and built a tower with the entrance to this shrine secreted away. They say he performed many dark rituals here and the shrine became corrupted."

"It's not remarked about in the chronicles I've seen."

"No, it's not. It's barely spoken about here, but the clerics —who came when the wizard summoned something he couldn't control—likely recorded that. I don't know which order came, but I doubt they'd show me their records if I knew. They ripped down the tower and purified the shrine as best they could, then sealed it away. For a while no one came here, but the land was still rich. The remaining farms here were prosperous, and a new town sprung up on top of the ruins, keeping the same name as the old."

"And the shrine?"

The fox pulled his hand back and the light faded. "It slumbers. The druids are long gone, and I wish not to see darkness embrace this place again. I do not know if the fact it responds to blood is the doing of the druids or the wizard. Slowly though the magic is fading."

"You think it needs to be fed?"

"Possibly, but I refuse to perpetuate that darkness. It is likely that when the magic finally fades Chaucer will fade with it. The land here has always been surprisingly productive for how poor the soil is."

The wolf frowned. "And the Sunstone?"

The fox turned toward the wolf. "It's possible it was here. It's possible it was used to capture the light of the sun and feed this shrine here in the darkness. There are no inscriptions that

I've ever found. There are no records that have survived here."

"I'm told the ancient druids were not big on recording things in paper. They used oral traditions."

"Indeed. Few stories about this shrine have survived. I looked hard for information. I never found anything beyond the scattered fragments of lore my family collected over the years. Even people like Pilth, whose family lived here when the tower still stood, do not know what happened here." Ibras sighed. "I've tried to decipher the enchantments, so I could understand what they do, but nothing I've done brings me closer to understanding the purpose of the shrine or how the enchantments work."

"I'm going to assume finding a druid is out of the question?"

"I've tried that, but the magic is just different. It's not from a tradition they could identify or knew of. To them, it's like you or I trying to read a spell book in a different language."

The wolf pondered and started to walk around the sacrificial altar. "They cut channels in the block to collect blood. Does it react to the blood of a feral creature?"

"I did not try it myself, but the druids I consulted with experimented with the blood of a chicken. The stone did not react to that. It appears only to react only to the blood of a sapient creature."

"You said dark magic was practiced here by the wizard."

"Necromancy, summoning fiends, the types of things that will get you thrown out of the college. The details are sketchy."

"Hmmm. Life and death. It responds to death." The wolf paused. "Have you tried life?"

"Life?"

"Yes, life."

"I don't follow," said the fox. "Just sitting on the altar?"

The wolf chuckled. "No no. The act of creating life."

Ibras blinked at him confused. "Have you tried fucking on top of the altar?"

The fox frowned. "I mean no, but…" he thought for a moment. "It might work?"

The wolf chuckled. "The ancient druids did not just worship death but the cycle of life itself. It's possible a spilling of seed might provide the recharge you need."

"That seems overly simplistic though. I recall quite clearly the warnings our teachers told us about mixing magic and sex."

"Oh, you can screw that up royally, but I recall someone was quite adept with a little telekinesis during foreplay."

"Twisting a nipple during sex is one thing. Casting complex arcane rituals is absolutely out of the question, at least if you're doing it right."

The wolf barked, amused. "Of course, but who said you needed to cast anything. You just need to renew the contract of life for the land. It should be a straightforward thing."

The fox considered and ran his hand over the surface of the stone. "The lack of any phallic imagery makes me wonder if that's the right path to go down, but it might work."

"Well, glad I could be of help." The wolf turned. "Shall we go back upstairs?"

"Not yet. We should test your hypothesis."

Charexin froze. "Test it? Ibras, we're not compatible. Not like I thought we were."

"Perhaps not, but I know deep down, you still care."

The wolf swallowed hard. "Indeed, but—"

"And who better to test such a hypothesis than two highly trained magic users who would be able to respond to any unintended consequences of that action"

The wolf blinked. "I'm not having ritualistic sex with you in a dungeon." He just shook his head. "It's not who we are anymore."

"Who we were never involved doing something like this

now, but I need someone I can try that with. Someone I trust."

"And you trust me?"

"I have had a while to think about my actions and realize I should have. I have always been too rash when it comes to matters of the heart."

In the back of his mind, he knew Ibras was right, if only to make sure nothing foul came out of the act, but it had been years since he'd seen Ibras. Years since they'd split up, years spent regretting what had happened.

The wolf softened. "You know make up sex has never been my speed."

"Who said anything about us making up?" The fox smiled. "It would just be an experiment, nothing more."

"Ah, but are you ready for it just to be an experiment? As you said, divination works much better when you know the target well."

Ibras walked up to Charexin, getting close so he could look him in the eyes. He was slightly shorter than the wolf, and a little skinnier, but that did not take away from the power he possessed. He'd always been a better student than the wolf. Spells and techniques that took time for Charexin to learn the fox had mastered easily. The threads of magic woven upon the fox were strong, and this close, he could feel the arcane energy.

"I have my own regrets. I used to think we'd be together, learning and growing, but magic tends to be a lonely endeavor. In the end, our different interests drove us apart."

The wolf shrugged. "You had a promising future working in the court. I was always more a hands-on type."

The fox looked away. "Yes, well little good my aspirations did me there. Being a courtier is far more work than I wish to spend my time on. The needs of nobility rarely prove to be interesting. I kind of washed out, and opted to return home when father became ill. There's at least something worthy of dealing with here. Where did you go, Charexin? No one mentioned you being around."

The wolf shrugged. "Oh, I did some traveling. I worked in the Scriptorium for a while as a cataloger. Not very exciting work, but it let me pursue my research. It's part of why they sent me to find the Sunstone."

"Do you really think it still exists? It's not been seen in a long time."

"Someone does. With stories that old, it's hard to say if they're really true or not."

"Hmm. Yeah. Obviously, the records we do have are also incomplete. We shouldn't be surprised. Even with the best of intentions, a lot of dreams never come to fruition either."

The wolf reached up to tickle at the underside of the fox's muzzle. "You're doing good work here. I know it's not the grand work you dreamed about, but I can tell you're doing the best you can."

The big ears splayed. "That's sweet of you." He leaned forward and licked Charexin's muzzle. "It makes me regret all the mean things I ever said about you."

"Still cocky I see."

The fox grinned and slowly pulled the wolf against himself. "Just shut up and let's do this."

"Hey now! I did not agree to do this yet."

A paw stroked against his trousers. "You say that, but you've already got a chub going."

The wolf shivered. "I never said I didn't like having sex with you. I just didn't like your smug attitude and the intrigue you got yourself tangled up into."

"That was a different fox, one who hadn't yet became bitter about the workings of the court. Someone who thought he could control the chaos around himself."

Charexin chuckled and traced a finger along the fox's muzzle. "You know that's a fallacy though. One of the first lessons they teach us is no matter how good a mage you are, there will always be forces beyond your control. Did you forget that?'"

The fox grinned, running his paws around the wolf's hips. "I thought I might be the exception, but later I learned some things I just couldn't steer no matter how hard I tried."

"Mm… and now?"

The fox licked his lips. "I need you to get naked and crawl up onto that altar."

"And if I do?"

He leaned forward and nuzzled the wolf so he could whisper into his ear. "We'll see if I can still keep my concentration to do a little telekinesis during sex."

The wolf shivered. He'd not slept with someone else who could do what Ibras could do in bed, even if they were a magic user.

The fox lowered his hands so he could grasp the wolf's rump and pulled him against himself. "I know you like that."

"I do," whispered the wolf already excited, "but should we first prepare ourselves in some way? This is a ritual."

The fox considered for a moment. "I have an incantation I could try, but that's all I've got. I wish I knew more about what rituals were practiced here."

It was risky. Nothing might happen or something bad could occur. They'd each had their own magical mishaps during their studies. Experimentation and practice were key parts of learning magic, but there was no way of knowing what would happen here. There was also the curiosity of learning something new that excited the wolf. It's what had drove him to study magic in the first place.

"Well we might as well see what happens," he said, breaking from the grip of the fox so he could undress.

They both took their clothes off and left them in front of the altar. They leaned their staves against one of the pillars. The wolf fished into the pocket of his clothes and pulled out a small vial of a viscous liquid which he handed to the fox. "I keep this to use as a spell component, but it also doubles as a lube."

The fox turned it over in his paws. "Ah, a grease spell. Sneaky, but effective for making an escape. After you then."

Charexin climbed up onto the block of stone and got on his hands and knees. The altar was cold to his paws and unforgiving. "I assume this time I'm the bottom?" asked the wolf.

The fox hauled himself up. "Yes," he said getting behind the wolf, kneeling on the stone. "I will say this is not a comfortable position."

The wolf didn't think being on the bottom was that great either, but he positioned himself, tail up, waiting for the fox to make the move. The air around them was completely still, the light coming from the braziers that threw long shadows across them.

"Ready?" Ibras asked.

"Yes."

"Then we begin." He cleared his throat and then intoned. "Oh great powers of old, we offer this sacrifice of seed, the white blood of life. From life shall come death, but from death shall come life."

The air in the room was silent and they both held their breath.

"Well, it was worth a shot," whispered the fox as he poured the lube onto himself and slicked himself up. He used the rest of the vial to slick up the wolf's tailhole, slowly working it into him with one finger, then two fingers. Charexin shivered as Ibras did this, methodically pressing in the digits, careful not to scratch the wolf with his blunted claws. A sudden flick of one his nipples by a hand that wasn't there told him Ibras had not lost his touch.

Soon enough, the digits were pulled out and the wolf felt something else being pressed against his rear. It had been a while since he'd had sex, years since he'd slept with the fox, but there was an old familiarity to it. The way Ibras lined himself up and slowly pushed in, it was different than the one-night stands Charexin had: it was gentle and not in a rush to get going.

The fox started slowly, pushing himself in and letting the wolf get comfortable before he pulled back. A paw gripped at his tail base as the fox slowly thrust into him before finally grabbing his hips. A third, invisible hand slowly stroked across his shaft.

Against the feeling of pleasure, it took Charexin a moment before he realized the stone he was on had begun to awaken. Gold light flicked out from the base of the altar, lighting the room.

"It's responding to us," grunted Charexin, as the fox thrust himself in again.

"I see," panted the fox and he started to work up a rhythm. Each thrust came just a little bit faster and the wolf whined under him. Slowly the pace grew, the moans getting louder, and the light in the room brighter. Ibras's magic faltered and the gentle invisible fingers teasing his shaft faded out. The fox was too preoccupied.

The stone thrummed under them, responding to the rhythm of Ibras's thrusts. Charexin could feel the pressure building as the fox kept repeatedly pushing into him. He moaned, ears laid back as Ibras took him with increasingly urgency. The altar had become warm against him and it was not from his body heat. Energy coursed through it now, and he could feel it growing in power with the fox's thrusts.

The wolf pressed himself back, arching his spine in pleasure as the fox slammed against him harder. The fox's knot started to swell and Ibras wanted to make sure he tied with the wolf. Magic far different than the type they wielded was at work here, and even in his bliss, the fox knew he needed to complete the ritual as best he could. He whined in need, feeling the tension in his shaft build, the climax slowly coming to him.

Finally, it was too much, and the fox popped the knot into the wolf, forcing the tie and emptying himself into Charexin. Ibras then leaned over and bit at the wolfs shoulder as he filled him. The wolf felt the invisible digits close upon his shaft again and stroke him. That was too much for the wolf then, and he lost control, finally climaxing, hot seed coating the stone below.

The wolf's legs gave out on him and they collapsed, still tied, panting against the stone, feeling the raw energy it contained as it crackled against their fur. In that moment, Charexin felt suddenly connected to the world. He was the dirt and the grass. He was the leaves in the trees. The crops growing in the fields swayed with the wind, and he could feel that wind against his branches. He and Ibras were one and together they were a part of the valley. The streams that crossed it ran through them like the blood in their bodies. Chaucer was the heart of the valley and in that instant the stones and the dirt were their flesh.

The valley was beautiful and they were beautiful. The wolf could feel Ibras as an extension of himself. It wasn't just the other mage's arcane power he felt but his heart his mind. They were linked in that moment like they had never been before and everything they had seen together, everything they had shared, it was there before them: their fights, their tender moments, the things they did to show they loved each other, and all the ways they had disappointed the other. The road they could have taken together unfurled in front of them like a banner being raised. They were a single entity unsure why it had ever quarreled with itself like this.

And as suddenly as the vision had started, it was gone, and the stone was still again, hard against the wolf with the fox on top of him. The light that filled the room only moments ago was gone, and they both gasped suddenly remember they still had to breath. For a moment or an eternity their bodies had become part of the stone, frozen in the act of copulation.

The fox shifted first, trying halfheartedly to tug his knot free. It only made the wolf more aware of the sticky puddle of his own seed he'd fallen into.

"Did you… did you feel that?" whispered Charexin.

"The vision?"

"Yeah. We were part of the valley there for a moment."

The fox took a deep breath. "I was the grain ripening in the field, the stones in the earth. I could feel the wind across my leaves as I stood as the trees."

All they could do was rest, dazed by the power they'd unleashed. They laid there joined until Ibras's knot softened enough and he pulled out. The fox rolled over to lie on his back on top of the stone altar.

"Do you think that worked?" asked the fox.

"If that didn't do it, I don't know what would."

"Yeah." The fox yawned tiredly, tongue rolling out of his muzzle. "That still doesn't help with you finding the Sunstone."

The wolf propped himself up. "Are you sure we aren't lying on top of it now?"

The fox didn't say anything, just feeling the warmth the stone still was giving out. Finally, he spoke. "*Upon the altar to the sky the Sunstone rests,*" He quoted. "That would make this room the altar to the sky, but I always thought that would be at the top of a tower."

"Me too, but what if this was an altar to the night sky?"

The fox got up and craned his neck looking toward the ceiling, He frowned and climbed down from the altar, walking over to pick up his staff. He then pointed it up at the ceiling, summoning light, but the ceiling showed no markings, no symbols carved upon it.

Naked, tail lashing in anticipation, he stalked between the columns until he came to the vestibule, and it was there a single symbol had been marked, above the door.

Charexin had also climbed down and he followed Ibras.

He was messy and spent, trying not to drip onto the floor. The scents of their love making filled his nose, but he had to see what the fox was looking at. "That does seem understated at best," he remarked, looking at the crescent moon glyph.

"It does." The fox frowned, ears laying back. "I would expect stars or some kind."

"There don't seem to be any."

After pondering for a minute, the fox reached up, craning his arm up and touched the moon with his paw. Suddenly the room lit up as thousands of little lights flashed in the ceiling of the room. A night sky shown above them.

"This really is it!" said the wolf turning around. "But it's nothing like we thought it was. They always said the Sunstone was a weapon, something that could be wielded in battle."

"You realize you can't tell them you found it. If the college comes here looking for this, they'll rip it out of the shrine, and who knows what they will do with it."

The wolf looked at the fox and gave him a wiry smile. "This must go unrecorded. We aren't the first to realize what is here could not be recorded for future scholars to find. My failure will be the same as those who searched before me."

The fox took his hand. "Don't be so hard on yourself. You pieced together a mystery that I couldn't solve on my own."

The wolf leaned down and kissed the hand gently. "No Ibras, we did it, together. Neither of us could have done this alone."

"You're right," he said squeezing gently, "but what will you do now?"

"I don't know. I have to go back to the college and report I didn't find anything. They'll likely send me back to the Scriptorium to catalog rare books."

"You could stay here," suggested Ibras.

The wolf flicked his ears and turned to look back at the altar.

"Not for that," said the fox hurriedly. "I miss you, and I'm sorry when I said you would never amount to much as a mage. I should have realized I was being foolish."

Charexin was quiet, his tail still as he looked over the fox carefully. "I like what I do at the Scriptorium, but it's not glamorous work," he said finally. "It at least lets me use my talents well."

"I'm afraid I don't have a vast library here, but I could use some help. There's still a lot I don't understand about this place."

The wolf smiled. "I would be happy to stay and help you conduct more research, but not because of the Sunstone."

"No? Why then."

The wolf leaned down and whispered into the fox's ear. "Because I've missed you too."

CONTAINMENT

NATHAN RAVENWOOD

"Just how much farther is this going to spread?"

Arno blinked, unsure if his superior was asking him a rhetorical question. "Sir?" he asked.

Captain Emeritus, a proud wolf, shook his head. He reached into the pouch at his belt and pulled out a thick syringe. "Arno, if you would."

Arno took the keys he'd gotten from the attending jailer and made to unlock the door. As soon as he put one of his webbed paws on the bars of the prison cell, the fox inside lunged at him with a snarl. Arno pulled his paw away at the last second, and the fox crashed into the bars. His thin arms pushed through the gaps, blunt claws trying in vain to grab hold of a bit of Arno's clothing. Emeritus moved like quicksilver, grabbing one of the fox's arms and pulling tight. "Arno, hold him!"

The otter did as he was bidden, holding the fox while Emeritus slipped the needle of the syringe into the fox's arm to draw blood. The fox whined in pain as he did. Arno felt something poke him in the leg and did his best to ignore it while Emeritus did his work. After a few seconds, the wolf had extracted enough blood. "Let him loose," he commanded.

Both of them let go, but the fox didn't retreat away from them. He remained near the bars, leaning his weight on them. He was young, a magistrate's son, at the age when he should have been out courting a vixen at a ball, dressed in finery. Instead, he was here underground, naked in a cell with wide, lustful eyes and a pendulous erection that never seemed to go away. Said erection poked through the bars of the cell, pulsing in time with the fox's heartbeat. "Come closer," the fox purred. "It isn't unpleasant, I promise."

Emeritus curled his lip. "Be silent."

A whine slipped from the fox's muzzle, and he sank to his knees, still pressed up against the bars that held him back. "Please," he whimpered. "Please. I need relief."

Arno's gaze lingered on the red length of the fox's erection for a moment before he forced himself to turn around. The otter folded his arms over his chest, scratching at his dark brown fur. All of a sudden, his paladin robes felt as heavy as a suit of plate armor. "If this tod is infected, it might have already made it to the upper quarter," he muttered.

"My fears exactly," Emeritus said. The wolf looked back at the cell. The fox had slunk back into the corner. "Come."

The two paladins walked the long hallway out of the underground prison, passing several other cells on their way out. The cells held males of varying species and ages. The fox that had accosted them was the youngest one, but there was also a stallion, a wolf, and a stag with silvery fur on his muzzle. All of them watched the paladins pass with eager eyes, their breathing heavy, all of them very obviously aroused—especially the stallion.

As Arno and Emeritus approached the door it swung open to admit two more paladins, both of them heavyset bears. They were dragging a struggling weasel between them. The weasel caught sight of Arno and strained to get away from his captors, his eyes boring into the otter's. "You!" he cried.

"You're the one who can satiate me!" For his species, the weasel was rather hung.

One of the bear paladins cuffed him. "Move," he rumbled, and he and his partner dragged the flailing mustelid down the hall towards the empty cell.

"Another one?" Arno muttered.

"The madness is spreading," Emeritus said, taking three claws and tapping his forehead, muzzle, and chest in sequence. "That's the fourth one this week. Soon we won't have enough cells, and we can't allow the indecency that takes place if we put more than one in a room."

Arno followed the Captain up the stone stairs to the main floor of the paladin barracks. The men and women there were going about their duties, as expected, but there was a definite edge to the mood of the room. Everyone's eyes were watchful, their attitudes mindful. Arno knew what the worry was. There was no telling what the true form of this madness was. Some thought it spiritual, a plague of the spirit that had spread through those who harbored hidden desires. Others thought it an infection, a malady like the Blue Plague from three years prior that would need to be treated with modern science. Whatever the case, everyone knew it was only a matter of time until a paladin became infected. With all the afflicted lying just beneath their feet, who knew how long it would be until the spirits or the vapors seeped through the floor?

Emeritus's office was on the second floor, a spartan room with a desk, bookshelves, and bay windows overlooking the island city-state of Hidrae. The wolf closed the door behind them. "I've contacted your old friend again to help us with this matter."

Arno clasped his paws behind his back, standing at rest in order to ground himself in his commanding officer's presence. It was hard to keep his thick tail from twitching, the appendage wanting to externalize the squirming he felt on the inside. He'd had a feeling this was coming. "With all due respect sir, did you *have* to?"

"Understand that I didn't do it lightly." Emeritus sat down at his desk, folding his paws on the smooth surface. "I trust alchemists about as far as I can throw them. But if we do not nip this now, we could be facing a far worse situation in the coming weeks."

"Can't we use another alchemist?" Arno asked. "There must be others in the city that we can contract to figure out what's going on."

"Perhaps, but Dian was able to figure out what the Blue Plague was and how to cure it within a few days, where we had others working on it for weeks and making no progress." Emeritus's face grew grim. "If we had gone to him straight away, we might have saved thousands of lives."

"But this is hardly the Blue Plague." Arno remembered the Plague in vivid detail, the smell of the dead and the unsettling color of blue it turned an afflicted tongue. "Nobody has died from this… frenzy."

"That we know of," Emeritus said. "We made the mistake of waiting last time, and I'd rather not make it again. If this madness spreads, the whole city could become a pit of orgiastic indecency." The wolf's ears went back. "Imagine if this made it to the city council and they started rutting each other during meetings. Or if it spread to the streets and everywhere you go you could not escape the sight and smell of perversion. Even if nobody loses their life due to this, it could still spell disaster for the city."

Arno clenched his paws together, sblunt claws scratching at his webbing. He knew what Emeritus was saying was true, but he really, *really* didn't want to have to go talk to Dian again. That first conversation three years ago had been painful and awkward, and the extent of his involvement with the alchemist during the Blue Plague had been to just introduce Dian to Emeritus. Then he'd stayed well away from the proceedings until a cure had been found. Dian had attempted to talk to him in the aftermath, but Arno had dutifully ignored him.

After a time, Dian stopped trying.

Arno sighed. "If that's what you think is best, sir."

Emeritus nodded. He opened up a drawer in his desk and withdrew several glass vials, the corks on the end sealed in place with heavy globs of wax. Inside the vials were blood samples, all of them labelled as to who they'd been drawn from. Emeritus unscrewed the barrel from the needle he'd used to draw blood from the fox, holding it mouth side up to keep the sample from spilling as he corked it. "It was blood that let him come up with a cure for the Blue Plague," Emeritus said, "So I'm hoping it's blood that will provide a solution to this madness."

The wolf placed the vials in a pouch and tied it shut, then slid it across his desk to Arno. "Where can I find Dian?" Arno asked. *Since you seem to be his best friend now.*

"As far as I know Dian still has that townhouse in the port quarter," Emeritus said. "Go. And may the Grace of the Eight go with you."

The otter took the bag of blood vials, holding them in his palm for a moment. For a moment, he thought about smashing them on the floor. Better that than having to face Dian again. But the paladins could just draw more blood and send someone else. If anyone were to deal with the alchemist, it should be him.

After all, they'd been friends once. Arno didn't dwell on his rural upbringing much, preferring to leave the past behind him. A lot of that past involved Dian in some capacity, the things they'd done with youthful innocence as their excuse. Things he could no longer do as a paladin of the Eight.

Arno left the paladin barracks, pausing only to strap his longsword to his belt and grab his red hooded mantle. The harsh crimson marked him as one of the Church's servants and allowed him passage anywhere in the city. The otter drew the hood up over his ears, tucking the bag of blood vials into a pouch on his belt.

It was late in the day, the sun beginning to sink towards the distant horizon, turning the cloudy skies a dusty orange. Arno's paws tread on warm cobbles as he made his way down from the Central District. Around him swirled a city preparing for evening—vendors packed away their jewelry and locked their shops, well-dressed socialites were already padding to their favorite social spots, and lamp crews were coming around with oil and torches to light the lanterns placed at regular intervals through the streets. The flow of people was in the opposite direction from him, going in towards the city center rather than outward. Arno wondered how many of them knew what was going on. The paladins had, by order of the Church of Eight, kept details about the disease to a minimum, so as not to incite a panic. But every man stuck in the cells below the barracks had a wife, a sister, a mother, *someone* who would ask about them if they were gone for too long.

Perhaps that was why Emeritus had contacted Dian. The alchemist had cured the Blue Plague in days. Whatever this was, he could probably deal with it in just as short a time.

As Arno made his way, the cleanliness of the city's center gave way. The streets in the poorer districts were rougher, the lanterns more sparse, and Arno lifted his tail up off the ground as he walked, lest it drag over a broken piece of glass or Eight knew what had been spilled on the ground that day. Instead of salons, the people gathered in taverns to drink themselves silly. Arno frowned on such libations, but he knew the common folk had to do something to fill the dearth of purpose. He tugged his hood up over his face more, hoping that presenting a purposeful visage would keep him from being accosted by a citizen he didn't have time for.

The smell of the port hit his nose long before it was in view. It was a rank, pungent odor, that of fish and brine and whale guts from the massive carcasses cut open and dissected for the valuable oil in their blubber. Another smell lingered under it, an earthy tone that only those trained to discern it could pick out. It was alchemical sulfur mixed with the tang of silvere, resulting from those who used the agents in conjunction with magic. It was the easiest way to know when an alchemist was about, though the scent was so peculiar that even those with sensitive noses often had to have it pushed directly under their muzzle to be able to identify it.

As he rounded a corner, Arno was treated to a lovely view of a whale on its side, hollowed out by the whalers with its vital bits neatly divided into piles on the dock. He almost walked past, until he realized that Dian was standing there among the dock crews, haggling with the foreman about something. The linsang alchemist was dressed in a black jerkin that accented the dark markings in his fur well, along with pants the color of ash. He had a calm expression on his face while making scale-weighing motions with his paws at the bare chested, one-eyed dock foreman. The foreman shook his head, and Dian shifted his paws closer together. With that adjustment, the foreman nodded. Dian handed him a sack of coins, and the foreman reached down into a crate behind him. He pulled out three large whale vertebrae, cut from the spine with a heavy duty saw. All three went into a burlap sack. Dian took the sack of bones and turned to leave, but stopped short when he locked eyes with Arno.

For a moment, they weren't in a smelly harbor surrounded by fish innards but at the edges of a small farming village half a continent away. Dian was standing on a path leading towards an uncertain future, looking back over his shoulder with those piercing silver eyes. Arno had stared back, the village behind him, feeling nothing when he should have felt anguish.

Then the moment passed, and Arno steeled his heart. He walked over to Dian, his steps careful to avoid the pools of blood and other refuse on the harbor walkways. "Dian," he said in greeting.

"Arno!" Dian pushed his way past a couple dockhands until he was close enough to Arno he didn't have to shout. He looked Arno up and down. "Got the mantle, I see?"

"I need to talk to you," Arno said, ignoring the question. "The Church needs your services again."

Dian looked around the docks. "Let's talk at my house," he said.

Arno followed the linsang through the port quarter, thanking the Eight when the linsang turned up an alley and led them away from the rancid stench of the harbor. They made several turns that Arno committed to memory for when he had to leave. A left took them past a tailor's with the door open, the proprietor shaping cheap fabric around a dress form that had seen better days. Down the street they took a right around a flower shop, the smell of which lingered in Arno's nose as they walked further down the street. Around the last bend, Arno nearly kicked a vase on accident. It was one of many displayed on a rug in front of a pottery shop. Arno's ears swiveled to hear two voices arguing in a language he didn't speak.

Dian stopped in front of a rather nondescript door that he unlocked and opened, beckoning Arno inside.Dian's foyer was similarly plain. A table stood by the entrance with some hydrangeas in a vase. Off to the left was a sitting room, and at the back was a staircase to the upper floors. The linsang ushered Arno into the sitting room, which held several heavy bookcases piled with tomes written in languages Arno had never even seen before. Dian snapped his fingers, and Arno smelled brimstone for a split second, then the logs in the hearth burst into flame. He blinked. The last time he'd seen Dian the linsang had still needed flint and tinder to start his fires.

As if reading his mind, Dian snapped his fingers and

conjured a small flame, holding it in the palm of his palm. "I've been practicing," he said, snuffing it out as quick as he'd created it. "I'll never be on the level of those born with the Gift, but it's still a nice practical skill to have."

"I didn't come here to tarry on parlor tricks," Arno said quickly.

Dian arched an eyebrow. "Then what did you come here for?"

Arno reached into his belt pouch and withdrew the bag of blood vials. He held it up, holding it in a way that made the glass tubes inside clink together. "We need your help again. There's something new happening, something-"

Dian sucked in a breath and scurried close to Arno. He snatched the bag from Arno's paw, ignoring the otter's protests as he yanked out the blood vials. His eyes went wide, the same way they always had when he found something new and interesting. "Oh, *yes*," he breathed. "Yes yes *yes*."

"What do you mean 'yes'?" Arno asked. "Did you already know about this?"

"You think there's something strange happening in the city and the underbelly of it here wouldn't know?" Dian tapped the wax-sealed end of the blood vial against his forehead. "You paladin types can hide the truth from the haves, but the have-nots will always sniff it out. Come."

Dian padded to the back of the room, paw reaching for a book on the bookshelf at the back. He pulled it, and a clunk came from within the wall. A section of the bookcase swung open, revealing stairs behind it. "Lab's this way," Dian said.

Arno gaped at the hidden staircase. "How did you even—"

"Lots of money and late-night work. Now come on." The linsang practically skipped down the steps, his long tail swishing behind him, forcing Arno to follow close behind.

The staircase was short, two flights that put them underneath the sitting room. Dian snapped his fingers to summon a flame again, then held it to a trough of oil affixed to the wall. The flame quickly spread around the perimeter of the room, bathing its contents in warm orange light. In the space were several tables piled high with instruments whose functions Arno could only guess at, glass apparatuses of all shapes and sizes filled with liquids in a rainbow of hues. There were several more bookshelves in the underground room, the texts on them looking even more esoteric than the ones on display above.

"I've been looking for a blood sample for *days*," Dian said. He grabbed a knife handle off one of the tables, pressing a button on the side that made a spring-loaded blade pop out. It only took him a few quick strokes to peel off the wax around the end of one of the vials. "But all the afflicted keep disappearing." The linsang looked back at him, silver eyes narrowed. "I don't suppose you know where they keep winding up?"

"They're in paladin custody," Arno said. "In case it's contagious and they could possibly spread it."

"So, you've seen them!" Dian moved over to a table near the wall. On it was an alchemical circle carved into a slab of granite, a solid piece of rock that looked like it should have collapsed the desk it was resting on. Next to it was a battered notebook, and it was the notebook that Dian grabbed and flipped through to a certain page. "Let me confirm some symptoms. The afflicted are all male, yes?"

"I thought you would have known everything there is to know by now," Arno said.

"It's not like the Plague where I could've stood on my old apartment balcony, thrown a rock, and hit someone afflicted." Dian grabbed an ink pen off the table, thumbing the little lever on the side for the ink reservoir. A bit of ink spurted from the tip, splatting into Arno's cheek fur and making him flinch. "Oh, dammit, sorry."

Arno reached up and wiped the ink off with his paw. Dian had always gotten fidgety when he was eager. "It's nothing."

"Now, symptoms. Describe them."

"It's a peculiar kind of madness. The afflicted all seem to be overtaken with a lustful state that not even..." He searched for a word that wouldn't make him feel disgusting. "Not even release can satiate. They remain in a permanent state of arousal no matter what."

Dian scribbled some notes in his book. "And they can't seem to control themselves?"

"No. We first tried putting them all in one cell underneath the barracks. Came back to find the floor *covered* in..." Arno bit his tongue, whiskers twitching. "There were a lot of fluids everywhere when we came back. Two were mid-coitus."

"Fascinating." Dian tossed the book and the pen onto the desk, then picked up one of the blood samples. "And you're not sure about the origins of this? Did you not do an investigation into what happened with the first person who caught it?"

"We thought it was an isolated incident. Just another degenerate who'd had too much to drink. It was only when he continued to stay in an aroused state that we began to suspect something else, but by then we already had another."

Arno hadn't missed how Dian's lip had curled a little at his use of the word 'degenerate,' but the linsang didn't press the matter. "Interesting..." Dian said as he took the blood sample to his work bench.

"What do you make of it?" Arno asked.

"To me it seems like symptoms resemble almost what occurs naturally in females when they go into heat." Dian uncorked the blood vessel and tipped the contents into a glass funnel, then lit the burner underneath with a snap of his fingers. "The raging, almost uncontrollable urge to mate, the constant state of arousal."

"But what might cause such a state?" Arno asked.

"Well, that's what we're here to find out." Dian ducked

down underneath the table and rummaged around, coming back up with an armful of bottles. Liquids of varying color and viscosity sloshed around in them, and Dian laid them out in a particular order. He made to uncork the first one, and had a bit of difficulty, so he wound up using the spring-loaded knife to pry the cork off.

Arno eyed the dark gray blade of the knife. In his head he could see a large, brawny ursine blacksmith hammering away at an anvil forging a knife just like it. The sight of that blacksmith had awoken…things in him. "You kept that all this time?"

"Are you kidding?" Dian stuck the knife point into the table, the whole implement remaining upright as he poured the contents of the first bottle into his unfathomable mixing instruments. "Knives from Weald forges last a lifetime and require a pass of a whetstone once a year. Why would I ever get rid of it?"

The fur on Arno's neck prickled, and he reached back to rub at it. A bit of the ink from Dian's pen, still tacky, smeared into the fur there. "I just always figured…"

"What? That because you turned your back on me and helped drive me out of the Weald I wouldn't take anything useful with me?"

Arno made a gagging noise. Dian wasn't looking at him, the linsang absorbed in his work. Whatever it was he was doing. The blood was boiling in the first tube, two other liquids heating up in others. "That's not how it happened," Arno protested. "We had to do it."

"Ah yes, that old argument. Because you all thought that I'd been marked by the forest spirit and the only way to keep it from coming back was to exile me." Dian kept working as he spoke, his paws steady as he measured liquids and mixed them in ways only he could comprehend. The blood had boiled into a vapor, a crimson cloud floating trapped in its glassy prison.

"It stopped coming around after you were gone," Arno said. "Therefore, it had to have something to do with you."

Dian made a clicking noise with his teeth. His tail lashed like a whip, but the crack was in his response. "It's whatever. I'm not bitter about it."

"Your tone says otherwise."

"Does it?" Dian swished a yellow mixture around in a bottle. Apparently satisfied, he hooked it up to the apparatus, the stopper of the bottle connected to the glass vial with the gaseous blood in it. He pressed down on a lever a tiny bit, and Arno watched as some of the gas filtered down into the yellow mixture. Dian yanked the bottle free, capped it, and shook it once. That simple motion turned the color of the liquid inside a deep black, so dark it seemed no light could escape from it. "Fascinating…" Dian murmured, holding the bottle up to the light so he could see how light played off the substance.

"What?" Arno said, stepping closer.

"The concentrated blood seems to have a reaction with the asteroid dust and gryphon venom." Dian pursed his lips, then set the bottle down on the table and took another blood sample. He trimmed the wax off with his knife and let a few drops drip out onto a small glass slide. Holding it gingerly between two claws, he took it over to his microscope and slid it into place. A quick twist of the knob on the side brought the lens closer to his eyes, and Dian bent over a little to peer down. The motion made his shirt flow with the contour of his back, and Arno blinked as he saw little hills and valleys crest and dip against the fabric. Despite his cozy lifestyle, Dian had managed to keep his wiry country-boy physique.

Arno shook his head, jamming his hand into his pocket and finding the Eight totem there. His fingers wrapped around the sharp edges, and he squeezed hard enough to draw blood. The pain grounded him, kept his mind focused and his thoughts pure. "What do you see?" he asked, keeping his voice level.

"I see evidence of a pathogen, but like none I've ever seen before," Dian said. He reached up to a nearby bookcase and took out a tome, his eyes never leaving the microscope lenses. He flipped through it, and Arno caught glimpses of drawings of viruses and diseases as he did. "It's like nothing I've ever seen before, but there's something about it." His tail flicked. "I wonder…"

Before Arno could question him, the linsang had darted back to his worktable and pulled another jar out from underneath. This one contained a silvery powder that glittered in the light that Dian took a pinch of between his claws. He added it to the pitch-black, oily concoction, then laughed as it turned the same color as the dust. "Brilliant," he whispered.

"Would you *please* explain what's going on?"

"It's a pathogen," Dian said, "but a brilliant one. Bears marks of magical construction, alchemical modification on top of an existing biological thing."

"Somebody *made* it?"

"And did a damn good job of it too." Dian took out even more alchemy ingredients and began combining them by the paw- and spoonful in a clean phial. "Seems like my original hypothesis about it inducing a heat-like state is right. It should be a simple matter to isolate it from the sample and create something to negate it using what we normally use to suppress heat cycles, combined with some other agents to render it more effective."

The linsang's paws became a blur as he mixed, measured, and poured until the phial was almost full. He gave it a shake, then held the rim up to the bottle fill of vaporous blood. Another push of the lever added a bit of the gas to the bottle. The linsang's face was focused, his silver eyes narrowed. Arno found his gaze lingering on that face, tracing the stripes there with his eyes. Had they always been so vibrant and striking?

Dammit, stop it. Arno squeezed his totem again, sending a new spike of pain up his arm. What was the matter with him?

Ever since he'd come back into Dian's presence he'd felt off. Was it the residual vapors of the port getting to him? Some gas loose in the workshop that the linsang was just used to?

"There we go." Dian swirled the concoction in the bottle a few times, then placed it over a lit burner. "Once that boils and sits for a bit we should have a viable antidote for you."

Arno scratched his forehead. "That's good."

Dian's eyes widened. "Are you okay?"

"Huh?" Arno looked at the tender webbing between his fingers, seeing the cuts there from him squeezing the totem in his pocket. "Oh. Don't worry."

"Like hell I won't, that's an open wound in a place where there very well shouldn't be any." Dian opened a few drawers until he located a roll of bandages. "Come here."

"I'm fine," Arno protested, jamming his paw in his pocket. The motion earned him another slice on the sharp edges of the totem.

"No, you're not, come *here*." Dian made to yank Arno's paw out of his pocket. Arno pulled his arm down, keeping his bloody fingers away from the linsang's paw. "Arno!" Dian snapped. He grabbed Arno's forearm with both hands and pulled with a surprising amount of strength.

"Keep your paws off me!" Arno snapped back in return, pulling his arm away forcefully. The touch alone brought back memories, less forceful touches that precluded other touches that were far from innocent. Things he was supposed to be long past.

"I swear to the Eight I'll—ack!" Dian was cut off by Arno trying to shake him off forcefully. The linsang hung on, and the motion of Arno's arm with the weight of the linsang tugging on it made the both of them lose their balance for a moment. They stumbled backwards into the table, their hips thudding into the heavy oak and Arno's thick tail slapping against the table leg. Dian caught them with a paw on the edge of the table, but the jostle from them bumping it and the sudden weight against the table made it shift, and Dian barely had time to curse before the phial in which the cure was boiling skittered off the edge of the table and shattered on the floor.

Both of them were engulfed in a plume of stinging gray smoke that burst from the shattered vessel, as if someone had tossed a smoke bomb into the lab. Arno coughed heavily a few times, holding the back of his bleeding paw to his muzzle. Dian picked himself off the floor, the linsang's striped body obscured by the smoke. "You absolute pillock," the linsang said, coughing a few times. "Why didn't you just let me bandage you up?"

"I don't *need* it," Arno insisted. He took a deep breath and coughed again. The smoke stung his nostrils, like the spices that came from overseas that Emeritus enjoyed on his food.

Dian reached down and picked up the shattered remains of the phial. "Well, we're in deep shit now."

"What do you mean?" Arno took another breath, managing not to cough with this one. "Can't you just make more?"

"I have the means to, yes, but that's not the problem here." The linsang waved a paw back and forth in front of him, the gray smoke swirling in eddies around his blunt claws. "That mixture needed to boil for a while for the pathogen to become inert. Since you acted like a petulant child and made it fall of the table, it didn't reach cure state."

"Meaning?"

Dian made a circular motion with his finger. "Meaning we're sucking in the pathogen more and more with every breath we take."

Arno felt the pit of his stomach drop out. "No. No no no no!" He spun around, thick tail whirling behind him with the force of the motion. He couldn't see a blasted thing in the gas! He stuck out his arms, took a few steps forward, then promptly ran hip first into another table. Something skittered off the other side and fell to the floor with a crash.

"Arno, calm down!" Dian's paw touched his shoulder. Arno whirled around and was taken aback by the fear that flashed across Dian's face. Was it already too late? Had the madness overtaken him and he didn't know it? "The more panicked you get the more you'll breathe, and the quicker the pathogen will worm its way into your body. There's no getting around it. Just stay calm, and let me handle this, would you? I'll make a smaller batch of the cure just for the two of us, it'll be ready quicker. Just stay calm, and stay out of my way. And bandage your paw, for the sake of the Eight."

Dian turned and stomped over to his workbench, fishing out a small glass jar and mixing up another batch of the cure. Arno stood still, the smoke beginning to clear out around him, trying to control his breathing. His entire body was hypervigilant, his heart hammering as he feared every twitch and motion. Before he even realized he'd pulled it out his totem was in his paw, his fingers sliding against the sharp edges.

"If nothing else, there may be a silver lining to this," Dian said. He raised the jar and swirled around the contents before adding pinches of dust from his supplies. "This may be a chance to document the mental effects this thing has."

"I know damn well what it does," Arno snapped. "And if I didn't know better I'd say you're perfectly fine with this happening."

Dian stopped mixing, his head turning back towards Arno with a sharp motion. His tail lashed back and forth again. "What's *that* supposed to mean?"

"You and me, locked in a room, both of us becoming indecent the further this progresses." Arno held up his paw, squeezing his webbing around the totem. "I won't let it happen."

"You think I *like* being exposed to diseases that do the Eight know what to my mind and body?" Dian set down the mixing jar with a thud and stomped over to Arno. "And quit it with that damn totem of yours!" He swatted the otter's paw. The motion caught Arno off-guard and he dropped the hunk of wrought iron on the ground.

Arno hissed and grabbed Dian bodily, leveraging his superior strength to back the linsang up against the wall. "Stop. Touching. Me."

"Why?" Dian spat. "You think you'll catch something other than this from me?"

"Shut up!"

The linsang's eyes were hard and merciless. "Why are you so scared of who you are, Arno? You smother it underneath piety, underneath self-mutilation. And for what? So you can feel superior to everyone else?"

"You could *never* understand," Arno spat. "Letting go of you was the hardest thing I ever had to do. But I had to do it. I had to become what I am now!"

"But *why?*" Dian's voice cracked on the second word, his haughty anger vaporizing like smoke. "What about the life you live now is better than it could otherwise be?"

The press of the linsang's body set Arno's tingling, and he realized with a jolt that their hips were flush and something hard was poking him in the inner thigh. Both paladin and alchemist came to the same realization and tore their gazes from one another.

"Just let me work," Dian said.

"Okay."

"You need to let me go first."

Arno did, scurrying away from the linsang as he turned back to his work. The otter retreated to the other side of the room, planting his back to the wall. He pressed back with all his strength, as if he could force himself through the hard stone and into the earth beyond. He tried to get his fingers around his totem, then realized it was lying on the ground somewhere near Dian's feet.

He could have walked back over to get it, but that would require getting close to the linsang again, and he was beginning to lose trust in his own body. The colors in the room were becoming sharper, enough that he could see a few motes of dust flitting through the lamplight like fireflies. Smells were becoming more potent, from the earthy scent of the wooden bookshelves and workbenches to the odors of the chemicals that Dian was working with. To say nothing of the otter himself—even yards away Arno could smell the linsang's musk as heady as if his nose were pressed into that spotted crotch.

He swatted himself on the cheek, trying to drive the impure thought out with brute force. But how could he? All of a sudden he was harder than he'd ever been in his life, his maleness straining against the fabric of his pants. Heat coursed through his body, and the shred of his mind that was still capable of rational thought could almost feel it pushing him towards Dian. Fires of desire that he thought he'd smothered long ago flared to life, like dropping pitch-soaked kindling on a coal.

For a moment he wasn't in the basement laboratory anymore, but on a sunny field far, far away. Dian was there too, reclining nude on the soft grass. He stretched his body out, toes shuddering with content. Both Arno and the linsang were sweaty and sticky, but the breeze kept them cool as it caressed their naked bodies. In the distance, the thud of an axe splitting logs could be heard. *That was the last time before...* Arno thought.

Before Dian had been marked by the spirit living in the woods. Before the monster hunters had figured it out. Before they'd needed to send him away.

Neither of them had known how their lives would change over the weeks after that day in the field. All they had known then was youthful desire and eager passion, not a care in the world for the integrity of their souls. Yet even now, seeing the memories in his mind's eye, Arno couldn't help but wonder what had possessed the Eight Gods to make Dian so beautiful, so tempting. His fur was soft, his body lithe and sensual.

Temptation had seeped from every pore then, and it did so now. His entire being was consumed by the desire to take Dian, to rut him until his need was sated. The more he resisted, the stronger the urge became. *No wonder those men in the cells went mad,* he thought.

"Dammit!" Dian cried suddenly. Arno jerked his head out of the cloud of memories towards the linsang to see Dian's paw scrabbling at the fastenings on his pants. "I can't..." He exhaled, a sigh mixed with a deep whine, as he fished his cock out of his pants. Arno salivated at the sight of the long pink length. The linsang moaned as he stroked himself. "I need both paws for this..." he panted. "But... dammit..."

Arno found that he'd crossed half the distance between them before he realized what was going on. He stopped himself short, and for a moment debated yanking out his sword and cutting himself across his chest. Perhaps that would be enough pain for him to think straight.

"Arno." Dian looked at him, his expression pleading. "I need you to use your muzzle on me. If you do that I can focus and finish making an antidote for this."

"No," Arno said, forcing the words out from a throat that desperately wanted to say "yes" instead. "Never."

"Dammit, Arno!" Dian cried. "Swallow your pride for five minutes and suck my cock so I can cure us! Otherwise we'll both go mad from this and who knows what will happen then!"

Arno moved as if he'd been fired from a bow. He almost tripped and fell in his haste to get under the table where Dian was working. *Nobody has to know,* he thought, as the smell of Dian's musk grew stronger in his nose. *Nobody has to know.*

The first touch of his muzzle to the linsang's erection was hesitant, but that touch was enough to bring back the knowledge of what he needed to do. Arno parted his muzzle and wrapped his lips around the warm length bobbing before him, sliding all the way down in one go. He heard a jerk and a clatter above him as Dian moaned. The smell in his nostrils grew sharper. His vision was filled with black spots and golden fur. The taste on his tongue was the same as it had been all those years ago, but the heady pleasure of having a cock in his muzzle was so much *greater now.*

As he worked, Arno decided in for a copper, in for an ingot. He reached down and undid the snaps on his pants, freeing his own maleness from its confines. He had free paws, after all. The first self-touch was enough to send a small band of precum jetting from the tip of his cock, the white spattering on Dian's stripes. The linsang didn't notice, or else pretended not to. Arno could still hear him working, the splash of liquids and the shuffle of powders. He tuned it all out, focusing only on the sensation of Dian's cock in his muzzle. He hadn't done this in a long time, but he remembered what he had to do: tongue up and curled to touch the sweet spots on the under-side, lips tight, mind your teeth.

"Arno, I'm almost done," Dian moaned. "Keep going, please."

He didn't specify whether he meant the antidote was almost done or whether he was close to coming, but Arno didn't care anymore. He'd forgotten how wonderful this felt, the heady warmth that overtook the body when you didn't care about decorum anymore and rendered yourself base. He took his time with Dian, keeping his ministrations gentle as he worked himself in turn.

"Done!" Something clicked into place on the table above them, and Dian leaned his full weight on the edge. "Well, it's boiling I mean. So long as it doesn't get knocked over again, it'll be ready in an hour." He exhaled, a long, breathy noise. "Gods I forgot how good your muzzle feels."

Arno whined as he shoved his face against the linsang's

inner thigh. "I can't take another hour of this, Dian," he murmured. "I need…"

The linsang's paw reached and found his shoulder. "Come here," Dian panted. "I won't tell a soul, I swear."

Arno let himself be pulled out from under the table. Dian grabbed a jar of something off the table and pulled Arno far away from it, towards the wall where the otter had retreated to earlier. "Can't risk it getting bumped," the linsang panted, grinding his body into Arno's. "Don't even want to think about what a double-dose of this might do."

It took a moment for Arno to realize that Dian was already naked from the waist down, his pants lying forgotten on the floor somewhere else in the room. Before he could stop himself, his paws were on the linsang's hips, digging the heels of his palms into Dian's pelvis. Dian made a mewling noise, jamming his muzzle into the crook of Arno's neck and inhaling. "Get naked. Get naked with me."

Forgive me, Arno thought, then surrendered himself to the madness. He tore at Dian's jerkin, making several buttons pop off in his haste to get the confounding garment off. The linsang's chest was as lithe as ever, though a little more filled out with a decade more of growth after leaving the Weald. Arno jammed his face against Dian's pectorals, inhaling his scent and nosing along his collarbone.

At the same time, he could feel Dian stroking him, the linsang making appreciative noises. Then his own clothes were coming loose, and Arno welcomed it. Before long he and Dian stood naked next to each other, grinding their hips together and panting into the space between their muzzles. "Just like we used to?" Arno asked.

"Yes." Dian kissed him, and Arno felt the world shift underneath him. He crushed the linsang's body to his own, turning and parting his muzzle to let their tongues meet. Warm stone touched his back, and he slowly sank down until his rump touched the floor, not breaking the kiss with Dian the whole way down.

The linsang retrieved his jar, and slathered something cool along the hot length of Arno's cock. He put a little more under his tail, then mounted Arno's lap, his wiry tail brushing the otter's ankles. "Just a little…there we go."

Arno howled in delight as tight, slick warmth enveloped his cock. Dian was right there with him, mewling into his shoulder as he settled down on Arno. The linsang's erection slid along Arno's stomach, a hot wand rubbing against the fur. Once more, Arno realized that things had not been buried as far as he thought, as his hips bucked automatically, the motion the same as it had been all those years before.

"Yes!" Dian cried. He hooked his arms around Arno's neck and hung on tight, his eyes boring into the otter's. "Take me…"

Arno shifted his hips once, then grabbed the linsang and took control. He bucked up into that tight warmth, that beautiful body, and the heat burning in his mind became all the more intense. Dian cried out, his body squirming in Arno's grasp, but the otter held on tight as he thrust up again and again. A part of him had been hoping that this would alleviate his need, allow him to think clearly. It only made it worse, but he no longer cared. All that mattered was the beauty in his arms, the scent in his nose, the warmth around his cock. He shifted again, allowing himself to get even deeper in the linsang's heat. Dian's teeth clamped on his shoulder, his breath hissing out into Arno's fur as he hung on for dear life.

Neither of them knew how much time they spent writhing together. Neither cared. There was only the heat, only the need crackling between them like a bonfire. Dian pulled away from Arno to look him in the eyes. There were tears beading in the linsang's eyes, but he said nothing. Arno pulled him into a kiss as his hips tensed, his release so achingly close. How had he forgotten how good this felt? The last moments before release, when the whole body is alive with energy, every fiber of your being beseeching you to go a little further, just a little, so that all the tension could snap free like a coiled spring— he'd forgotten all of it.

Which meant that when he did finally come, his hips slamming up into the linsang's body, his release was like none before in his life. Arno became almost abstract, everything fading into a blur as his cock pulsed within the linsang's tight tailhole. Dian himself was already a quivering mess, his own cum splattered all over the otter's belly. All Arno could do was take hold and ride the wave, still inhaling the sweet scent that came off the linsang's fur like a cloud. They remained as they were for a while, shuddering against one another, neither saying a word.

The sight of Dian slumped against him, his body quivering in bliss, made the last of Dian's mental blocks vanish. Things he hadn't thought of in years all of a sudden came back to him. He remembered the day the monster hunters had come seeking the forest spirit, how he and Dian had watched them venture into the woods. Later that day, they had returned, and done some strange ritual in the town center that had led them right to Dian.

Two days later, Dian had been sent away. The linsang had begged Arno to intervene, or even to come with him. But all that Arno had ever known was in the Weald, and there was little but hardship that awaited him if he went with Dian.

His only option was throwing himself into faith, to bury everything he'd once felt under piety and self-control. It was the only way to escape the throat-constricting despair.

He knew he wasn't the only one. Most paladins came from backgrounds where they had left things they would rather forget. That unspoken commonality between them bonded them together, telling them 'we serve the people for the common good.' It was easier to be Arno the paladin rather than being Arno, the coward who hadn't stuck up for the one person he was closest to.

Arno blinked as something shattered. "Eight dammit," Dian muttered. The linsang wasn't in his lap anymore, instead standing across the room, and Arno realized that he'd actually dozed off for a time. The heat in his mind was still there, though it wasn't nearly as intense as it had been.

Dian bent over to pick up the broken jar he'd dropped, catching Arno's eye as he did. "Welcome back," he said. He pointed to Arno's side. Sitting on the floor a couple feet from the otter's hip was a small cup full of thick blue liquid. "That's the antidote. Drink the whole thing, don't miss a drop."

Arno grabbed the cup and tipped it to his muzzle. The liquid tasted like peanuts and blueberries and had a thick consistency that made him gag, but he forced himself to suck it down. It settled in his stomach like lead. Arno folded his arms across his chest and pulled his knees up.

"It took a minute for it to work for me, so don't panic if the feeling doesn't go away just yet." Dian leaned on the table, writing with a pen. He was still naked, his cock limp between his legs like his drooping tail. "Couldn't do anything about the taste. Sorry."

"It's alright." Arno leaned back against the wall, settling into a cross-legged meditation position. True to Dian's word, the concoction radiated a chill through his body that snuffed out the remnants of the heated pathogen that had scorched his veins. "I've drunk worse. What are you doing?"

"Documenting what we experienced," Dian said. He paused and made broad strokes with his wrist, drawing a diagram of some kind on the page he was working on. "These are for my personal notes, mind you." He held up another sheet of paper between his fingers, folded down the middle. "This is the formula for you paladins. I already set another antidote batch cooking. Seems like orgasm gives you temporary clarity."

"Fascinating," Arno muttered. He suddenly felt very vulnerable, sitting naked on Dian's floor. He cast about for his clothes, finding them in a heap nearby. He dressed quickly, not wanting to look at the linsang.

"I'll do some digging, see if I can figure out whose pawprints are all over this." Dian set down his pen. "Maybe convince them not to make any more of it."

"Sounds good."

"Are you going to say anything other than monosyllabic grunts?" Dian asked, his voice irritated. "Don't pretend like what just happened didn't happen."

"Or what?" Arno's tone was just as snappy.

Dian deflated, his ears going flat and his tail dropping. "I… don't know."

"You promised you'd keep my secret."

"Because I thought that maybe I could turn this to my advantage!" Dian balled his fist, arm shaking with controlled anger. "I thought that maybe if you could let yourself *feel* something again, rather than suppressing every natural impulse at the behest of your superiors, then you might be willing to see me again!" He slammed a paw against the table. "Three years, Arno! Three years I had to keep myself in check knowing that you were just up the road. But you wanted to be a paladin. You wanted to serve the church. And I let you."

"You didn't 'let me' do anything." Arno moved close to the linsang. "This is what I wanted to do."

"Do you have *any* idea how much it hurts to hear you say that?" Arno had to lean close to hear Dian speak. "I love you, you fool. I always have. But I held myself in check because I didn't want to control you. But all this time, you *wanted* to not feel anything for me?"

Arno stood still for several moments. The silence stretched between them, as vast as the years they'd spent apart. "I had to, to better serve."

Dian made a noise, then sagged like a balloon released of its air. He reached over and grabbed the bottle of bubbling blue antidote and corked it, then handed it and the paper with the formula written on it to Arno. "Then I have nothing more to say to you."

Arno took the bottle and the notes and left. He reached the stairs expecting to hear the linsang call after him, to continue their back and forth argument. But nothing followed him up the stairs, nor did anything come on his way through the foyer and out the front door.

Dawn was breaking in the distance. The whole ordeal in the basement had taken the entire night, yet Arno didn't feel tired at all. He stood on the street for a few moments, breathing in the cloying harbor district air.

He'd gotten what he'd come for, a cure for the affliction. But somehow, he felt like he had found something he hadn't realized he had lost, and just as quickly it was gone once more. Arno reflected on it as he hiked back up the road to the upper quarter of the city, as the lantern crews emerged to snuff the lamps in preparation for the day to come.

STOLEN LOOT

IAN MADISON KELLER

Elrad started, staring out at the horizon with a sinking feeling in his stomach. Up on the Crow's nest the lookout rang the alarm bell, but the pirate ship on the horizon was already visible to him on the deck. This was bad. His ears were flat on his head and his tail lashed behind him with agitation.

Captain Shells strolled up behind him and clapped him on the shoulder. "Quite the voyage you picked to join us on, eh?" Her tail curled high behind her and her ears perked forward. Her long braid of slate-gray hair flapped behind her in the breeze.

Elrad had braided the long locks of his mane in his front to keep them out of his eyes, but the rest of his hair was gathered at the nape of his neck with a black ribbon that matched his horns. The lion straightened his coat, making sure it was buttoned tight against the stiff breeze.

The captain seemed awfully calm, considering the black flag on the horizon that was rapidly getting closer. "They're catching up to us!" he growled. "What do we do?"

"Well, depends on what symbol I can make out on that flag as it nears. Some of the pirates will just take our cargo and let us go."

Elrad flicked an ear, a snarl pulling at his muzzle. He lifted a hand as the ship crested a large wave, drawing on his magic to part the spray of ocean water. Water splashed onto the deck on either side of him and the captain, leaving the two of them dry. "Not going to happen on my watch."

"We may not have a choice, sir." The captain glanced at him and her muzzle drew back to display her bared fangs in the first display of real emotion she'd shown since the sound of the alarm. The captain's blue-gray fur stood up and she shook her head. "It shouldn't come to that. Our air mages will keep the wind in our sails, and we should outrun the blighters in short order.

Even as she said this the ship's two air mages conjured up a gale and the sails, which had previously been hanging half limp, filled to bursting. The ship's bow raised and they began skipping across the water.

The captain grinned and flipped her braid over her shoulder as she went back up to join the helmsman at the wheel. Elrad stayed, eyes fixed on the pirate ship and hands wrapped around the railing, his claws digging into it. The ship rapidly receded behind them until it was hidden behind the crest of a wave, and he relaxed. But only for a moment. The ship appeared again, a wake of water spraying off the back of the ship, the sails billowing full despite the wind blowing the other direction. He straightened back up in alarm as the ship closed the distance between them.

"What now?" he roared, staring at the ship. It was close enough now that he could almost make out the name of the ship on the bow.

The captain looked up at the Crow's nest. "Well?"

"The Disfigured Lion!" the lookout called down.

The captain frowned and her tail lashed.

Elrad left the railing to run up and stand next to the captain at the ship's wheel. "Is that bad?"

She shrugged. "Could be worse. We'll probably survive. But, well, our cargo is doomed."

Elrad's tail wrapped around his legs. "My father won't be happy."

"Your father would be even more upset if you died," the captain said. "Thank Unda it's Captain Skane, and not someone else."

"How did they catch up with us?"

The captain sighed. "Fresher air magic users. Ours have been working overtime trying to make up time after that big storm yesterday put us behind schedule."

"What should I do?" Elrad asked. The ship was close enough now that he could see the pirates lining the deck, waving cutlasses, spears, and even improvised clubs. Flashes of fire, water, and earth magic sparkled in the hands of others. Presumably all the air mages were busy. The figure he guessed to be the pirate captain stood at the prow of the ship, dreadlocks whipping behind him in the wind. His dark-blue fur was the color of deep water with white streaks that reminded Elrad of whitecap waves. The fluff of fur at the end of his tail was white and matched the underside of his curved horns. The captain had his hand up and blue magic sparked from his fingertips. Elrad frowned, wondering what magic he could possibly be doing, but when his eyes trailed down the ship he saw the massive wake the ship was throwing up fluttered white in the breeze, he realized that the captain was using his magic to have the water propel the ship forward. Advanced magic. Elrad was impressed despite himself.

The pirates caught up with them rapidly. The pirate captain yelled over the roar of the waves as his ship came even with theirs. "Weigh anchor and prepare to be boarded."

"Furl the sails and weigh anchor," the Captain yelled from her place at the bridge.

"What!" Elrad snarled in frustrated. "Why are you doing what this bastard says?"

Captain Shells gave him a patient, condescending look that he often saw on his own father's muzzle. Frankly it just made him angrier. "Sir, they've got out us outgunned and outmagicked. We already tried, and failed, to outrun them. Our best chance of survival is to not fight back."

He hated that she was right. He clenched his fists, his claws digging into the pads of his hands and tail lashing behind him.

The ship slowed until it was drifting on the waves. The sailors worked quickly, yelling instructions back and forth. Most of them were water mages, or those without magic, with a few scattered air users. No fire or earth like on the pirate ship. Elrad wondered how the pirates had gotten those types of magic users on a ship. Usually they hated to leave dry land, and for good reason.

While the sailors worked, the pirates watched them, and Elrad watched the pirate captain, trying to distract himself from his growing ire with Captain Shells. He looked so regal in his coat and with his dark fur, unusual in one of their kind.

The pirates threw grapples across the broadside, lashing the vessels together, before running out long planks that spanned the distance between the ships. They flooded onto Elrad's father's merchant vessel. The sailors all raised their hands as the pirates surrounded them, herding them into a group near the ship's prow. While they did that, the pirate captain stalked up the stairs to the bridge with a cocky swagger that had Elrad having to adjust himself in his pants to keep his growing erection from showing.

"Good call, Captain Shells," the pirate captain said with a grin, resting his cutlass on his shoulder. "I'm Captain Skane, of the *Disfigured Lion*, and I'll be relieving your ship of its cargo today." He swept down in a low bow, sweeping his arms out to the side before straightening back up. "No need to move. Just wait peacefully while my crew relieves your ship of its cargo, and we'll get home to our families."

"You can't take it!" Elrad blurted, clenching his fists.

The pirate's gaze slid off Captain Shells and settled on him, giving him an appraising look up and down as if seeing him for the first time. Elrad self-consciously fiddled with the buttons of his coat, realizing how much his upper-crust formal outfit set him apart from the rest of the crew. "And *who* is this?" The pirate captain grinned, coming up uncomfortably close, until they were almost muzzle to muzzle. The pirate was a little taller than him by a good six inches, and he reached down and rubbed Elrad's head between his horns. "So cute…" His gaze locked on Elrad's crotch and hung there for a moment, and when he raised his head he winked, "that he thinks he can stop me."

Growling, he slapped the pirate's hand away. "I *can* stop you."

The pirate laughed at him, deep in his belly. "You think you can, do you?"

"I do!" Elrad roared, narrowing his eyes and shoving the pirate away from him.

The bustle on the deck stopped, all of the pirates turning to stare up at them, and Captain Shell gasped. She grabbed his arm and hauled him back away from the taller man. "The young master didn't mean that, sir."

"I did too," Elrad growled, tired of being treated like a mere child. He'd taken this voyage to prove himself to his father that he was old enough to help run their shipping fleet. He was more than a dandy about town, and he wanted to prove that to his father, but that wouldn't happen if this voyage ended in disaster.

She moved to place herself between him and the pirate, but he stopped her with a lazy swing of his cutlass, placing it between her and Elrad. "Now, now, this *man* is old enough to speak for himself." He kept the blade hovering there, but turned the sharp edge to face the young lion. "Did you mean what you said?"

Inside, his stomach was twisting in fear and not a little excitement with how much attention the pirate was paying him. The man was even more handsome up close, with chiseled features and lithe muscles that showed between the open flaps of the greatcoat he wore and made the thin fur of his chest ripple. "I did," he said with as much conviction as he could and managed to get it out without his voice cracking.

"Hear that boys?" the captain guffawed. "This one thinks he can take us all on. And him without even a weapon." The crew roared along with him.

Elrad gulped and glanced around at the hardened pirates below them. "A wager then. I take you on and come out on top, you leave empty handed."

"A wager?" The pirate's laugh deepened. "That takes some balls, boy. What's your name?"

"Elrad Ayizan." He stood tall and stared the pirate in the eyes. His tail betrayed his nervousness though, curling around his legs no matter how much he commanded it not to.

The pirate gave him a lazy grin, letting the cutlass bob up and down as he thought. "A wager has two sides. What would I get if I win? I don't see any gain here for me and lots to lose. The cargo is already mine for the taking anyway."

"If you win, I'll give you triple what this cargo is worth," he said on a whim. "As soon as I get back to shore."

The pirate's eyes went wide for only a moment, and he quickly recovered, covering his surprise with a smirk that showed his fangs, but Elrad knew he had him. "That's an... interesting proposal. Come." He sheathed his cutlass and slung an arm around Elrad's shoulders.

The captain stepped back, the fur on her hackles raised, her teeth bared, and her tail twitching. "Skane, don't hurt him."

"No promises," the pirate waved a hand over his head at the captain as the two of them descended to the deck. Louder, to the assembled pirates he yelled, "Someone lend this boy a cutlass!"

"I'd prefer a spear," Elrad said, the stupidity of his words beginning to sink in as the pirate's musk hit his nose. The pirate smelled of unwashed fur, a smell he'd become a bit used to over the last few weeks, but Skane's musk covered that with a pleasant tang that was attractive. His erection grew larger, and his tight pants, so fashionable in the capital, seemed like a very stupid idea now.

"A spear, eh?" Skane's claws dug into Elrad's shoulder as he pulled the smaller lion close to whisper in his ear. "I, too, enjoy my *spears*."

Elrad swallowed, hard, and glanced up at the pirate. The man's golden eyes were twinkling, and he winked at him as one of the pirates thrust a spear into his hands. Skane gave his shoulder one last squeeze and then stepped away to address his men.

"In order to save the boy embarrassment and keep away the temptation of using water magic, we shall be having our… duel… in private." Skane made a little bow to the jeers of the pirates. "I know, I know. Don't worry, I shall regal you all with a tale of my epic victory during our celebration of our take." More jeers, and not a few laughs.

"That boy won't last more than a few seconds," a pirate yelled.

"Perhaps not," Skane smirked, looking over his shoulder at him and winking. "But I hope to be surprised."

Elrad was glad the blue fur on his face was dark enough to hide his blush. Skane was right, inside neither of them would have any water to magic, putting them on equal footing.

Skane strode to the door to the captain's quarters off the foredeck and flung it open. "We shall have our duel in here. Do not disturb us. No matter what you may hear."

Elrad shuffled inside, his tail curling between his legs and his head ducked low. His borrowed spear almost knocked into the ceiling.

"Don't worry," a pirate called. She came out of the crowd and took up position by the door. "We know a slip like that couldn't take you, Captain."

"That's the spirit." Skane whooped and shut the door behind him.

Shaking, Elrad lifted his spear and held it at the ready. Skane lazily withdrew his cutlass and dropped into a fighting stance. "Come at me then."

He charged, stabbing at the pirate. His tutor at home would have scolded his bad form. Skane deflected it with a flourish. With another flick of his wrist, he put the tip of the blade against Elrad's throat as he stumbled to a stop with his spear tip jammed into the wall.

Elrad widened his eyes, but the pirate just gave him a lazy smile and slashed the cutlass down. He winced, but surprisingly didn't feel any pain. But he did feel a breeze on his chest where his stylish coat fluttered open, all the buttons having been cut off. Snarling, he wrenched his spear free of the wall as Skane jumped back with a snicker.

"Can't end things so quickly. That's no fun." The pirate put a hand on his hip and made a fancy move with his cutlass. "I'll wait for you to take that ruined coat off. The way it's flapping it'll just get in your way."

Startled, Elrad straightened and took a step back. "That's awful decent for a pirate."

"Maybe, or maybe I just want a better look at your chest, eh?" Skane laughed as he ducked his head, his ears flattening in embarrassment and not a little excitement.

Propping his spear against the captain's side table, Elrad pulled off the coat and tossed it over the table before picking the spear back up.

"Come at me then." Skane spread his arms and took a swaggering step forward.

Elrad dropped into a defensive stance and circled to the side, wary now. "I'm feeling a bit overdressed." His fur bristled as he shifted, looking for an opening. His tail tip flicked restlessly. Meanwhile, the pirate looked relaxed as he swayed, moving effortlessly with the rolling of the deck as a large wave rocked the ship. Elrad stumbled.

"Still not gotten your sea legs yet?" Skane chuckled and sheathed his cutlass. "But you make a good point. I did say I wanted this to be a fair fight." He stripped his long coat off and tossed it carelessly aside.

Elrad lurched back and raised his spear, eyes riveted by the play of muscles under the pirate's dark blue fur. White stripes crossed the pirate's back, and a white stripe of fur started at his belly and disappeared into his pants, drawing the eye to his crotch. Elrad licked his lips, knowing he was staring but unable to help himself.

Skane redrew his sword and brandished it. "Since I got first hit, I'll let you strike next."

Elrad shook himself, all the way down to the tip of his tail and took his spear in both hands. He lunged forward and feinted at Skane's off hand, forcing him to cut across himself to try to block it. Then he reversed his strike at the last moment, scoring a shallow cut across the back of the pirate's hand.

He winced and tossed the cutlass to his other hand. "First blood. I'm impressed."

Skane pulled his left arm back and then flicked his wrist, sending the cutlass flying at Elrad. He yelped and stumbled back, falling on his rear and landing painfully on his tail. The sword flew overhead, barely missing him. But the throw had just been a distraction. The pirate jumped forward onto his hands and launched himself forward head-over-heels in a backflip.

The pirate landed one foot on his spear, driving it the rest of the way to the floor and mashing Elrad's hand. His other foot landed on the floor on his other side, straddling his furred chest. Skane fell into a squat, landing his weight on his stomach and pinning him to the floor. He rested one knee on the arm that held the spear, grabbed his other arm, and wrenched it up and to the side, pinning it to the floor.

"Yield." The pirate grinned down at Elrad, letting his tail tip brush down the inside of Elrad's thigh. Where the pirate rested on his stomach he could feel, and see, the pirate's erect cock straining to get free of the thin linen breeches. The back of the pirate's ass rested on his crotch, where his own erection was making itself known. The pirate gave a wink and wiggled his ass, letting his tail-tip dip lower, to press against Elrad's groin.

Despite the serious situation, he was greatly enjoying himself. "But if I yield, you'll get off me," he said almost without thinking about it.

Skane barked out a laugh. "Let us change the field of battle then, and choose new weapons." He kicked out with the foot that rested on the spear, sending it clattering away. With his free hand he reached down and tugged at his pant's drawstring, loosening it, and pulled his cock out and laid it on Elrad, gently stroking the length of it with his palm, claws gently brushing the fur there. "I choose this. Do you accept the new terms of our duel?" Skane smirked down at him.

Gasping, Elrad got his free elbow under himself and propped himself up as far as he could with the pirate's weight pinning him down. "I do, but you have me at a disadvantage. I cannot reach my own… spear… like this." He knew he was blushing, the tips of his ears felt hot under the thin fur there.

Skane's smirk deepened. "Let me free it for you." He let go of Elrad's hand and crawled backward down his legs, until he sat on his thighs. Then he put his hands on Elrad's hips and used his claws to shred his pants down either side. He let out a yelp of surprise that turned into a groan of pleasure as the pirate grabbed his throbbing dick and began stroking it with the soft pads of his hands. His tail thrashed, and the pirate twinned his own tail around it, a purr rumbling in his chest.

Elrad fell back with a shudder as the pirate quickened his motions, sliding his hand up and down the length of him. His claws dug into the captain's rug that lay beneath them as he fought to not cum, knowing without asking that would end the duel with him as the loser. As the pirate worked, he used the claws of his other hand to finish shredding the remains of Elrad's pants down to the knees. Then the pirate took his own cock in his hands, spat on it, and rubbed himself until he was hard again. His palm glowed with magic as he worked, foaming the spit up until it covered the length of him.

"You gotta teach me that spell," Elrad gasped.

The pirate snorted and let go of Elrad's throbbing cock and shifted onto one leg. Elrad bent his knee and lifted his leg up and to the side to give the pirate access, reaching down with one hand to spread one cheek out further. Grinning, the pirate pulled himself closer, resting Elrad's extended leg on his shoulder, and pushed his dripping cock against his rear. "There's a good lad."

Elrad cried out again as the pirate slowly pressed himself inside. Skane went slow at first, inching in and out until he was loosened up enough to take him down to the balls. They found a rhythm quickly after that, Elrad's hips moving in time to the pirate's thrusts. As the pirate's breathing came faster, he felt himself getting closer to the edge, and knew it was time to move.

Sitting up abruptly, his extended leg screamed at the stretch. He grabbed at the pirate's horns with both hands and rolled them over, until he sat on top and the pirate lay with his back on the floor.

Bending his leg back so he could rest on his knees, Elrad rocked back and forth on Skane's cock, riding the movement of the ship with the waves. The pirate shuddered and cried out, and Elrad could feel his cock pulsing inside him. Now Elrad began stroking himself, clenching his butt around Skane's cock trapping in him, until he too came all over the pirate's furry stomach, staining his white-and-blue fur with his cum.

Elrad slumped back, panting with effort, and the pirate did the same, moving a hand back to rest his head on his arms.

"I'd say I won our little duel." Skane beamed up at him, white teeth flashing from his dark-blue muzzle.

"Oh? I'd say I'm the winner." Elrad gently rocked his hips again, tightening his sphincter on the pirate's now-soft cock. The pirate winced, but didn't lose his grin.

"Do you now?"

"I did." It was his turn to smirk. "I took you and came out on top." He wiggled his butt again, making their twinned tails dance. The pirate's grin faltered and then he let out a deep belly laugh so loud it startled Elrad.

"I suppose you did." The pirate chuckled again as Elrad canted his head. That had not been the reaction he'd been expecting. Skane's cock had slowly slid free, so he climbed off, shaking off the final torn remnants of his pants.

Still laughing, the pirate climbed to his feet and re-fastened his pants. Elrad put his coat back on, trying and failing to get it to stay closed. Finally he held it closed with one hand, glad at least it was long enough in front to hide his assets from the crew. He hung back as the pirate flung the door to the cabin open, trying to stay in the shadows.

"The boy won our duel, so as promised we'll leave the loot," he announced to the assembled pirates, who'd formed a ring around the doorway.

"What!" one of them yelled. "Captain, you can't be serious?"

"I'm a man of my word." He turned back to Elrad and made a flourishing bow. "But, I won't leave without a souvenir." He drew his cutlass, and before Elrad could react, lunged forward and grabbed one of his braids. He sliced it off with a deft flick of his wrist, planted a quick kiss on Elrad's gapping muzzle, and vanished, slamming the captain's door behind him.

Shaking, Elrad slid to the floor, reaching up to finger the short lock of hair, as the sounds of the pirates leaving the ship drifted in to him. He wondered what his father would think if he joined them. It didn't matter. But by the time he climbed to his feet and threw open the door, the pirates were gone, their ship already disappearing behind a large wave.

Still, Elrad mused that the pirates hadn't left totally empty-handed. He hoped the captain would take good care of his heart.

THE NIGHT'S DANCE

JADEN DRACKUS

Raj'arr swore under his breath at the sight of the bear standing behind the throne.

As if this wasn't challenging enough already, the caracal thought as he fought back a snarl. Then he saw the gold cage covering the bear's nose. His heart stopped when he noticed the shimmer of enchantment on the gold as the brown furred ursine surveyed the hall. Raj'arr's ears folded before he caught himself and forced them back upright. The last thing he needed was to make their target suspicious. While the assassin had heard that Ak'adirr was paranoid, he wasn't prepared for the lengths the crime boss would go to protect himself. But then, very few of the marks he'd pursued knew that the Nightguard was after them—and Ak'adirr was well aware that he was being hunted by the Emperor's personal assassins.

Here in the town of Zundal, at the very southern border of the Empire, the chase had ended. Though if they couldn't figure out a way around an ursine guard who'd had his already impressive sense of smell enhanced, it could end with the sand cat evading their grasp. Not the mission Raj'arr would have chosen as the first outside the Imperial City for a new partner. But then, the caracal had never had a partner like Shadow.

Shadow, the twenty-year-old who'd just been promoted from a Dagger-Tail trainee, was already in the Emperor's sights as a favorite agent, so it made sense to send him after Ak'adirr, the confidence man who'd worked his way so deeply into the Imperial court that there was talk of him marrying one of the Emperor's grandnieces. The sand cat had put a stop to that himself by skipping town with a small chunk of the Imperial Treasury, enough to allow him to vanish from the court and buy his way into the crime clans of the Southern Province. For a year, he'd run the town of Zundal, thinking himself untouchable. Tonight, he would learn that no one was beyond the Nightguard's reach.

If they could figure out how to get around this new obstacle.

Raj'arr's gaze drifted around the hall. Ak'adirr was holding court from a throne on a dais at the far end of the room. Trestle tables lined both walls, and the floor was filled with the typical south province crowds. Antelope, gazelle, coyotes, and cheetahs dominated—though the omnipresent foxes and wolves were numerous as well. In the center, a small troupe of feline dancers performed accompanied by a flute and a lyre. Armed equines, bovines, and lions stood at intervals down the hall and as well as the doors. And that one bear behind the throne. That damn bear.

It wasn't that killing Ak'adirr was *physically* going to be difficult—that was never the issue. Raj'arr and Shadow had been sent to kill the cat, but to do so in a way that wouldn't ruffle the crime clans *too* much. After all, the clans had their uses in the political underworld of the Empire. So the pair had planned for months on what to do. Schemes had come and gone until one day they had been indulging Raj'arr's passion as a painter. As Shadow posed, he'd jerked out of position without warning. He'd been so excited he'd pounced across the room onto the caracal. A smile passed over Raj'arr's muzzle as he remembered what they'd done after that discussion.

A smattering of applause brought his attention fully to the present again. Memories of sex with his lover would have to wait. If they were going to figure out how to get around the bear, Raj'arr had to talk with Shadow without bringing any attention to it. For a long moment, he just stared at nothing, trying to come up with a way to get to his partner. A pair of antelope passed in front of the caracal, making the distinctive giggles of lovers sneaking off for a tryst. As Raj'arr watched them pass, the solution dawned on him. He moved his way towards the dais, snatching a drink from a servant's tray as he passed. He sniffed it then downed it when it proved to be a fortified wine, sweetened in the southern style. It would do to give the impression that he'd been freely imbibing well enough. He took another and let his movements become a little less controlled. With one eye on Ak'adirr to make sure the sand cat wasn't looking in his direction, he undid one of the buttons on his silk vest and tugged his tunic out just a bit. A quick swipe over his head ruffled his fur. He sipped his wine and studied his reflection on gilded rim. Disheveled, but not overly so, exactly the look he was going for. Just enough to give the appearance of a minor noble who'd indulged a little too much. He made his way through the crowd, making sure to stagger every now then until he reached the crime lord's dais.

"Ah, Lord Kar'sha," Ak'adirr called to Raj'arr in a South Province accent he hadn't had in the Imperial court. "I trust you are enjoying yourself?"

"Oh, I am," the caracal replied, resisting the urge to throw a slur into his speech. While the noble he was playacting as was a minor one, he still had the dignity of the Imperial Court to maintain. "Your reputation for hospitality is well earned."

"But?" The sand cat asked, his tone making clear that he'd heard the word unspoken in Raj'arr's statement.

Behind the crime lord, the bodyguard sniffed. Clearly the ursine had no trouble detecting the wine, even without whatever augmentation the nose piece was giving him. Raj'arr took an unsteady step forward and leaned in. Sure enough, the bear growled as his paw dropped to his side. The caracal jumped back in mock surprise, even as he heard an armored guard shift behind him. Ak'adirr chuckled. "You'll have to forgive them. When you've been gifted with Imperial generosity, others get jealous and try to take it from you. One can't be too careful."

"Of course. My apologies," Raj'arr said with a bow. He steadied himself and raised his voice as the musicians began again. "I was just going to ask how you could let those lovely ladies work so hard and not be comforted after such exertions."

Ak'adirr's eyebrow raised in surprise at the mention of "ladies" before a sly grin passed over the sand cat's tan muzzle. "Ah. I had wondered if that might cross your mind." Ak'adirr took a sip from a glass at his left paw, guarded by the bear, before giving a sniff that sounded disapproving. "Your reputation for enjoying the *finest* companionship precedes you."

Raj'arr returned the crime boss's smile with a flick of his tufted ears. There was no mistaking the sand cat's disapproval, and the caracal could guess what offended him. *Oh, so you're one of those that looks down on those who have relationships with males. You are going in my painting of The Battle of Dragonbreath Falls as a dead body, ass.* "Life is too short not to enjoy the finer things."

"Of course," the sand cat purred, though the twitch of his nose betrayed his disdain. "It's just as well that you are feeling like female company tonight, as my guards are off limits and there are no male dancers in my employ. Did you have one in mind?"

Raj'arr turned back to the floor, pretending to study the dancers to hide the smirk on his own muzzle. His tail swished behind him before he let his gaze pause on a slender black panther, dressed only in a top that covered her chest, white linen bands around her forearms, and a skirt that came to mid-thigh. It was a modest outfit compared to some of the others, as the red fabric of the outfit was opaque, but still showed off a good deal of silky black fur. She was just taking a bow at the conclusion of performance, and her green eyes briefly met those of the caracal. A hint of white appeared on her muzzle as her fangs were exposed by a smile before she turned away.

Raj'arr pointed. "Her. That lovely panther."

Ak'adirr nodded. "Ahh., She is new. Arrived a few weeks ago with the new troupe. I haven't caught her name. Perhaps you could inform me of it once you're done preparing her for me?"

"I think that can be managed," the caracal replied, managing to hide the growl that threatened to escape from his lips. He bowed to the sand cat and held it until the crime boss waved him away.

Without another glance, Raj'arr straightened up and headed off to the dance floor. He passed through the crowd, maintaining the slight stagger he'd been mimicking as he went. Finally, he reached the dancers and clapped his paws together. They looked him over as he locked eyes with the panther. He looked up and down her frame. Her green eyes gazed back at him and her paws opened and closed nervously.

She was slender, though still on the large side for a panther, and taller than the caracal. Her thick tail twitched behind her as she shifted from paw to paw. Her outfit was of a deep scarlet, accented by gold piping and a row of tiny bells that jingled with each of her movements. This close, he could smell the spicy perfume tinged with a hint of artificial musk she was wearing. She licked her whiskers and gave Raj'arr a nervous smile. "My lord?"

"My dear," Raj'arr replied, this time slurring his words.

"You have been working ever so hard this evening. Surely those lovely paws of yours are growing tired?"

She looked down at the polished wooden floorboards before responding in a husky tone. "My paws are used to long performances, my lord. But I suppose it has been a long night."

"Indeed," Raj'arr said as he offered an arm. "But I know a way you can get off them for a while. If you're willing."

She looked around, and the caracal saw a few knowing smirks, a few sympathetic smiles, a nod or two of encouragement, and even one or two jealous looks. The troupe leader, a fennec, nodded and waved his paw dismissively at them. "Just have her back in an hour! She is performing the K'orath Nor, and I don't have anyone else that can fill the role."

"Of course," Raj'arr purred as the panther took his arm. "I wouldn't have my favorite dance ruined."

With a wave to the dancers and a nod in the direction of the nearest guard, the assassin led his companion out of the hall and into the corridor. The guards at the entrance didn't manage to hide their snicker as they watched the couple head to Raj'arr's guest room. The panther took two steps into the room as the caracal turned and locked the door. When he turned back, "she" had her paws on her hips and was glaring at him in a much more confident manner then she'd displayed back in the hall.

"Just what," Shadow growled. "In the hell do you think you're doing?"

———

The jaguar held his stance as his partner looked him over, waiting for an answer to his question. He didn't get one—at least not a verbal one. Instead, the caracal took two strides forward and wrapped his arms around Shadow before pressing his muzzle into the younger feline's. Shadow was taken off guard and let it happen, his own muzzle opening just enough for Raj'arr's tongue to enter it and find his. It had been too long—a month at least—and the young assassin wanted nothing more than to melt in his mate's arms. Instead he planted his paws in Raj'arr's chest and pushed the smaller feline backwards. "That's not an answer!"

"I know," the caracal said as he closed back into another embrace. "But it's what they expect, and I needed to talk to you."

"About what? What's so important that you'd risk the mission by meeting with me?"

"It's already at risk," Raj'arr hissed. "If we don't think of something quick, there's no way we can kill the sand cat and get away."

Shadow blinked, his anger going cold. "What? We have it all planned out."

"The bear, Dagger Tail. Didn't you see the bear?"

"Don't call me that," Shadow snapped reflexively. He wasn't a trainee anymore, but Raj'arr always called him one when he thought the jaguar was making poor decisions. The assassin frowned, his ears folded down. "What about the bear?"

"You saw his nose? With that thing on his snout, he'll know what you are before you even get close."

The jaguar's nose twitched as he closed his eyes and brought the images back to his mind. He saw the bear complete with the gold cage on his nose, and with the image came memories from training where ursine guards had been the most difficult to get around with their extremely sensitive noses. "What *is* that?"

"I'm not completely sure," Raj'arr said. "My guess is it's to enhance his sense of smell. It definitely shimmered when he growled at me."

Shadow nodded—he'd wondered why the caracal had been so aggressive in his approach to Ak'adirr. Of course he'd been trying to get a better look at the nose piece that was bothering him. But knowing what they were up against was only half the battle—now they had to figure out what to do with that information. And with their plan hinging on everyone thinking Shadow was female, a bear with an enchanted jewelry augmenting his sense of smell was a huge problem. The perfume and musk he wore was common enough among athletic females that it had fooled everyone so far, including the fennec, but if Raj'arr was right, it wouldn't work on the guard.

"We need to think fast, Spots."

"I know! But it's hard to focus with your paws wandering all over me."

"Sorry," the caracal said. He stopped, but didn't let go. "Can you blame me? It's been over a month. I'm guessing not from what I'm feeling down here…"

Raj'arr's paw moved again, sliding over Shadow's hip and then between his legs. Shadow tried to growl, but it became a moan as the caracal took hold of the jaguar's groin. A binding held his sheath and balls tight to his torso and back between his legs, respectively. But as Raj'arr rubbed, the illusion was broken as Shadow's shaft began to emerge.

"You're not wearing the sheath," Raj'arr breathed into the jaguar's ear. His tongue followed, pressing a warm wetness into Shadow's ear.

"It was… too noticeable," the jaguar huffed. Little shocks of pleasure ran through his body. His lover was right—it had been too long. He wanted this.

But they had a job to do as well. Even as the caracal teased him, Shadow's mind raced. Their plan required Shadow to get close enough to Ak'adirr to make the kill and then get away in the confusion. The getaway depended on everyone thinking that they were looking for a panther lady, and not a male jaguar. But the bear would be able to tell that Shadow was a male, even with the perfumes. Raj'arr was right—unless they did something, and did it quick, everything would come to naught. And with Ak'adirr expecting someone to come for him, they might not get another chance. *What can we do?* Shadow couldn't come up with anything, and the scent of aroused caracal was making it difficult to focus…

The assassin's tail went still and stiff as the revelation hit him. Raj'arr noticed and paused, only to stagger as the jaguar threw himself at his lover. Shadow growled as he nipped at the caracal's tan neck fur. His paws went to Raj'arr's belt and began working at the buckle.

"Gods Spots," Raj'arr whispered. "I was just teasing."

"It's what they expect," Shadow reminded him.

That made Raj'arr pause, long enough for the jaguar to finish unbuckling the fancy knotwork buckle and send the caracal's trousers to the floor in a puddle. Instantly, the room filled with the sandy, sun-kissed-grass scent of his arousal, Shadow growled and took hold of his mate's tan furred balls as he rubbed his neck against Raj'arr's cheek.

All at once, the older assassin caught on. His body went taught, then he let out a growl of his own. In an instant, the dance of love shifted leads, as Raj'arr shoved himself against Shadow. The caracal aggressively rubbed his face against the jaguar, his paws tracing the lean sides of his lover before finding the cord that kept Shadow's skirt on. The red silk puddled on the ground as Raj'arr lifted his mate off his paws and carried him to the bed. Shadow left off his groping, and wrapped his arms around the caracal's neck, huffing and moaning as his chest was nuzzled and nipped at.

Raj'arr dropped Shadow to the bed before pressing himself against the jaguar. There wasn't going to be a need for foreplay—his shaft was already fully exposed against the muslin hiding Shadow's own equipment. Though the cloth was losing that battle, as Shadow could feel his shaft pressing against the smaller one outside the binding. The caracal leaned forward and pressed his tongue into the jaguar's ear. Shadow moaned as the warm, wet pressure moved along.

"You need to get ready?" Raj'arr asked in a breathy whisper as he leaned back to loosen the cloth prison around the jaguar's groin.

Shadow favored him with a sly grin. "Didn't you always tell me that 'A Nightguard is always prepared?' I got ready for this before I came up to the hall." *I also did it every damn night for a month to think of you.*

"That's my girl," Raj'arr said loudly for the benefit of any eavesdroppers.

He smacked the jaguar's hip playfully. Shadow took the hint and lifted his rear to allow the caracal to pull the binding free. He sighed in relief as his balls and shaft fell away from his body. His cock sprang fully erect, the reddish-pink contrasting sharply with his all black fur. Raj'arr purred as his paws ran over the jaguar's lean form, following the curves and pausing occasionally to trace rosettes hidden by the dye. The older feline rubbed his face over Shadow's chest, marking him aggressively.

Shadow's lower body got a different attention, as Raj'arr humped his thigh and ground against his groin and rear, leaving fur matted with trails of pre from his leaking shaft. The jaguar shuddered as Raj'arr pressed some sensitive area. Little shocks ran down his spine as his tail flicked against the bed in ecstasy. He'd missed this so much. The plan, the reason they were doing this, left his mind leaving only the joy of participating in this dance with his lover. Then Raj'arr's weight was gone.

Shadow let out a puzzled meow and tried to push himself up on his elbows but was met by a caracal paw that shoved him back down. Raj'arr hissed, but when Shadow blinked and met his golden eyes, there was no malice—it was just part of the game. The jaguar leaned back and watched as his mate took two strides and retrieved something from his bag. He returned holding a small vial, and Shadow dutifully spread his legs.

Raj'arr poured a good amount of the liquid onto his paw before setting it aside and reaching down to the jaguar's exposed rear. The young assassin moaned as the caracal rubbed the cool liquid over his hole, fingers tracing the ring before one slipped inside. He gasped, then groaned as a second digit followed. His back arched as Raj'arr swirled his fingers, making sure to get everything slick before withdrawing them.

The pressure of his lover's weight again left Shadow as the caracal poured another measure of liquid into his paw and rubbed it over his own shaft. Raj'arr neglected to make his usual effort to keep things tidy, and a good amount splashed over Shadow's groin and legs. The jaguar huffed in annoyance before the part of mind that wasn't losing itself to pleasure realized what his lover was doing. He lay back and let Raj'arr lead. The caracal's paws caressed his flanks before slipping under Shadow's hips to lift the slender jaguar's rump to the proper level. Shadow looked down past his wobbling erection to his lover's face.

The pressure between his cheeks returned as Raj'arr positioned his tip just against the younger feline's ring. The caracal's golden eyes met the jaguar's green ones, an unspoken question in them. Shadow took a deep, calming breath and nodded.

Raj'arr pushed forward, slipping inside Shadow's rear in a smooth motion. The young assassin let out a gasp that quickly became a moan as the caracal hilted him completely. Raj'arr paused and held himself tight allowing Shadow to adjust to the feeling of his lover inside of him for the first time in months. The jaguar babbled incoherently as the caracal rocked, working his shaft back and forth at a gentle pace. Shadow sighed in contentment at the feeling of his mate's thickness filling him, the barbs on the shaft stimulating his insides.

The caracal purred, wiggling his hips before slamming against the jaguar's rear. Then he began in earnest —or would have if he hadn't pulled back enough to slip out of Shadow. Raj'arr cursed and muttered something about it having been way too long. He re-positioned himself and went back to work before the jaguar could say anything. The growl that had been building in Shadow vanished in a groan of pleasure. The jaguar's eyes rolled back and he wrapped his legs around the caracal's hips as he gave himself over to the sensations.

Every time Raj'arr's hips met his rear, a shock of pleasure went up Shadow's spine all the way to the tips of his ears. The warm thickness of the caracal's cock pressed against his insides, filling him in that way he'd missed so much. His own cock throbbed and bounced, slapping against his thighs and lean stomach in time with Raj'arr's thrusts. His fur was matting with the constant dribble of pre leaking from the tip. Not that Raj'arr was doing any better, if the feeling in the jaguar were anything to go by. Shadow panted as his lover's pace increased—back and forth, back and forth. The jaguar's heart hammered in his chest and he felt the warmth of ecstasy fill his face and ears. His paw wandered down towards his cock…

Only to be pinned to the bed by Raj'arr. Shadow whimpered and tried to lift his pinned arm, only to be answered with a growl and an aggressive thrust that forced him deeper into the mattress and put an end to any thoughts of resistance. The jaguar leaned back and shuddered in pleasure as the caracal picked up his pace. Raj'arr leaned in further, keeping Shadow's wrist pinned as he took a muzzle full of the jaguar's neck scruff. Shadow could only moan and whine at the feeling of the warm thickness filling him, occasionally gasping as the soft barbs of his mate's shaft stroked an especially sensitive spot and sent a jolt through his body. He could feel the pressure building inside him, but he'd never gotten off from just being fucked before. And he doubted he would now—Raj'arr's lean stomach wasn't rubbing his shaft enough to get Shadow close, probably by design. He whimpered at the injustice of the situation.

Raj'arr didn't notice, or pretended not to. Instead, the caracal growled, and his pace became frantic. From the way the thickness inside him was throbbing, the jaguar knew it wouldn't be long. He closed his eyes and waited for the pleasurable sensation of his lover's climax. It didn't come. The weight of Raj'arr vanished from on top of him, and the thumps against his rear ceased. The thickness spreading his hole vanished, leaving him to whine at the numbness of its absence. He opened his eyes as the caracal's panting changed to a hiss, and just as quickly closed them again as a spurt of warm seed splashed against his chin and into his face. A second pulse followed, coating his groin and balls. Then a final one dribbled over his right thigh. For a moment, all he could hear was Raj'arr panting, and his own arousal waved in the air with the need for release. He was *so* close…

Then he let out a gasp that threatened to become a scream as something ice cold pressed against his exposed shaft. Shadow hissed and squirmed but the freezing pressure stayed with him stealing any arousal away. The assassin pushed himself up and found Raj'arr pressing the flat of a dagger that shimmered with the blue-white of a frost enchantment against his rapidly retreating shaft. The caracal gave the jaguar an apologetic look as he pulled the weapon away from Shadow's sheath.

"I'm sorry Spots," he whispered as he leaned down and began licking his mess from Shadow's face. "But we can't have you going off. I'll make it up to you, I promise. Just not now."

"I understand," the younger feline hissed. One some level, he did, despite not feeling it at the moment. All of it made sense—the scent of sex would explain away why the supposed panther lady smelled like a male, with the strong scent of dried caracal seed covering even more. But if Shadow finished, then the illusion would be broken. It had to be this way.

Shadow slipped from the bed and began rebinding the cloth around his groin. He tried to ignore the matted fur and the sticky wetness seeping into the fabric. He'd had worse things in his fur. The jaguar tied the fabric up and cinched it tight before looking up to find Raj'arr watching him. His ears folded in embarrassment as the caracal smiled.

"I don't care much for that look," Raj'arr commented as he wiped a cloth over his retreating shaft, balls, and groin. The dagger he'd used to "encourage" Shadow's arousal to go away was sitting on the nightstand. He walked over and opened the window before returning to the bed. "Nothing to play with."

"I know," the jaguar replied as he pulled his skirt back on. He accepted the cloth the caracal held out and did his best to get the cum out of the fur on his thighs, or at least tried to make it less obvious. "But it's only for tonight."

"Yes. And I promise, as soon as we're far away we'll take care of you." Raj'arr smiled and pulled his pants up and tightened his belt before stepping over to help Shadow with his outfit as the jaguar adjusted his top. That "help" consisted mostly of ruffling the fabric to make sure it didn't sit right, making it obvious to the careful observer what they'd been doing.

"Needed more encouragement," Shadow muttered, his voice coming up an octave into a more stereotypical feminine range. They moved across the room and back to the door, and Raj'arr took his arm and patted the fabric wrapped around the jaguar's wrist.

"Well, you are performing my favorite dance my dear," he said loudly as he opened the door. "And there's only one chance to get it right. A little extra encouragement can't hurt."

"Of course, Milord." Was all Shadow could reply with now that they were back in public.

———

"You're late," the troupe master hissed. "I should have known that High Court lay-about was too drunk to get his rocks off quickly."

"Relax," Shadow assured him. "I am here and still able to perform."

"Ha! Spoken like someone who knows she won't have to face the consequences of her actions!" The fennec folded his ears flat and bared his teeth. "Listen here, girl. The K'orath Nor is the pinnacle of Dash'arrad style, I still can't believe that I have to rely on a novice like you to perform it! It has to be done perfectly! Or else our host will be displeased, and I don't have to tell you what would happen if Ak'adirr is displeased! Oh, but you don't care! You've got an Imperial toy to protect you!"

Shadow sighed, putting on a show of being displeased though he was anything but. The fennec bouncing from paw to paw and jabbing at the "panther" with a finger would only help with what was about to happen. He had no particular love for the fox, but he didn't want him hurt when the hornet's nest got kicked over. Shadow knelt down to be eye level with the troupe master. "You're making a scene. You wanted someone who knew a dance as obscure as the K'orath Nor. That's me. You wanted a panther, and a black one to be as close to the original as possible. That's me." He let his voice drop to a growl. "Now get on your stool and announce the dance."

The fennec blinked as the musicians moved to their instruments and the other dancers took their spots. The fox's muzzle opened and closed a few times before he glared at the panther.

"Fine," he huffed as he turned away. "Just don't forget the stakes."

"Oh, I won't," Shadow muttered as he moved to a side table to collect the items he'd need for the performance. *You have no idea what's at stake.* His partner for the dance, a lion, gave Shadow a sympathetic smile before moving to take his own place as the fennec clapped his paws and called for the hall's attention.

Shadow took a breath and looked over the crowd. Raj'arr flashed him a brief smile. The jaguar took two steps forward to the center of the hall and gave the area one final look. Ak'adirr's throne was pushed to the edge of the dais, leaving the short sand cat close to the floor. The ursine guard, with the golden cage on his muzzle that had caught Raj'arr's attention, stood behind and to the left of the throne. Shadow closed his eyes and ran through the plan again in his mind. If they had managed to cover his scent enough, there wouldn't be any need to change. The jaguar nodded to himself and slid the specially made fans the dance required over his paws as he moved to the center of the floor. The lion nodded and adjusted the cuffs of his own costume, a vague imitation of a nobleman's jacket and short pants, before turning his eyes to the fennec. The fox was reaching the conclusion of his pitch, describing the beauty and difficulty of the K'orath Nor and how only the most skilled of dancers could perform it properly. He tellingly skipped over the part where this would be the first time this pair preformed together.

Shadow tuned the fox out, though a tight smile played over his lips. The K'orath Nor was an old dance, so old that its origin was lost to time. All people knew was that it was an energetic dance involving a female and a male dancer, with the lady in the leading role. It was a storytelling performance, and had become known as the Fan Dance for the ornate fans used in the wooing of the male dancer. In reality, it was anything but. Hidden in the archives of the Nightguard, tucked away to be forgotten or ignored, the K'orath Nor's original name could be found—The Assassin's Dance. The fennec finished his spiel and clapped his paws again. Shadow and the lion bowed to Aka'dirr and took their places as the music began.

The assassin centered himself and let the sounds and scents from the room flow over him. His body moved, almost of its own accord, which left his mind free to analyze and process as the dance went through its steps. He flowed through the first part of the dance as he watched the sand cat and the ursine. Both were leaning in to watch the panther— the bear with a slight look of disgust and an annoyed look in Raj'arr's direction. Aka'dirr ran a tongue over his whiskers and favored Shadow with a lecherous grin. Shadow let a fan flutter slightly as he passed it in front of his face, but otherwise appeared to be focused on his performance.

The story told in the dance was old enough that the names and locations had been lost to time, even in the Nightguard's library. But the details remained the same—a young panther was making her way through the world as a dancer, until one day she performed at court and caught the eye of a powerful noble. He was smitten with the dancer—which the lion was in the process of demonstrating by moving with Shadow, his paw tracing the curves of the "panther" while remaining a few inches off the fur. The lion sniffed and let out a quiet, but disapproving grunt.

"Should have cleaned better," the lion whispered as the steps of the dance had his muzzle blocked by Shadow's head.

The jaguar twirled, running the fans up the lion's flanks before passing them in front of his face. "He was drunk. Didn't leave me enough time."

The lion's smirk was actually part of the performance, but Shadow could see a twitch of the whiskers that said it was a bit more genuine than it needed to be. He reached out to spin the jaguar again, entering the part of the dance that no one understood. In most modern interpretations, the noble's expression wasn't supposed to be a smirk—it was an expression of desire. Of course, in the forgotten original, it was an expression of his power over the panther, which explained the reaction Shadow was supposed to have when, after a few moments of sensual twirling around each other, the lion reached up to brush his face—which in the dance sent Shadow spiraling away. Following the modern practice, the lion pranced forward to catch the jaguar and brought their noses almost together before pulling away again to leave Shadow alone on the floor.

The assassin let himself collapse to his knees as the music slowed and dropped to a whisper. Then, he pulled himself back up waving his fans and prancing around the hall. This was the sequence that had earned this performance the name of the Fan Dance. Originally, it was supposed to represent the panther retraining herself in her previous profession—an assassin. The dance was supposed to end with the female lead rejoining and brushing the face of the male partner—symbolizing their reunion and shared love in the modern telling, and her taking of revenge in the original. This performance would end in the spirit of the original, but with the Nightguard's unique twist.

Shadow let his movements carry him towards the throne. He passed the fans in front of his face, first one then the other. The bear was still annoyed, if the fact that his eyes kept flicking from the jaguar towards a caracal was any indication. Aka'dirr still wore the same smile on his fluffy cheeked face as he watched the lithe jaguar, but looked up as the ursine muttered Raj'arr's cover name. For a heartbeat, his throat was exposed.

That was all the time the assassin needed. He focused his thoughts, and beneath the wraps, the dragon shaped brand on his right forearm glowed—even through the cloth—as he summoned the Shadow Edge dagger bound to him. It materialized in his paw hidden by the fan. A graceful pirouette brought him within arm's reach of the throne...

With a quick pass of fan, it was done.

Aka'dirr's eyes went wide as he realized what had happened, but the Shadow Edge's paralysis enchantment ensured that the sand cat could do no more than that. A thin collar of bright red appeared on the tan fur of his throat. Shadow locked eyes with the dying feline, making sure the smaller cat knew that this was no accident. If the thief knew who had ordered his death before he crossed to the other side, the jaguar didn't know. The assassin couldn't risk exposing that the Nightguard had done the deed. There was no covering the scent of blood as it ran down the sand cat's chest, turning the white fabric crimson—especially not from the bear. He sniffed, then roared as Shadow twirled away. He dismissed the dagger, and Aka'dirr slumped over.

Instantly the hall was in a panic. Screams filled the air as the crowd was suddenly running everywhere at once. The guards stood rooted in shock, save the bear who was already shoving the throne aside to lunge at Shadow. The body of his former employer flopped unceremoniously to the floor. The assassin threw his fans in the ursine's face, and bolted, his long tail streaming behind him as he dashed out of the hall. The guard at the door was in no position to stop the jaguar, as a pair of panicking antelope crashed into him.

Shadow was the first one out into the corridor. The jaguar took the first turn at a dead sprint, his mind already going over the rest of the plan. Between himself and Raj'arr, everything should be ready. Ten yards and two corridors later, he reached the closet that he'd found—a small room with only a set of shelves and a window over the lake. He ducked inside and slammed the door behind him. He already had his clothes off before he was halfway to the window. He flipped the latch and threw his outfit into the lake. He turned back to the shelves, not taking time to rejoice in the feeling of walking with his balls not trapped against his groin for the first time in weeks. There would be time to relish it soon—but first he had to escape. He had only moments before the guards figured out where he'd gone, and he'd need a full minute before he could leave this room.

Sitting on the second shelf was a large glass flask containing what looked like a purple liquid. Shadow snatched it and moved back towards the window. He hesitated for a heartbeat, as his instincts screamed at him not to do what he had to. He closed his eyes, whispered a curse, and slammed the container into his chest. The bottle shattered with a sound like broken glass, but the shards disintegrated as the liquid splashed all over the jaguar's fur. There was a loud *foomp* like a fire starting, and the assassin fought back panic as the coolness of the liquid suddenly became a wave of heat that washed over his body. The sensation started at his chest and rushed down his legs and up to the top of his ears, becoming more intense when it reached places that the potion splashed. Shadow winced as the feeling reached his groin and then went between his legs, but it wasn't unbearable. The feeling raced down his tail, and as suddenly as it had come it was gone.

He opened his eyes and shook the last of the purple flames from his paws then looked up to see a black jaguar in the window. He saw the rosettes on his fur, little darker circles against the rest of his fur and for the first time in a month recognized Shadow looking back at him. But there was no time to take joy in that. Still nude, he lunged out the window, stepping as close to the ledge of the sill as he dared before turning to face back to the building and lowing himself over the edge.

Even with a jaguar's claws and skills, the hand-over-hand climb across the four rooms to Raj'arr's guest room was harrowing. Shadow had to stop once to force himself to breathe before continuing. The cold air coming into the oasis off the desert and blowing under his tail didn't help matters.

The jaguar barely managed to pull himself into the caracal's window before he heard shouting coming from the closet he'd left. Four rooms separated him from the shouts. He had to hurry.

The scents of sex still lingered in the room, but he had no time to worry about the stirring they raised in his sheath. Two steps brought Shadow to the side table, and the outfit that was laid out there—a simple tunic and breeches that any servant might be expected to wear. There were no undergarments, he noted with a sigh, but realized it was a good bit of foresight on Raj'arr's part. As he threw them on, the assassin's nose wrinkled as he realized they hadn't been washed and still had sand and dirt on them. The caracal had thought of everything. Now it was the jaguar's turn.

He just managed to get the breeches on and the belt buckled when the door flew open. Three lion guards burst in, followed by the bear and Raj'arr, who was doing his best to look betrayed and angry. Shadow put on a relieved expression. "My lord! I was looking for—"

The jaguar was cut off by the lions, who sprang forward and shoved him to the floor. Shadow gasped and writhed on the floor as they roughly searched him. "My lord!" He called again in surprise.

"That's not her!" Raj'arr growled. "Tra'iska just arrived from the Imperial City!"

The lions hauled him upright and held him off the floor as the bear stepped forward and sniffed him. Shadow swallowed, and let a hint of the genuine fear he was keeping down to show through. His ears folded back as the bear blew a hot breath in his face. The jaguar let out a hiss of shock as a meaty paw clamped on his groin. An investigative squeeze seemed to satisfy the bear, and he motioned to the lions to release Shadow. He stepped forward and bared his teeth.

"Just got here, huh? You see a panther run this way?"

"No," Shadow stammered, letting his eyes drift to Raj'arr

as if seeking reassurance. His tail thumped the floorboards. "The. The corridor was empty when I came in looking for Lord Kar'sha. I, I heard someone run past a few moments later. Then a splash from outside the window."

The bear stared at him for a moment, then snorted and turned away. The lions followed suit. Raj'arr growled and paced the room, looking surprisingly ferocious for the smallest one in the room. Shadow worried that the caracal was over-playing the "innocent but worried he looked involved" role. But that was what Raj'arr was going with as he punched the wall. "She got away. Godsdamnit!"

The bear shook his head. "She won't get far. But as for you, Kar'sha, I would not want to be here when the rest of the Families arrive to start asking question. The Imperial Court's protection only goes so far…"

"Generous of you," the caracal said with a sardonic grin tinged with just a hint of concern. He looked around at the guards, his ears flat and his tail still. Then he straitened up and tugged on his vest. "Yes. Well, the Court no doubt has gotten into all sorts of trouble without me."

"No doubt," the bear said, not bothering to hide rolling his eyes. If Shadow had to guess, he was weighing the desire to know if the caracal was involved against the risks of drawing official Imperial attention. Caution won, and the ursine sighed. "Won't look for you tonight. But come morning, I'll want to know if you just have bad taste in women, or had something to do this."

Without another word, the guards left the room, leaving the two Nightguard alone. As soon as the door slammed shut, Raj'arr smiled at Shadow. "Well, I believe we should get going then."

"Already, sir?" Shadow asked, letting a pleading whine creep into his tone. "I was looking forward to sleeping in a real bed tonight."

Raj'arr chuckled in reply, but his short tail was a blur behind him as they began packing up the room.

———

Dawn found them miles north on the Imperial Highway and looking for a place to camp. A mile outside of town, they'd stopped at a hidden cache to collect the rest of their gear. They'd destroyed their disguises and were now dressed in the brown and green leathers of Imperial Rangers. Raj'arr patted Shadow on the shoulder.

"You did well. That was quick thinking using sex to get around the bear."

"I'm just glad the dye remover also got rid of that mess," Shadow replied, shifting at the memory. "Still not sure how I feel about setting my groin on fire—even if it didn't actually burn."

"A bit late to worry now," the caracal said with a laugh. "But com'on. A mile up ahead there's a hollow that's out of view of the road. You've waited long enough, and I want some spotted dick in my muzzle."

Shadow was too excited to react to the joke. He grabbed Raj'arr's arm and took off at a run, his tail flicking rapidly behind him.

TO HEL AND BACK

TELEVASSI

Sword in paw, I circled my opponent. The snow crunched under my claws. My heart beat in my chest. The wind tousled and grabbed my fur. I felt none of that. I was a proud huskarl; the elite, oath-bound bodyguard of famous lords! Disciplined. Skilled. Devoted. We were the pinnacle of warriors.

Indeed, when the valkyrie Skade carried me to Valhalla, she only told me to keep up my guard. It would only take one moment of weakness for a foe to humble me.

I took her words to heart because I had a secret. If anyone found out it would be the end of me, yet keeping it just got harder and harder.

"Stop denying *us*!" I demanded.

The husky countered. His battle-snarl was bestial, sword flashing as his blade caught the moonlight. I parried and the steel-clash rang in my ears.

I held him there. And he held me. Our swords sharp, locked together, growling and grinding against each other. Neither of us was willing to give ground.

I swung my leg and swept his paws out from underneath him. That curly tail of his softened the fall, but at least his swordplay was improving.

"Aelfrith," I panted, offering him my paw as he lay sprawled in the snow. "We've done nothing but make eyes at each other since we made it here!"

Instead of savouring my victory my eyes ran straight to what I desired: down the husky's subtle curves, his lithe frame, and slender muzzle. The tips of his fangs glistened inside his muzzle, guarding his soft lips and slender tongue that I longed to kiss.

The very thought brought me to my knees, a soft whine escaping my lips. We hadn't even shared a kiss here; I was so afraid of getting caught. I'd lose my reputation and place at the mead hall. Who would ever stand by me in the shieldwall if they knew I lifted other males' tails? They'd banish me from Valhalla, and send me to freeze in shame and dishonour down in Hel, in Niflheim forever.

That was my secret and my shame. Yet regardless of the consequences, I ached to be with him.

"Please." I reached out and touched his muzzle, paws trembling as if he were sharp.

"You always wanted to come to Valhalla," the husky reminded me. "You followed your lord into a pointless battle, fought to the death to avenge his stupid mistake." He growled, reminding me how my 'blind loyalty' to warrior culture angered the skald. I'd explained a thousand times I had no choice. My honour was my word, and it was unbreakable. But for him words were to be moulded into whatever tale he wished to weave. "Admit it," he retorted. "Just like in life, we can't be lovers here."

The husky was right. The days in Valhalla were constant training for Ragnarok, the gods' final battle at the end of the world. The nights weren't any rest either, just unceasing feasting and endless drinking. There was no time to feel his warm breath on the back of my neck as we slept late into the morning, or how we'd tremble, giddy as our bodies forced us to break the kiss to breathe. Aelfrith always called me a pawn in life for being a huskarl. The afterlife was no different.

I sighed, tossing my blade aside. I was never any good with words. He always got the better of me in our arguments. Being a skald, of course it was his strength.

"I'm sorry." My ears drooped.

The husky growled at my refusal to admit it, scrabbling to his feet. He clutched his sword, scowling as he brushed his fur. Despite being half-naked and covered in snow he wasn't cold.

"Would you rather be in Niflheim?" I asked.

He scoffed, tail bristling at the thought. Being a storyteller, he knew the rules well. Niflheim was the place you went if you didn't die heroically in battle. Sickness, old age, or even just dying without a weapon in your paws condemned you to freeze your miserable tail off for eternity. Ragnarok would come as sweet relief down there.

I decided not to press him about it. Despite its flaws, Valhalla was the best we could do. Instead I closed the gap between us, pulling him close to me so he could share my warmth. He melted briefly, accepting my touch.

"Remember how we fell in love?" I murmured, nibbling his ear the way he liked it. "You were that dashing young skald who came to the hall, showing off your clever verse and that cute, curly tail of yours."

"You were so shy about us." Aelfrith huffed, shaking his head. "I caught you staring so often. When you got brave enough to meet my eyes, I flashed you a smile from the other side of the crackling hearth."

"By the end of it, only you noticed it wasn't the fire that got me panting."

Aelfrith giggled, but that memory held a sombre note. That very evening my oath-lord called me to war, to the battle that killed us the very next day.

I wasn't ready to admit it, but I was tired of being a pawn, tired of having to hide who I was.

The thought wormed through my mind as the husky gripped my hips. I ran my paws through his soft fur. He was a beautiful beast, his fur a gossamer sheen as it caught the pale moonlight. As a huskarl I'd seen lords and ladies married, but never had I seen one imbued with so perfect a betrothal gown as he was now. I let my paw run lower. We never managed to consummate our desire, but perhaps here, perhaps now.

"Athelstan," Aelfrith warned me. I closed my eyes while my mind raced through all the consequences if I gave into my feelings.

Screw it.

I kissed him.

I forgot the rest of the world for a sweet moment. His lips tasted of juniper berries and his tongue was like honey. He thrust back into my muzzle, swirling about mine as we grappled, full of vigour to win the only important fight tonight.

When we withdrew, we gasped like swimmers spent from the sea. Aelfrith tried to warn me a final time, but I silenced his clever tongue with another kiss.

The rush of air as we broke away from the second one brought only a keener edge and no relief. Perhaps that was his warning? Love seemed the opposite of fire; smothering it never extinguished it. Instead it only burnt brighter.

I'd suffocated ours for too long.

"Don't make me beg," I pleaded, pressing my hips against his. The way our fur rubbed together set my skin tingling as if my body was about to dissolve.

"I need you."

"Someone will find out," the husky cautioned me.

"I don't care."

I was desperate, and for once I wanted to live without worrying about the consequences of loving him. My body wanted to rebel against the indignity of it—why should it matter if we were gay? It had no effect on how well I wielded a sword.

"I don't care!" I affirmed my vow with a growl, inhaling his scent. "In life we hid it. I can't spend eternity hiding it too."

Aelfrith sighed, slowly wagging his curly tail.

"Shouldn't I savour this one time I'll get to hear the great wielder of war-rods whimper?" He always enjoyed teasing me with kennings, short riddles, but clearly I'd put him off his game.

"War-rod?" I giggled. It wasn't his finest at all. "Surely that silver tongue of yours can do better?" He ignored me, growling needfully as he unbelted my trousers. My pointed tip greeted him, sliding out slick from my sheath, while my knot continued to swell inside.

"Let me make up for the poor wordplay." The husky grinned, licking his lips. He pinned me down in the snow, massaging my knot with a paw while he flicked his tongue over my sensitive tip.

"Was this always what you meant when you said you were good with your tongue?" I shivered as he took my head in his warm, wet muzzle.

Gods, why had I missed out on this?

I gasped, begging him for relief. Aelfrith paused, slowly releasing me from his muzzle. Gingerly, I reached down and pulled my swollen knot free from my sheath, panting as I tried to steady myself.

"Perhaps I should let you set the pace?" Aelfrith teased and got down onto all fours, his tail barely inches from my muzzle, wagging gently.

I couldn't hold back. He smelt better than ever this close. And when my nose touched his ring? I lapped away at his tail-hole hungrily while he quivered and whimpered at the touch. Every taste stoked greater desire inside me.

"Come on!" Aelfrith huffed impatiently. He looked over his shoulder, a sense of urgency in his golden eyes. He needed this as much as I did.

I whimpered, forgetting what to say as I entered him.

He was tight. Slick. Warm. I slid deeper into him. He twitched and squeezed around me. I ground my teeth and held him as if he were part of me, savouring the completeness of our bond.

"Aelfrith!" I whined, resting my hips against him for the first time. The pleasure was too much for me. I pulled back and thrust against him with growing desperation.

My instincts took over, scrambling my senses. His tight ring squeezed down on me. My knot throbbed desperately; the pleasure doubling. I thrust my hips, eager to tie him.

Instead I climaxed, collapsing onto his back. My legs wobbled as we held each other. I wanted to bathe in the after-glow and let him feel my breath warm his neck, but my senses began to return, dragging back my old fears with a vengeance.

We'd been missing from the hall for too long.

I pulled out, tail and ears drooping. The fleeting nature of the moment we'd stolen only filled me with greater remorse.

"I'm sorry," I said. Aelfrith bristled, but I went on. "We can't risk being found tied." But even as I apologised, my mind was racing, trying to figure out how we could indulge this forbidden pleasure in secret. "We can sneak out again." I panted. "Meet here every night…"

The husky twitched as if I'd stuck him with a pin.

"You said you didn't care!" he snapped, pulling his curly tail back against him. His scent changed too, becoming sharp and acidic, his anger clear. "Stop hiding the truth about us."

"And what, suddenly all the grizzled warriors wish us well on our honeymoon?" I scoffed, focusing on brushing my fur so it didn't look like I'd just rolled out of bed with him.

"How do you know that for sure?" Aelfrith snapped, shaking his head. "I love you, but by the gods, didn't I just teach you that when it comes to love you can't be a coward?"

I let him stride across the field, his curly tail bobbing indignantly behind him while my seed leaked from his hole. Even when he was angry he was still unreasonably cute.

As usual he came out from our argument on top.

———

I returned to the mead hall after the evening's feasting had reached its climax. Snoring wolves lay spread-eagled across the benches, fur covered in crumbs and muzzles sticky with honey. Broad-chested horses clattered their hooves as they struggled to stay upright, and delicate felines mewed indignantly as the world spun, trying to make sure they would at least fall on their feet.

They were all too drunk to notice me or the scent that lingered on my body. One quick wash and no one would ever know. We'd not be thrown out of Valhalla, and then I'd figure out how to patch things up with Aelfrith.

I dodged between the tables and the beginnings of a brawl, skipping towards the door just on the far side of the hall. Despite the size of Valhalla, to get anywhere I just thought about where to go, and *poof*! A bit of simple magic made the hot springs appear behind the next door I opened. Convenient for traffic, convenient for my indiscretion…

I wagged my tail in relief as the cool night greeted me. The steaming pools never featured in the festivities. They lay at the bottom of a steep trail, and despite boasting a magical view of the auroras, it was considered too much of an unmanly activity for any self-respecting warrior to be seen here. I still quickened my pace down the steps, pausing only to strip once the wafting clouds of steam concealed me. Tossing my tunic and sword-belt aside, I skipped down the final couple of steps, claws clacking against the stone.

"That's another evening of feasting and drinking you've missed!" A pair of blue eyes pierced the clouds, followed swiftly by a slender muzzle and perfectly white fur.

I yelped, fanning my tail around my sheath and clutching the bushy tip tighter than a sword. It was Skade, the valkyrie who brought both of us to Valhalla. She laughed, dipping her shoulders back into the water, the strong tang of the mead on her breath.

CrapFuck! What was she doing here?

"You know mortals can't drink like you," I replied, trying to distract her and prevent her smelling the scent on me.

"I know!" She grinned, tying back her long white hair. "I drank the whole hall under the table. Just wait 'till I start training tomorrow! Heads will be ringing!"

My ears throbbed at the thought.

"Sounds like I made the right decision," I muttered.

"Oh? What's more important than feasting with your comrades?" she asked, ears twitching. "You need to do it if you want to get stronger."

"Practicing my swordplay," I gulped. "And now I'd quite like a bath."

She paused, running an eye up and down me.

"You know, earlier I had Erik and Magnus duel for the pleasure of joining me?" She blew me a kiss, giggling as she tried to splash me, but I was too far away for her to hit me.

"Skade, I'm really not interested." I ground my teeth.

Gods, why did she have to be here?

She cocked her head to the side, scratching her chin.

"Fine." She swam to the opposite side of the pool and dropped the act. "You could knock some sense into the other recruits though." She fetched her mead horn and took a deep slurp.

"Particularly Erik and Magnus?"

"Especially," she groaned.

I half-listened as she vented, paying more attention to the now slippery steps, thanks to her splashing. I kept my tail tucked between my legs, hoping it would catch the scent, but it made it hard to keep my balance.

"Anyway, who was it you were training with?" Skade cooed, fiddling with her mane as she waited for me. "Let me guess!" She paused and shoved her muzzle deep inside her drinking horn, mead sloshing about inside as she gulped away.

"Aelfrith!" She belched.

"No!" I snapped, waving my arms about as I tried to keep my balance.

"Yeah right," she snorted. "He barely eats or drinks because he wants to keep his figure, and no other sparring partner would leave you without some blood and bruises…"

"We were working on our footwork!" I shot back, picking up the pace as I skipped down the final couple of steps, tail still curled-

My paw slipped.

I tumbled into the water, sending a plume of water up into the air. When I surfaced I was greeted with a very wet, and unimpressed, wolf.

"Stick to playing with sheaths rather than swords," she grumbled.

It was over. They'd throw me out-

"Oh come on," she sniffed, taking another drink. "It's obvious you love him."

"I do not!"

"I brought the two of you here." She sighed and waded over to me to squeeze my paw tightly. "Of course I knew. Lovers always die together on the battlefield."

My shoulders drooped. "Please! Don't say anything! I don't want to go to Niflheim! I'm still a great warrior!"

"Ugh! Snap out of this!" She chided me. "Warriors don't grovel or apologise, they act! Like I care if you prefer to bury your bone in curly-tailed boys," she teased, flicking me with a drop of water. "If I had a knot, I would."

I tried my best to give Skade one of her icy stares in return, but she just laughed, the silver beads tied into her mane clacking together. "Relax. I'm not going to throw you out."

Easier said than done.

"But if the others find out, the entire hall will mock me." I replied.

She shrugged.

"I can only speak for myself," she admitted, stepping out the water. She shook the water off her back and groomed her fur with her claws. "You're not the only one who comes here to wash away a scent or two. If some blockhead makes it a big deal? I'd punch his lights out until he's learnt the lesson."

"I can't beat up everyone, and Aelfrith can't even beat up one guy!" I complained. He was just too soft in some places, too thin in others. He wasn't a warrior and that was the problem. How could I even begin to hope they'd accept *us* when he could barely wield a sword? He didn't have the victories, the fame, to command respect.

Skade rolled her eyes.

"Fine, keep fucking in secret until Ragnarok."

"No!" I hissed.

"Then earn their respect. Fight for it," she said, as if it was that simple.

"Who? Fight you?"

She snorted.

"As if you'd win." She smirked. "Warriors are simple. They only respect strength. You should know this!"

"We shouldn't have to fight for acceptance! We should be able to love each other!" I wasn't arguing anymore, just repeating Aelfrith's arguments back to her because deep down, I believed them.

"True. But on the other paw, we shouldn't have to prepare for Ragnarok," she shrugged. "But if you want to win fame for the both of you…" She lowered her tone. "There's a creature roaming the halls each night. It stole one of the gods' enchanted arm-rings, and spitefully goes about eating the new warriors who haven't built up their strength from the feasting. We haven't managed to catch it yet because of the treasure's power, and upon our honour we dare not tell the gods of our lapse in security. The shame would be great. Deal with the problem and I'm sure you'll both be famous enough that even Odin wouldn't care whose scent you rub into your fur."

With that, she gave my ear a supportive lick, threw on a tunic and strode up the weathered steps, leaving me alone. I stayed in the water and watched the stars, stewing in my own thoughts.

―――――

As we waited the shadows grew.

The great hearth in the centre of the hall glowered among the ashes like a sleeping dragon, while the shadows leapt large about the hall, getting up to all sorts of mischief as the fire drifted off to sleep.

Finally the hall was plunged into darkness. Aelfrith's fur bristled beside me, speaking his thoughts. *I can't believe I let you talk me into this.* Even his curly tail was straight as a bolt.

I was glad he'd come. His presence gave me courage and eased any doubt about the plan; we'd kill the monster and then be respected enough to survive coming out. But also, and I dared not say it, the beast would likely go for Aelfrith anyway. He barely ate anything.

Nothing stirred in the darkness. Every now and then a couple of mice scurried about underneath the benches, squeaking as they devoured the crumbs. I focused on that, wondering how on earth they managed to get here, whether they were heroic warriors among their people. Whether any of them were gay.

But what if we can't kill it? What if they don't accept us? What if Aelfrith got hurt?

My tail twitched behind me, trying to balance my body as

my mind raced ahead. The husky grabbed it, halting my runaway thoughts.

It was here, an obscure cluster in the dark. It grew as it approached, snuffling the empty benches, shuffling across the floor. It prowled about, offended by the fine cuts of meat, ignoring the half-eaten plates and golden cups of mead.

It plodded closer, sniffing loudly, licking cheeks of warriors so drunk they were out cold, trying to find the tastiest, freshest meat.

Aelfrith huddled close to me, both of us feigning a deep sleep as it caught our scent. Fear kept my ears from twitching at each step. Its hot breath hovered above my face. My husky squeezed my arm—

I struck.

The monster shrieked but the blade bounced off its hide. I struck again, a sure thrust straight at the chest, but the blade shattered into a thousand glittering pieces.

It threw itself at me and flattened me against the floor. The force cracked the painted tiles and knocked out my breath. I held its jaws open, desperately trying to push it back as it thrashed and gnashed them. Muscles strained and sinew cracked as we fought, and each frantic breath I took was filled with its rotten breath.

"Aelfrith!" I screamed, panting. I couldn't hold it back for long. "Help me!"

I couldn't see—couldn't hear him doing *anything*. Where was the sound of his sword swinging through the air?

"Almost!" he grunted, slurring his words with a snarl as he spoke. "Almost!" He grunted as he heaved. Then there was the clatter of claws and armour as he tumbled across the hall.

My heart sank.

"Got it!" He held in his fist a rune-etched band of gold, glowing with power. Somehow, he'd pulled it free of the monster.

I was such an idiot. How could I have forgotten about that?

I didn't have time to chide myself. Instantly the beast weakened, wailing like a limb had been ripped off. It lurched toward my lover with those crooked, cruel fangs, desperate to reclaim its power.

I threw myself at the beast, arms fastening around its neck. I bellowed in its ear as I tightened my grip, strangling the life out of it. It wheezed and spluttered, trying to throw me off. But I needed to defend my mate.

The hall had now awoken to the struggle, swarming the rows and rows of overturned mead-benches about us as the warriors gathered to cheer us on.

I couldn't hear them. My blood roared in my ears. The beast's efforts became frantic, panicked, erratic, until it gurgled one final breath and tumbled down onto the floor.

When I came to my senses the cheer was deafening.

I broke into a nervous laugh, then a confident one. Elation rose in my chest, and I felt giddy with the praise. Lions roared. Dogs barked. Austere wolves howled, bulky horses nickered and stomped their hooves, while slinky felines purred in muted approval.

"What a fight!"

"Bare paws alone!"

We'd done it! We were heroes!

I searched for Aelfrith, but couldn't find him as the crowd swelled about me. He must have been swept up by the crowd too, but as I called out his name I realised what the hall was shouting…

"Athelstan! Athelstan!"

They were only cheering my name. They'd forgotten him even though he was crucial to the victory. As the crowd lifted me up I caught sight of his curly tail slipping out the door. I struggled free of the crowd, ignoring their dismay as I chased after him.

———

I tracked Aelfrith to our sparring spot. This time things felt cold. It wasn't the snow but the taut way he held himself, his fur bristling like needles.

"At least you remembered me." He huffed, folding his arms.

"I came as quickly as I could."

"Of course." He snorted. His words smelt acidic. He held the armband in his paws, turning it over and over.

"I tried to tell them," I began, but I let my voice die as Aelfrith clenched his fists. A vein on his forehead throbbed, prominent even under his fur.

"Tried to tell them?" His chest heaved, rising and falling heavier than after the fight. He stalked right up to me, his muzzle an inch from my own. "You said nothing!"

I twitched as he sunk his sharp words into my heart. He was right. I'd kept making excuses for myself, that we needed standing, renown, and fame before we could come out. But my belief in the currency of heroic culture was just a way to delay the moment I'd have to risk it all for love.

Aelfrith continued his assault.

"You asked me to make a sacrifice so we wouldn't have to hide, but I'd already made one for *you*." He shook his shoulders as if limbering up for a fight.

"I could have left you on that battlefield," he continued. "I was a skald, not a huskarl. No oath that compelled me to fight. I could have continued my life, wandering wherever the coin led." He paused, taking a deep breath. "Instead I held your paws around your sword so you'd make it to Valhalla. When the enemy struck me down I held on. I held onto you until I could see the valkyries coming, not because I sought a place in Valhalla, but because I'd bound my heart to the only wolf that mattered."

We were in love.

"What would you have me do?" I pleaded, "take you back into the hall, hold you in my arms and kiss you in front of everyone?"

"Compared to risking our lives to save the valkyries' tails? Of course it'd be *actual* bravery!" he shouted back.

"I did my best!" I snarled. Now he was being unfair. The words echoed around us, mocking me. "We have to get them on our side, remember? We have to earn their respect *their way* before they'll even consider seeing things *our way*!" My voice was breaking.

Gods, I knew hiding our love hurt, but why did he have to be so unfair? This wasn't like in life. He couldn't pack up his things and go tell tales at another hall. For once in his vagrant, oathless life, he was bound to something, just like I was. We didn't exist in isolation.

"If we never proved our honour, they'd just cast us out! Would you rather spend eternity freezing your tail off in Niflheim?"

"They're never going to accept us! Haven't you learned anything?" He hissed, baring his teeth. "The evening before we died, you could have come to my bed. You could have got a taste of what our life could have been—I'd even have let you knot my tail," he snapped. "Instead you chose not to because you were afraid they'd smell my scent on you when we were in the shieldwall, because you believed there was no other way to live other than that stupid warrior's life of yours. You made us live a shadow of our lives. I won't do the same in the afterlife!" He spat.

"Aelfrith! Please, just—"

"You wasted that night. That life. *Our* life," he shook his head. "You're not going to change."

"Please! You don't mean that—"

Gods, am I crying?

"As far as I'm concerned, I wish I had told Skade to send me to Niflheim!" At the final word there was a thunderclap.

The runes on the arm-ring flashed brightly, but it was the tears that blinded me. I rubbed them and tried to wipe them away with my paws, but they were clumsy things, better suited to hacking at things with a sword than delicate work.

Aelfrith was gone.

I called his name, whining and lashing my tail. But he'd left no footprints, no scent to follow.

———

Skade found me kneeling in the snow, longing for it to cover me.

"Seems you two really went at this session." She sniffed, knowing better than to ask if I was hurt.

"You should have never brought us here," I sobbed, giving in to self-pity.

Skade growled, grabbing me by the scruff of my neck. I'd never seen her so livid. Her fur flushed crimson even through her snowy fur, and her eyes were sharp with anger.

She disagreed.

"You think an army of hot-headed mead-brains will be enough when Ragnarok comes?" she snapped. "You think Odin plucked out his eye because he thought it would make him look like some tough guy?" She scoffed and held my muzzle shut. "I took him to Valhalla because unlike half the blockheads here, he wouldn't charge straight into a shieldwall. He'd have the sense to go around it!"

She let go of me, rolling her eyes as her words did little to console me. She softened her tone, that fierce warrior becoming convincingly maternal.

"I watched you fight the beast. You both performed admirably."

"Then why did everyone ignore Aelfrith?"

Skade didn't directly answer. Instead she pulled me close, trying to instil some of her will into me as she hugged me.

"I told you, they're blockheads. You'd have to shove their muzzles in the truth to make them understand what he did," she sighed. "Let's go clear this whole mess up."

"You know where he is?"

Skade rolled her eyes.

"Do you really need to be told where he's gone?"

I winced—I knew the answer. I really was a blockhead too.

———

Niflheim.

The last place a warrior wanted to be. It was the resting place for those who died unworthy deaths: sickness, old age, or simply a death without a sword in your paw.

It was cold. Unbelievably cold. Cold like the Fimbulwinter would be; when the snow would come in all directions and swallow the world.

It was silent too, without colour. A bleak winter's day stretched on without end, under a pale sun too weak to burn through the thick mist. Unused to the utter silence, my ears rang. Every breath seemed loud, and every footstep that cracked the ice felt like disturbing a funeral.

Up ahead a mead-hall loomed out from the mist. As Skade guided me towards it, the building grew. No light came from it. No song spilled out into the wastes, nor was there the heartening sound of merriment. Instead sadness clung to it; ice spiralled down from the gables in intricate patterns, sealing decaying woodwork and tattered paint.

"A word of advice." Skade stiffened next to me. "Hel doesn't take kindly to valkyries. She thinks we cheat the system by choosing just about anyone for Valhalla…"

I raised an eyebrow.

"Of course, she's wrong!" She blushed. "Don't mention I helped you. Or look at her bad side. Just remember, Hel wasn't given a glamorous lot and she came out best from the rest of Loki's brood."

I raised my other eyebrow, but she refused to elaborate.

"Hey!" she hissed. "I'm the one who's risking my tail to fix your screw-up!" With that she gave a friendly shove towards the open doors.

The scene inside wasn't welcoming, but a pale imitation of Valhalla. Row after row of empty benches stretched out under the squat, cave-like ceiling. Frozen spreads of ancient food furnished the tables, closeted by bare walls hung with lightless torches. When I stepped inside the gloom shifted, revealing pale, translucent bodies that sat motionlessly at the benches. As I crept down the hall they remained still, as if the slightest breeze would blow them away.

A stern voice rang out ahead of me.

"You can start with an apology for disturbing the mirth of my hall." Hel lounged across a gilded throne of silver, curling a finger through her mane as she spoke. One side of her radiated divinity, a greater beauty than even Skade. But the other? Misshapen, rotten, skeletal. Barely lupine, barely living, let alone divine.

A bad side indeed.

"You're so inconsiderate with your footsteps, and so loud with your infernal breathing," she snapped her bad half, while her good side rolled its eye.

I knelt on the floor, flicked my tail back and folded my ears, trying to placate her while remembering Skade's advice. How could I have screwed this up so quickly?

"I can't believe you fell for that!" she whooped, the sound echoing throughout the hall as both her sides laughed in unison. "Family trait," she sighed, resuming a quiet tone as she gazed across the hall. "I don't get to laugh often down here. They couldn't even hear the clash of battle when Ragnarok comes, my poor, forgotten souls."

"What have you done to them?"

"Everything I can," she said, bristling at the accusation. "When the Aesir don't want you, there's not much you can do," she muttered, clearly speaking from experience. "I don't have the power to comfort them, but I'm the only one who loves them." She sighed, her dead half drooping.

"That's not true," I replied, risking her anger. "I love someone here more than you ever could." I didn't know what else to say really. I wasn't the great speaker; I didn't have Aelfrith's power to make others see things his way. So buried my pride and spoke honestly.

Hel cocked her head to the side, sniffing loudly, snout twitching, rotten flesh squelching as she cast for a scent. When she got it from me, she grinned.

"Yes yes, I know him," she smiled at me. "But don't blame me, lover boy. I was simply doing my job. I don't make the rules."

"He doesn't belong here!" I growled, baring my fangs at the goddess.

"Excuse you," she huffed. I bit my lip and folded my ears, but that was as much an apology I was willing to give.

"It's not every day someone makes the choice to come here themselves."

Aelfrith stepped out from behind her throne. He looked cold, austere, serene. There was none of the life I knew in his eyes, none of the warmth that animated him, or that smile of his whenever he saw me… But even so, without a coat of mail or sword weighing him down, he looked free.

"He told me all the details of the story. Four paws on one blade?" Hel shook her head. "I love a bit of creative accounting, but if I don't stomp my paw down on it I'll be all on my own down here."

"Let him go! You don't even quibble when old wolves with all their teeth fallen out make it to Valhalla by barely touching a sword!" I retorted, but despite my pleas I understood. He was the only reason I wasn't here. He died to save me from this place. No wonder he was angry with me. No one could know of his heroism, that he died rescuing his lover from this misery if I refused to speak the truth about us.

Hel stood up, her rotten half leaving a trail of sticky black residue on the throne.

Had I pushed her too far?

"Sounds like you've been speaking to one of those damn valkyries!" She snapped, forking her half dead tongue between her teeth as her dark side took over. "No wonder you know the rules so well."

"He's here by accident!" I shouted.

"He's here because he wants to be!" She snapped, the skeletal half of her muzzle clicking together with each word. "I know all about the cruelty of your gods, the cruelty that forces you to be brainless fodder, training forever for their war! I've given him peace, which is more than your love can claim to have given him!"

I bit my lip. I felt the fight slipping from me. It was another argument, another tongue lashing that I lacked the tools to counter.

Screw it. At least no one in Valhalla would hear this...

"I hurt him." I called out. "That's why he's here! I should have just swallowed my pride and told everyone that I loved him. Instead I risked our lives because I thought the glory would make them accept our love. But I didn't have the courage to say it, when he'd saved my life for a second time," I stumbled. "I'm sorry, but coming out is the scariest foe I've ever had to face." I hoped that poor reflection of the husky I loved could hear me.

Aelfrith's icy spectre softened, his ears drooping as his eyes met mine.

"Why couldn't you just have said that in the first place?" he said. "Why does it take so much to make you see it?"

"Finally!" Hel groaned. "I thought he was never going to fall for it!"

I ignored the goddess and rushed towards him, fervently declaring my undying love and affection for him while Hel stamped her feet, sighed, and waited.

"Fine," She harrumphed, grumbling about how no one acknowledged how well she tricked me. "You can both go. But I want fair compensation for helping out with your mess!" she snapped. "I'm not here to mediate for any more lovers' tiffs."

I nodded, eagerly accepting her terms. I offered Hel my sword, my fine set of armour, but she rejected all of them with a laugh.

"What about that runed band you carry on you? It has power. I could use it to make this place less miserable!" Hel clapped, both sides of her bristling with joy.

Aelfrith however, looked dismayed.

"That's the only thing I have to prove my heroism to the others."

"You've got me." I kissed him, promising him that this time, I'd do things his way.

I'll admit it. I felt the nerves grow as we left Niflheim. I felt them as Skade carried us back to Valhalla, where behind the gates lay a sea of glittering mail.

Suddenly I felt at peace. I had sworn an oath to Aelfrith that I would proclaim him as my love, and keeping my oath was what a huskarl did. I didn't quite understand it, but I felt the two antagonistic parts of my life had found peace.

I kept hold of his paw as we entered the hall. We were both unfamiliar with the feasting and drinking, but as we entered there was a roar. Fists banged on tables. Hooves clattered on the floor. And then they all fell silent, waiting for the tale to be told.

I took in a deep breath, thinking how to say it. I guessed there never was going to be a perfect way to do this.

So I kissed him like I'd never get the chance again.

Perhaps there was silence. I couldn't hear over the rush of

blood in my ears, the thud of my heart. Yet somewhere I heard Skade cheer, leading a growing applause.

"You idiot," Aelfrith chided me, breaking into a smile as the tables began to thunder in applause.

Everyone drank a lot of mead that night, enough that us mortals gave Skade a run for her money.

THE DRAGON'S WISDOM

TJ MINDE

"Stop me if it's too much, okay?" the bear said, petting Jamie's hip.

"Just fuck me already, Dawson!" The goat nudged his hips back, pressing his bare rear against the stiff shaft behind him. "We both want this, so let's go."

Dawson nodded. "Alright. But stop me if it's too much." After pressing his lubed thumb to the goat's entrance, Dawson placed his tip against the smaller male's flesh and pushed.

Jamie pulled the pillow tighter to his muzzle as, little by little, the bear split him open. His breath shuddered.

"You doin' okay?" Dawson asked.

The goat nodded and answered, "I'm fine. Keep going."

With half his shaft in Jamie's rear, the bear began to pull back. And, just before slipping out, he pushed in again.

"Ah!" Jamie cried out, clenching around the bear's cock.

Keeping his hips still, Dawson leaned forward. "Do you need me to stop, love?" Jamie grunted a no, but his face was screwed up in discomfort. The bear sighed. "I've seen that look before. It's okay, Jamie. It's not easing taking what I got." He pulled his hips back, sliding out of the smaller male.

As the bear's shaft left him, Jamie let out a breath he'd

been holding. "Dammit. I really want to though," the goat said.

"Hey, hey," Dawson cooed, "I know you do. But, it's not the end of the world. Trust me, I love the," he paused for thought, "skillful way you work what magic you got. Your oral skills are bar none. And your digits play me like a piano." With a smile, Dawson pushed Jamie over and spooned the smaller goat.

"I just want you fill me with your hips," Jamie said.

Dawson reached around to scratch the rough hair against the goat's belly. "Babe, I'm not your ex. I really enjoy all the time we spend together. I'm not gonna leave you just because you can't take my dick this minute."

Jamie sighed in response.

"Hey, none of that now. It's only Friday night and you promised to spend the whole weekend with me." He hugged the goat tighter. "Besides, you get to meet the rest of the table in less than an hour. You excited for the game?"

Jamie cuddled against the bear behind him. "As ready as I can be. I've only played in one game, and that was just a three-month campaign in college. I've never got above seven, so I have no idea how this high level stuff works."

Dawson laughed, hugging the goat. "You'll be fine. I'll be sure of it."

"Well, if the DM says so."

"He does." Dawson kissed the back of Jamie's head. The two snuggled together for a moment, just enjoying each other's company.

After a pleasant bit of silence, Dawson cleared his throat. "I don't think the table would like us to show up naked and smelling of lube."

Jamie smiled again. "Want to grab a shower with me before we go?"

"That's exactly what I was thinking."

"Well, great minds think alike," Jamie said. Dawson

planted another kiss on the goat's forehead before letting him free.

———

The four warriors stood in the middle of the cavern. Behind them was a waterfall splashing into a pool, and on the far side was a hoard of treasure, piled high. And between mountains of loot, set on a pedestal made of a mixture of adamantine minerals, was their prize: a gold chalice studded with emeralds and peridots. But there was one last obstacle in their way.

With a mighty roar, the red dragon breathed out its second breath of fire of the combat. The barbarian and wizard rolled out of the way, dodging the flames, but the paladin couldn't avoid all the damage.

The barbarian called out to the armored warrior, "you alright?"

"I'll be fine, keep fighting!" the paladin shouted.

The barbarian raised his great-axe high and charged with a cry, "take this, foul beast!" and swung his weapon forward…

"That's a nat-twenty," Jamie said with a fist balled up in excitement.

"And the confirmation roll?" Dawson asked.

The goat picked up the die and rolled it a second time. "Seventeen plus," he looked back at his character sheet, "thirteen is thirty."

"Plus one from haste," the rat across the table added.

"Make that thirty-one." Jamie looked over to his boyfriend.

Dawson smiled. "That's a confirmed crit."

The goat tossed a few dice and poked at the calculator on his phone. "That's thirty points of damage."

"Very nice," Jamie exclaimed. "Your great-axe sinks into the dragon's hide and blood seeps from the wound. This creature is not looking good at all. But he's still up."

Paula looked closer at her character sheet. "Oh, sweet, I can actually use this! As an immediate action in response to the confirmed crit, I cast decapitate on Barb the Barbarian."

Dawson looked down behind his screen. "An immediate action? I forgot it was that fast."

"Yup. Want me to show the page to confirm?"

"And possibly stop you from making Jamie's character look more bad ass? Hell no." The bear grinned. "Roll for spell resistance."

She grabbed a spherical die and rolled it. "Twenty-two."

"Nice! It goes through." Dawson rolled a die behind his screen. "And the dragon fails it's fort save."

"Yes! Jamie, roll four more d6s of damage and up your crit multiplier by one."

"Okay," the goat said as he grabbed the extra dice to roll. The whole table was buzzing with excitement as he added the numbers up. "That's another eighteen points of damage; forty-eight points total."

"The hide your great-axe sank into was actually the dragon's neck, and with the addition of Lady Roxanne's spell, your muscles swell and continue to slice straight through. The dragon's head falls to the floor. A breath later, the rest of the creature's corpse follows." The bear smiled wide. "Congratulations. Y'all killed the fearsome dragon of Mount Gorath."

"Are we out of initiative order?" a badger beside Jamie asked.

Dawson nodded. "Yup."

"Then Maldin runs over and grab the chalice."

Paula rolled her eyes. "Of course the rogue runs for the prize."

"Damn right," the badger said back.

"And while he does that," a tiger added, "Ja'kin casts cure serious wounds, just in case we need to fight something else. That breath weapon kept fucking me up."

"That's the life of a walking tin can, Mike," Paula added.

The tiger crossed his arms. "Yeah, yeah."

"As Maldin grabs the chalice," Dawson said, "the cavern you're in begins to rumble."

"Oh shit," Mike and Paula said at the same time.

"And that's where we are going to leave the adventure for tonight."

Everyone groaned and gave their own words of protest.

"Hey, that's all I had prepared for today, sorry."

"You gotta have something else," Paula said.

"Actualy, one last thing: go ahead and level up before the next session." Dawson smiled.

"Might as well get it started now," Paula said and began typing on her phone.

"If folks are gonna level up," the tiger said as he stood from the table, "I'mma grab a beer, anyone else want one?"

Everyone but the badger accepted the offer.

Jamie looked at his sheet. "Hey Dawson, could you to help talk me through some of the options?"

"You just can't wait to get your hands on him, can you?" Paula teased with a smile.

The goat rolled his eyes. "I can wait until we get back to his place for that." He nodded to Dawson. "Besides, I didn't have an opportunity to get all hot and bothered."

"Not enough hot guys in the session?" Mike asked as he placed beer bottles in front of the others.

"Oh no, the dragon was hot enough. I wasn't the right class to try and seduce it."

"There's a reason I didn't let you play a bard," Dawson said with a grin as he moved closer to the goat. "And it let me keep the dragon, so your imagination could run wild and get you worked up."

Jamie crossed his arms with an exaggerated look of shock on his face. "You meant to tease me? That's not nice."

The bear pressed his head to the side of one of Jamie's

horns. "Maybe a little. You'll just have to wait until we get home to find out."

"As long as your pants stay on here," Paula said with her eyes on her character sheet. "I don't know Jamie well enough for that."

Dawson almost spat out his beer. "You mean I can lose my pants, but he can't?

The rat didn't look up from her sheet. "General pantlessness, maybe. In the right situation. Outright orgy? Not yet. Maybe after a few more sessions." She looked up and winked at Jamie.

———

"Glad to know I'm welcome back," Jamie said as they entered Dawson's apartment building

The bear smiled. "I told you they'd like you."

"Well, you know what I didn't like? Intentionally making me squirmy."

Dawson led the way as he climbed the stairs. "I tried to get you off before we left," he said softly, "but you insisted on something else."

"What can I say, I'm a size queen at heart," the goat said as he followed Dawson.

Dawson laughed. "Maybe at heart, but your ass sure isn't." Bright playfulness shone through his voice. "Though not for a lack of trying," he added as he switched keys. The bear opened the door and held it for Jamie. "After you."

The goat walked in with a shake of his head, and Dawson followed.

As the bear locked the deadbolt and took half a step inside, the smaller male pushed him back against the door. Standing on his tip toes, Jamie pulled himself up—and the bear down—with one hand on Dawson's shoulder, passionately pressing his muzzle to his lover's.

While Dawson's ears were up in surprise at first, they relaxed as the goat's free hand explored his body. The bear's paw rested on Jamie's side while his other braced against the door. As their eyes closed, Jamie's hand slid along the bear's soft chest, circling until it found the nipple hiding under the shirt. With a gentle pinching and teasing, Dawson moaned into the kiss and his nipple firmed. Jamie opened his muzzle ever-so-slightly and pressed his tongue to the bear's lips. And with a tighter squeeze of Dawson's nipple, the bear's mouth opened and their tongues danced in passion. As the kiss heated up, Jamie's hand traveled lower, sliding along the soft padding that was the bear's belly.

The goat finally broke the kiss. "Do you know how sexy your body is?" Jamie asked, reaching under his lover's shirt and burying his digits into thick brown fur.

"Honey, you're the sexy one," Dawson replied.

As an answer, the goat's hand traveled lower and found Dawson's trapped erection waiting to greet him. "If you say so," Jamie said, planting another kiss on the bear's muzzle before moving to his knees. He made quick work unbuckling the belt and freeing the bear from his pants. "But your body – and your cock," he added as he pulled down Dawson's boxer briefs, "turn me on so much." He tugged the bear's foreskin back, and the tip shined with arousal. Jamie eyed the bit of pre the formed and licked it clean. "And while my ass might be tight, I know what treats I can get."

The goat ran his tongue around the tip again before wrapping his muzzle around the shaft properly. With a moan of his own, he pushed himself further on Dawson's cock, sliding an inch down, then back up. Little by little, Jamie worked his way further, getting his nose closer to the bear's pelvis.

Dawson's jaw fell slack at the attention he got. His paws wandered to the goat's head and found his horns, just long enough to be more than a pawful. He didn't push or pull, but simply moved with the motion. As his arms got into it, his hips joined in. With each cycle, Dawson got more energetic.

Taking the bear's enthusiasm as encouragement, Jamie worked faster, sliding more of the length into his muzzle. Time and again, strands of fur would tickle his nose, but he was shy of taking the full scent in. He reached his paws around Dawson's warm, thick thighs and roughly squeezed the bear's ass, pulling his hips forward. As his muzzle was filled with thick cock, Jamie's nose was buried in fur.

Before he could enjoy the fullness, the goat's throat protested, gagging around the flesh. With involuntary tears in his eyes, he pulled off and coughed.

"Don't push yourself, honey," Dawson said, letting go of the goat's horns.

Jamie nodded and swallowed. "I know." His gaze was right back on the bear's cock, and he licked the glistening tip in front of him again before stroking the bear's length. "Just a little eager tonight."

"Ya don't say?"

Jamie rested his head against the bear's thigh, staring at Dawson's shaft as he stroked it. "If I can't get you to come in my ass, I want you to come in my muzzle."

Dawson rest his paw on the back of the goat's head and scratched at the rough hair along his neck. "Well, we could get there."

The goat shuttered. "That sounds splendid."

Raising an eyebrow, Dawson looked down Jamie. "What if I said there was something else I wanted to try?"

"What's that?" Jamie asked, looking up at the bear. There was a special shine in his eye that made Dawson grin.

"Something I thought of on the way home."

The goat's hand stopped. "Really now?"

"You think I'd lie?"

Jamie shook his head.

"Okay," Dawson continued. "Then strip and get on the

bed." His tone made it clear it wasn't a suggestion, but the smile on his muzzle brought no malice.

Jamie stripped and made his way to his lover's bed. Hopping from foot to foot, he finally took off his socks and flopped on the bed. "Where do you want me?" he asked, looking to the bear coming through the doorway.

Dawson's eyes wandered over the naked goat—from his slim belly, down towards the firm length between his legs, all the way to his toes. The bear licked his lips as he started taking his own shirt off. "I want you in the middle of the bed, laying back comfortably. Whatever 'comfortably' means to you."

Without a word of reply, Jamie moved two pillows to the top-center of the bed and scooted into position. After he finally laid back, he laced his digits together and rested his hands on his belly. The goat watch Dawson finish stripping and move to the closet.

"So what's this idea you had?" Jamie asked eagerly, staring at the bear's ass.

Dawson didn't reply right away. Instead he remained bent over until he pulled a gym bag out from the back of the closet. With a smile on his muzzle, he walked over and set it beside the bed. "Well, I've found self-guided meditation rather helpful for relaxation and, I'd wanna see if it works for you too."

Jamie raised an eyebrow. "Is that it?"

"No," Dawson chuckled. " I'd walk you through a scene, touching and manipulating you throughout the encounter."

"And that would help me take you?"

"Well, I didn't say I'd only touch you with my paws," Dawson said with a sultry grin.

"Okay," the goat said with apprehension in his voice. "And if I'm not comfortable?"

Dawson nodded and reach down into the bag. "Then you have this," he said as he placed a plastic box in the goat's hand.

Jamie held the item closer to his face. The small, rectangular device had a space just big enough for his thumb. As he dipped in and pressed the surface there, it gave way with a loud, sharp, *click*.

"If you ever feel uncomfortable with the scene—be it the words being used, the suggestions being given, or if I'm too rough in any way—give this a click and I'll stop." As he spoke Dawson began to slide his paw along the goat's thigh. "For this to work, I'd need your full trust, and all in all, you have the final say. You're the one in control."

Dawson continued to stroke the goat's thigh, waiting for Jamie's decision.

Taking a deep breath, Jamie laid his arms at his side, clicker loosely in his left hand. "I trust you."

The bear nodded. "Then let's start. I want you to close your eyes and take a deep breath." Jamie did as he was told. Dawson continued, "keep your eyes closed. All I want you to do right now is focus on my voice. My voice and my paw, here at your thigh. Let all other thoughts drift away.

"As you take your next breath," Dawson continued, "I want you to fill your lungs with all your most recent thoughts, and as you exhale, let them rush out with it. But, in the back of your mind, you know you have your rip cord via the clicker in your paw. Otherwise, your mind should be free of thought."

Dawson guided Jamie through relaxing his body, from head to toe. As he cited each body part, Jamie relaxed further. Feet, legs, chest, arms- with the exclusion of the hand with the clicker - and head.

"And as we breathe out all the tension from our neck and head, we relax even further, ensuring, with your consent, no outside thoughts or feelings will interrupt us. The more you relax, the more you allow my words to become your thoughts.

"As you listen to my voice, imagine yourself walking through a forest. You've heard there is a cave nearby, and deep in that cave is the answer you've been looking for. But what's the question? Of course, it's 'how do I take a big, thick cock up the ass.'" Dawson licked his lips again. As one paw pet Jamie's thigh in a smooth, even pace, his other moved to his own shaft, bringing himself back to full arousal.

"It doesn't take you long to find the cave. You imagine the most erotic scent coming from deep within. Breathe this in deeper and let it push you closer to your heart's desire. The more you inhale this relaxing aroma, the further into hypnosis you go.

"As you peek into the cave," Dawson continued, still petting the goat's thigh, "you see the wide hallway is flanked on either side by torches. There are ten pairs of torches, leading you deep into the cave, and we'll count them down from ten to one as you pass them.

"Ten. The smell of the forest is gone, leaving you with the erotic scent, filling your muzzle, relaxing you further and reminding you there is nothing to worry about. Nine…"

———

As I walk deeper into the cave, I don't hear much of anything. There's a soft crackle of fire, and maybe a drip of something like water in the distance, but nothing else—not even my footsteps. Hell, I feel more like I'm floating along the dirt floor than walking. To be fair, I can't see much either. The cave is pitch black, and though I know I can walk safely, all I can see is the flame from the torches I pass. Pair after pair.

The scent of sulfur and… Dawson's arousal reaches my nose. And deep inside me, this combination makes me squirm, but I don't respond as much as I expect I would. Still, I walked on. I have to find whatever is here that will help me take my bear's cock.

I pass the last set of torches and keep walking in complete darkness. I feel calm and free, but still apprehensive. I'm not tense, but I'm still expecting something.

A bead of light appears at the end of the tunnel. It isn't much, but it's enough to give me a goal. I hurry towards it, feeling its warmth embrace me the closer I get. It's so bright, I can't see past the entrance until I'm break through, into what looks like a massive hall.

Well, maybe not a hall. More like a cavern. And really, it's huge, running fifty feet from left to right and at least one hundred feet back. Over by the wall closest to me are falls splashing into a pool. On the opposite end of the space is a massive pile of treasure and gold.

As I look around, I feel like I've been here before. *The game! This was where the chalice was in the game today. Then that might mean…* I look to the back of the cavern. Near the top of a massive pile of loot is a dais with a chalice on top. *That has to be what I'm looking for. It must contain something that will let me take Dawson's cock.*

I start walking toward to the treasure trove of goodies, planning to climb the pile to get to the chalice. *This feels too easy.* Looking from right to left again, I don't see anything. Moments later I hear a deep growl from above. I look up in time to see a dragon with bright copper scales—not red like we fought earlier—staring down at me. It leaps from the stalactite it clung to, and I fall back just as it hit the ground. The creature stands as tall as any mount. And it's a massive wingspan, rows of teeth and broad chest make him—and I finally see it is definitely male—an imposing creature.

"I assume you are here for treasure, adventurer?" he asks. The words I want to use won't leave my throat, so with a hard swallow, I nod. "Very well," he says with a lilt in his voice. "If it is treasure you seek, you may have it. On the condition that you satisfy my needs first." Before I can question him, the dragon jumps into the air and flies off to the pool.

I scramble to my feet and follow, watching as he lands on all fours and fell on to his side, slamming his tail into a boulder and lazily dusting the remains into the liquid beside him. As he lay there, I caught sight of his belly and my gaze wanders lower. His thick cock, long and curved, rests against his leg, awaiting attention. I get closer and his scent seems familiar, like Dawson's, but still subtly different.

I watch as the dragon's tail sinks into the pool, stirring the contents. The scent of the dragon's arousal mixed with another familiar smell: lube. Whatever that stone was, it created a pool of lubricant.

With a raise of his brow, I am instantly on the ground beside the dragon. I can't explain how it happened, but he looks at me from above. His serpentine neck rolls in anticipation as my head rests on top of his arm. The scaly surface is surprisingly comfortable. As I look down along our bodies, I see the dragon's cock is inches from mine own hard in excitement. His legs stretch further down, and his head over mine, but the middle of our bodies match well.

"Let's start by stretching you out, little goat." the dragon says. The thick base of his tail grazes under my thighs, and I slide my feet back, raising my knees and spreading my rear. "There you go. Already know what to do."

As the tip of the dragon's tail slides between my cheeks, I take a deep breath. And as it starts to enter me, there's very little resistance. What's more unusual is that I don't have the urge to touch myself. All I want is to lay back and let the dragon's tail slide in and out of me—fill me again and again, going deeper each time. A soft moan escapes my muzzle at that thought.

"Look at you getting into this. You must really want the treasure. But if you are to satisfy my needs to get it, you must work your way up to it." His thick, warm cock presses against my hip and I moan again. "But it seems like you're enjoying this well enough, isn't that right?"

I give him the barest of nods.

"Very good, little adventurer. I'm going to roll you over

now. You don't need to think about the action, just go with the flow, alright?"

I nodded again.

With his tail still inside me, the dragon set a clawed foot on my right knee and slid a digit into the bend. Next, in a slow, easy movement, he lifts and pushes me, rotating my hip. My left leg flattens against the ground as my lower half twists. "Keep your breaths even. You'll be fine," the dragon says. "If it's more comfortable, we can move your arm around my neck, if you'd like," he says as he curls a clawed hand around my wrist. The grip is firm and secure, but not tight. And I know if I give the slightest hint, he won't move me. But with my hip as it is, my shoulder's elevated off the ground, leaving my arm limp at an awkward angle. It takes most of my effort to nod my head, and when I do, the dragon lifts my arm, draping it comfortably around his neck.

With my body in place, he slides his tail in deeper than I thought it could and I let out another moan. "I think you're ready for something bigger," the dragon says. I try to look down at his cock again, but I can only see the black tip. "Eager adventurer, aren't you?" The dragon chuckles deep within his chest and the warmth of the fire in there flashes briefly. "No, no. I won't give you that yet."

He raises his head to the treasure pile and whispers something between his teeth. The words aren't comprehensible, but a soft glow of magic is bright in his eyes.

I follow his gaze and from deep within the pile, rises a gold idol. It's bulbous in nature, but not as thick as the dragon's shaft. It has a wide base and, the closer it got, the more I realize it's a golden plug, thicker than any other I'd ever seen in person.

It floats closer to the dragon's muzzle, then changes course, disappearing beyond my hip. Sliding his tail from inside me, the dragon places the new device against my entrance. Slowly, inch by inch, the dragon pushes the plug into me. The material stretches me, not uncomfortably so, but noticeably. Once my insides tense against the material, the dragon slides back, then in again. Little by little, deeper each time. And as the item stretches me more, it pulls further energetic moans from me.

"You're really getting into this. I'm happy to see that," the dragon says. "You're almost there. I know you can do it." The pace of the toy in me slows as the dragon focuses on trying to fit the device in place.

He leans closer. "One last push, little goat," he says into my ear. I feel his hand on my shoulder and another bit of pressure at my rear.

As the implement slips past my ring, I let out a gasp that quickly becomes an elongated moan. While the dragon stops pushing, I can feel the item still inside me, spreading me, exhausting my muscles. And it is erotic. I may not be hard, but I know my shaft is leaking pre and creating a second pool at my side. It's… different to say the least. Not bad— not in the slightest—but certainly a fullness I've never experienced.

With a happy rumble from his throat, the dragon changes his position, running his front claws through the hair on my leg as he taps the base of the plug in my ass. Each pleasant jolt of pressure pushes a new moan of bliss from my muzzle. Without saying a word, he keeps this up. *Growl, scratch, tap. Growl, scratch, tap.*

"I'm going to create fire, then cast a spell. The next scent you smell will help you relax even more, understood?" The dragon's words are a question, but they sound more like a command. Either way, I give the softest of nods.

His head moves to my left and the smallest of flames shoots from his muzzle. The warmth surprisingly doesn't reach me, and the brightness is gone almost as quick as it started. But moments later, an earthy scent reaches me. Smoke and pepper and other notes fill the air, and like the dragon said, I relax further. I take a deep breath in and, as the air escapes my lungs, the plug is removed from my rear.

"There you go. Just like that. Nice and relaxed. I think you're ready for the main event, don't you?" His lower half shifts about and I feel his length press against my entrance, but he waited.

Yes, I really do want this, I think to myself. I try my hardest to nod.

"Then here we go." The dragon presses his hips forward and his tip enters me.

It's slick and my rear doesn't fight like I expect it to. He takes his time as he fills me. At first, the dragon leans over my body with his hips against mine. And little by little he works himself back and forth, slowly getting deeper each time. And what pain there is from being stretched by his dick is lost by the present feeling of fullness —almost like taking a toy that's too big. And it feels wonderful.

The earthy scent of his spell reaches my nose again and between that and the dragon's motions, I can't help but moan. "You liking that, little adventurer?" He waves his arm over me and the scent grows stronger. I try my best to nod as I whimper in pleasure again.

"Then let's get a little closer," he says as he wraps an arm around my shoulder and drapes his body over me. His other hand rests against my thigh and I feel the added weight on my hip and chest. At the same time, I can still breathe easy and he can move his hips.

His grip on my body tightens and the dragon pulls me down while slamming his hips forward, going at a much faster pace. The weight and closeness of his body pressing against me again and again was incredibly erotic on its own. But feeling his cock in me, knowing it was sliding deeper in me and will fill me, that turns me on even more.

My hand over his shoulders tighten in need.

He presses deep into me and made his cock swell, holding

himself in place. He wasn't finished, just pausing. "Remember little goat, if this is too much, you have that spell in your hand. You can escape if you need," he whispers into my ear.

And while I felt the device in my hand, I don't need it. Instead, I turn my head and kiss the side of his muzzle.

His chest and throat rumble in approval. "Then I'll keep going." And when he did, his pace was faster still. The dragon must have paused when he was already getting close. And now he must be even closer. His grip on my hip tightens as he thrusts into me as deep as his cock could go. At the same time, the dragon starts nipping at my neck. The teasing attention is heavenly and another moan escapes my lips. Each time he thrusts in, he pulls my hips and shoulders down while pushing in as deep as he can get.

"I'm close. You ready?"

My tongue lolls out in pleasure. This is what I want. This is what I came looking for.

With a growl from deep in his chest, the dragon shoves one last time, and his cock throbs as it filled me. Each pulse spreading my ass more, adding to that pleasurable pain. We lay together as he emptied his load, filling the deep recesses of my insides.

I close my eyes and enjoyed this feeling of fullness. I haven't finished yet, but I'm certainly aroused.

As the dragon's climax wanes, he rests on top of me. His hurried breath slows little by little, and when it is even again, he sits up and set both hands on my knee. "Now that you've gotten your treasure, let's see if we can get you a proper reward." Keeping himself inside me, the dragon rotates my knee, ending with my legs flanking his hip. I look down at my cock and, as I figured, it isn't hard. But it is sticky with pre and the hair around it and my hips is matted and messy. The dragon set the palm of his hand on my shaft, rubbing and stimulating it. He doesn't use his digits, but the rough flesh is certainly arousing on its own.

As I watch, his eyes glowed bright again and the scent of magic wafts over me. "I want you to get hard, little adventurer. And once you do, I have one last item we can play with." With a wave of his hand, a bronze cylinder with an opening at either end floats over. The dragon guides it into the pool of lubricant and back out. It glistens and the sight urges my cock harder.

"There we go. That's what I wanted to see." Using his claws, the dragon carefully points my tip to the entrance of the cylinder. "I doubt you'll last long after all that stimulation. Don't you agree?"

Without any preamble, the dragon slides the device around my cock and down my shaft. When it reaches the base, a jolt of pleasure ran through my body as my tip pokes out the other side.

"Maybe I need to get a longer one," the dragon muttered. "Oh well, that's a problem for another time." He makes his cock swell in me again and I give another moan. He watches as a bead of pre forms at my tip. "My, my! You must be very excited." With a comfortable grip around the sleeve, he pulls it halfway off, then slides it all the way back down. Again and again, sending pulses of pleasure through my body. "Come on, little adventurer. You got filled with thick cock, now show me the mess you can make." While my body feels heavy, I started to rock. Just slightly, squirming in pleasure.

"I can tell you're on the edge. Come for me."

And that's the last command I need. I wrench my eyes shut and my breath hitches, but a long moan still escapes. I heard the dragon chuckle as my rear tightens around his member, and he starts thrusting again. The pitch of my moan rose and, a second later, the first shot of seed burst from the opening of the toy. The dragon keeps stroking, but times it with the pulses of my cock and ass in order to milk me for all I'm worth. Shot after shot splatters my chest and belly, as well as the surrounding floor.

"There you go. That's what we wanted to see. Just like that," the dragon coo'ed.

As the last of the seed dribbles down the outside of the sleeve, I let out a long sigh.

"Very good, little adventurer. Now that you have your treasure," he swells his cock one last time, still hard enough to keep it in, "and you've gotten your reward," he then slides the sleeve off my cock, making my body shudder and protest at the stimulation, "it's time to wake up on the count of five. One… remember the lesson you've learned here as you start to gain control of your body again…

———

"Five. Eyes open and wide awake. One, two, three, four, five. Eyes open and wide awake," Dawson counted. When Jamie opened his eyes, he looked around and saw a candle flickering beside the bed. The goat then rolled his shoulders and stretched his arms out. Dawson continued to run his claws along the goat's inner thighs. "You back, honey?"

Jamie nodded. "And did it work like you hoped?"

Dawson nodded and made his shaft swell, still buried in the goat.

"That was you?" Jamie asked, smiling. In response, the bear leaned forward and thrust his hips. Jamie gasped and moaned. "Holy fuck."

"Relaxation is the key. For both of us. It isn't something we can just jump into. At least not yet. But toys helped, too." The bear nodded to the floor beside him. On a towel sat three devices: a thin, long dildo and a thicker butt plug, all slick with lube and one cock sleeve covered in come.

"Well, you were right," Jamie said as he laid back on the bed. "This *was* a fun way to relax. And how many guys can say they were fucked by a dragon?" He winked at his lover.

The bear chuckled. "The funnier thing is that you already

know this lesson. You know you have to go slow when sucking me off. You just have to remember that when we have anal sex, too."

"You're right, you're right." Jamie held up his hands in mock surrender, but the smile on his face told the truth. "I've relearned my lesson."

Maybe we could try again. Without the trance this time? Ensure I understand the ins and outs of how this works?"

Dawson finally pulled out and laid beside the goat. "Well, you aren't going home until late Sunday, so we have plenty of time."

Jamie pulled the bear's arm over him. "I was more hoping in about twenty minutes?"

Dawson laughed. "Then let's not change the sheets yet."

THE JOURNEY

ALKANI

"There it is, friend. Jhalathein," Devon said to his client as he gestured down the hill with a leather-gloved hand. The road on which they stood lead to a city nestled in the rolling hills near the coast. Small, angular fishing boats trolled the waters out in the bay while a triple-masted barque sat docked, sails drawn tight. People of all species wandered the town, looking like ants weaving across the sandstone cobbles of the streets. "Just in time as well. The sunsets are beautiful."

Devon's traveling companion was, like him, a Jubat. His thickly-built, tall companion bore a pale-blonde cheetah pelt which reminded him of his younger brother, Nicholas. The Jubat took a few more steps down the path, inhaling the scents of the sea as the sun cast gold light onto his damaged, blood-stained military officer's uniform.

"Look at that," the Jubat said. "Were the sky a poem, I would think it was written to welcome us." He turned to face Devon, smiling, ears perked, and eyes alight with excitement. "Will you be joining me for a drink and a meal before you depart, friend?"

Devon shook his head. "I cannot. I must return to my

waystation." He shifted his weight from one foot to another, flexing his toe claws and crossing his arms over his chest.

"Is it not dangerous to go alone?" The Jubat stepped closer to Devon, his golden fur and the ocelli on the back of his flattened ears going shades of blue in the shadows of sunset. "You must stay. You can leave in the morning. Please, allow me to entertain you as best as I can."

"Again, I cannot," Devon growled. His tailtip flicked as he forced himself to relax. " I must leave. Immediately."

The Jubat muttered an apology, then gave Devon a curious look. "Would you at least do me the pleasure of seeing your face before we part?"

Devon drew the cloak's hood lower over his face. "I am not a sight to behold, friend. Please, spare me the need to."

"Then your name, at least," The Jubat asked as his tail thrashed behind him.

"It is of little consequence—"

"Then how can I thank you," the Jubat snarled at Devon. "Is my company so loathsome that you would give me no way to repay the debt of kindness I owe?"

Devon, unphased, nodded. "There is a small favor I would ask of you, if you insist on repaying me."

The Jubat straightened up, his hackles lowering while his tail's energetic lashing slowed to a gentle wave. "I would be happy to. Just please let me return your kindness, Warden."

"Pass this message to my brother." Devon reached into a satchel, drew out a thin, cloth-wrapped parcel, and offered it to the Jubat. "Open it when you are safely behind the gates. It will guide you to him."

"Of course," the Jubat said as he tucked the parcel under his arm. He was about to ask another question when a horn blared a single note that echoed into the hills. "What was that?"

"A warning. You must go. The gates will soon close and the watch will not open them until morning." Devon gave the

Jubat a stiff bow from the waist. "Goodbye, friend. Be safe, be well, and may the elements guard your steps."

The Jubat saluted, placing his hands over his heart. "And to you, Warden. I shall deliver your message."

Devon watched as the Jubat hurried down the path past the city gate stones, and vanished from sight. "Elements damn you," Devon spat. He brushed tears away from his eyes. "Why did it have to be you?" He turned and started walking back up the path, sighing.

"Goodbye, Nicky," he muttered, his tail lashing behind him as he stormed off and the horn sounded again. "I hope you choke on that letter."

———

Devon sat at the edge of a scenic horseshoe gorge whose bottom couldn't be seen and whose open side revealed only the shifting, glimmering landscape of the Shift. A waterfall flowed on the other side, its roar subdued by distance.

Devon appreciated the white noise of the waterfall. Most days it was a welcome, calming distraction that took his mind off the day's events. Today, it wasn't, and he found his thoughts going back to his brother, Nicholas, or Nicky, as he used to call him.

Seeing Nicholas off wasn't something Devon had expected. Had he known the call was for his brother, he might've asked Duarcogatl if he could reveal himself to him. In the end, perhaps it was for the best that he maintained secrecy: who knows how Nicholas might have reacted.

While crouched next to the fire, Devon felt the air go still. The fur on the back of his neck stood on end and the faint scent of ozone floated to his nose. He watched as something slithered up from beyond the edge of the cliff.

"Duarcogatl," Devon said as he stood. His tail flicked behind him and his ears twitched.

"You insist on using my full name; I am honored," Duarcogatl said without words as she slithered up from the cliff and directly towards Devon. Her form was that of a massive sand boa as thick as Devon was wide. Brilliant purple pupils glowed like stars set against black sclera. Bright, nebulous blotches peppered her ventral side against a star-speckled void. Her dorsal side was a cool white color that glowed from within, brightening the area without adding light. She glimmered as she moved and the patterns of her scaly skin shifted as if she was a living window into space. *"But why do you insist when you may call me Coga, as a friend would?"*

"Are you a friend right now," Devon asked, crossing his arms. "Why would you have me escort my own brother?"

Duarcogatl froze mid-movement, her tongue rapidly flicking as her lidless eyes dimmed. *"I thought you would be pleased to see your brother one last time. You were worried about him. I thought if you knew his fate…"*

"I—yes. You were not wrong." Devon sighed, coiling his tail around his leg and shaking his head. "I think I would have, had he not gone and done something stupid."

"Which was?"

Devon shook his head. "He joined the Loyalists."

"Ah," Duarcogatl said, flicking her tongue. *"For that I am sorry. An unfortunate turn, but nothing stays the same, especially here in the Shift."*

"No. I suppose it does not."

"Do you know why?"

"No." Devon crouched. Though he was facing Duarcogatl, his gaze was unfocused and distant.

Duarcogatl flicked her tongue in a quick motion, moving her gaze from Devon to the unlit fire. *"Did you need help with the fire?"*

"What? No. Forgive me." Devon snapped his fingers. A small red spark erupted from them and leapt to the kindling.

Red flames danced over the branches and leapt into the sky, burning away the glimmering air.

"So you have learned? Good," Duarcogatl said as she coiled by the fire and let the silence linger between them for a while. *"It was risky, what you did today,"* she finally said. *"Careless. Some might say foolish. Pointless."*

"I know." Devon pulled a strip of jerky and an apple from one of his satchels. "I'm not sorry for what I did. I hope you weren't expecting an apology."

"I was not."

"You're not upset?"

"Concerned for a friend," Duarcogatl said as she looked up at Devon, her head resting on her coils. *"It is hard to tell what is coming sometimes. I do not want to hurt you again."*

"You won't, Coga. I assure you," Devon said. He took a bite from his apple. "Escorting family was something I should have expected. It was bound to happen. It was just another day—"

"But it was not. I can taste your anger, see your sorrow. You need time to grieve, time to think, time to simply be."

Devon scratched behind his ears and leaned back. "It is kind, but I cannot shirk my duty—my responsibility—as a warden."

"Look at it not as shirking. Look at it as time for yourself to rest, explore, do as you please. The Shift can take you anywhere. Maybe you should take advantage of that." Duarcogatl looked up at Devon while her tongue made long, fast flicks at the air.

"But the calls—"

"No," Duarcogatl said as she raised the tip of her rasp-scaled tail and rested it gently on Devon's lips. *"Consider yourself and what you need. Think on it and and let me know later. Please?"*

Devon nodded.

"Good," Duarcogatl said as she let her tail slide back to the ground. *"Would you mind if I stayed in your camp? The fire is warm, the stars are beautiful, and I would like to spend time with you."*

Devon sighed and glanced up at the stars. "Please. I think I could use a friend right now, too."

———

In the morning, Devon woke just as false dawn broke. Determined to try and enjoy the last day of the two-week break Duarcogatl and he agreed to, he ate, packed up camp, and was on the road before the first rays of sunlight crept over the treetops. He enjoyed the brisk hike, taking in the scents and sounds of the forest, refreshed and ready for whatever tomorrow might bring.

Then the call tugged at him with the same force a cruel puppeteer might use when tugging a marionette's strings.

Devon crashed into a tree near the path, catching himself with gloved hands as dizziness overtook him. He lay at the base of the tree, feeling sick as the world spun around. This wasn't a sensation he'd experienced or expected from the call.

Devon shook out his head and groaned as he pushed off the tree. Should he ignore this? Should he just go home? Another warden was covering for him. Duarcogatl wasn't expecting him to check-in until tomorrow. It would be okay, wouldn't it?

The call tugged at him again. Harder. The world spun as the scent of blood flooded his nostrils. As he knelt on the ground, Devon covered his eyes to keep himself from dry heaving. Something felt...

Different. Familiar. Dangerous.

Devon concentrated, focusing on the otherworldly emotional threads that pulled at him through the call. They were fresh, raw, and tender. He strummed them with his will, listening to the ephemeral, haunting sounds they made. Anger. Rage. Fear. Desperation. Longing...

Devon barked, standing as if someone had swung a blade at him, his pupils blown wide, ears flat against his head, and tears coming unbidden to his eyes. His hands were alight as flames danced around them, burning nothing despite bright blue searing heat. Devon felt many things through the call, but he'd not felt anything specifically directed at him before. The flames faded as Devon calmed himself, fearful and worried at the same time. Who was issuing this call?

He grabbed his things and ran in the direction the call beckoned, hoping he could find out. He had to know.

———

The call drew Devon up into the foothills around the base of the Broken Spine Mountains. He'd only been into them once before, when Duarcogatl offered to show him where she'd hatched and spent her youth. He wandered past the fork in the road that lead to the Boundless Edge, a jagged, craggy cliff that spanned for days and whose bottom seemed endless, passed the wardens' waystation further along the road, and finally entered a forest of silver-barked conifers huddled along the western side of the mountains.

The forest was silent aside from the occasional rustle of leaves or bird call. Devon disliked this forest and these mountains: he always felt as if they were changing while he was in them; morphing, twisting, turning him around like a rat in a maze. When asked, Duarcogatl explained it was the Shift playing tricks on his mind. The Shift was unpredictable, ever-changing. It wasn't just because people ended up here, but because it, too, was alive.

The call strengthened as Devon powered his way through the forest. He chided himself as he huffed and puffed up the road. Once he'd spent years in the mountains with his beloved, his "strongheart" as he called him. Maybe, he thought, that was why he'd stayed away from them.

Maybe the memories of a lifetime ago still hurt too much.

The path rose to the top of a plateau which opened onto

an alpine plain dotted with tough shrubs and low trees. Devon stopped and leaned against a tree near the edge of the plain. The call throbbed in his mind while a stitch ached in his side. He took a few minutes to recover and study his surroundings.

Then he saw the overturned wagon.

Devon ran, as the call pounded inside his head. He could see smears of blood, broken crockery, ruined cloth, and the shattered timbers of the Hultaran wagon. The scent of spices and perfumes floated into his nose along with char, blood, and gunpowder. Arrows and buckshot peppered the wagon's remains. The ceorarkra pulling the wagon were gone.

Devon slowed to a walk, then fell to his knees and gasped for breath. His field of view narrowed, slowly but steadily dimming as darkness crept in from the edges of his vision.

"Devon?" A felinoid creature, clothed like a warden, with large ears and a short-striped tail hurried over from behind the wagon. They knelt next to Devon, concern in their brilliant cerulean eyes.

"Felt—call—" Devon said, gasping for air. The felinoid's ears splayed to the side, making her look almost like a child.

"Hold on," the felinoid said. Her eyes glowed brightly as she made a gesture with her hands. Her fur pattern changed, resembling a starry void with splotches of stars and nebulae. The space seemed to fold around her hands as she molded it into a bubble and gently pushed it toward Devon.

Devon gasped, swallowed, then coughed. His vision blossomed, the darkness leaving as his strength returned. The glow from the felinoid's arms faded, and her pelt returned to its previous state.

"Thank you," Devon said as he stood. "Ah—"

"Kei Lakem," she said with a small, patient smile. "And you're welcome. Sorry to be direct, but what are you doing here? Shouldn't you be on your way home?"

"I—wait." Devon's ears flattened and his tail wrapped around his leg. "Have you…"

"Not yet. You arrived right as I was going to take it." Kei blinked, then her ears perked.

"Could I—"

"I—don't think that's a good idea. Might be best if you just sit this one out." Kei gave Devon a nervous chuckle.

Devon felt the call drawing him toward the wagon. He grunted and winced as the dull throb of a headache started to set in. "I don't think you understand—"

Kei shook her head. "I don't think you understand. You're not getting this call. Coga would be furious if she knew you were here."

Devon gulped as the headache intensified. The back of his eyes started to itch. "No." Devon growled as he glared daggers at Kei. "I need to take this call."

Kei shook her head. "Devon, and I say this from a place of caring and love, you—don't—want—this—call."

"Why," Devon asked, his ears splayed as he licked his chops. The itch was turning into a burning fire. "For what reason?"

Kei winced, then shook her head. "You know, I heard this coming. I should have known this would be unavoidable."

"You…heard?" Devon heard a high-pitched ringing. He swallowed again. He couldn't get enough air.

"I'm Leptan. You know?" Kei pointed at her ears. "Oh, right. Not the Leptan people you know. Those were my ancestors. Charming, but not too friendly. Or chatty."

"I still—d-don't see—"

"Ah-pa-pa! Look, the ink's drying on the page and I only have so many words, so let's save it for another time, okay?"

Devon felt as if he was on fire. The ringing in his head was deafening. The headache threatened to tear his skull apart. The sensation, directed at him when he read the call, returned at full force.

Kei's ears splayed. "Devon? Are you—"

"Get out of my way," Devon snarled, as he shoved Kei out

of the way and ran behind the wagon. He paused, looking over the wreckage and debris. He studied the figure lying on the ground—

And froze where he stood.

Tears ran down Devon's cheeks. His face contorted into a mask of grief as he fell to his knees. The figure was, as all the others whom he'd escorted had been, without injury and seemed only to be peacefully sleeping. He reached out to touch the Hultaran's paw-like hands, recoiling when he made contact. He was real. He was here.

"Oh, no. No, no, no. Not like this," Devon muttered as he leaned back and took a shaky, quivering breath. "Oh, shit, elements and spirits, no…"

"For what it's worth," Kei said as she walked over to Devon and put a hand on his shoulder, "Duarcogatl didn't want you to see this."

"She knew?" Devon put his muzzle in his hands as tears welled at the corners of his eyes. "Oh, spirits, she knew."

"Yes. She did." Kei withdrew her hand and sat on one of the shattered timbers on the ground, careful to avoid jagged edges.

"I'm so sorry. I should have listened to you," Devon said. "Oh, why didn't I listen?"

"Because like you said, there was clearly something special about this call," Kei said. "But you still have a decision to make." Kei stood, brushed the detritus from her clothing, and offered Devon a hand up. He took it, sniffling and wiping his face with a kerchief.

"Will you accept the call and escort him to Jhalathein, keeping him ignorant of who and where you are and letting him think that you're part of the Fabric, or," Kei shifted her hand to rest over her heart. "Will you let me take this call for you, and spare yourself the suffering?"

Devon took a deep breath. "I would never forgive myself for knowing I hadn't taken him."

Kei gave Devon a small, sad smile. "I can erase your memory. You'll awaken in your camp ignorant of the fact that you were ever here and that we met."

"How would you do this?" Devon's ears perked and his tail lashed behind him.

"I have my ways, I assure you. It's not painful or harmful." Kei crossed her arms over her chest. "Consider, but don't take too long. I'll be nearby." Kei smiled, then walked off, giving Devon some space.

Devon stood staring at the figure on the ground. Time had been kind to the Hultaran: the fine white fur that chased the edges of his muzzle and eyes complemented the cream-toned fur along his chin, throat, and chest, and contrasted the cinnamon-colored fur covering the rest of his body; he'd managed to keep his saber teeth where others had lost them; his horns, curving back with points forward, were polished and chip-free; his silver mane was beaded, braided, and tied with the red and silver ribbon that he'd loved. He was a sight for sore eyes.

Devon never thought he would see him again, especially not like this. He'd always imagined that after the incident, he'd settled down for good, found someone to make him happy, and had a peaceful life.

Perhaps he had. The question Devon was asking himself was whether he could be trusted to respect the life the Hultaran had possibly led once they'd parted ways, or would his curiosity and impulsiveness be his undoing? Would it be this Hultaran's undoing? Would it hurt either of them to know?

"Kei," Devon said, calling over to her. "I've made my decision."

———

"Thank you for all your help. I'm grateful for it," Devon said.

"Help? I failed." Kei shook her head. "I should be apologizing to you."

"You tried. That deserves my gratitude."

Kei sighed. "If I may, can I give you a piece of advice?"

"I'm all ears."

"As if I've never heard that one before," Kei teased, then sighed again. "Remember that you don't have to do this alone."

Devon chuckled. "I shall remember that."

"Goodbye, Devon. Call for me should you need anything. May your paws lead you down the right path."

With Kei gone, Devon faced the Hultaran laying in the rubble. He steadied himself, cleared his throat, and then spoke.

"Awaken, Lohal, child of Noka and Cin, that I—" Devon stopped as his voice cracked. He cleared his throat, then tried again. "That I may greet you as a friend and companion here at the end of all things."

Devon watched as Lohal stirred. The Hultaran shifted, uneasy, as if experiencing a nightmare. "Devon," he shouted as he bolted upright, eyes wild with fear.

"Easy, friend," Devon said. He felt a stab of sadness at hearing his name. "Easy…"

Lohal drew fast, short breaths. "Where am I? This is not the road to Trrvash."

"Are you Lohal, friend," Devon asked as he stepped forward and offered Lohal a hand and a smile. Lohal gave him a look of confusion and suspicion.

"Who are you," he growled at Devon. "A Loyalist? A vagabond? A deserter?" Lohal stood, bringing himself to his full height. "Have you come to rob me? Answer me!"

"I am a warden passing through these parts. I saw the wreckage of your wagon and came to help." Devon withdrew his hand, using it instead to gesture at the destruction.

"I don't remember wardens on the road to Trrvash."

Lohal narrowed his eyes at Devon. "Have you dispatched my attackers?"

"They have been scattered to the winds. Surely, Aktik's justice shall be swift."

"You know of our spirits," Lohal said, eyes still narrowed as his long, ropy tail whipped behind him. "How is that?"

"Once upon a time, I was welcomed by and walked among your people ." Devon said, smiling. "I was even soul-bound to one."

"Soulbound? You?" Lohal smiled, all teeth and fangs; if Devon hadn't spent a great deal of his life around Hultarans, he might have found it unnerving. "You were fortunate, and I'm sure they were as well." Lohal relaxed, letting his posture curve forward.

"Your face is strange, friend warden," Lohal said. "I can see it, but it feels as if I cannot." Lohal openly stared at Devon, as if it would bring his face into view.

"Truly? Perhaps you were knocked on the head too hard."

Lohal laughed. "You don't know me well yet. You know my name, friend," the Hultaran said, gripping Devon's hand in his own as he looked him over. Devon was loathe to let go, but he did when Lohal narrowed his eyes.

"We should gather what we can and get moving," Devon said, his tail-tip twitching wildly. "I know of a city near here, Jhalathein, where you may find refuge. We can be there in three days. I know safe places we can stay on the journey."

"The name Jhalathein eludes me, but I don't relish camping in the open." Lohal asked as he looked at the debris around him. "Are we not on the road to Trrvash?"

"On an offshoot of it, actually. We should be back on that road soon." Devon sighed, then drew his hood over his face as Lohal stared at him.

"Fine. Are these places safe?"

"Safe enough. Waystations are dry with a warm fire,

serviceable food, and a nice view, if that persuades you." Devon said without missing a beat.

"It does." Lohal, with Devon's help, gathered some supplies from the remains of the wagon. When they were ready, Lohal hefted his pack over his shoulder. "Lead on, Warden."

Lohal and Devon left the wreck and made their way out of the mountains. Though Lohal was courteous, Devon couldn't help but feel as if Lohal was watching him closely. Was his heart ache was giving him away? He tugged the hood of his cloak down a bit further, but it only made him feel more exposed.

———

"How is it again that you knew my name," Lohal asked Devon as they walked. Despite the sun hanging low on the horizon, there was just enough daylight left to make it to the wardens' lodge near the fork in the road.

"I have a great many skills with which to acquire information," Devon replied. Lohal scoffed at him and he smiled. "No, really! To be quite honest, it was a chore to determine yours."

"Truly," Lohal said, doubt tinging his tone as his tufted tail waved behind him.

"Indeed. You spoke it as you were awakening."

"Is that so?" Lohal's tail flicked back and forth.

"It is." Devon gestured to the squat, square building ahead. Its windows were shuttered, but it otherwise looked in good condition.

"Behold," Devon said, jogging towards it. Lohal followed, jogging on two legs then dropping to all fours as his wild sabretoothed ancestors had done.

By the time Lohal reached the door, Devon had already

unlocked it and stepped inside. Lohal followed, brushing the dirt and grass from his hands and paws beforehand.

"Time to banish the darkness," Devon said as he tugged on a pulleyed cord near the door. A cloth blind drew back from a skylight.

The dimming evening light revealed high ceilings with exposed beams. A wide, square, stone hearth sat in the center of the room. There were chairs, a table and benches, some cots and blankets, and cupboards for cooking and dining supplies. While the room had a slight musty smell, the building was in good condition. A door off by the sleeping area led into a private room with a writing desk, a cot, and a small wood-burning stove.

"Ah. A proper lodge," Lohal said as he set his pack and bundle of goods at the foot of a cot.

"Large enough for a warden and their guests," Devon said as he rolled back the last of four blinds. Meanwhile, Lohal busied himself with unshuttering windows. They snuck looks at each other: Devon felt his heart jump into his throat every time he thought he'd had made eye contact with Lohal; a few times, Devon had caught Lohal looking at him, only to turn away when he'd suspected that he'd been seen. Could Lohal know who he was?

After opening the windows, Devon sighed; there was still much to do, even with the help of magic and muscle. Butterflies fluttered in his stomach as he glanced at Lohal one last time. The questions and his uncertainty would have to wait.

———

"Yes, I'm an elementalist of sorts," Devon said as he took a drink from his cup of sour ale. "One of the benefits of being awakened to the elements themselves by one's soulbound."

"So, this flame doesn't consume the wood in the fireplace?" Lohal asked while nursing a jug of stout. Devon was grateful that the food stores were ensorcelled to never run out; if his memory of Lohal was right, he might go through several jugs before being satisfied. He seemed a little tipsy, though; that wasn't like him.

Devon and Lohal sat across from each other at the table. Lohal was in his smallclothes and Devon wore a loose linen tunic and cropped pants. Dirty plates sat in a neat stack, and the leftovers were covered with cheesecloth. A pile of sweet corn cakes lay between jars of honey and persimmon jam.

"Not this one, no," Devon said as he blew on a clawed finger. Its tip burst into a red-colored flame. "I can change how quickly it burns." Devon willed the flames' color to change from red to violet and all the shades in between, letting it turn pale orange as it lingered on his claw.

Lohal took a long pull from his jug, glancing at the little flame on Devon's fingertip. "I was once soulbound," he said as he glanced at the corn cakes. He took one and popped it into his muzzle, chewing it slowly. "I guess I still am. He was a flamebearer, like you."

Devon nodded, smiling to Lohal. "I've known a few. Each seems to embody the element they voice in their own way."

Lohal chuckled. "Indeed, they do."

Devon blew on his claw, extinguishing the flame. "What became of them?"

"He met his end," Lohal said, taking another pull from the jug. He looked at Devon for a moment, then at the plate of corn cakes.

"I'm sorry—"

"It was his choice," Lohal said, gripping the neck of the jug harder. "He did what he felt he had to."

"I'm sure he felt there was no other way—"

"There was another way," Lohal growled, his cup-like ears flattening as he curled his lip. "He just couldn't accept the cost."

"His decision rests not on you—"

"It rests on me!" Lohal snarled. "I could have stopped him. I should have stopped him. I should have jumped right over his head to the warleader."

Devon quietly summoned a mote of flame, shifting its color as it moved between claw tips. Lohal said nothing but quaffed the last of the jug and set it aside.

"Is there more of this," Lohal asked as Devon paused his hand and flame movements. "I think I need some more."

"I would suggest against it: we have an early start tomorrow," Devon said coolly, "but I cannot make that decision for you."

"You learn fast, warden. Besides, the flavor is wonderful, and it doesn't hit me hard. I've missed good stout."

Devon sighed. "Downstairs, through that trapdoor." Devon watched Lohal work his way down the trapdoor and into the root cellar. The portal was just large enough for his bulky frame to fit.

Lohal pushed up bottles of stout, sour ale, and lambic as Devon thought about what Lohal said. In the end, Devon had decided his way was best. Clearly, it wasn't the best for him. He was here, after all.

And if Lohal was killed by Loyalists…

"Will you join me, warden," Lohal said as he set an armful of jugs and bottles on the table. "You have bottles I've not laid hands on for years."

"One more drink. The blueberry lambic, if I may," Devon said. He blew out the little flame on his fingers, quaffed the dregs of his cup, then pushed it forward.

Lohal grinned. "My favorite," he said as he poured some for Devon.

"You don't say," Devon said with a small, knowing smile. He sipped the dark, sour-sweet liquid.

———

"Warden?"

Devon awoke in an instant. By the way the stars lay in the sky outside his window, it was the small hours of the night. Devon rubbed his face and sat up, regretting drinking as much as he did.

"Warden? Wake up," Lohal hollered, slurring his speech. With a sense of concern and no small amount of dread, Devon donned his trousers in the dim starlight, opened the door to his room, and stepped into the main hall.

"Ah, there you are," Lohal said, huffing as he got up. A variety of jugs, jars, and bottles were neatly arrayed on the long table across the main hall. "Join me, Warden. Come. Speak that I might know my enigmatic and gracious host better." Lohal sat on the bench hard enough to make it creak, then took another drink from a clay bottle.

"We've already spoken quite a bit, friend Lohal," Devon offered, hands out and slightly raised as he stepped towards the table. "Surely, some sleep—"

"Slumber is for the weak-willed, friend warden," Lohal bellowed, then laughed. "I shall not sleep, for this place..." Lohal lowered his head and closed his eyes.

"This place?" Devon asked. Lohal started at the question, snorting and shaking his head, his braids jangling and his horns whipping about.

"Tell, me, friend warden," Lohal said with a bit of a growl as he fixed a bleary, blood-shot eye at Devon. "What is your name?"

"It is of little consequence—"

"Oh! So you refuse to share your name then?" Lohal pointed a clawed finger at Devon and stood. "How inhospitable."

"If the scores of bottles I see and me awakening in the middle of the night to check on you aren't hospitable—"

"Then tell me, warden, why can't I see your face, eh?"

Lohal took a long drink from his bottle, liquid spilling out of his maw and onto him and the floor. "Why. Can't. I. See. It?"

"Because—"

"And how, most benevolent and puissant elementalist lord warden, did you know what my favorite meal was—"

"Lohal—"

"And my favorite dessert? Corn cakes common around here? And my favorite beverage?"

"Kind sir—"

"I'll tell you why," Lohal said as he stood to his full height. He crossed his arms in front of him, muscle clearly defined under his short coat of fur. His tail whipped back and forth behind him, its tufted tip beating on the bottles so neatly placed on the table. "Because I'm dead—"

"Please—"

"And this is all a trick! An illusion where I'm tormented by memories of my lover—"

"Lohal, stop! Listen to me—"

"Because I should have stopped him—"

"It wasn't your decision—"

"Don't give me your false platitudes, demon!" Lohal roared and leapt over the table at Devon, who darted out of the way just in time. "I will not listen to the words of my tormentors!"

"Lohal, I am not a demon—"

"Then why do you know so much about me while I know next to nothing about you?" Lohal charged at Devon again. Devon pivoted out of the way. Lohal reached to grab Devon, but missed as the jubat spun away, knocking a jug off the table.

"You said—" Devon said with the large table between him and Lohal.

"You said I spoke my name, demon!" Lohal stalked around the table, growling, claws sheathed. "But I never spoke about my favorites. I never said a thing about my soulbond, yet you speak with Yrrtir the Bright as easily as he did—"

"Surely it is coincidence!"

"No!" Lohal bellowed. "You made me corn cakes. Devon's corn cakes! With just the right amount of cinnamon and nutmeg," Lohal roared. In one swift motion, he was over the table. Bottles and jugs crashed to the ground and against the wall. Before Devon could dart away, Lohal grabbed him in one massive meaty hand, slammed him against the wall, and pinned him against it with his body.

"It is a common recipe," Devon croaked as he gasped for breath. He was about to say something else when he felt cool metal against his throat.

"Give me one good reason to not slit your throat, rip out your stomach, and use it as a wineskin," Lohal growled, muzzle pressed against Devon's face.

Devon could see the moisture marks from tears at the corners of Lohal's eyes, smell the liquor he was sweating and breathing out, and feel the warmth of his body against him. Were he not in so much danger, Devon might be turned on, but he was in a tremendous amount of danger.

"Hurry up or I'll—"

"Because," Devon said, recalling something that both Duarcogatl and Kei had said to him. "Because I promised that I would greet you at the end of all things, though you might not know my face—"

"What?"

"And that as we took our journey together, from one world to the next, you might feel the comfort of a friend, though not know why."

The pressure from the dagger on Devon's throat eased.

"And at the end of the journey, as you passed through the gate, you might look back and recognize me for just a moment, as a reminder, and then the door would close."

The dagger dropped to the floor with a clatter.

"And I would wait to see you again, because—"

"—you chose to." Lohal's bloodshot eyes, clouded by enchantment and lost to a memory, snapped into focus. They locked with Devon's, and Lohal gasped as tears welled at the corners of his eyes. "I can see you," he whispered, choking on the words. As he stepped back and let Devon down, he brought both hands up to Devon's cheeks. "I can see your muzzle."

Devon reached up and thumbed Lohal's cheeks just below his eyes. "Still think I'm a demon?"

"No," Lohal mewled as his eyes drank in Devon.

"And you realize you're dead, right?"

"Yeah."

Devon cocked a brow. "I'm surprised you're not upset by that." He reached up and gently pet on Lohal's cheek. The Hultaran openly wept as he pushed his cheek against Devon's palm.

"No," Lohal said, eyes lidded and suddenly looking very tired. "I've got you, flame blossom. That's all I need." Lohal pressed the top of his head against Devon's and cried.

———

The next morning, Devon woke in Lohal's arms on the floor of the main room. Devon sighed; it had been a long time since he'd had the warmth of anyone against him. As he lay there, his mind wondered what was going to happen next. Lohal was still expected to go to Jhalathein, the City of the End, in two days. Could he stay here?

Assuming that Lohal wanted to stay, of course.

Devon's stomach rumbled as hunger teased at the edge of his gut. After reluctantly freeing himself from Lohal's arms, he started working on breakfast.

"Wake up, strongheart," Devon said sometime later, poking his companion in the back with a toe and setting a plate on the nearest bench. "Breakfast. Come, there is much to do, lodge-wrecker."

Lohal sat up, immediately bringing a hand to the bridge of his muzzle. "Ugh, what did I drink?"

"Everything," Devon said as he set a plate down on the bench for himself and handed Lohal some bread. "Come eat. Eggs, boar, and we still have corn cakes and honey from last night."

"You spoil me," Lohal said as he picked himself up off the floor, grabbed his plate, and sat on the bench. Devon joined him. "I'm sorry for last night."

"You should be. This place is a mess."

Lohal ducked his head, plucked at a large piece of boar meat and tossed it into his muzzle. "I'll make it right."

"We both will. But first, eat. I think you'll find that you feel better." All that Devon got in response was a grunt as Lohal's movements sped up and a shine came back into his eyes.

"Feel better," Devon asked at the end of the meal.

"Yeah. Thanks. How did—"

"I didn't. Remember where you are."

"Right. Not Sorrsh." Lohal said as he stood, stretched, and grabbed his now empty plate. "You know, we should talk."

"We should," Devon said he sopped up some yolk and meat drippings with his bread. "But first, we clean."

———

"This is the place," Devon said as he put his pack down on the ground. The horseshoe gorge greeted them under the light of a waxing crescent moon. The waterfall rumbled across the gorge, and the remains of a campfire from almost two weeks ago lay in its cradle of stone and earth.

"Reminds me of that one place," Lohal offered as he, too,

dropped his pack and supplies on the ground. "The fishing was good there."

"Yes, it was." Devon turned to the extinguished campfire and snapped his fingers. Embers flew to the logs, burning a bright red, then calming as they floated over the wood.

Lohal set up camp while Devon foraged. In no time, bedrolls were laid out to accommodate them sleeping together along with a pot and a large spoon. "I know you said we didn't need to eat, but…"

"It's nice and comforting," Devon replied with a smile. "And I always liked my own cooking."

"I did, too. I missed it so much I used to dream about it." Lohal chuffed at Devon as he drew out cumin, roasted boar, and a bundle full of corn cakes. Devon tipped the boar and cumin into the pot with water and the forage for soup and set the cakes aside. They sat together looking out over the gorge, listening to the waterfall, and looking up at the stars while the soup cooked.

"So," Devon said as he looked over at Lohal.

"We should talk."

"Yes. We should." Devon reached over, placed a hand on Lohal's forearm, and ran his fingers through the short fur. Lohal took a shaky breath.

"I missed you so very much, blossom." Lohal said, his voice cracking. He coughed and cleared his throat.

"And I missed you, strongheart." Devon sniffled and kept running his fingertips through Lohal's fur.

"How long have you been waiting for me?" Lohal reached over and gently rubbed on Devon's back through the cloak.

"I—do not know. I've escorted many down these roads." Devon slid his hand over to Lohal's knee, spreading his fingers out like a starburst. "Some dangerous, some pleasant. Mostly confused, or angry, or both."

Lohal grunted and kneaded the back of Devon's neck. "I

sensed something about you when I first awoke," he said as he shifted to face Devon more directly. "A connection?"

"I sensed it in the call, too," Devon said, letting his hand slide from Lohal's thigh to the ground.

"When I awoke, I expected to see you."

"And instead, you saw a stranger whose face was like something out of a dream." Devon reached over and rested his small hand atop Lohal's massive one. "Terrifying?"

"Angering." Lohal grinned. "I wanted to shred you to ribbons."

"Glad you decided against that."

"Me, too," Lohal said, sliding his hand under Devon's cloak and tunic near the shoulders, letting his fingers stroke the warm fur underneath.

"Did you ever couple with anyone else?"

"Yes," Lohal said. "Does that bother you—"

"Lohal, no! Of course not! I was gone. What, did you think I would have you shrivel up and die because I did?"

"More like explode," Lohal grinned. Their laughter echoed into the night, lost in the waterfall's low rumble. "You?"

"Me? No." Devon sighed and shook his head, the mirth fleeing his features. "No. It would have been inappropriate."

"Ever the chaste and virtuous. Pure as the first sprouts of the spring season."

"Yes. Well, not that pure." Devon slid his hand higher up the inside of Lohal's thigh and dug his fingers into his fur. "Or should we put that to the test?"

"Hmm. Let me think about that," Lohal rumbled, looking up and away, "hmming" and "hawing" as he feigned deep, serious thought. "Yes."

Devon smiled as he traced circles with his fingers along Lohal's inner thigh, his touch grazing and teasing the fur. Lohal grinned, leaning on one arm while Devon scooted in and brought his other to tease at the fur on Lohal's cheek.

"Best not tease me," Lohal said, a low rumble in his voice. "I hear teasing cats can be dangerous—"

"Oh, so you're a cat now?"

"Sort of," Lohal replied, sticking his tongue out through his grinning muzzle. "Enough of a cat to make you squeal when you want it."

"I think the only one who might be squealing tonight is you." Devon slid the hand up deeper against the inside of Lohal's thigh. Lohal grunted as the back of Devon's hand grazed his crotch, teasing at his sheath.

"Maybe. I think I deserve it." Lohal gently shifted his hips, pressing his groin against Devon's now wandering hand. Devon was only too happy to oblige as he toyed with Lohal's concealed sex without hesitation, tracing the precipice of his sheath with a finger while using his thumb to gently rub his sac.

Lohal purred and leaned back, spreading his thighs, and Devon scooted closer, running his other hand down Lohal's neck to his chest. Devon worked a hand up past Lohal's small-clothes, teasing through soft fur until he found the sticky mess of the tip of Lohal's sheath.

"Are you enjoying yourself?"

"Oh yes, blossom," Lohal said. He looked at Devon through half-lidded eyes, pupils wide from the stimulation and ears askew. "I have missed your touch so very much."

"Good."

"May I—"

"No, my heart," Devon replied. "Tonight, I want to pleasure you, if I may?"

Lohal gave Devon a curious look, then reached over and rested a hand on Devon's knee. "Always, blossom."

Devon stood, followed by Lohal. They undressed each other, exploring each other as if it were the first time. They spoke with their touch: light and firm; soft caresses and claws gently dragging along flesh; a squeeze, a rub, or a stroke.

Their hands roamed freely as they stood naked to the world together.

When they were satisfied with their exploration, they rolled their clothes into bundles that would serve as pillows. With Lohal's hand in his, Devon guided them to their makeshift bed.

Lohal looked to Devon, who nodded at him, then lay on his belly and tucked his long, ropy tail to the side. His hips were slightly elevated, thanks to the bundles he was laying on, enough that Devon could get at his sheath.

Devon knelt between Lohal's thighs and gently stroked along the back of them with his claws, enjoying Lohal's shivering and purrs. With a snap of his fingers, Devon summoned motes of flame and waved them onto Lohal's body. They traced patterns along his fur and muscles, leaving warmth in their wake. Devon, meanwhile, kneaded his hands in the small of Lohal's back just above his tail, squeezing the base of it. Lohal grunted, squirmed, and curled his toes.

"You torment me, blossom," Lohal purred as he squeezed Devon's waist with his thighs.

"Not enough, I suppose." Devon smiled as he slid his hand in the gap between Lohal's groin and the ground, gripping as much of Lohal as he could. Devon stroked Lohal, teasing some of Lohal's slickness from his tip and spreading it on his shaft.

"Need more lube," Lohal said as he slowed his thrusting.

Devon focused and set his hand aflame, then gripped Lohal's length. The flames flowed like water, leaving warm, oily residue wherever they went. Devon stroked a bit faster. Lohal eagerly thrust into his hand, moaning.

Devon's length eased from his sheath, poking out and forward. A mote of flame traced along it, pulling a soft gasp from his muzzle. He summoned a handful more and directed them to his groin, giving them free reign to go where they pleased.

"Enjoying yourself," Devon asked, squeezing Lohal's length as he stroked.

Lohal grunted, thrusting into Devon's hand. "Think I want something else, though." Lohal turned his head and licked his chops.

"Careful what you wish for," Devon said, directing the flames on his hand to form a ring around Lohal's long, tapered sex. With another gesture, the ring contracted. Lohal moaned.

"Damn that's tight," he said as he thrust again.

Devon chirped and shifted the flames away from his rod, sending them to Lohal's hole instead. The Hultaran moaned and shuddered as they oozed warm oil on him. Devon's length, fully extended, glistened in the light as he rose to his knees and positioned himself behind Lohal.

Devon willed the flames under Lohal's tailhole to his hand and gently teased his partner with his fingers, careful of his claws. Lohal pushed back against him, eager to have him within. Devon's finger slipped into Lohal, followed by a second one not soon after.

"Please, blossom," Lohal begged. He turned his head, panting and whining and pushed his hips back towards Devon.

Devon removed his fingers and shooed the flames away, positioning his sex against Lohal. Gently, Devon pushed into Lohal, causing the Hultaran to moan, both joyous and sorrowful. The fiery ring continued to squeeze against Lohal's own erection, directed by the timing of Devon's thrusts.

Lohal groaned as Devon sped up, Devon's grip guiding both of their thrusts and timing. He felt every one of Devon's thrusts hit home, prodding against his prostate as he pulled in and out. A tightness tingled at the base of his spine and grew as his cock started to tense.

"Devon," Lohal panted. "Slow—down. Gonna—" Lohal groaned as he came, thin, narrow spurts splattering on the blankets and bedroll. His length jumped, smearing seed on his belly, and the knot-like bulb at the base of his length expanded. Lohal pushed his head against his forearms. "Fuck…"

Devon slowed his thrusts and rubbed on Lohal's hips in slow, broad circles. "Strongheart, are you okay—"

"Yeah, just—" Lohal pushed his head against his forearms, panting. "Been a while. That was intense."

"Sorry," Devon said as he started to pull out.

"No! Don't stop. You really think I want you to stop?"

"Lohal?"

"Just." Lohal sighed and looked back at Devon, then grinned. "You know what to do."

Devon smiled at Lohal. He slowly hilted himself into his lover as Lohal watched. They grinned at each other as they started thrusting and pushing in time with each other.

Lohal's length, half-tucked in his sheath, peeked out as Devon thrust into him. By the time Lohal was panting, his length was hard and dripping droplets of precome onto their bed and sprinkling his chest.

Devon grunted, picking up speed. He thrust hard and fast, his hips solidly striking against Lohal's ass with each thrust His cock twitched as Lohal clenched down on him, but it wasn't enough. He slid out and tapped Lohal's back.

"Swap," Devon asked, shivering, his cock rock hard and pulsing in time with his heartbeat.

"Really?" Lohal turned over, his throbbing prick pointing up at the sky.

"Yes. Right now."

"But—" Lohal didn't get to finish the sentence as Devon summoned another round of oily flames to dance along Lohal's length. He shuddered as they faded away, leaving only their oily residue behind.

Devon straddled Lohal's hips, pulling his tail up and resting his hands on his partner's chest. "Oh, ancestors, please let this be enough," Devon muttered as he started to lower himself down onto Lohal's lap.

With Lohal's help, Devon lowered himself onto his lover's sizeable prick. He gasped when he felt his hole press against Lohal's tip. Devon focused for a moment and summoned flames to leave their oil on them. With a grunt, Devon shoved his hand behind him and impatiently fingered his eager hole." Let me," Lohal offered, gently pushing Devon's hand out of the way and using his fingers to smear the oil onto and into Devon. The jubat moaned as Lohal pushed against, then into him with a thick finger. Devon pushed his hips against Lohal's fingers, eager for him, and Lohal obliged with a second finger.

"Easy, blossom," Lohal said as he adjusted. "Ready?"

Without a word, Devon lowered himself onto Lohal, slow and steady. He winced, then paused for a moment. "Fuck, were you always so big?"

"Yes."

"How in all the hells did I take you before?"

"Patience. And a lot of lube."

Devon sat with his head pushed up against Lohal's chest as he panted. Lohal leaned over and groomed the back of Devon's neck, purring at Devon in encouragement.

Devon squirmed, trying to get a few more inches of Lohal into him before stopping. Seated on his length, Lohal gently gripped Devon with his other hand, helping hold him up.

Comfortable with things, Devon slowly pushed himself down on Lohal's rod, eliciting a hiss from the hultaran. Up and down Devon went trying to keep balance while Lohal provided the supporting grip. Soon enough, Devon was taking more of Lohal's rod, pulling and tugging along his length with each stroke, and Lohal pulled his hands back, letting Devon take control.

Devon's slow pace built. Faster and faster he moved his hips. Lohal joined him, trying to time his moves to his partner: with each dip, a thrust; with each gentle gyration, a counter.

"Blossom, are you..." Lohal asked, panting and huffing.

"Almost..." Devon shuddered, then barked as come erupted from his cock, smearing on Lohal's chest and abdomen. Spent, he panted and rested his head against Lohal's chest with his partner still inside him.

"Did you—"

"No. and I—already did—once tonight."

"I thought—you said—you had another..."

Lohal grinned, "Do you really want to finish me off?"

"Yes."

Without waiting, Lohal grasped Devon's waist and started thrusting in to him. Devon shivered and squirmed, still sensitive from his own orgasm. It wasn't long before they were both a panting, sweaty mess for the third time that evening.

With one final thrust, Lohal buried his length inside of Devon, crying out as he did so. He felt his knot-like bulb swell, locking him in place as Devon wriggled, trying to make himself comfortable. Lohal gently ran his claws along Devon's spine as the jubat lay against him, a sticky, sweaty mess.

Once Lohal's bulb receded. Devon eased himself off his partner's length and lay face to face with him.

"Did we still want that soup," Devon finally asked as he nuzzled Lohal.

"Not hungry."

"Then we'll leave it for the morning," Devon said. With a thought and a wave of his hand, the campfire doused, the flames faded from view.

Lohal pulled Devon close to him. They both slept soundly that night.

———

Lohal awoke in the pre-dawn morning to birds chirping. Careful not to wake Devon. He rose and padded around the camp, lighting the campfire, setting the soup to reheat, and taking stock.

Once Lohal was finished, he sat at the edge of the gorge and watched the waterfall on the other side. A smile came to his face as he leaned back against an arm, tailtip tapping against the ground all the while.

"May I join you," Devon asked as he sipped water from a skin and ate an apple.

"Always," Lohal said, patting the ground next to him. Devon sat and leaned against him.

"We should talk," Devon said.

"Yeah, we should."

"Last night was—nice. I'm glad we did that." Devon took a bite of his apple and chewed.

"Just nice?" Lohal peered at Devon and smiled.

Devon returned the smile. "Would you want to do it again? I mean, would you want to stay here with me?"

"Can I do that?" Lohal's ears perked.

"I—think so. I don't know. Either way, you only have one more day."

"I do?" Lohal frowned. "How does that work?"

"Something about transitioning from one place to another consuming energy," Devon said, scratching at his neck. "There's only a limited time."

"And—after that?"

Devon shook his head. "You fade from the Fabric."

Lohal's ears lowered, then rose. "Oh. Well, I can visit, right?"

Devon's face fell and his ears flattened against his head.

"What aren't you telling me, blossom?" Lohal stroked on Devon's back as the jubat sighed.

"If you go to Jhalathein, you'll return to the Fabric. You will forget me, the journey…"

Lohal's ears pinned against his head. "Everything since I arrived?"

Devon nodded. "Everything."

Lohal sat, rubbing on Devon's back. He didn't want to forget what he'd just experienced. He'd not had an easy life, but forgetting this journey wasn't an option for him. And he'd found Devon again. The thought of leaving him behind for who knows how long…

"Who would we ask?"

"I—don't know, to be honest. Maybe Duarcogatl—"

"Wait, Duarcogatl is here?" Lohal's eyes widened. He peered around as his tail zipped behind him.

"Yes. I—"

"Why didn't you say anything?" Lohal's ears lowered and he curled his tail on himself.

Devon chuckled. "I speak with her all the time."

"All the time? You. Speak with a god. All the time?"

"I even feed her, sometimes—"

"She eats?" Lohal paused and scratched his head. "Wait, she eats? Like us?"

"There is a lot to talk about, but regardless, I think we could ask Duarcogatl."

"Well, why don't we then?" Lohal stood, stretched and flexed his neck, causing the bones to pop.

"Now?"

"Yeah, now! I only have a day left, and what happens if we need to do something?"

"We're naked and stink of sweat," Devon said, standing with Lohal and looking at him. He picked at a spot of matted fur on Lohal's abdomen. "And sex."

"Okay, so how about this: I make breakfast this time, we get cleaned up, then we ask." Lohal crossed his arms over his chest. "Does that work?"

Devon nodded. "That…works." He smiled, looking at Lohal for a moment. "Are you sure—"

"About what?"

"That you want to stay?" Devon's ears perked and there was a glint in his eye.

"Blossom, you jest! Of course I want to stay," Lohal crowed as he wandered over to the pot of warming soup and stirred it. "But for now, less chit-chat and more work! Go bathe!"

───────

"Are you ready?"

"As ready as I suppose I can be," Lohal said. He was dressed in breeches, and boots that left his toes open to the air. A short leather vest adorned his chest and a faded crimson mantle covered his shoulders and upper arms. He carried with him a quarterstaff scrawled with elaborate patterns. "Does this really suit me?"

"It does," Devon said, circling Lohal. He poked at Lohal's exposed abdomen, then rubbed the fur. "The view is quite nice."

"You always liked it when I wore this," Lohal rumbled, smiling. "Shall we?"

They left the southern waystation and headed south along the road to Jhalathein. The sky was cloudy, but the day was bright and a breeze on the wind helped keep them both cool.

"Are you nervous?"

"Yes," Lohal said, grumbling. His long, ropy tail bounced behind him. "Were you when you answered your first call?"

"Oh, yes," Devon said. "You never get used to it, you know. But you do get better at it."

"I'm glad you're by my side, blossom," Lohal said, casting a glance at Devon. "I wouldn't want to do this alone."

Devon slowed his walk, then stopped.

"Devon?"

"You know, a few weeks ago, I never thought I would see

you again. I thought this would be what I did for was left of my existence. Alone."

"Devon—"

"And now," Devon continued with a bit of a chuckle, "you're here. You're really here. Somehow you found me, or I found you. We found each other."

Lohal's tail was still as he walked over.

"And I'm grateful to the spirits and the elements and the ancestors," Devon said as the words tumbled out of his muzzle and his calm, cool composure shattered. "But I keep wondering if…"

Lohal wrapped his arms around Devon, and Devon pushed his forehead against Lohal's exposed chest as he wept.

"I keep wondering if this is a dream."

"If it is, we're sharing it," Lohal said as he rubbed Devon's back. "We're in it together."

"Together," Devon said as he leaned against Lohal.

"For however long it lasts," Lohal said as he leaned down and nosed at Devon's head.

"Yes," Devon said with a chuckle as he sniffled, coughed, then let Lohal go. "I love you, strongheart."

"And I love you, flameblossom," Lohal said with a smile. "We still have a bit of of a walk ahead of us. Shall we?"

And they both journeyed south along the road to Jhalathein, leaving laughter in their wake.

TALES OF A QUIXOTIC KOBOLD

MIRIAM CAMIO CURZON

Long-Tail slept curled around a large dire wolf despite the unseasonably warm temperatures. Beside the pair lay a set of leather armor piled haphazardly in the grass which left the kobold in nothing but his smallclothes. The dire wolf was a large mass of dark gray fur, offsetting the wiry golden-brown kobold. Long-Tail's broad muzzle was curled and moved in his sleep. Rust-colored eyelids twitched. He was dreaming; spittle dripped down Hanor's flank.

Hanor huffed, already awake, the large beast's breath blew up a mini whirlwind of dust. "Master," he growled, "Wake up before you make a mess of my fur."

Long-Tail only snorted and pressed his snout deeper into Hanor's fur. "Five more minutes." The still unconscious kobold's words were muffled. He grabbed a fist of fur and ground his body tighter to the warm softness. His hips shifted and the tented loincloth rubbed against the wolf's chest.

Hanor raised his head and kicked his hindquarters, slamming the kobold face first into the dirt. "Master, please," he whined, rising to all fours, "Keep yourself sheathed."

"Hanor? Where's Patron Tiar?" Long-Tail rubbed at his eyes with a jaw-cracking yawn. His long tongue flicked over his nose brushing the dirt away. Looking around, his eyes grew wide and shoulders slumped as his hands flopped to the ground at the sight of their campsite in the middle of nowhere. "This isn't home! And that bleeding sun is still stuck there."

"Home is still a fair way off." Hanor's tail swayed, eyes pointing away from the rise between Long-Tail's legs.

Long-Tail noted the signs of Hanor's agitation. "What's wrong?"

"Are you not going to apologize for humping my leg like a… like a common town dog?" If dire wolves could blush, Long-Tail was sure Hanor would be blushing.

"Would you be so lucky to have the one favored above all by the illustrious Tiar favor you in such away!" Long-Tail gesticulated wildly at himself, attempting to appear as heroic a small kobold could in only undergarments with an erection. "I was dreaming of the rewards and favors to be showered upon me when I return to the divine Tiar with my mission complete."

"I don't really think they sent you out only to bring back news of the end of the world. The sun never setting nor truly rising tends to herald apocalyptic catastrophe."

"But now we know it's magical and not natural. After all, the temperature cannot remain constant, nor the sun and moon fixed in place on the horizon. That's something!" Long-Tail pulled on his over-linens with his chest puffed out. He clearly accomplished the task Tiar presented to him. The riding leathers were tight and took some pulling and squeezing to get on.

"You really should treat your gifts with more care."

Long-Tail finished buckling the leather armor pads around this arms and torso. He buckled his long, slim sword to his left hip. Lastly, he swung a small rucksack on to his back. It was light. He only ever traveled with dried meat and water canteens. After all, he was a prince among kobolds, and kobolds were the most ingenious travelers. Or so he always thought. "Finished." The kobold was breathing hard from the exertion of dressing, his forehead clammy. "Now, which way?"

"Mas—"

"Purely rhetorical, Hanor, I assure you! Of course, I know my way back to Tiar. Like I could ever be lost with their pure heart shining on the horizon!" A chuckle with the air of nervousness followed is haughty speech. "We just follow the setting sun."

"But was the sun rising or setting when it got stuck like that?"

"Kobold ingenuity. I can always tell. And you call yourself a wolf, for shame."

Hanor growled in response but remained silent as Long-Tail pulled himself up onto wolf's back.

———

Long-Tail slid off Hanor's back with a groan. His butt hurt and he was certain his tail was bruised. In between the pair and the frozen sun was one of the largest settlements he'd ever seen. "What? What is this Hanor?" The kobold fell to his knees.

"That is a settlement."

"I know that, but what is it doing there?"

"Looks like nothing. Being a settlement."

"But it shouldn't be there…"

"From the looks of it, it's been there a long time. If you carried maps with you, maybe—"

"Kobolds don't need maps," Long-Tail interrupted.

"Just admit you're lost, Master."

The kobold sputtered. "Just because this settlement popped out of nowhere doesn't mean we're lost."

"Correct. I'm not lost."

"We'll just go through the settlement. It's their fault for

getting in our way." Long-Tail's eyes narrowed, and he stood claws balled into fists.

At his words Hanor bowed his head and his ears flattened. "We'll be caught." But Long-Tail was already barreling forward towards the settlement. "Wait, Master. You'll get us killed."

Long-Tail patted Hanor's side. "I'm touched that you are so willing to sacrifice yourself for me. Tiar will certainly reward you in the after-plane." The kobold strode, snout up, knees high, as though he hadn't a care in the world. Hanor bounded after, head bowed and tail between his legs, whining.

Fortunately, when Long-Tail pushed his way through an outer fence, all seemed quiet. Given that the day-night cycle ceased to function, it could be any hour of the day. Or night, for that matter. Long-Tail grinned wide, his long lizard tongue flickering out between his sharp teeth. The settlement was sleeping. He immediately slunk to his best creep.

Looking back at Hanor, he put one claw up to his muzzle. His grin was still plastered there: a silent declaration of his ineffability to his faithless companion.

They crept side by side through wagon-hewn streets. The extreme angle of the sun left plenty of long shadows, but also plenty of spots of bright exposure. It was like creeping around at night except with a bunch of lamps focused in single areas. Long-Tail certainly played up the danger Hanor felt. After all, he was brave and reckless hero crossing deep through monstrous territories. If they were caught, they would be roasted alive.

So serious the pair was they didn't notice how dry and cracked the ruts in the road were. Or how uncharacteristically quiet the whole settlement was. They paused in the shadow of a tall brick house. Long-Tail crouched low holding an arm out to stop Hanor. The center of the settlement lay exposed before then. It was a large rectangular quadrangle with a three-tier fountain in the center. Obviously, it wasn't running as even Long-Tail whose eyes weren't as keen as Hanor's noted there was no sign of flowing water.

"We should make for the shadow of the fountain," Long-Tail declared. His legs wobbled ever so lightly.

Hanor's ears were on detection duty. "I hear nothing Master."

Long-Tail inched forward, coaxing Hanor along with the arm he'd been holding the wolf back with. They made it about halfway to the fountain with ever-careful step. Crashing glass echoed through the plaza and Long-Tail yelped his way into a sprint on all fours.

Ducking behind the carved limestone fountain, he marveled at the craftsmanship as he labored to catch his breath. Hanor came crawling on his belly in the shadows.

"This must be a grand settlement for them to have such an extravagant fountain." Long-Tail patted the stone. "Of course, not as good as ours, but still superb craftsmanship."

"Not now, Master," the dire wolf whimpered.

Glass crunched somewhere out of sight and Long-Tail dove for comfort, wrapping arms and legs around Hanor. "I don't want to get roasted," he cried into the wolf's fur. Even Hanor quivered slightly beneath the embrace.

Silence followed the breaking and cracking of glass. There were no voices, no alarms, no torches or pitchforks. Long-Tail sniffled and peeked out from Hanor's gray fur. The settlement remained deserted, even after the sounds of burglary in process.

"Master!" Hanor exclaimed, "Tell me you did not soil yourself in fear."

There was a distinctive smell to the air. Long-Tail only just noticed. "How could you accuse me of such indignity!"

The pair crept up out of the shadows. The smell seemed to emanate from around them, particularly from the fountain. It smelled of refuse and rotten eggs. Despite the beauty of the white limestone carved fountain the water was murky and warm. Long-Tail's eyes fluttered at the waves of heat coming from the fountain. "It's warm," he said, sticking a claw in the water.

"Master, I don't hear anything. This settlement is empty. I can't smell anything other than the—" As Hanor spoke Long-Tail was unbuckling his armor and scrambling up the side of the fountain. "Master! We're out in the open! There might be someone watching."

Long-Tail shrugged, siding off until only his smallclothes remained. "Don't care." He jumped in. The splash wasn't large but did spray Hanor with foul smelling sulfurous water.

"Master..." Hanor shook his fur out with a quiet, exasperated growl.

The wolf looked around as Long-Tail paddled about the small fountain base.

"Look!" Hanor pointed to a wooden sign swinging from a storefront on the far end of the plaza. "If you want a bath go take one properly."

Long-Tail launched out of the fountain and sprinted down the cobblestone dropping his remaining clothes along the way. He marched naked right into the door, which was locked. Telling a kobold a door was locked was futile, because a kobold would find their way through even the strongest of locks given enough time. All it took Long-Tail was putting a claw into the lock and whispering a simple incantation. There really was no reason for a bathhouse to have high security.

The building was wood and lacked the same polish as the fountain. Long-Tail saw nothing worth stealing, not even door handles. All that mattered to him was the rows of barrel basins hopefully filled with water. Reaching one of the bathing rooms, Long-Tail nearly tripped over a pile of discarded white towels. Steam wafted up into little light let in through the second floor-high windows. The sulfuric smell was stronger in here, mixed with iron and minerals, and mildew from the abandoned towels left in the humid room.

Many of the barrels were low on water, but there was one in the corner that was still receiving a steady stream of water from a pipe that had been left open. That whoever lived here had left the settlement seemingly overnight did not concern Long-Tail. The kobold's mind was fixed on one thing and that was scrabbling up the side of the one barrel. His claws scratched into the wood and then he tumbled in with a satisfying splash.

Long-Tail closed his eyes and just floated. His butt, sore and tired from riding, began to tingle, eliciting a moan. There'd been no rest since he'd set out on his journey to discover the truth of the suspended planetary cycle. Never before had he the chance to bathe in one of these constructed bathhouses. Always cold rivers or rare hot springs, never one of these cushy indoor places. Empty as it was, he could just relax and let his senses drift. No need to watch for hunters or other predators.

Water trickled peacefully into the tub and Long-Tail wished he could be there forever. All he'd need is to convince Tiar to leave the mountain and take over this abandoned settlement. That was the dream. He rubbed his stomach, through the mix of fine scales and fur. It'd been awhile since he'd had what he'd call a fitting meal, but his stomach was warm. Blood moved through his veins more freely. His tail floated languidly beneath him, helped to keep him floating near the surface.

Parts he hadn't consciously felt in weeks awoke. Particularly at the thought of Tiar's pearlescent scales that radiated rainbows in the lunar light. It wouldn't hurt to, he reasoned as he stroked lower on his belly. His mind didn't go to some graphic fantasy as he wrapped his hand around it. He focused on praise as he started to stroke. It's what he lived for.

His legs stretched, causing bones to pop. Rust scales bobbed to the surface of the bath. The mottled brown tip appeared as foreskin drew back, breaching the rippling surface

MIRIAM CAMIO CURZON

as Long-Tail's cock hardened in his grasp. It was longer than it was wide, a fair match to the grip on his sword. This was all horribly self-indulgent of him, he knew, to perform such a flippant and scurrilous act while in service to Tiar. But the praise he'd receive upon his return…

He stroked faster. Water began to splash in the barrel more violently. His toes stretched apart, and he rocked against the wall on his horns. There was no need for rhythm, not that he could stop his hips from thrusting.

From Tiar's slender, perfect muzzle they'll whisper in his ear how well he accomplished his mission. Only he could've done it. His heart beat faster, his breathing grew erratic. There was no other kobold as perfect as he. Long-Tail bent forward, using his tail to balance and legs to brace. His muzzle neared the part of his erection that poked through the water. As he grew closer, his pace slowed, and his tongue flicked out across his tip.

"Master? Master Long-Tail?" Hanor called out of the blue.

Long-Tail jolted in the tub, sending his horns crashing backward into the wood. Through his quickened breath he called back, "What is it?"

"I've collected your things and piled them *neatly* outside the door."

"What, is that all?" At least even if Hanor entered the extremely humid space he wouldn't be tall enough to have immediate view on him. So, he kept stroking himself, although more subdued and stealthily.

"Yes, Master. I've seen no hide nor hair of anyone. Shall I widen my patrol?"

"That's a good idea." Long-Tail grunted, using both hands for stimulation this time. "Whatever you think is best. I may be awhile." He heard claws scraping against wood heading away from him.

Long-Tail stretched and flexed his shoulders as he sank

back into the job at claw. Something was bothering him. His erection was doing just fine,, but rather than pleasure he felt uneasy. With all the steam and sulfurous fumes, he didn't have much luck with his senses and ears were simply unreliable.

Better to ignore it he figured. After all the settlement was deserted. So, he closed his eyes, focused his mind, and imagined the celebration Tiar will throw for him on his return. There will be much ale and fresh meat. His shaft jerked in this two-handed grip that covered it completely.

"Oh, illustrious Tiar," he moaned as his hips quivered. Glass crunched again, and he yelped and jumped from the bath. Someone was spying on him! "I am ashamed at you Hanor! Sneaking around and spying." He inched his way to the entrance, darting between basins and barrels, clutching his dignity. "If you want to watch, just ask!"

There was no response, as though the dire wolf was not there. But he was sure. And he was always right. He slipped into his clothes, hissing as he forced his slender erection into the tight leather. Obviously, normal leathers could not accommodate such a glorious kobold specimen. Drawing steel, he pushed out into the courtyard.

The courtyard was as deserted as before, but Long-Tail didn't trust the silence. Hiding in the shadows of the open door, he surveyed high and low. There were no wolves or enemies to find. Across the way, on the opposite side of the fountain was another grand building with tall columns. Fear forgotten the kobold felt the call for treasure. Such grandeur could only mean hidden wealth. Maybe it's where the thing called a king lived, but obviously the entire village had fled in terror when they saw him and Hanor approaching.

With steel drawn, Long-Tail charged through the courtyard. Better safe than sorry. Anyone left would be running scared anyway. The door was already cracked when he arrive and he slammed forward, sending the oak door swinging open to neatly rest against the inner wall. Whoever had lived here had left in a rash, destructive hurry, he assumed, stepping through splintered furniture. He flicked his tongue out but sensed nothing except dust and sand. The walls were comprised of large sand colored bricks. Nothing too interesting. These monster humanoid settlements were boring. Aside from the baths. And beds. And shiny jewels. But from room to room, he found nothing of value. No food, no baths, no beds, and nothing particularly shining. Guess that meant no king lived here. Even the torture utensils they ate with were made of wood. Dull, dull, dull. "Rawrhg!" Long-Tail roared his displeasure. They should've left spoils for their kobold conquerer.

Long-Tail approach a spiral staircase leading up and down. Still believing spoils were to be had he flicked his tongue at either option. Certainly, the bedroom would be below ground where it is safest. He kept his own small horde in his room. But there was a thing called a vault. Could the vault be with the dungeon which is obviously upstairs? Closing his eyes, he clutched a rainbow jeweled amulet under his shirt. "Illustrious Tiar, may you guide your greatest devotee." He took a step up. Of course! Had he only thought logically, if he were to flee, not that he would ever have cause to take such a cowardly action, he'd grab from his horde first. So any left over spoils would be in this inconveniently located vault. Tiar was a genius and he was a genius for trusting Tiar.

Stairs were a curse of the devil. They were unnaturally tall steps designed for horrible monsters. Nevertheless, Long-Tail huffed up the stairs to the devious dungeon muttering unfathomable curses at the evil creatures who would ever build such a terrible dungeon. Their poor victims would be forced to march up these same steps. The thought sent shivers through his small horns. He tugged reassuringly on his horns. His knees trembled, making each step closer to the top a Herculean labor.

Fear mounted in the small kobold's chest, but he would

never let that interrupt his ascent. He about cheered when he reached the final step and arrived at the landing. But where were the bars and the torture devices? There was a raggedy rug and large windows letting in the in between morning twilight. There was a dresser against one wall, but its drawers were strewn across the ground. Maybe there was a cage beyond the rectangle of curtains against the far wall.

Long-Tail started skipping towards the moth bitten curtains. He should've paid better attention to his footing, though. Halfway there he stumbled and his right foot caught in a loose floorboard. As he spilled on to his hands and knees and his sword skittered across the floor he only thought of one possible explanation. Treasure. Once recovered, he rapidly set to ripping open the boards around the hole he'd made until it was large enough to stick his head in. It was dark, but his vision was keenest in the darkness.

At first all he saw were cobwebs and the beams supporting the floor. Most of it was varying shades of gray-brown with little distinction between shapes. On closer inspection he saw a leather pouch tacked to a beam. Pulling his head out he reached his arm deep inside until his claws brushed the pouch and then yanked. The pouch tore as he retrieved it for his inspection. It was well-worn leather, the kind that screams long forgotten. Like many things forgotten, the inside was empty except for fine silver dust. Long-Tail leapt up and poured the fine powder into one hand, raising it close to his eyes where it glittered in the permanently fading light. He had a vial for this very purpose.

"Master!" Hanor barked from down the stairs, jolting Long-Tail from his delicate task of securing his new treasure. In a moment the dire wolf bounded through the opening by the stairs.

Long-Tail kept his back to Hanor, hunched over as he poured the last specks into the glass vial trying not to think of how naturally Hanor had ascended the cursed stairs. Any number of terrible catastrophes could've befallen the dire wolf if he'd only stopped to think. But thinking was his job, so he couldn't fault Hanor for behaving like a wild beast.

"Master, you shouldn't wander off on your own in weird settlements."

Fixing the vial in a protective pouch, Long-Tail retrieved and sheathed his sword. "There is nothing to fear here. They've all fled when they heard we were at their gates. They even left behind their valuables to appease us. And look, evidence of their wickedness." He pointed to drawn curtains. "Behind that is their hideous torture machines."

Hanor sniffed the room. "I—I don't think…"

"Behold!" Long-Tail threw back one of the curtains to reveal a large bed. "Why those sneaky… They hid their bed in the dungeon!"

Hanor padded forward and stood beside the kobold. "They don't appear to share your predilection for sleeping below the earth."

"They must truly be monsters. Look at that floor, completely unsafe. That ceiling could fall at a given notice. They might as well be flipping birds roosting at precarious heights in flimsy twigs."

With a sigh, Hanor answered, "I am tired." The dire wolf pulled himself up on to the bed. "Draw the curtain back, at least it'll keep that infernal light at bay."

With no day or night cycle, they'd spent weeks without the comfort of lightless peace. "You're cranky," Long-Tail muttered and tugged on the heavy drapes. They were rough and the color of mud, which irked the kobold. Such tasteless-ness. He couldn't help but consider taking them; they blocked the sun wonderfully, almost as well as a deep cave. Fighting back a yawn, Long-Tail stripped down to his loincloth. Hanor was already snoring in a high-pitched whine, sprawled out across the bed. He flopped beside the wolf and rolled so his head rested on along Hanor's spine and fell asleep.

Once again, Tiar came to him under the guise of his dreams. They loved him best of all, Long-Tail was sure. Why else would they visit him so often, so far from home? Why else would they press against him like they were? He was already responding, rubbing against the deity's warmth, the firmness of their form. Tiar was a god of dreams with how well they danced through his. How far would they take him tonight? Long-Tail groaned and licked along Tiar's shimmering scales but got a mouth full of fur.

Long-Tail hacked and coughed away, sputtering the memory of fur from his tongue. Stupid dog, he thought immediately, but his ears shivered at the low, rumbling growl. Hanor writhed on the bed beside him with his muzzle buried in the bed covers. Clearly, the wolf was in his own dream world. No doubt he was clearly dreaming something horribly inappropriate and impossible. An uncouth wolf like him… He was red in the face, though he wouldn't notice a thing like that. As it was, Long-Tail was pressing down on the rise in his loincloth and biting his lip.

Tiar had left him… *needy*.

Hanor did not appear to be faring much better as he thrust against the bed. His long pink tongue lulled out of his muzzle. The kobold reached out a hand and brushed the start of the wolf's tailbone. Beneath the fur Hanor's muscles spasmed, like his whole body was circulating to his hidden groin. This was new. In all their time together, Long-Tail had never witnessed the wolf in such a virile state. He brushed Hanor's back, and the wolf snarled in response, leaping from his repose.

"Master?!" he huffed.

Long-Tail drew back, masking his alarm with an indignant scowl. "You were going to make a mess of things," he muttered, covering his lap again.

The wolf's erection, deep and red and large bobbed

between Hanor's haunches. It seemed to beat and bob like a heart suspended in the air.

"I-I'm sorry, I couldn't control it! This bed... it smells something fierce."

Long-Tail pressed his nose to the covers where the dire wolf had lain. All he could smell was the permeating arousal of wolf. Even his scent was buried deep behind the odor. Even so, under his leather loincloth his heart fluttered at his scent. Tiar was here in the radiant warmth that even now compelled Long-Tail to lean toward Hanor. "Listen Hanor, Tiar came to me in my dreams so that I may wake as needy as you. As we are both servants of Their divinity, we should share this burden." In the dimness of the sheltered bed, Long-Tail could see the red pink flesh that flared out of the darkness of Hanor's sheath. His was naught but a dagger in comparison, hard but still contained within the protected sheathe of leather.

"You cannot be serious!" Hanor's muzzle contorted in surprise as he sat up. His position caused his erection to bob between his front legs.

"Nonsense." Long-Tail slid onto his side, pushing his hips forward so his bulge was blatant. "As Tiar's servants and adherents we are obliged to follow Their Will. I ask you, why else would Tiar bring me this pleasure two cycles in a row?"

"Because you are a single-minded dunce!" Hanor's eyes narrowed, but his erection persisted.

"You protest, but I know you wish to share my body with Tiar." Long-Tail trailed a claw down the length of body from neck to groin. "This belongs to Tiar but it is clear They wish to share me with you. This is a high honor, no one else has such a privilege." He rolled his claws along the band of his loincloth. There was no way anyone could resist such a sight; he was Master Knight Long-Tail Spitfang.

"You presume to know my desire, master?" Hanor leaned forward.

"Of course. Anyone would with just one look at me." He nodded and closed his eyes, failing to sense the growing aggression in his partner. "I know how you sneak glances while you feign disinterest even while brandishing a mighty spear in my direction." It was so simple, really. Very easy for a kobold with his level of perception and insight. He stretched out onto his back pushing the palms of his feet together and spreading his knees open, a final coup de grace. All his assets were bare and it was simply a matter of seconds before Hanor would realize his pride was beaten by the height of Eros his prime kobold flesh produced.

"Have you ever lain with my kind before?" Hanor asked with a shift in tone Long-Tail could not miss.

"Of course I have! I am a Master Knight." He could taste the shifting scents in the air, even the wolf simply blinking.

"Not slain, but lain, as no knight ever does." Hanor inched forward, despite his bulk he managed without a sound or disturbance. "You have a habit of getting in over your head little Spitfang."

Long-Tail immediately raised himself in his elbows. "Who're you calling little?" His face went straight up into Hanor's chest. The kobold's entire body fit easily underneath the wolf. Any light would've been easily sucked up by the dark fur that filled his vision. Within Hanor's great chest came an earthshaking rumble. A challenge! Their weapons touched, Hanor's tip burning through the leather sheath. This was surely a predicament, snared as he was, encased by large muscle and fur, but he was Long-Tail. He pulled himself up against Hanor's underside with arms and legs until only his tail remained in contact with the bed, parrying the wolf's lance which glanced off along his groin and down between his thighs. He delivered his riposte, but his thrust was dulled by the leather his dagger was still sheathed inside. Dull as it was, it was still of minor effect, drawing shivers from his toes.

Hanor appeared unfazed from Long-Tail's offensive; he

simply sat back on his haunches again as though the kobold was a smock. His red lance now skewered Long-Tail between the kobold's tight asscheeks. This lit a fire under the kobold's tail. He dug his hind claws into Hanor's pelt and raked them across the wolf's thick hide. Hanor grunted and shifted, catching the leather cord around Long-Tail's waist with his hind claws and tearing.

With their movements the garment unraveled easily, leaving the kobold's dagger free to rub and thrust against the wolf's fur. Long-Tail pushed himself away, meeting Hanor's lance with his freed weapon. They locked together in their duel, but the kobold was more dexterous and flexible than the powerful dire wolf. He could grip where Hanor could not, a skill he exploited to lock their weapons together. Their fervent need moistened the exchange like oil. His hands were small, barely able to grasp them together, but it was enough. Hanor was clearly out matched. Long-Tail's tongue flicked out as he concentrated on showing the dire wolf why he was Tiar's favorite.

Hanor was far from done. Given the right preparation any kobold was capable of the move he made, but Long-Tail's focus could not compete with canine flexibility. The wolf's giant head shot between them and wrapped their duel in his large muzzle. It was a particularly effective blow to the kobold who gasped and bit his tongue hard enough to draw blood. Damp drool and smooth teeth brushed his fingers. Were he a kobold of lesser fortitude he would've given up, afraid of losing a finger or two to the dozens of razors delicately wrapped around them both. But Long-Tail was the bravest, so he kept a tight hold on the parts of them that were not buried in the moist furnace. Their dueling pleasures forged together, and Long-Tail started striking hard with his hips. He slid while Hanor was fixed in place, thrusting fast and deep into the opening the wolf left.

Unfortunately for the long-tailed kobold, his stamina was

fading fast and he could feel the energy still surging from Hanor. It'd all been a trap and now he was stuck, locked between a lance and an army of rapiers. Like any good attack, he had to plan his follow through, think ahead, prepare his next moves. Certainly, the hulk of a wolf lacked the foresight of kobolds. He snuck a drool covered claw into his hole, easing his walls open for his defensive retort. Even if he faltered now, he was determined to rise again.

They panted their passions and Long-Tail's groin grew exponentially, unbearably hot. Like with the fire of the forge, his dagger beat along the lance. The harder he struck against Hanor, the more he started to crack from base to tip. The culminating waves of Long-Tail's swift fall spewed forth over Hanor's length and tongue. He fell back, breathless, and the wolf's muzzle retreated. Hanor's lance fell strong on his now soft and wrinkled dagger. But he'd made the preparations to continue unarmed and his efforts were not in vain as his entrance stretched open.

Hanor dropped back to all fours, once again standing over the length of the kobold. The gray fur around his muzzle was wet and streaked with their musk. His breath came in deep, heavy bellows that combined the scents of their combat as an airborne aphrodisiac. Long-Tail clenched around his claws as he angled his hips to disarm the wolf. It was a shift, but violent plunge. He hiked his hips up to accept Hanor in, wrapping his legs up around the wolf's back. Grunting, Hanor sheathed his lance in Long-Tail's waiting trap. Every time he tried to pull out the kobold pulled him back in.

Long-Tail showed his expertise at fighting unarmed, even as he started to rearm himself. He thrust and ground against Hanor. The length of Hanor's spear would only work against the wolf as it was trapped up to the hilt inside Long-Tail. He capitalized on his advantage, constricting himself around the invading pole. Hanor would fall, he would see to that. His rump slapped against the wolf. Each thrust dragged his shaft through hot fur. The hairs grew damp and slick, increasing the ease with which the kobold sliced against the stomach.

Hanor began a whining growl.

"I told you, you were blessed by Tiar with me," Long-Tail grunted beneath Hanor and the kobold consumed the rest of the wolf. The knot squeezed locking the wolf in place. Hanor couldn't withdraw even if he wanted to, now.

With a final cry, the spear of flame erupted its death bellows. Long-Tail gasped triumphant as the wolf violently shot his virility inside. Hanor's chest shuddered in deep, uneven breaths. His fur brushed Long-Tail's horn crown. Long-Tail relaxed, letting his arms and legs drop from around Hanor. His hips were still locked in place, but the kobold did not mind. All he had to do was lay back and relax. "Just don't fall on me," he warned, jabbing the heaving chest above. "Tiar will curse you for your weakness."

Wordlessly, Hanor sunk down onto his side with Long-Tail cradled in placed. The kobold wiggled, drawing resistive groans from him. "Big baby." Long-Tail jabbed Hanor with his reborn erection. Such a weak wolf, to be so tender after one round. With a sigh he wiggled more carefully until he could rotate around. He snuggled his back into Hanor's warm chest and wrapped both hands around his tool. Some final servicing before returning to slumber. Tilting his head, Long-Tail sensed the deep, rhythmic thrum of the wolf's breathing, no doubt already asleep. He noted he'd have to get the wolf some proper endurance training.

Long-Tail closed his eyes and lightly caressed his hard organ. He could take his time, let his thoughts of Tiar guide his hands. Nothing too hard or too fast, make each touch ephemeral like a divine aura wrapped around him. When it was time, Tiar would finish him off.

———

Long-Tail awoke with a start to an empty bed. The sheets were a mess and stunk. His ass and tail were both terribly sore. Sticking his nose out of the curtain he could tell from the path of scent Hanor had left the tower. He collected the sticky remnants of his loincloth and wrapped it around himself. No sense trouncing around naked, but he could at least rinse off before putting clothes back on. He snatched up his belongings and dashed down the stairs, not slowing down until he felt the cold stable earth under his claws.

The air in the plaza was different today. Charting differences in days was impossible, but something felt different the moment Long-Tail entered. Hanor was cleaning himself in the fountain. He would jump into the water and then out, proceeding to attack his fur with his tongue. Forgetting the air of misgiving, Long-Tail strutted the rest of the way to the fountain, plopping the pile of belongings on the ground as carelessly as he could.

"Good morning, Master."

"Is it?" Long-Tail asked, slipping into the shallow pool.

Hanor looked up from his current task of digging his tongue into his sheath. Growling, he answered, "Yes, it is morning because we both just woke up, not because the sun and moon stopped doing their fucking job."

"Testy." Long-Tail clicked his tongue as he rubbed at his scales. The sulfur in the water obscured the finer flavors of the air. "It smells like home, doesn't it?"

"If you have time to daydream about home you have time to start marching toward it." The wolf paused for a moment. "In the right direction this time."

"I only follow the Divine Light of Tiar. In their guidance we follow." Long-Tail stretched his arms out wide in reverence.

"Whatever gets your rocks off," Hanor muttered.

"Didn't They help us both with that?" Long-Tail answered with a wide smile aimed directly at the wolf.

Hanor stood up suddenly. "You do yourself. I'll go somewhere else." Without waiting, he took off at a swift trot away
from the plaza.

"Grumpy grumpy..." Long-Tail lay back until he was
totally submerged in the fountain. He scrubbed his muzzle
and then focused on his rear and leather loincloth, both
covered with copious amounts of crusted cum.

"Who's'at? You know we'nt s'pposed to swim in 'da foun-
t'n," came a voice from high above him. "I'll tell them you
were doing something naughty."

Long-Tail yelped and flailed, plunging down to the smooth
tile the bottom. Water sprayed from his nostrils when he resur-
faced. "Wh—who is there?" He tried to hide the quaver in his
voice.

"I'm Kim," the voice answered, still somewhere above,
probably on one of the surround roofs. "What's your name?"

"I am Master Knight Long-Tail Spitfang, servant of the
Divine Tiar."

"You a monster, ent' ya'? But a small one. Otherwise you
wouldn't fit in our fountains, or our beds, or our baths."

Long-Tail giggled nervously, still unable to spot or even
place the voice. Apparently, the settlement wasn't as abandoned as they'd thought. So, he bolted. He snatched his
belongings, juggling his sidesword as he dashed to the nearest
doorway.

"Hey, wait, I've never seen a monster before," the voice
called out as he fled.

In the cover of the alcove he spilled his belongings on the
ground. Hastily he started throwing on clothes, barely
managing to get his limbs in the right holes. He tore his
undershirt on his horns. When his shirt cleared his muzzle,
he was standing snout to snout with a dark-skinned creature
with no fur or scales but wore stained clothes. They didn't
even have horns. Long-Tail gasped. *Human.* He was done for
sure.

"My parents don't like monsters. They were scared of them. But I'm not scared of anything, I'm twelve."

Long-Tail was speechless. He had no idea what to say. Never once had he ever approached a human or been approached by one. What could one say? "H-hhhello," he stammered backing up against the building. "Where is everyone?"

The small human Kim shrugged. "They left. They came back a bit before, but I 'id. They been weirding e'er since the sky broke. 'Pocalypse dis, judgment dat. 'Then they said we 'adda leave. W'enthey came back lookin' for me, but they smelled bad. My parents weren't wif' hem. They didn't wanna go, they scared 'hem fierce."

What little Long-Tail knew about humans was from distant observation. He knew enough to recognize Kim was one of the mini-humans that were never far from other mini-humans or giant-humans. Mini-humans were always pack creatures when he'd seen them. For Kim to be alone, without a pack, he knew this was wrong. He swallowed and moved to speak just as Hanor came rushing in between him and Kim.

"Master!" Hanor growled and bared his teeth, saliva dripped from his teeth.

Kim's wide brown eyes bulged, and they stepped back. The wolf, much larger than the mini-human, stepped forward. Long-Tail recognized the fear. He'd just felt it. Tiar had no kobolds other than him. So, he was the same. "H-hanor... Stop. You don't need to scare them."

"But they'll roast us and skin us," Hanor snapped, side eying his master.

"I..." Kim's lips trembled as they addressed them. "I'm a vegetarian." They started to cry.

Hanor tilted his head. Long-Tail stepped forward, brushing a hand through the wolf's pelt. "It's fine Hanor, they left their pack. Mini-humans never leave their packs."

"I'm not a mini-human, I'm a child," Kim sniffed.

Long-Tail took a step back in surprise. "Child? What's a child? I thought you were human."

"A *human* child."

"Same difference," he muttered. "Anyway, this is my mount, Hanor. Hanor this is the mini-human child Kim." He whirled around and went back to dressing himself. Kim wasn't a threat thus no longer worthy of his attention.

"Where are we going?" Kim asked, pulling Long-Tail's attention. The mini-human child patted Hanor's head and looked at him expectantly. "Long-Tail, where are we going?"

Long-Tail sputtered. A mini-human child was asking where *we* were going. "We aren't going anywhere. I am returning triumphant to Tiar and not getting roasted or skinned."

"But 'dey may come back. They were 'ere earlier, a bunch of 'em with mean spiky swords and... and..." The thing looked like they were about to cry again.

"Absolute forbidden," Hanor barked.

"But I wanna go with you Mister Spitfang. I wanna meet this Tiar thing! 'Sides I dun' wanna stay around with the weird robed fo'k."

A new servant! His eyes brightened. Tiar would be pleased to be brought a new devotee. Then the praise. His tail began to wag slightly at the prospect, just as Hanor's was. The dire wolf had flopped on to his side as Kim attacked him with their claws. Just as he'd seen settlement dogs do from afar. He put on his biggest smile. "Very well, you may accompany us mini-human child Kim, but only if you pledge yourself to the beauteous Tiar and to follow only Their word."

"Ohhhh. Does that mean I don't have to listen to parents or adults?"

"Of course. Tiar is not a parents or adults."

"Don't move! I'll go get my things!" Kim ran off and Long-Tail didn't move a muscle.

———

Among Kim's things was a map. With that map Long-Tail finally figured out where they were and which direction they should move in. They had to keep the moon to the right of their right eye. Because the moon was now a fixed point, they didn't have to correct their direction. It's not like he'd been totally wrong, just a little bit right. He'd gone a little bit north after all, or maybe south. Either way it was a tiny bit in the right direction.

They kept a mini-human child pace. Though, Long-Tail had to admit, Kim had quite the energy, almost on par with a kobold. He rode Hanor, always, it was a matter of rank. As they grew closer to the mountains that were to the left of the moon, he started to recognize the shape of the peaks. They had to forage regularly. While Long-Tail was thankful he didn't have to share his rations, they lost time searching the fields and woods for grains, herbs, and berries. A vegetarian. Really?

The first few rests were ineffective. Kim had too much energy. Long-Tail tried to blindfold them to calm them down, but it just took a few marches with no sleep to wear them down. Then he tried the blindfold and stuffed socks in his ears. When Kim did sleep, they only managed a few hours before waking up screaming. Long-Tail wondered about this oddity of human sleeping patterns, but apparently they regularly slept high above the ground. Who was he to question this practice in particular?

Since they didn't travel by road, or at least human road, they didn't really see anyone. He was hardly surprised, with the world as big as it is and in its current state. In the wilderness there was nothing to keep proper track of time. So, there was no reason to expect that they'd run into anything. That's what he told himself at least. As they neared the mountains, they entered the outskirts of an alpine forest. Tiar loved spruce tips. Kim needed to forage for some food as well. Whole they hadn't covered as much ground as he'd have liked, Long-Tail decided it was worth stopping and foraging.

"But I wanna meet Tiar," Kim protested.

The sound of Kim's dedication sent his pulse racing in ecstasy. "I must bring Tiar an offering of spruce tips. And you can gather what you need for rest of the journey. We won't stop again."

After some time passed, Hanor's ears perked up. Long-Tail was too busy plucking what he believed to be the best spruce tips to care.

"Master."

Long-Tail was trying to whistle, but his tongue and teeth and muzzle shape meant he only hissed. In his head it was a pleasant tune, not unlike the sound of Tiar's voice.

"Master."

The spruce tips on this tree were terrible. He tossed what he'd accrued into his knapsack and moved to the next tree. These things tips were great.

Hanor bit his hand.

"What is it!"

"Giant-humans," Hanor answered in a harsh whisper.

"How? Why all the way out here? There aren't any roads here."

"Only us."

"And Tiar." Long-Tail abandoned his tree. "We should spy, Tiar would want us to."

Hanor agreed, "Can't have them encroach on our domain."

"Lead on brave Hanor!"

With a quiet yapp, Hanor stalked off toward the thinner part of the forest. Long-Tail followed, but something was nagging him like a forgotten thought that had slipped out. He tried to connect the dots in his mind in hopes that it would lead back to what he felt he was forgetting. But that just led him on a convoluted wild goose chase through unrelated thoughts, including what he was planning to eat for dinner.

When Hanor stopped, Long-Tail was too busy doing mental gymnastics to notice. He would've barreled head long into a clearing had Hanor not grabbed his sword belt in his teeth. There were three of those giant-humans in the clearing all pale faces and dark hair. None appeared armed, but Long-Tail knew better than to trust a giant-human at a glance. These were wily, unsavory creatures who'd sooner skewer you and roast you than leave you be. Then he noticed what was nagging him. Kim was a mini-human, just like the one standing in the clearing covered in blackberry and juniper juice staring down the giant-humans.

"Maybe it's just Kim's pack come to collect her," he whispered to Hanor.

"Could be. You say that mini-human child don't leave their pack so maybe."

It was a plausible idea. At the very least, Long-Tail didn't want to get caught and roasted for taking a mini-human child from their pack. However, Kim had the same posture as they did when Hanor confronted them in the settlement. They also looked about as alike as dire wolves and coyotes. One of the humans stepped forward. Kim stepped back holding the strap of their bag in a tight fist at their side. The giant-human stepped forward again raising an arm toward Kim. This time when Kim stepped back, they raised the bag to strike. One of the other humans leapt for Kim, reaching out.

Kim screamed, "Master Spitfang! Hanor!" They swung the bag down against the outreached arm, but there wasn't anything substantially heavy in there, just soft berries and mini-human child supplies.

Hanor growled and Long-Tail gripped his sword and scabbard at his side. Three giant-humans against a kobold and a dire wolf. His arms shook. He was used to choosing his encounters, but there was no choice here. Kim pledged to

Tiar, as Tiar's kobold-in-charge Long-Tail knew there was only one response. He charged into the clearing and drew his sword, swinging it at the two giant-humans closest to Kim.

They shouted and jumped away from him. Nervous, Long-Tail's shoulders rose and fell with labored breath. His tongue darted out and his tail twitched. But Hanor was nowhere to be seen. He rested his left hand on the scabbard. It was sturdy and made of hardy leather, which he used sometimes in the past as a surrogate parrying shield. But it would serve Kim better right now. He pulled it loose and held it out to the child. "All servants of Tiar must fight," he said. He'd seen mini-human skirmishes before and knew they could fight. But fight giant-humans? That he wasn't sure of.

"Disgustin'. One of those demihuman lizards. Things stink," the third human said.

"Come away, now, Kim," the first human ordered.

"You en't Tiar, you en't even my parents. You pr'bly scarificed 'dem or somethin'. I watched you take away Elder Maggie and she 'ent come back."

The second human drew a dagger, but it looked more like a sword to Long-Tail. "Get'ter," they said, gesturing to Kim.

Kim held the scabbard out in two hands like a sword as the two giant-humans approached. This match up was certainly uneven. Long-Tail would say it was downright dirty, but that's how these giant-humans did things. He still had his own problem, the dagger looked sharp and pointy, and the giant-human was big. Long-Tail tried to concentrate on the human coming toward him, but the two advancing on Kim kept distracting him. He let out a screeching vibrato that brought one of the humans to their knees. With a howl, Hanor bounded from the far side of the clearing jumping on the human still threatening Kim. The one with the knife turned to his pack member, but Long-Tail was nearing with his sword pointed up at them. Kim started whacking the human on the ground about the head. They kept trying to get their hands up around their ears, but Kim kept whacking them back down.

Long-Tail swallowed. The human was at least twice his height, tall even for a giant-human. Even at full height he could barely reach their neck with his sword. Even their arms looked massive. They could probably grab his sword and pull it if they tried. So, Long-Tail leapt at them, going for their left leg. Attack, the thought drove him on. To stop would be to die. Keep them defending against low blows. Even as they jumped back or parried with their dagger, he snarled into another attack.

Then the boot landed right in his stomach. His sword fell and he was thrown back, landing hard on his shoulder. From his peripheral vision he saw Kim still beating on their assailant, who was managing to stand. Hanor was playing with the third one, and here he was swordless and on the ground. He struggled to breathe. He struggled to rise. His shoulder protested, bursting with pain. The giant-human's boots cracked the undergrowth. Long-Tail tried to scramble backward with his still good arm. He was able to find purchase on small roots that his claws helped pull him along. It wasn't enough, though. A large hand wrapped around his ankle and pulled him under the giant-human.

Long-Tail flailed as they knelt down, pinning his body to the ground. They were gonna crush him. He threw a handful of soil with whatever little twigs and pebbles were present at their face. He snarled, snapping at them, but there wasn't much he could do. His legs were trapped. They had a knife. All he had were his teeth and one good arm with claws. The human's free hand pressed into his chest. He slashed with his claws. They laughed even as his claws dug into their arm.

The laugh morphed into a breathless gurgle. Dark blood splattered his muzzle, he could taste the iron in the air. The dagger fell silently to the ground. Long-Tail saw the point of his sword sticking through the human's neck. They teetered and then fell forward. The point of his sword came straight at him. He closed his eyes tight but was too pinned to move. And then pain as the sword cut across the top of his scalp. Well, he was still alive, but trapped under over two-hundred pounds of weight slowly crushing him.

Long-Tail pushed the body up as best he could, but without leverage and the strength to push that much weight it was useless. Then weight shifted and the body fell on him again, but this time off to the side. Kim was pulling and pushing. Grunting with each attempted. Long-Tail continued to push, and they managed to get him out. The two other giant-humans were gone, as was Hanor. There was a distant howl from a very happy wolf.

"Did I do good Master Spitfang?"

Long-Tail could only pat their head as they cried.

———

"So, where's this Tiar thing?" Kim demanded.

They were walking up unevenly hewn steps in a cave. "Just ahead." He'd made the child carry his bag. He was injured in battle after all. So, he may tend to exaggerate a bit, but that's what kobolds do. But even this hurt too much to boast about. His left arm hung useless at his side.

They came to a clearing in the cave. "Behold, Kim, for this is the great and wondrous Tiar!" he announced with a drop bow.

"Where? I don't see anything." Kim started jumping about like it was a matter of height.

"Right in front of us. Are you blind? Don't be disrespectful!"

"The crystal?" they asked, tilting their head in puzzlement.

"Their scales glisten like the purest diamonds."

"Okay, I guess." Kim followed Long-Tail's example and

bowed before Tiar. "Happy 'ta serve at your plea'shure." Then, turning to Long-Tail, they asked, "What do I do now?"

"Now? Umm… just go explore those cases behind Tiar. This is all Tiar's domain. I must reveal the astonishing details of my mission."

"'Kay, where's Hanor?"

"Getting some dinner, it's been a while since he's had a good meal."

"Kay," Kim said with a nod and started running off to explore the caves.

At last. Long-Tail had dreamed of this since he had left on his mission. He told Tiar exactly what he'd discovered. It was, as they suspected, the work of magic. He then proceeded through a smaller opening in the wall beside Tiar, one that only a kobold could fit in. With Tiar's blessing he disrobed as he approached Tiar's sacred spring. The water would heal his wounds and he had more than earned this as a reward.

Tiar had been most pleased with Long-Tail. He grinned as stepped into the warm spring. In fact, Tiar had praised him most auspiciously. He was hard before he was even submerged. Tiar had told him he was a great kobold. He rubbed himself. Great kobolds get great rewards. His toes curled; eyes closed. They had granted him a vacation. His left arm popped, and its hand joined his other, toying with the tip. After all, the world was in crisis, what better time for a heroic kobold like himself to go on vacation. He gasped, running his claws up and down his length.

This was all before he'd told Tiar about rescuing Kim and Hanor from evil cultist giant-humans. He rolled his shoulders back and rested his neck against the edge of the pool. There'd been three of them. His hips rocked as his hands continued to dance up and down the length of his cock. They'd all been armed. Long-Tail pressed a claw at his tip, which tickled his foreskin with each return trip. With giant swords. He bit his lip hard enough to draw blood. He won. His stomach tightened.

Maybe Hanor could use a bit of this reward, too. Tiar was clearly proud of their reverent dire wolf. He stood up with a splash and water cascaded over his length. A title, that's right! He could bring Hanor his reward with the title Tiar just bestowed upon him.

Snatching up his loincloth, he snaked through the hole, pausing for only a moment to make sure the garment was fixed around his waist. Kim, curled up at the foot of Tiar's divine glow, glanced up at him, blinking with drowsiness. "No time! Tiar has given me a message I must deliver at once to Hanor, with no delay."

"But I thought ya' said 'e was out getting din..." they began, with the slow rhythm of impending sleep.

"We operate at Tiar's behest, not schedules of our own, you know. Now, Tiar isn't used to normal sized humans let alone the miniature child ones, but they do not object to you sleeping right there. After the adjustment period you will be entitled to go about the place at will. Just stay there." By the time he'd finished he was practically screaming from the opposite end of the cavern. They'd survived a deserted settlement all on their own, certainly they could handle Tiar's cavern alone.

The short bath had reenergized Long-Tail, and he cavorted and skipped down the stair-like rocks to the valley below. He followed the trail of blood in the air, first to the carcass, and then to Hanor. The wolf lazed beside a small pond, licking his fur. His ears perked as Long-Tail approached. "Master, you have left your clothes behind."

"No, I made sure I was decent, my rush necessitated a swift response. As I was lying in repose, cleansing myself in Tiar's divine water, their word came to me of their desire to reward their faithful servant. So here I am to grace you with Tiar's blessing."

Hanor's eyes turn up to the kobold attempting to tower over him.

"Now…" Long-Tail glanced around the pond. Back at the cavern he could use Tiar's ledge, but here he needed a suitable pedestal on which to deliver the address. Spotting a suitable rock jutting from a far corner of the pond, he gripped Hanor's neck scruff. "Come over here." Long-Tail guided Hanor over to the gray stone. "Sit down, right here," he pointed as he scrabbled up to kneel on the rock. From his vantage point he could look down at the dire wolf whose muzzle was level with the top of the rock. Long-Tail cleared his throat. "Our divine master Tiar has bestowed upon me, Knight Commander Lord Long-Tail Spitfang, the duty of dispensing their divine will upon the honorable mount Hanor the dire wolf who from this day forth shall be known as First Class Knight Hanor Swallowtail." He reached down and clasped the sides of Hanor's muzzle raising it up. "Congratulations, Knight Hanor," he brushed his muzzle to the wolf's.

"Thank you, Master."

Hanor's breath was hot and close, reminding the kobold of his state of dress. His muzzle curled. "Now," he began, leaning back on the rock. "I promised to deliver the entirety of your reward." His legs slid out, one to either side of the wolf's large muzzle. The swift and loosely tied loincloth rose from the pressure of his expanding length, a declarative statement as to Hanor's reward.

PLATINUM

KUROKO

Click

Uh—oh. That had sounded... firm. C'aer didn't have time to really dwell on that sound, though. He had to get the item off the grounds with him somehow, and the easiest way had been to wear the damn thing. Between that little bauble and the information he'd managed to learn and confirm, it had been a profitable night, now he just had to get out of the estate without losing his head.

Easier said than done, he had to hide out in a gardener's shed until the guards started to get dozy. There was plenty of worry about someone sneaking in, but with some care to avoid lamplight and patience, he was able to get clear of Duke Mac'Rael's estate.

Back to his place to change, get out of the flimsy harem girl's outfit. He was dead certain none of the actual harem girls back east would dress that way outside of events to impress the outsiders. He'd met a few passing through, and they were practical women. Fancy, near—invisible silks were pretty, but not suitable for most tasks, and the gaudy jewelry that the Duke's girls had been wearing was just silly. Half of those necklaces were clearly just tin with a shiner charm on them. Form over function. Expensive crap. Tin wouldn't keep a charm well. Silver was the usual. Simple charms could last a lifetime, and the complex ones would at least last a year or two.

Platinum was the big boy, though, and could hold even intricate charms for multiple lifetimes without need for recasting. No one made pure platinum items for any purpose other than enchantment, so spotting one just sitting on a desk had been too much of a temptation to resist.

Harem outfit off, he looked down. He really, really wished that the silly outfit had involved something like a pocket, so that it hadn't been necessary to actually put on the platinum chastity cage. But it was worth a literal fortune, enough to retire on, even if it wasn't enchanted at all. Duke Mac'Rael was well known as a perv, it was certainly enchanted in some way or another.

C'aer pulled the lock pin out of the toy and sighed as he pulled the barrel of the cage off.

Pulled the... pulled...

It refused to budge.

He looked again at the lock pin, the only thing that had been connecting the two halves of the cage and was very clearly in his hand.

"Well fuck."

———

"—is good enough. Here's your fee, I'll transcribe it and send it off to Madame."

C'aer shifted uneasily in the chair. He hadn't been willing to delay this meeting. Intelligence work often meant narrow windows between acquiring information and delivering, else the information would be outdated and useless. Caravan timetables and inventory was only good if there was time to intercept and sell the stolen goods. So his little 'why won't this come off' problem had to wait.

"Great, thanks. Dietrich, you know anyone with a good handle on cursed charms?"

The scarred little kinkajou tilted his head and shrugged. "No specialists, no, but Trystan might be able to help. He ought to be waking up soon."

C'aer nodded, then left the room, tucking the pouch of silver coins into his vest.

———

"Come in, come in, what can I help y— oh. It's you."

"Look, I can explain. I didn't know you had guild protection when I made the bet."

"You literally stole my shop from me with a drunken wager."

"I gave it back!"

"I had to threaten to turn you in to both the guards and the guild!"

Trystan had him there. C'aer had rigged the game of cards, egged the ferret into a large wager, then sprung his trap. He hadn't expected to find his newly acquired shop squarely in the middle of his own guild's territory, with the very clear "I paid my fees, leave me alone" glyph on the front door.

"Okay, yes, I did that. I did pay everything back, and then some. More than you would have made over the fortnight that things were messed up."

It was his turn to be uncomfortably right. But the bookish little fennec wasn't going to leave it at that. "At most that makes us even, it certainly doesn't give me any reason not to send you and whatever you've decided needs my help off to go rot with the guards."

C'aer flattened his ears and his tail tucked down between his legs. "I'd, uh... very much prefer you didn't do that. Look,

Dietrich said you're the best one to look at this, and honestly, I'm pretty much fucked if I don't get this taken care of. Probably fast, I don't know enough to be able to read what this thing does, and I have a very personal interest in getting it off of me."

"Ugh, fine, I'll take a look, but Dietrich owes me one, and so do you! Come in the back room and show me whatever it is."

Trystan led the way into a cramped back room. The curio shop was already stacked with cases and shelves of weird stuff, and the back room was only slightly less chaotic. The obscure wares were up front, the actual valuables back here. There wasn't a lot of space, but it was mostly private. The fennec started pulling out books and devices while C'aer slipped his trousers off.

Trystan turned back toward him, saying "okay, show me what you've g—PUT YOUR GODDAMN PANTS BACK ON BEFORE I CUT YOUR D—oh… Oh! So that's what your dumb ass got into."

Rapid shifts in speech and attitude and mood, not unusual for a fennec. "Yeah, I get it. The fucking lock pin comes right out but the cage won't open up."

The little fennec leaned in close, then grabbed a jeweler's loupe. "Mm. Looks like pure platinum, too. No chance of the charm just wearing off naturally, either. Engraving is super fine. Probably done by a fae." One hand twisted and turned the cage to take closer looks here and there. Which rapidly made the cage uncomfortably full, too tight for the cock inside to do anything but throb.

"C-could you maybe do less touching? That's already pretty uncomfortable, Trys." The fennec ignored his protest and kept turning and touching.

"Shut up. You're the one who stuck your dick in something without knowing how it worked. I can just leave you in it, if you like? It won't ever come off on its own, nor let you. I can tell that just off the top layer inscriptions. It looks like there's a few other incentives to submit, too."

"Incentives?"

"Oh sure. You haven't tried lockpicks or anything on the pin, have you?"

"The pin comes out, why would I try to unlock it?"

"Because magic? Dumb ass? But if you haven't already, you probably don't want to."

"Why?"

"If you want to know exactly, you'd have to try it. The rest of that inscription is on the inside of the cage, but it's very particular about a key, not lock picks, for good results. You didn't happen to grab a key?"

"No, I was kind of in a hurry. I saw a bit of platinum and figured it was worth at least a few thousand silver. It's obviously magic!"

"It's cursed, you dumbass. Hold still so I can figure out how to get it off."

"Fuck I need to get off. Get it off. Get me off. Fuck fuck fuck."

"Oh, looks like you tripped something on it. See the glow there on the base ring?" C'aer was a little too distracted by the sudden surge of need to really focus on what he was being shown. The cage was too tight, too tight, and he needed to relieve the pressure somehow. Instinct said he needed to cum, but he wasn't going to be able to, not with the cage on.

"Can you get it off me, like right now?"

"Maybe? There's some sort of trigger clause here at the tip, something about a liquid. Clearly not pre, you're drooling enough of that to have triggered whatever it was."

"Water?"

"Pfft, no. Maybe saliva?" Before C'aer could protest, Trystan had his mouth around the cage, the little fennec pushing his tongue between the bars, licking, sucking, enough stimulation to make the wolf's knees weak, make his need even sharper, but nowhere near enough to actually get him off.

He held on to the smaller canine's ears and panted, until he was finished. "Nope, not saliva."

"Fuck that hurts. Too tight." A glance down confirmed that his dick was bulging between the bars, aching from the tightness and desperate for release. "Maybe cum?"

"Sure, could be. Do you want some of mine?"

C'aer looked down at the grinning fox. "You're enjoying this, aren't you?"

"I'm not the one sticking my dick in random cursed items. If anything, I'm going to stick mine in a dumb wolf, but only if he asks very nicely for me to help him cum. Otherwise I can hand him a nice bottle of oil and he can try to handle it himself."

The wolf frowned. "What the hell kind of oil are you talking about?"

"Just some gearworkers oil. Super slick stuff, you can fit anything inside of anything else, almost."

"Like you inside me, for example?"

"Now you're talking my language."

"Oh for the love of— fine. Fine, let's see if you can get me off in this damn thing, and if that will let me take it off." C'aer got down on his knees and bent over, lifting his tail. The cage was achingly tight now, and he felt two strokes from exploding, if he could only actually get those strokes in. The little fox shed his robes and grabbed a flask off of his workbench.

Rather than straight jumping his bones, Trystan seemed more concerned with playing around. Dripping the oil, strangely warm, under his tail, rubbing it in with a few fingers while his other hand played around with the wolf's aching balls and trapped shaft. "Fuck please, please that hurts, stop. Just fuck me already."

"I'll bet. Your balls feel like they're about to explode. You're going to cum a bucket load when we get you to pop."

"Quit talking about it and do it, or do I have to beg?"

"Oh, would you? That would be fun." Trystan didn't wait for him to do that, though, just drizzled more oil on his shaft, and started to push himself in under C'aer's tail. That felt good. The fox was small, a comfortable fit, and C'aer had spent several of the last few days playing harem toy. Definitely more pleasant than some of the guards had been. The worst he could say about Trystan was that he'd rather be on top.

Granted, if he didn't get help from the fox, he might be bottoming for the rest of his days. And terribly uncomfortable, too, it honestly felt like the cage was shrinking around his trapped cock. He could see that it wasn't, thankfully, but it felt that way.

The first catch of knot against his pucker was unexpectedly quick, and he had to put a hand back to slow the fox. "Fuck, you gotta drag it out Trys. I'm nowhere near, I need relief. Even if it doesn't get the cage off, please, I need to drain this out or I'm going to have balls so blue I could sell them as sapphires."

The little fox slowed his hips, shuddering excitedly as he pulled back, knot popping back out without catching and inflating fully. C'aer would have given damn near anything to have his own knot out, have it swelled and squeezed.

"Oh, I have an idea, then!" Trystan hopped off, came around in front to hunt for something on the table, cock bouncing in the air as he moved things on his work bench. "I was fixing this up to sell to Widow Mac'Rory, but it could use a test-drive and you're here and in need."

"This" was some sort of silver device, egg-shaped and big enough to fit comfortably in his paw. And when the narrow end was pressed on, it lit up with carefully engraved runes and started to buzz like a jar of pissed-off bees. "Go ahead, try rubbing it around on the cage. The vibrations should help you get off even with it on. It might not be exactly pleasant, but it should do the trick."

Worth a try. C'aer raised his tail again and moaned when the fox buried himself under it again and went back to fucking away. The egg was powerful enough to set the whole cage to buzzing, a unique sensation. It was an all-encompassing sensation, pleasure coming from every direction, but also the discomfort of tightness rising as well. It was a balancing act, the uncomfortable restriction kept pace with the rising pleasure, but it was working, he could feel himself getting closer and closer to release, even if it was far slower than he wanted.

Things got suddenly stronger when the little fox's knot caught in his ass, pulled, tightened, locked, and he kept with those short, hard thrusts, pulling back sharply to really drive his pleasure up. Good timing, because release finally poured over C'aer as well, and it was a powerful thing. Not the same as if he'd been topping someone, nor if he'd been bottoming and taking himself to hand as well. Not sharp pulses of cum but almost a stream, softer, slower, but so damn much of it, pouring on the floor.

The almost musical ping of metal hitting the floor wasn't lost on him, either, nor was the sudden sense of freedom that came with it, his aching cock finally able to fill and swell like it ought to. Even if he was spent, it still felt fucking good to get hard again.

But there was a strange lure to the thing, to put it back on, to wear it again. To learn how to be used, to be obedient to be—

"Fuck, I need to get the other half off, this thing is fucking with my head."

"Alright, lemme... uh. I'm kinda stuck, there's a bucket to your left, stopper on the top. Yeah, no magic, just ice, that'll get your, uh... "swelling" down so you can slide the base ring off. Probably some pretty solid mind-affecting stuff to make you want to put it back on."

C'aer wanted to put the cage back on more than anything, and it was an act of will and focus to knock it out of reach and grab for the ice. That was good enough, it let him calm down and pull the ring off. There was still a need to put it all back on, but it was less potent.

They had to stay together for a good twenty minutes before Trystan's knot softened enough to part, and both of them just sat on the floor. Had to find dry spots for that, which took some looking.

"You okay?" The fox was the first one to break the silence.

"Probably. Sore as fuck, and I can feel the damn thing trying to lure me back in. That's some insidious magic."

"Sure is. You want to keep it? Try and resell it? Breaking it and reforging would be a lot of investment, but there's enough metal there to do quite a bit."

"I'll spend the coin and time to break that cursed thing."

"I'll cut you a deal. No coin up front, but I get half the metal when it's broken down."

"Outrageous! One sixteenth."

"Who else is going to do the job and not turn you into the guards? Three eighths."

"Three others I can think of, and they'd be smart enough to take coin and shut up. One quarter, or nothing."

"One quarter, done and bargained. Got any plans for your share?"

"I've been wanting some jewelry for special occasions. Do you know any charms for—"

———

The message had been terse, but that was expected. Too much explanation would give details away if the message were intercepted, and when dealing with extremely illegal goods, one couldn't be too careful. Trystan had simply sent him a time.

The front door to the little fox's workshop was closed, and

all the lights were out. The ground floor windows had been shuttered and barred, but that was simply a sensible precaution, and not enough to keep C'aer out. He took a few steps, pushed off the neighboring building, and leaped to grab Trystan's roof and pull himself up. There wasn't a true second story, but the workshop had a loft that the little fox used mostly for storage. And the window was unlocked, as he'd expected. Small, he had to crawl through into a cramped little space full of boxes. He could hear a faint hum, see a blue glow somewhere below, but working through the boxes without knocking anything over took a bit of time, and both hum and glow were gone by the time he dropped from the loft into the workshop.

"Right on time. Aren't you a punctual thief?" Trystan was sitting at his bench, with only a single candle left alight. "I've just finished your last piece."

The last week of work was spread out on the bench in front of him. Four stud piercings, four rings, and a pendant. A suite of clever little enhancements to assist him both in getting into places he wasn't supposed to be and in avoiding the consequences. Nothing dramatic, but an edge. Nine of them, really.

"Oh, those look good. No trouble with the enchantments?"

"Simple things like that? Not a chance! Hear clearer, see brighter, react faster, jump higher, and always know where you've been. Single-task enchantments are easy. I had a lot harder time with my own reward. Want to try it out?"

The fox was nude? Had he been bare-assed when C'aer came in? Probably, but it was conspicuous; The tone he'd asked in had made it so.

"What did you make?" Better to ask than find out the hard way.

Trystan stuck out his tongue, and the glint of candlelight sparked off the barbell pierced through it. "Forever minty fresh, and that includes a bit of a chill when I lick things." The dart of eyes from C'aer's face to his crotch and back up was telling. Then he gestured to a small cloth on the end of the table. "Cock ring. It was a stone bitch to get a resizing charm to work right, but it will fit on anything from a finger to a forearm. Endless stamina, you can fuck all day without worrying about blowing early or running out of breath."

"Want to try it out, he says. If you wanted to plow me again why didn't you say so?"

"Actually I wanted to be on the receiving end, if that's okay?"

"Oh. Mmmmm so this is why you were willing to bargain with no coin. A little alternative payment?"

"Not like that. You don't have to say yes, your stuff is done and yours, I bargained it as we agreed. This is outside the bargain. An offer, a request. There's two of the rings, we'll each wear one. It'll be fun!"

Well, compared to the previous encounter with enchanted dick adornments, this one sounded downright fun, and if he was going to get back on that metaphorical horse, it might as well be with someone small enough to manhandle as necessary. Plus he was kind of curious what noises the fox would make when he was stuffed so full of dick he could barely breathe.

"Eh, sure. Let me get my purchase all tucked away where I'm not going to lose it." C'aer folded the jewelry up into a neat little velvet bag, then tucked that into a concealed pocket in his doublet. "So what, you want to put mine on, and I'll put on yours?"

"Not what had crossed my mind, but I like your idea better." Trystan pulled the two rings off of their little cloth. They looked heavy, thick, and too small. Resizing charm, he'd said. C'aer had just pushed his trousers down off his hips when he felt a tongue and nose down there, nuzzling into his underwear, seeking and finding and teasing his dick.

"Eager little thing. What, last week wasn't enough for you?"

"Katan's maw, no. I hadn't gotten laid in six months, been too busy to go looking. Then this big wolf stud shows up on my door wanting me to play with his junk? Like divine providence answering my prayers."

"It was a little more complicated than tha—OH! Shit, cold. That stud isn't kidding around, that's some chilly mint."

"I like it! Might have been a little strong, but the way you shivered… good stuff." Another slow drag of that tongue up his shaft, leaving a trail of aching cold that sent another shiver up his spine. "Hold still." The ring was way too small to fit over his shaft, but true to expectations it expanded and contorted to slide all the way down. Tight, all the way down, consistent pressure. Like shoving into a tight ass in one long, smooth, well lubricated thrust.

It settled in around the base of his cock, then tightened down a tiny bit more. Trystan grinned up from there, nuzzling his balls. "Okay, it won't come off, and you won't cum until—"

"Fuck, another cursed item, why the hell would you—"

"Shut up and listen, asshole. I don't want a wolf slave or anything, you have control, it's just actual control. It's stuck on you, and you can't get off until you twist it a half turn left. You can fuck all day and you'll just keep building and building and building without blowing until you turn the ring. I want you to fuck me into a coma and leave me covered in spunk, not beg me for a key or some shit like that. You want to take it off, you turn it a half turn the other way after you blow. *Don't* turn it to take it off before you cum."

"What happens then?"

"I don't want to talk about it."

"Oh, so unintended side effects. Now I'm really curious."

"It took me four hours of continuous masturbation to get every drop out and I had to clean my entire workshop."

"I thought it was surprisingly neat in here."

"I put down a tarp in my room, in case you said yes."

"That messy?"

"Gods I hope so."

"I trust you've got more of that gear oil?"

"Of course! I don't think I'd be confident handling this," he kissed C'aer's tip and gave it a long, cool lick, "without a lot of ease for the friction."

There was still a ring on the table, and the wolf grabbed it, then turned toward the second door of the workshop. "Going to show me in?"

Trys bounced to his feet and led the way. He probably thought that was a seductive sway in his step, but really, he was way too bouncy and buzzy to really do seductive in a traditional sense. Enthusiasm was more fun, anyway.

Trystan's bedroom was sort of a mess. There was clutter around the periphery, books and candles and odds and ends, and a little hammock dangling from the ceiling. But the floor was clear aside from a wide sheet of wax-treated canvas and a bunch of pillows. "You were really ready for this, weren't you? Well, come on, let's see about getting you so completely fucked you can't walk."

The little fox paused. Having second thoughts? Worries? Not good. Time to push a little. C'aer took the ring in one hand, and the fox's tail in the other, then used the latter to steer him, push him down on his back. Bigger wolf, time to loom over the fennec. Show the ring, set it gripped in his teeth, neatly bracketed by canines as he went down on the sand—colored squeaker. The sensations were wild. The ring was close and tight, and he could feel it expanding slowly to match the topology of the excited little fox's erection. It moved his jaw to match, left room for him to rub tongue along the underside of the fox's shaft.

That got a shaky sigh of pleasure from the little guy, one that rose in pitch and urgency until all at once he let out a gasp. The ring tightened in place neatly, and the way he shuddered said a lot. He'd been close already just from the excitement and the rub of his tongue. And all of that cut off instantly. He gave a few more bobs of his muzzle, to see if he could push the issue, see if he could make him blow even through the restrictive charm. No luck, but he squirmed and bucked with all the enthusiasm of someone right on the edge.

"Oh no, no no no little fox. I'm going to enjoy what I'm going to do to you. You put us both in cursed jewelry. It might not be permanent, but these are certainly curses you've tied together, so I'm going to make you pay for tricking me into another cursed evening." Trystan's eyes opened wide, possibly alarmed, before he saw the grin on C'aer's face.

"What are you gonna do, big bad wolf? Fuck me to death?"

"Oh, somebody's feeling brave. Where's that oil?" Trys pointed to a jar on the floor off to one side. "Good, why don't you just get comfortable. Lay back, relax."

While he worked the stopper from the jar, the fox arranged a couple of pillows and sprawled backwards on them, lazily pawing himself, not that there was even a half chance of losing interest or excitement. If both rings were done the same, every little bit of lust was stored, accumulated, a slowly growing need even without actually doing anything. Every damn heartbeat was a tiny tremor of pleasure added to the stack.

If Trystan had done his charms right, this was going to be great. If he hadn't, this was probably going to result in one or both of them dying of dehydration after twelve hours of fucking. There were worse ways to go.

The jar was full of the vaguely mineral smelling oil, thin and slick, so prized for being able to lubricate even the finest gears so smooth they'd never waver. Also very good for ensuring there was no unpleasant excess of friction during buggery. It only took a little dripped on his cock and massaged in to get him slick enough for the job. Two fingers of the other hand daubed in, then pushed to rub at the little fox's pucker. He moaned nice and loud for that. pushed his hips up, eagerly. "God, you're such a slut."

"I'm a fox, you asshole. Get it right." Which was not exactly arguing against the statement. And any argument would have been void anyway, given the way he arched his back and eagerly shifted to line himself up. Presented with that invitation, C'aer could hardly have said no.

Someone had been preparing himself, C'aer slid in with little issue, the fox tight but not uncomfortably so, not a problem. Tight enough to be fun but not so much as to make it an effort to get hilted nice and deep. He'd been right, it turned out, the fox made the most adorable noises when he was overstuffed, dick bobbing and pulsing against his tan-furred belly.

It was pretty easy to get a rhythm going, hips working back and forth as the little fox adjusted himself, angled or twisted to get a new take on the sensations. More than once he felt himself getting close to the edge, only to have the sensation snapped away, his lust knocked a few pegs back down. He didn't get winded, either. "Hey let's try a little change!" C'aer didn't wait for questions or argument, just grabbed the fox by the throat and by the thigh and lifted him up. Up on his knees with the fox supported by both hands and his cock, the wolf started bouncing him, watching for signs of dismay or dislike. The fox getting good handholds to steady himself was the opposite, and urge him to bounce harder, lifting and pulling the fox back down, spearing him again and again. Twice more his edge came and fell away, and he could hear the frustrated gasping from the fox, too.

There was no good way to tell how long they'd been at it. Candles were burning low, but how high had they been? The windows were shuttered and barred, no sign of dawn light outside either.

"Hey little fox, you want to call it? See how much we've stored up for you?"

He shoved himself back down, hilted on the wolf, then nodded. "You want to go off first, or me? Or try for both at the same time?"

"Fuck it, we can do both. About the only way to guarantee it. You wanted to be soaked in it so, uh…" No instruction needed, the fox disengaged, got a pillow to prop up under his hips, then folded his arms behind his head.

"Go ahead, fuck me a little more, get us right up to the edge, then turn both rings. Remember, to your left for your own, to your right for mine."

"Right. Left for me, right for you." He was pretty sure he'd remember that in the heat of things. Back to fucking, pounding. Surprised how durable the little fox was. The size difference was enough to cause concern, but he was stretching just fine and moaning up a storm.

Things were going just fine, but then mistakes happened. C'aer pushed harder than he should have, and his knot sunk fully in. Trystan clenched, which pretty much sealed the deal, there was no getting out after that. But there also wasn't a good way to reach the ring to turn it. It was awful and awesome at the same time, that feeling of being ready to blow, washed in the hormones of impending climax, rutting away with the instinct of a wolf about to empty himself. But the actual climax didn't come. Logically he knew what he needed to do, but his brain wasn't getting a response from his body, overrule by raw instinct. He'd never been good at restraining himself in the middle of things.

Trystan wasn't faring much better. His knot was all the way formed, bouncing and extra-taut in the empty air, and the fox reached down to stroke and squeeze it, fingers unsteady, trying to get that last little bit of relief that obviously wasn't going to happen. C'aer had no idea how long it took to get things fixed. Trystan at some point slid a hand down between them and twisted the wolf's ring, then his own, breaking the dam on two long overdue orgasms.

Vulpine capacity was something of a wonder, but even that couldn't contain everything that C'aer was pulsing into him. Minutes, multiple, that's how long the continuous release took, spasm after spasm of overwhelming pleasure, until there was too much inside the fox, and it started to leak out, then puddle, then thoroughly soak the cloth under them. The same was true on top, his belly, chest, face, ears, the cloth behind him, even a little of the wall was liberally coated, and more joining it as they both jerked and twitched and humped through the long—overdue release.

Neither was entirely sure how long it took, how much was emptied out of them, just that it was a huge mess, and the euphoria left behind was more than any prior sexual encounter either had been through. "Fuck, little fox, this is addictive. I'm sore and tired and I still want to go again for another few hours."

"My ass disagrees, even if my cock is on the same page as yours, so unless you want to bottom for me, I'll have to say no. Come on and let's twist these things again so you can eventually get out of my sore behind."

"Seriously, you should market these things. Charge a mint for them."

"I'd need someone dumb enough to get me the platinum. And maybe model them for prospective customers. What do you say, want to add sex demonstrator to thief on your calling card?"

THREADS

UTUNU

I mean no harm! Please, lower your spears. I merely saw your silhouettes in front of the fire—I thought you were the Fupisi that I know, but I am mistaken.

Here, I'll lay down my weapons. The atlatl and spear, the bolas, and my knife… there. Now it is just me, not that I'd be any threat to the group of you!

I have some spotted hyena friends, Fupisi like you. Though by your piercings and the bold colours dyed into your fur, I see you are clearly from a different tribe. May I be so forward as to share your fire? It has been a long day.

You seem hesitant, and still hold your spears.

Aren't you curious why I speak your tongue, at least? That's part of a story, and conveniently enough I am a story-teller. I can offer a story in return for your fire and, if you still wish me begone after, I shall happily depart.

Ha, I'll take the one slightly lowered spearpoint as assent. Well then!

There are three types of stories.

I don't mean the typical stories, like the ones told by a friend to a companion, or a tale-teller to a rapt audience. Those are important, of course, for they bring people together. They paint vivid pictures, whether true or false or something in-between, and invite listeners to be a part of it.

No, I mean the stories that define us. The ones that are true yet not often told, that tell of who we are, that embody us. That is the first type of story.

Then there are dreams, the hopes and desires we all have, both awake and asleep. These are often what we want our own stories to be, and wish that our paths might bend towards them.

And finally there are the stories that might be, the stories to come; the ones that become true when each branch in our path is decided.

———

I was merely a cub when I realised I was different. Not that much different, mind you, from the rest of my tribe, the Kishundwa. We aardwolves are storytellers to begin with, and the keeping of lore and the telling of tales hold great importance to us. When I was young, and the shaman would speak to us of our history, of past hunts, of long-dead heroes, I would listen, enraptured. She bristled with stories, their threads almost bursting to escape, and when she would finally release them I would surreptitiously grab them out of the air as their threads writhed, and make them my own. My collection grew, until one day she finally noticed.

"Othi, what are you doing?"

Embarrassed, I told her of the threads.

The next day she made me her apprentice.

Apparently seeing these threads, these manifestations of lore and stories, is a rare thing… even scarcer in males, like myself. So Umaluki—that was the shaman's name—took it upon herself to teach me. I learned many things: medicine, living and growing things, other tribes and their cultures (at least the little we knew of them), and I threw myself into these studies with the eagerness of a youngster who understood the privilege being offered.

Yet Umaluki told me nothing about threads. She told me stories, and there were threads there of course, but she told stories to everyone. I grew frustrated, for the stories provided fewer and fewer threads different from the ones I already held. I saw other threads, woven inside the people of my village, but none as close to the surface as the story threads Umaluki let drift forth.

"You took me as an apprentice, Umaluki, but tell me nothing of the threads I see!" I complained one day.

"They can be dangerous," she responded, and my confused expression prompted her to continue.

"Stories are freely given. The threads you see as I tell you tales—they are there for the taking. Not all threads will be, and you must take care you do not take the wrong ones. Come, let us hunt."

Puzzled, I followed her. She had not asked me to hunt before, and my curiosity warred with the dread her words had evoked.

We hunted together in silence, and I entangled a hare with my bolas. It lay there, panicked and wide-eyed, quivering with fear as I approached. I reached for my knife to kill it.

"Wait, Othi. See its threads?"

It had very few; it was a simple creature, after all.

"Take one."

I was nervous—I had only grabbed threads before that drifted unanchored. This was embedded deep within the being of the hare. But I took it, and it slid out.

And the hare unraveled.

The creature was still there, of course, but it also *wasn't*. It lay there passively, blinking stupidly, and did not even struggle as I drew my knife across its throat.

"You see the threads within the people of our tribe. This happened once to one of them, not long ago. Afterwards he lay there much like the hare—empty, unresponsive, no recognition, no speech, no thought. He was not truly there any more, for there were no stories left to him. So. Othi, be careful."

She didn't need to say anything further; I understood.

———

Ah, I sense a prickle of uncertainty now—and you grip your spears tighter. Do not worry! Like any ability, the magic of threads has varied facets and complexities and dangers. As we learn skills, we learn restrictions. I'm sure when you learned to use a spear you were quick to realise that you don't hold the pointy end! In any case we aardwolves are smaller than most, as you can see, and it's just me compared to what, seven, eight of you? I pose no danger.

———

Seasons passed, and I came of age. I realised then that I saw more than did my teacher, for I could discern the faint echoes of the other types of stories. It frightened me; I did not want to peer too closely and see the hopes or truths, let alone futures, of others. So I pulled back from it, letting only the faintest touches of those other threads impinge upon my senses. But even that was sufficient to be able to read others with an empathy that reached well beyond the cues of normal intuition.

Amongst the Kishundwa, like many tribes, sexual intimacy is freely and often shared. Yet in those raw, open, primal acts there is a letting-go, a lowering of walls, and that gives wing to dream-threads and desire-threads that might normally be hidden. With my newfound sensitivity the touch of these threads could often be overwhelming.

I told Umaluki of this.

"Ah, I am sorry, Othi. I truly am."

"But why?" I asked.

"Khulu. The shaman before my mother, remember? He could do this too. And so he could never be close—it was too much for him. Your friends, your tribe, your village… you know them too well. And knowing them further can be painful, let alone the dark lure of strumming their threads for your own ends."

She paused briefly, eyes downcast.

"I fear you may always be alone."

Some young Kishundwa go out into the world when they come of age, for it holds distant lands and different peoples, all with their own stories and lore. There is no better way to collect those stories than to seek them out.

At least that was the reason I gave my friends for leaving.

———

I'm relieved that at least some of you have decided to sit! A few of you, though… your scent still carries impatience. Fidgeting with your spears! I'll skip forward to something more interesting—perhaps my first encounter after leaving the protection of my village?

———

It so happened that a lone hunter and I crossed paths, quite by accident. My bolas had briefly slowed a dik-dik, and as it tried to escape into the undergrowth nearby, a spear—not mine!—impaled it. We both seemed surprised to see another; in silent agreement we built a fire and shared the kill, glancing at each other curiously across the flames.

I had not met a Mapaku before, but there was no mistaking him. He was tall—but then most everyone is to the Kishundwa—and had the distinctive large ears and tricoloured fur of his people. But what drew my attention the most were all the threads around him. Unlike Umaluki, these were not story-threads simply waiting to be released, but rather they stuck to him in clumps, almost like scars. Damaged, somehow. I let my sense drift closer, then immediately pulled back from the dissonance of it. His orange eyes met mine across the fire, and for a moment I thought he had felt my gentle probing; his gaze held mine briefly, then away, and I did not need any special senses to feel the sadness there.

I decided to tell him a story.

Quickly I realised we shared no language—my words had no meaning to him, and his questions to me were unintelligible. Sighing and giving him an apologetic smile, I got to my feet, brushed the dust off my fur, straightened my rather rumpled loincloth, and began to act out one of my hunts. It was one of my earliest attempts at hunting after leaving the village, and had resulted in significantly damaged pride and a modicum of relief that no-one was there to see it. But it made a funny story, which I attempted to convey with as much exaggeration as I could muster, both in words and motions.

I must have looked the fool, but he was engaged—he quickly understood the gist of my meaning, and laughed at my antics. Othi the Great Hunter was thwarted, pride wounded and stomach empty! Panting, I plopped myself back down and grinned over at my companion, staring at him expectantly. His smile slowly faded as it dawned on him that I hoped for a story in return, and he tilted his head down and to one side, avoiding my eyes.

I waited for a while, but he didn't move or talk. I assumed our day would end that way, and as evening slowly turned to night, I fetched some nearby wood with which to stoke our fire. But after I had returned and poked at the flames awkwardly, uncertain whether I should stay or go, he began to speak.

He started slowly, haltingly, like he was afraid of the words even though I did not understand them. But he continued and I sat quietly watching him, listening. He would glance up from time to time and notice me sitting there attentively, which perhaps gave him the incentive to keep going. Threads detached from him as he spoke—not the peculiar clumps of them, but others—and I absorbed them as they drifted near. And with them came context and rudimentary understanding.

I did not know the Mapaku's language, but I started to feel the events of his story and the feelings they brought. He had lost someone—no, multiple someones—who were close to him, and now he was directionless and far from home. Loneliness was paramount in all the threads that leaked forth from him, and my heart ached with it.

I waited silently until his words slowed to a stop, and the sounds of our camp were just the crackle of the fire and the insects of dusk. Together we sat there quietly, the weight of his words pressing down upon us both, until I caught a whiff of the heavy scent of approaching rain. I got up then, walked over and sat crouched on my haunches facing him. He did not flinch as I reached up and gently touched his muzzle, stroking it softly, my eyes bright with sympathy.

He looked away again as the rain began to fall.

A nearby kopje provided an overhang under which we could stay relatively dry, and we made our way over to it. He said nothing more—he seemed resignedly empty after his speech, and I did not wish to prod further. For a while, I sat near the edge of the overhang, listening to the rain fall in the darkness as he slept behind me. Eventually I decided to join him and laid nearby. Not too close, though. I wanted to leave him his space, even as his loneliness called out to me.

It was late at night when I awoke. The rain had stopped, and our small, sheltered area was lit with moonlight. I felt the Mapaku pressed against me, his chest to my back, an arm cradling me. I heard the shift in his breathing as he realised I was awake, and I turned to look at him. His contented scent turned quickly to agitation and embarrassment, and his ears were flat against his head as he started to roll away.

I gently set my paw on his chest, stopping him. His ears were still back with dismay, but I shifted closer and began to run my paws through the fur of his neck and shoulders. I quietly stroked him for a time, my claws combing through his fur, tracing the patterns of the moonlight-muted colours on his chest and belly and the shape of muscle beneath. His scent changed, a sharp tang of arousal, and a glance down to his loincloth confirmed it. He shifted, embarrassed, and started to speak, but I just smiled and continued to trace his fur until he had settled again.

I paused, and looked up at him. He lay there, his expression betraying nothing, but I could feel the tension in him. I reached down and carefully untied his loincloth, setting it to the side; he did not stop me, merely continued to watch me quietly. I cupped his maleness gently with my paw and started to explore his length, pink against his fur. His was a different shape than I was used to—the bulge at the base especially. I stood, and his eyes followed as I rid myself of my loincloth, revealing my own arousal jutting forth from its sheath.

I then crouched straddled atop him, guiding him beneath my tail; slowly I lowered myself, feeling him stretch me and slide in. His breath quickened as bit by bit I took him further until I sat impaled by him, pressed against that bulge, my paws resting against his chest. I gave a shuddering satisfied exhalation and opened my eyes to find his gaze on me, his face intent.

I rode him then, slowly and methodically, feeling him shiver and pant beneath me, and it was not long before he groaned in release. I paused with him there, buried inside me, until his pulses slowed and his gasps lessened.

Only then was I aware of the threads around us both; I closed my eyes and took them in, reveling at the wealth they contained. Desires were there, and raw emotion and need, all coloured by the loneliness I had seen earlier. But that was not all they held—there was understanding and lore there too, and I found myself suddenly aware of more of his story. Because with the threads came language—not its entirety, but pieces, fractured bits of a tongue that I began to comprehend. I wondered then if I just had not noticed this back in my village, since there was little in the way of language or lore to pass between myself and my lovers. But here, with this Mapaku?

I smiled at him, and his smile back made my heart ache in a different way. There was still that need in his eyes, and I obliged, starting to move against him. He slid easily now, slippery with the seed he had left, and he moaned as I began riding him again, more insistently this time. His paws found my eager hardness, coaxing me, and when he again began to pulse deep inside me I spilt my own seed across his belly, panting with the exertion. I lay there atop him until I felt him slip out, and his breathing slow with contented sleep.

The night air around me thrummed with threads; it felt as if they had spilled forth when he did, and I collected them to me. I had a smattering of his language now—a thrilling discovery, I decided—and even some of the scarred threads across his body seemed to have less of a hold. I knew our brief time together would be but a temporary respite, and as I absently ran my paw through his fur I wondered if there were another way.

I formed some threads then—threads he had given me, but I bent them a bit, repurposed them. I pulled them taut and lay them back upon him, a guidance for the paths that bifurcated ahead. Hints of where to go, where my village was, and the comfort he might find there. Perhaps he'd find the closeness there that was no longer mine to claim. When morning came and we would go our separate ways, I knew he'd find them. I just hoped he'd still be there if my journey brought me back home.

———

I see a glimmering of understanding there now!

Picture the savanna stretching out before you, its long grasses rippling like an ocean in the breeze. If you took a blade of that grass and examined it closely, it has a wealth of detail and intricacy, but limited by what it is. It is a blade of grass, but it does not describe the savanna. The grass blades individually do not contain the context of the larger whole.

Threads are similar; singularly they contain information, but much of it might make little sense without the whole. They are fragments—detailed fragments, but still just pieces. Although those pieces may offer glimpses into the totality, whether by its colour or texture, or how it might match with other pieces nearby, or—

Please, put the spear down! Clearly I digress. I'll try to refrain from the hows and whys of threads, but now you can likely guess as to how I speak Fupisi with the fluency I do. Shall I speak of the first time I encountered hyenas such as you? I can promise that encounter will do much better at holding your interest!

———

The world can be a lonely place. I do not understand why other tribes seem so few and far between… perhaps there is lore about that somewhere, I don't know. So when an opportunity arises, my curiosity gets the better of me. It's why I approached your fire, after all!

Their voices carried far in the still night air, and I heard them long before I saw the glow of their fire limned against the edge of an outcropping. I crouched in the tall grass for a while, listening, my urge for company warring with the carelessness of approaching the unknown. Words overlapped words loudly in a language I did not understand, but there was laughter, and that I understood. So I made my way around the rocks and into the edge of the firelight.

Four heads swiveled immediately to face me, suddenly silent. I absently noted I had left my short spear leaning up against the rocks a number of paces back, but then realised that even with my weapon, I probably didn't look particularly threatening. Four hyenas stared at me and I halted midstep, staring back. Suddenly one laughed, pointed at me, and then said something to his fellows, which resulted in their collective amusement. They were all seated near the fire and had made no move to stand or grab weapons, which I took to mean I had been dismissed as a threat. I sat down within the range of the firelight but a number of paces away, looking curiously around their camp.

I knew they were Fupisi, that was certain—I had heard spotted hyena tribes often decorated themselves with jewelry of bone, and these ones were no different. They had clearly feasted on an impala kill, for there was still a good portion of it left, cooking by the fire. One of them noticed the direction of my gaze, and said something; there was a discussion, and another one stood and grabbed part of a cooked haunch, tossing it my direction. I retrieved it, somewhat nervously, and smiled my thanks before sitting back down. I ate in silence, and it seemed as if the hyenas had almost forgotten I was there.

I watched as they talked, and their interactions were a story in itself. They all looked to be the same age—young males, barely into adulthood like myself—and there was clearly a camaraderie there borne of many years of friend-ship. They continued animatedly, gesticulating to each other and laughing, the aardwolf disregarded, shouting in disagree-ment only to chuckle and agree moments later, punctuated by playful shoves and mocking tones. Threads leaked from them, and even without their stories made manifest I feel I could have discerned much about them.

It was their first hunt together, that I could tell. They had been given the opportunity and had taken it well—a large kill, more than they could eat, and all that was left was to boast to each other about the parts they played. It had gone so well, they even were magnanimous enough to feed a wandering aardwolf! I smiled as I listened, and the threads drifted. They were writing their own story here, and it was one that would stick with them for years hence—a promising start to a lifetime of friendship and intimacy and successful hunts. I wished I could be a part of it.

And I could, I thought bravely to myself. I wanted to learn more about them, but they didn't need me like the Mapaku had. They had each other and their own story to share. But could I be part of that shared story, part of their successful hunt, part of the threads they would carry with them and spread to others? I looked over at them and I noticed them watching me, laughing and shouldering each other over a shared joke. A suggestive tone from one made another growl, amidst the good-natured jeers of his friends.

There was a tension there, I could feel it. They were all young, like me, seeking their place. Their success together stoked a flame and pitted them against each other in a subtle wrestle for dominance, even as their threads wove them together. It was a war of confidence, and their scents spoke of barely restrained energy and strength and challenge, almost bestial in its underlying sexuality, bubbling beneath the surface.

The encounter with the Mapaku had opened new possibilities to me which I found difficult to resist. These young hunters needed someone to boast to, someone to whom they could demonstrate their strength, their prowess, but not each other. So why not me?

I stood then, and strode over. Surprised, the largest got to his feet—they were all significantly bigger than I was, much like all of you—while the others watched, deferring to him ever so slightly. I walked up to him, meeting his gaze directly. There was a hushed silence, taut and dangerous, as they all eyed me. I stood there, desperately trying to control my nerves yet knowing my scent betrayed me. My expectant arousal strained against my loincloth, painfully obvious, and my ears flattened as panic bloomed—had I done this all wrong? I lowered my muzzle submissively.

A flood of words and laughter broke the silence, and the one standing in front of me growled an amused response. My eyes were still downcast, my field of view containing just the hyena's belly and below, where his colourfully dyed loincloth barely hid his own burgeoning interest. In a brief surge of fearlessness I crouched down on my haunches in front of him, pushed the flap of his loincloth to one side, and took him into my muzzle.

The hyena tensed with a surprised gasp, but did not move. I heard amused exclamations from the others, but the one I was tasting was silent, and his erection swelled in my mouth. I closed my eyes, focusing solely on his pleasure, working his length with my tongue then vigorously with my muzzle, switching my attentions in time with his grunts and slight movements against me. This night was theirs, and I would add to their successful hunt; I would give them another conquest, another shared story, and the threads would intertwine them all for years to come.

His paw rested on my head as I worked, absently rubbing my fur. Their conversation began again, excited now, the verbal sparring and friendly boastfulness painting the tone, the chatter and laughter swirling around me. I continued to service the hyena in front of me; his breath hitched, and then he gave a long low groan as he reached the edge and over, his release filling my mouth. I held still, while he pulsed against my tongue and the threads circled around me. Then, finished, he withdrew, the last spurts of his seed trailing down the side of my muzzle.

I felt a paw between my shoulders, pushing me gently forward and down, then paws near my hips as another divested me of my loincloth. Naked now and on all fours, I held myself motionless, caught in that stretched expectant moment amidst the excited discussion immediately behind me —until a paw lifted my tail and a hardness pressed beneath, entering me. He began to thrust and I moaned with the primal urgency of it, my paws slipping slightly in the dust beneath as he pushed. His vigor seemed almost desperate, and it was not long before I felt him shudder and growl and pulse, and his seed spilled hot inside me as his claws raked the fur of my back.

No sooner had he slid out then the next hyena mounted me, gripping my hips and pulling me back against him as he thrust, and I braced my forearms against the packed dirt, gasping with the intensity of it. He stopped and held me there, buried deep, quivering in release as he added his own seed to that of his friend.

Detachedly I could hear my overwhelmed whimpers and groans and feel the threads spill forth, as they took their turns one after another. I soon lost track—it was a whirl of incoherence and overstimulation. I painted the ground beneath me and still they took me and each again, a show of strength and competition and threads that wove together until, finally, they were spent. I lay there curled near the fire, beyond exhaustion, leaking seed and threads and finally consciousness.

When I eventually awoke late the next morning, I was alone. My muscles ached, and I was sore in other ways too, so I was glad that the hyenas had stoked the fire for me before they departed. I was happy as well for the gifts they had left behind, some purposeful, some not.

The remainder of the impala was one. I was famished.

The threads they had so enthusiastically provided the night before remained with me, of course. And, as I sat there,

I realised I now knew their language. Not fully, but certainly enough for basic communication.

And there was the bone bracelet one had playfully left behind, hanging from my sheath.

———

Ha, well, that seemed to prick up your ears! Not the only thing to perk up, I see; you all seem to have set aside your spears for rather different ones! And yes, the bracelet on my wrist that you've now noticed is the same one.

Ah, and thank you... I am hungry. Even just this remainder of your meal is more than enough. Yet I can't help but notice your expression, amongst other things, as you handed it to me. Am I to assume you wish to perhaps reveal something of your own stories to me? To provide me with threads of your own?

A moment though.

You, the one so kind as to offer me some of your food. How long has it hurt?

Do not look so surprised. Threads spring from all of you and their weave defines you. It is one of the reasons Umaluki taught me medicine, since when coupled with the ability to see threads it helps to see when something is wrong. One can see frays, kinks, knots, tears— obviously they don't necessarily look like that, it's more that they're just... *wrong*, somehow.

That's what you have there. A tangle of threads, curled in upon itself, dark and invasive. Do not anger! This damage is not a weakness of yours, and neither you nor your friends should think it so. May I? I'll press lightly; it's right here, within your abdomen. It has grown, has it not? Ah, the prickle of threads that leaks from you now—fear, worry, fury, despair —why would I tell you something like this, do you think?

It's because I have another small story to tell you, for I may be able to help.

———

I made the connection between healing and threads quite early on, and brought it up to Umaluki one day.

"Can't we just fix threads if there's something wrong?"

"Yes and no. As you know, a thread is not an isolated piece —it is connected to a flood of others, and we may not know why they're linked that way. So what happens if we straighten a bent thread, but in doing so it mars the weave it's in? We could touch one and unravel hundreds.

"That's not to say it couldn't be done. But it will always be a risk. Especially if the thread is where it should be."

"What do you mean?" I asked.

"Someone comes to you, knowing you are a healer. Their paw is bent awkwardly, and it has been since birth. That someone's threads are where they should be—it is who they are, and who they have been. That difference in them is woven throughout their being, and any attempt to alter it might be catastrophic. What if, in attempting to fix something simple, the threads just unraveled? Remember the hare?"

I remembered.

———

Ah, no, do not despair. I have not finished my story yet. Listen!

———

Not long ago, in my travels, I met some jackals. They were a hunting party, much like yourselves, and quite friendly. And much like tonight, we found ourselves sharing a fire. I knew they were Bweha, but uncertain as to the tribe, for the jackals often have slightly different fur patterns and colours. These ones had clearly been together a long time—much was left unspoken in their interactions, a comfortable quiet that comes with knowing one another deeply. Even when they spoke, there was little in the threads that drifted between them; it seemed similar to my first experiences with those I grew up with in my village, where we knew each other so well that little needed to be said.

The jackals' easy camaraderie, their quiet words and soft chuckles, made me feel like that much more of a stranger. I had been feeling quite lonely long before I met them, since what Umaluki had told me about the past shaman, Khulu, weighed heavily on me. I was afraid that I would continue to be alone, unable to truly get close to others for fear of the intensity of threads that might be shared. I was young and probably foolish, I don't know, but I wasn't convinced that that would happen to me. I wanted to prove her wrong.

When morning dawned, the jackals chatted amongst themselves, preparing for a larger hunt to bring game home. I knew a scattered word or two from the threads that had drifted my way the night before, so in my horribly broken Bweha I asked if I might accompany them on their hunt. I was a lorekeeper, I explained, and hoped that I could learn more about them while offering stories and lore in return. To my surprise, and in a gesture that makes my heart ache even now, the Bweha invited me not only on the hunt, but to stay with them a while as a guest in their village.

It proved to be quite a bit larger than my own village, and as I stayed, I learned far quicker than any would have expected. The Bweha proved to be an open and friendly people; they treated me as one of their own, and shared their time with me as if I were Bweha myself. Rarely did a night pass without company and I made the most of it, thrilling in the intimacy and closeness and the threads I added. And I learned. Of them, their dreams, their gods, their culture, and more. In return I wove stories for them, stories that reflected them and involved them and touched upon their dreams, and it fascinated them. It brought them yet closer to me, and my heart swelled at their acceptance.

Days passed into weeks and months, and there was still much to learn. I regaled them every evening with stories, and every night they shared something of themselves with me. Even with all the stories I told, I could not come close to what I had been given in return.

A day came, though, with a hunt. A hunt much like every other day, but it went badly. One of the young warriors was severely injured, and the healers in the village could do nothing but ease his pain. His wound was a mortal one and all knew it, including him. I sat at the edges of their agony, seeing them all struggle, seeing the threads of their worry.

Later that night, I approached his tent. The powerful, acrid scent of fear and blood and pain permeated it in its entirety, and I flinched from it as I entered. Another warrior stood at his bedside, but I told her to rest; I would watch him for a while. I sat beside him, and his agonized gasps hurt to hear. I shifted closer and he looked at me pleadingly, his amber eyes barely lucid. So I tried to help, even though in my thoughts Umaluki chided me for a fool.

I laid threads on him to strengthen him. Threads he himself had given me on nights together, threads that defined him and his desires—I took them and aligned them with his body and willed them into place, setting them there to redefine the warrior who was so badly damaged. He steadied, but not enough. I took the dreams and needs of his tribemates then, all their concern and worry for him, all those threads that were gifted to me freely; I pressed them upon him, attempting to fix the broken things, bending them to choose the correct path. His eyes watched me the whole time.

I awoke three days later in my own tent, feeling drained and desiccated, utterly exhausted, and it took another three to get my strength back. The Bweha were profoundly grateful, even though their warrior would not be quite as strong as he once was. But at least he would live. They rejoiced in that, as I did, and at the feast of celebration that night I realised I would always have a home there with them, should I wish. Yet I knew I had to leave—I had gotten so close that the threads had become almost too sharp to bear. But I told them I would return someday, and I will.

———

You, with that tight tangle of threads, clustered and darkening even as they slowly spread—it does not define you. It is foreign to who you are and so, I hope, not as inextricably linked to the rest of your being. Much like the Bweha warrior I helped—his injury was new and not part of who he truly was, which made it possible to heal. I told you this last story so that you realise there are paths open to you, and paths that I can help you follow. Threads exist for all three types of stories, and they can all be twisted to change what comes. So don't despair.

Even now I can see that that shadowed clump of threads has loosened—even now you see that there are possibilities ahead. Embrace them, for I will help. Your friends, as well, are all still rapt with attention; sights and scents lead me to realise that I've managed to arouse their interest, too; the evening air is heavy with threads waiting for release!

Are those your desires? I have befriended Fupisi before, and twined my threads with theirs. Shall we write our own story together? Come, share your stories and dreams with me; let us make it a memorable night!

ABOUT THE AUTHORS

Faora Meridian: In the distant land of Australia resides some of the most deadly and dangerous creatures in all the world. From potent venom to paralysing stings, nearly every creature on the dystopian, sunburnt continent tries to kill you. Faora Meridian, however, appears to be an exception. This dragon has penned furry prose for over a decade now, has been published in such anthologies as *Heat*, *FANG* and *Hot Dish* among others, and so far he remains just outside most lists of the top fifty most dangerous creatures found in his homeland.

Linnea Capps is a three -time August Derleth award winning poet and Leo Literary Award winning author. She's also a smoking hot grill on the internet constantly getting up to shenanigans and out exploring the world. When not seeking out adventures and experiences, she happily plays songs on her ukulele and writes the stories she dreams up every night before bed. You can find her on Twitter @LiteralGrill and on her website www.linneacapps.com.

Skunkbomb currently lives in Arlington, Virginia in an apartment that is running out of space on the bookshelves. He's been writing in the fandom since 2015, and his other erotic stories can be found in *FANG 7-10* as well as *CLAW Volume 1*. When he isn't writing, Skunkbomb thinks about going outside to rollerblade or hike, but often ends up watching another episode of Game Grumps on YouTube or one of the hundred shows he needs to catch up on. He is the editor of *Give Yourself a Hand: A Furry Masturbation Anthology* for Goal Publications, which is due to come out in early 2020. Skunkbomb can be found on FurAffinity as Skunkbomb123 and on Twitter as @skunkbomb123.

Alison Cybe is an award nominated author who specialises in fantasy and horror fiction. Their work has appeared in several horror and sci-fi/fantasy publications. They are the manager of the gaming website CybesWebsite.com in which they write articles, editorials and reviews. Their work has been featured in several horror and sci-fi/fantasy publications, and they have worked as a freelance writer for companies including tabletop RPG publishers Sanguine Publishing and Green Ronin Publishing, and have written extensively on inclusion and positive representation within the gaming community, and have contributed short fiction to multiple gaming publications. Recent published works includes a series of LGBTQ+ comedy novels, and they are currently working on *Realms of Valeron*, a light-hearted comical fantasy romp set in a digital age which explores how bonds of friendship form across the online world. Alison was born in Scotland and lives in England, and is a co-manager of a large gaming club. Their interests include celtic mythology, transhumanism, garage kits and pet rats, and they have a degree in Film & Media. They are non-binary and my pronouns are they/them, and favourite colour is green.

NightEyes DaySpring is a known troublemaker who is rumored to have a penchant for coffee and an interest in dead, ancient civilizations. He has been actively writing furry fiction since 2010. His stories have appeared in *Werewolves vs. Fascism*, *Gods with Fur*, and *FANG*, along with other anthologies. He also co-edited *Dissident Signals*, an anthology of dystopian furry literature. Currently, NightEyes resides in Florida with his boyfriend, where in his spare time he masquerades as an IT professional. For updates on his writing, visit nighteyes-dayspring.com, and for day-to-day nonsense, follow @wolfwithcoffee on twitter.

Nathan Ravenwood dabbles in many genres: sci-fi, fantasy, horror, romance, and combinations thereof, and also likes to write both erotic yarns and tales of anthropomorphic animals. He's been writing seriously since high school, where he fell in love with the furry community. While it's not the only fandom he writes for, it is an ever-present fixture in his life and a constant inspiration. His debut story "The Paledrake" was published in Uruk Press's *Sex and Sorcery 3*, followed several months later by his first novel *The Cordax Mondotta*. Since then, he's published more novels with Uruk Press and short stories with furry publishers: "The Road to Macluske" in *The Rabbit Dies First* and "Card Subject to Change" in *Heat #16*. You can find his ebooks on Amazon.

In his free time, Nathan enjoys video games, metal concerts, cooking, and geeking out over professional wrestling. He lives in Florida, which continues to provide him with inspiration in it's gorgeous natural beauty and eccentric people. His goal is to make each story and novel better than the last, and to one day own a great number of cats."

Ian Madison Keller is a fantasy writer currently living in Oregon. Originally from Utah, he moved up to the Pacific Northwest on a whim a decade ago and never plans on leaving. Ian has been writing since 2013 with eight novels and more than a dozen published short stories. Ian has also written under the name Madison Keller before transitioning in 2019 to Ian. His short stories have also been published in *CLAW* and *Purrfect Tails*, and he has an M/M urban fantasy novel coming out from Fanged Fiction. He can be found at http://madisonkeller.net or on twitter as @MaddieKellerr

Jaden Drackus, or Jay Dee is a dragnox from Maryland. He has been writing furry stories since 2010 and writing for publication since 2016. A historian by training, he was inspired in his youth by science fiction and fantasy, he tends to work in those genres as well as historical fiction when he writes. Jay Dee lives with his boyfriend and 3 cats. When not writing he plays video and card games, builds plastic models, and reads. He is an alumna of the Regional Anthropomorphic Writers Retreat. His stories can be seen in *FANG 8, 9,* and *10*—the last of earned a Cóyotl Award nomination. He can be found on FurAffinity as JadenDrackus. His silly observations on life can be seen on Twitter: @JadenDrakus.

Televassi is a wolf from the UK, who writes poetry, prose, and has a 'slight' obsession with Beowulf, The Elder Edda, and Celtic La Tène culture. Considering those interests in all things before 1000AD, it is ironic that others decided to nickname them TV. Yes, as in a television. You can find Televassi's work in a number of furry publications, such as *Heat, Dissident Signals,* and *Give Yourself a Hand* to name a few. If you want to keep up with their latest writing and ramblings, you can find them on twitter regularly yapping about writing, history, and rock climbing.

TJ Minde found the furry fandom after moving to Ohio. It's there that, after a few motivators, the rat had the urge to pick up a pen – or grab a keyboard, as it more often is these days. Since then, he's been creating characters, writing stories, and started a novel. The more he's written, the more friends he's made though different writing circles. When not focusing on words, TJ enjoys other nerdy activities, like Magic: the Gathering, table top RPGs, and video games.

TJ's other stories may be found in issues of *FANG, Heat* and other anthologies both in and out of the fandom. For thoughts, comments and replies in bite-sized chunks, he can be found on Twitter @TJMinde.

Alkani is a a small cat who enjoys scientific and creative pursuits. A fan of speculative fiction, fantasy, and any number of other genres, he enjoys writing stories that prominently feature characters and their interactions. When he's not writing, he also volunteers for a furry residential writing workshop, RAWR (http://www.rawr.community), and the non-profit that runs it, APAW (http://www.apaw-inc.org). He also plays Guild Wars 2 (as a charr, of course)! You can find Alkani on Twitter (@ServalScribbles). He also has a blog (Chirp!: The Musings of an Anthropomorphic Serval [http://chirp.theirvoices.org]).

Miriam Camio Curzon It is easier to say Miriam does not exist, but rather only manifests words on pages for *FANG* through magic. If they did exist, they would be a marbled polecat-satyr masquerading around as a fox. You can read such fine literary manifestations in various volumes of *FANG* and *Foxers or Beariefs*. In some not to distant future, they will appear regularly in blog post in MCPolecat's Pillowford (pillowfort.social/MCPolecat). For now, the magic is dampened by a veil cast by doctoral education.

Kuroko Carol (or Kuroko) is fairly new in furry writing, since she only really got back into it in 2018. Since then she's found a decent groove, and a handful of anthology publications since, like *The Furry Cookbook* and *Breeds: Foxes*. She's often found on Twitter @interfectorem9 or behind her sewing machine in the middle of nowhere, Montana.

Utunu Since the mythical early 90s, Utunu has been a video game developer, and is currently working at BioWare in Austin, Texas. His interests include gaming (especially Eurostyle boardgames and good old-fashioned pencil & paper gaming), African fauna (*lycaon pictus* in particular), playing squash and proper football, commissioning artwork, studying languages and linguistics, writing, worldbuilding, commissioning more artwork, long sentences, and the Oxford comma. Unfortunately he has time for very few of these.

ABOUT THE EDITOR

Sparf is a writer, actor, narrator, and podcaster currently hailing from the Washington, D.C. Metro area. He can often be found running around furry conventions with his hair on fire because he seems to keep collecting responsibilities.

He is an aficionado of so-called 'genre' fiction, including science fiction, fantasy, horror, mystery, and even the occasional romance, with target audiences ranging from middle grade to adult. His own writing has featured in past volumes of *FANG*, *ROAR*, and other anthologies from FurPlanet, Rabbit Valley, and he has a story in *Patterns in Frost: Stories from New Tibet Vol 3* from Sofawolf Press.

ABOUT THE ARTIST

Rukis lives on a farm, where she spends most of her time working on art, caring for her animals, and hanging out doing tabletop gaming with her friends. She is a huge fan of old school D&D, White Wolf, and Warhammer, as well as studying and collecting exotic fish (Cichlids, mostly) and drinking a lot of Dr. Pepper. Her menagerie includes a rabbit, some fish, two wonderful dogs, and a whole mess of chickens.

She is the author of *Heretic* and the *Off the Beaten Path* trilogy, which also take place in the world of *Red Lantern*.